ORPHANAGE 41

Victor Malarek

Produced by:

FriesenPress
Suite 300 – 852 Fort Street
Victoria, BC, Canada V8W 1H8

www.friesenpress.com

Distributed to the trade by The Ingram Book Company

DEDICATION

For the tens of thousands of orphans and abandoned children of Ukraine.

CHAPTER ONE

Maria Demianenko stared anxiously at the large wooden crucifix looming ominously over the room on the wall behind the director's desk. Her heart was pounding rapidly in her tiny chest as she gazed up at the imposing bronze figure of Jesus on the cross. In her mind, she crossed herself three times. Wiping her palms on her faded blue jeans, she whispered an odd prayer.

"Forgive me Father for the sin we are about to commit." She squeezed her pale blue eyes shut, deathly afraid to face Jesus.

Her boss, Natalka Matlinsky, the director of Orphanage 41 in the western Ukrainian city of Lviv, was uncharacteristically happy this morning. She was humming as she worked.

Matlinsky was a model of productivity sitting ramrod behind her battered, military-issue, green metal desk, scribbling notes into files and tossing them onto a growing pile to her left. Glancing up for a second, she saw that her assistant was wound tight.

"Oh, come on now!" she chided her young charge. "We are making a deserving family very happy. And we get a bit of spare change for the orphanage. No harm done."

The director could see that her assistant was deeply troubled by the events about to unfold, and despite her self-imposed good mood, Maria was starting to annoy her. "You *see* how we struggle month after month. We would be destitute were it not for the paltry handouts from the state. We have nothing for the children. No toys. No sweets. With this baby we can buy them some treats, maybe a few story books. We will be getting 5,000 hyrvna! It's not a lot of money but it will help, even if just a little."

Maria was still unconvinced.

Her boss had had enough.

"Stop your silly fretting!" she snapped. "Go make me some tea.

Maria retreated from the office, thankful to be out of the room.

Natalka Matlinsky stood a mere inch above five feet. Her long, jet-black hair was pleated into a single braid and wrapped around her head like a loaf of bread. Attractive, though austere, she lacked any fashion sense; her color palate ranging from carbon black to what in her eyes was a more cheerful charcoal grey. She never married. She could never visualize cooking, cleaning house or attending to the carnal needs of a man, let alone popping out one baby after another.

After graduating from university with a major in economics and a minor in English, she dedicated her life to the Communist Party. Her goal: to climb the ranks. In no time, she gained the reputation of a determined and ruthless bureaucrat, and in the process, grated the nerves of a stream of Party stalwarts. The men decided she was a cold fish and made her the target of vulgar, sexist jokes. The women plain loathed her. They thought her too ambitious. Everyone wanted her gone and on a bleak February afternoon in 1990, the regional Party boss executed a backroom scheme to do just that. For her 15 years of dedication and good work as a community activist and organizer, she was *rewarded*. Matlinsky was appointed director of Orphanage 41.

The woman was no fool. She knew she had been shafted, exiled to a backwater institution to languish in obscurity. She had no choice in the matter. The decision to move her was not up for negotiation. But Matlinsky was not one to surrender to obscurity. She left the Party firm in the resolve to somehow engineer a comeback, no matter what it took.

One year later, Matlinsky saw her ambitions decimated by the unforeseen events of August 24, 1991. The Iron Curtain crumbled. The Union of Soviet Socialist Republics was no more and Ukraine was granted independence. The Communist Party was in a shambles as most of its former leaders abandoned ship for the lush pastures of graft and corruption. She was now trapped, stuck in a hellhole that reeked of urine, curdled milk and crying babies with no way out.

At 39, Matlinsky had been director of the orphanage for four years. From the moment she took over the post, she made it clear that she was the undisputed power. She demanded loyalty and lorded over her staff. She did not accept any challenge or criticism, and from day one instilled a regime of fear – a trait she'd honed while clawing up through the Party ranks.

Maria Demianenko was her first hire. The director had interviewed dozens of eager prospects and found the young hopeful's passive, timid behavior an agreeable asset. In fact, it had been an unwritten pre-requisite for the job. Matlinsky wanted someone who wouldn't question her. She needed an assistant with no backbone, someone who'd be too scared to reveal any secrets from the inner sanctum. She found it all in Maria.

As Maria returned to the office, the phone rang. She almost dropped the tray of teacups and cookies. The director shot her an exasperated look and answered after a second ring.

"Yes. What! I don't need this problem," Matlinsky said, the familiar impatience creeping back into her voice. "We discussed this earlier. You were to tell her the baby will be born with defects?"

Maria winced. Over the past several days, she had overheard snippets of phone conversations between her boss and the doctor about the impending arrival of this baby, and it had been driving her to distraction. It wasn't difficult for her to figure out the plan they'd concocted to take the newborn from the unsuspecting mother. The assistant knew it was immoral and illegal but she lacked the mettle to stop it.

There was a long, tense pause as the director listened impatiently to the doctor's explanation.

"And given all that you have told this silly woman, she still wants to keep the baby after it is born? She is a fool," Matlinsky said as she throttled the black receiver in her right hand, her knuckles turning white. "Do what you need to do. One way or another, you must get her to sign the adoption papers. I need that baby. Do we understand each other? We have an agreement!"

With that, she slammed down the receiver and turned to Maria. Her good mood had totally evaporated. "If you so much as look at me one more time with that stupid expression on your face, I will fire you. Do I make myself clear? Now get out of my office! "

The following morning as Maria arrived at work, Matlinsky was pacing in the corridor like an expectant father.

"The baby has arrived. It's a boy and he is healthy. Get the bassinette. It's time to go," she shouted to her assistant.

A moment later, they were racing out the side door of the orphanage. Maria tossed the bassinette into the back seat of Matlinsky's black Russian-made Lada. The director cursed the nine-year-old rust bucket as it sputtered and choked before finally starting up. Maria said nothing. She kept her eyes closed as her boss maneuvered aggressively through the narrow, clogged streets of Lviv. At the rear of the hospital, she spied a spot for the disabled, jammed on her brakes, shifted gears and expertly backed in. Retrieving a worn disabled sticker from the glove compartment, and to Maria's dismay, she tossed it onto the dash with a smug grin.

Matlinsky leapt out of the car, barreled through the emergency doors, and made a beeline for the maternity ward on the third floor.

"So many foolish, unwed teenagers having babies," she muttered as they wound their way through the corridor. "Then when one of these fools is offered an opportunity to give up her baby for adoption to a loving family so that it can have a good life, she decides she wants to keep it. What is wrong with her? Has she no common sense? No decency?"

The director was on one of her rants and Maria knew she didn't expect an answer. She learned long ago to keep her head down and say nothing. Still, she was feeling sick to her stomach at the cruel deception that was about to unfold.

Dr. Ihor Kowalchuk was waiting in his office. He was a tall, rakish man with slicked back, salt and pepper hair, bushy eyebrows, a thick moustache and a long narrow face. His looked stressed. On a tiny cot beside his desk, a newborn infant slept peacefully, wrapped tightly, Soviet-style, in a pale blue, cotton blanket.

"You are certain the baby is healthy?" Matlinsky demanded. "No diseases … no addictions!"

"The baby is healthy," the doctor reassured. "The mother did not drink and did not take any drugs during the pregnancy."

"Do you have all the papers?"

"Yes."

"Signed?"

"All signed." Kowalchuk replied, handing Matlinsky a file. She quickly flipped through it.

"And do you have…?" the doctor began.

Matlinsky pulled a thick envelope from her purse and discreetly slid it across the desk. Dr. Kowalchuk nervously shoved it into the inside pocket of his suit jacket. The director turned and nodded at her assistant. Maria bent over, picked up the baby and gently placed him in the bassinette. At that moment, a spine tingling scream reverberated through the corridor. Maria froze, staring at the doctor, his entire face creased with worry.

"A grieving mother," he said, turning to Maria. "Her baby was stillborn. She demanded that she see him. She was hysterical. We needed to calm her so I sent a nurse to the morgue to get the baby so she could hold him for a moment."

Maria's heart sank. As she glanced over at the director, she noticed Matlinsky glaring with icy disapproval at the doctor. It was a look Maria knew well; one her boss flashed whenever a member of her staff slipped-up. Maria wondered what he had done to set her off.

"Are we done then?" Matlinsky snapped.

Dr. Kowalchuk nodded.

"Then let's go."

Matlinsky turned on her heel and walked out the door. Maria picked up the bassinette, holding it close to her chest as though to protect the newborn from the evils of the outside world. As she passed the ward where the grieving mother cradled the dead baby, she willed herself not to look in, but she could not drown out the woman's desperate pleas.

"I beg you, Lord Jesus, don't take my baby's life. He has done nothing wrong. Take me! I am the sinner. Give my baby back his life! Take me. I beg you!"

From the corner of her eye, Maria noticed a large, swarthy man with a drooping, black moustache sitting on a wooden bench across from the ward. He was hunched over, looking grim and staring intently at the cement floor, his muscular arms folded tightly across his chest. He didn't look up.

Back in the car, the ever-subservient assistant looked down at the baby and caressed his cheek. He was still asleep. Maria's mind drifted back to the glorious day she landed what she felt was the job of a lifetime - assistant to the director of Orphanage 41. She was 22 and fresh out of college. Armed with a diploma in childcare, she believed she could make a profound difference in the lives of the tiny souls entrusted to her care. She was overjoyed and very proud. However, that euphoria was short lived. The seemingly permanent knot in her stomach was now a part of her psyche. She had been hired to be loyal, and that loyalty is what kept Maria afloat.

In her heart, the assistant knew what they had done was morally wrong and she suspected that if the scheme were ever discovered, there would be a huge price to pay. And there was no doubt in her mind that she would be dragged down in the mess that would ensue.

"I will drop you off at the orphanage," Matlinsky said, breaking the icy silence that had enveloped them like a glove. "Make sure the baby is washed, fed and glowing. I'm going to the Grand Hotel to pick up the couple. They will be so happy. And wipe that annoying look off your face!"

The baby stirred and woke up. Maria was instantly captivated by his deep brown eyes. As she watched the tiny bundle, she let him clasp her finger.

Despite her angst, she couldn't help but smile. She began to wonder whether Matlinsky might, in fact, be right. Unlike most of the babies abandoned on the steps of orphanages across Ukraine, this child would grow up with a real chance at a good life.

CHAPTER TWO

Mykola Yashan was bored. He hated the class. All he wanted was to escape into the cool, sunny Edmonton spring afternoon and spend it with his girlfriend. But he was stuck in the University of Alberta's cavernous main auditorium propping his eyelids open with his thumbs while half listening to Professor Vasyl Romaniuk drone on about the brutal genocides committed by Soviet leader Joseph Stalin in Ukraine in the 1930s. It was Slavic Studies 101. Mykola was in his third year and, for a student majoring in civil engineering, this was one subject he neither wanted nor felt he needed to take. But he was required to take it. Either that or suffer the wrath of his father. The thing is, Mykola knew the subject inside out, probably even better than the professor. Throughout his childhood, he had been Slavic-grilled to the brink of madness – at the dinner table, at social gatherings, at youth conferences and at Saturday Ukrainian school – accounts and stories all delivered in finite, blood curdling detail by his famous father, Stepan.

Dr. Stepan Yashan, (always "Dr." never "Mr."), was a distinguished historian and respected scholar in the expat Ukrainian community throughout North America, Britain, the European Union and Australia. He was a tenured professor of International Studies at the University of Alberta, holding two doctorates – one in Eastern European Studies from the University of Toronto and the other in International Politics from Oxford.

For Mykola, living in his father's gargantuan shadow was an unforgiving trial. As far back as he could remember he was made to feel like he could never, and would never, measure up. Yet he was expected to play the role of the dutiful and respectful son who, on occasion, was sternly cautioned by the doctor not to do anything that might embarrass the hallowed Yashan family name. Mykola profoundly loathed his father. He found him cold, aloof and arrogant. The man never hugged him. On Christmas, birthdays and Father's Day, he'd offer up a limp handshake to his son's outstretched arms. He never gave Mykola any praise and rarely attended an event that featured the boy. He was always too busy with more pressing matters. In the professor's world, academia trumped family.

Dr. Yashan was a celebrity among the intelligentsia of Ukraine and throughout the so-called Diaspora. His meteoric rise to international acclaim had its genesis in the spring of 1993 while on a yearlong sabbatical at the National University of Kyiv. After delivering a lengthy dissertation on the Holodomor: "1932-33 Forced Famine in Ukraine" in which millions of peasant farmers were deliberately starved to death, Dr. Yashan was approached by a dapper, elderly gentleman who made him an offer that sent his brain into overdrive. The silver-haired stranger identified himself as Ivan Borovsky, a retired colonel in the infamous Ukrainian Secret Service or NKVD. He was clutching a battered, black leather briefcase which he claimed, in a hushed, nervous whisper, contained top secret documents, files and photographs that dealt with a particularly horrific incident in Ukraine's history. It involved a venomous purge ordered by Joseph Stalin in his fanatical drive to crush Ukraine's spirit of nationalism. Borovsky said he possessed documentation of the systematic extermination of an estimated 300 kobzari (wandering bards). The minstrels, who were all old and blind, traveled throughout the countryside singing songs of Ukrainian tradition and patriotism while playing the bandura, the national instrument of Ukraine. As the story was told, one of Stalin's more brutal henchmen, Lazar Kaganovitch, was dispatched to Ukraine with instructions to liquidate the kobzari. On December 4, 1933, the minstrels were invited to a symposium at the Opera House in the eastern Ukrainian city of Kharkiv, where they were brutally tortured and summarily executed. For more than six decades, accounts of the slaughter were relegated to the stuff of urban legend. It could not be proved or disproved.

For Colonel Borovsky, a 40-year veteran of the NKVD, leaking the documents was not an act of altruism or a wish to see the truth revealed. He was a mercenary, plain and simple. He wanted money. Having recently been put out to pasture, he realized that his meager government pension was a grim sentence to a life of poverty. What doused any embers of loyalty to the secret service still lingering in his blood was observing Ukraine's fat-cat oligarchs grow incredibly rich from the unbridled greed and corruption that swept Ukraine after independence. It was the straw that broke the once unflappable and dedicated agent's back. The officer decided it was time to stick his head into the trough.

Borovsky targeted Dr. Yashan for two reasons. From a simple search of secret files amassed on the academic at NKVD headquarters in Kyiv, he learned that the professor was a wealthy man, having inherited a large sum of money and property when his parents died twenty-five years earlier. Secondly, and more importantly, the notations in the files cited the professor's Achilles' heel: his titanic-sized ego, which, it was noted in the margins, could be exploited should the 'need arise'. The colonel quickly and accurately surmised that the man craved the spotlight and worldwide acclaim. He was ripe for the picking.

After a brief meeting in a grove of blossoming chestnut trees on the grounds of Kyiv University, the two men headed for Dr. Yashan's hotel room. While perusing the yellowing documents, the professor's hands began to tremble. He could not believe the treasure trove in his possession. The colonel smiled knowingly. He knew he had hooked his self-centered quarry and began to reel him in. His asking price: a modest $50,000 in U.S. currency. A bargain considering the return on the investment and the international fame and glory it would garner. The professor shot out his hand and the deal was sealed. The transfer took place three days later in the back pew of the Saint Sophia Cathedral, a stone's throw from the Verkhovna Rada (Ukraine's Parliament). Dr. Yashan slid a tattered prayer book over to Borovsky. The agent reached inside and retrieved an envelope. He shot the professor a nervous smile, took a moment to verify its contents, then got up and left the church, leaving the briefcase on the bench. The professor grabbed the handle and pulled it toward his chest, cradling it as one would a newborn child.

Dr. Yashan made international headlines with the publication of a scholarly tome on the massacre. The book detailed the entire operation beginning with cables from Stalin giving Kaganovitch orders to carry out the mass slaughter of the kobzari. When the blind minstrels were assembled in the grand auditorium of the Kharkiv Opera House, a platoon of secret police in black leather jackets fanned out and forcibly confiscated their banduras. Those who refused to release their grip on their beloved instruments were severely beaten with wooden clubs and bare fists. With the heart-ripping sounds of banduras being smashed against the walls and stomped on by cackling thugs, the minstrels suddenly broke out in song – defiantly singing the national anthem of Ukraine. The commanding officer shouted from the stage, ordering them to be silent. The bards continued to sing. One by one, under the cloak of darkness, they were dragged from their seats to a walled, side courtyard where they were photographed before being shot in the back of the head. Their bodies were loaded onto trucks, transported to the outskirts of the city and dumped into a hastily dug trench in an abandoned field.

Among the aging documents was a crude, hand-drawn map showing the precise location of where the mass burial took place. On a visit to Kharkiv,

Dr. Yashan had located the gravesite, which was now within the city limits. To his horror, it was a football field. He stood at the edge watching school children run up and down chasing and kicking soccer balls. With deep reverence, he closed his eyes, dropped to the ground and offered a prayer for the dead. The children stopped playing and stared curiously at the weeping stranger, wondering why he was on his knees.

The most chilling find in the briefcase was an envelope that contained the black and white numbered photographs of the 292 minstrels taken moments before their execution - KZ001 to KZ292. They all died nameless. Dr. Yashan spent hours staring into their faces. Not one showed the slightest hint of fear, remorse or cowardice in the face of death. The kobzari were defiant to the end, hence the title of the professor's 458-page tome: Blind Defiance. The photos became the linchpin in a travelling exhibition undertaken by the professor on the release of his book.

Two years after the publication of *Blind Defiance*, and during a visit to Kyiv, Dr. Yashan received a cryptic fax from the colonel saying that he had another "gift" for the professor. It was a brown attaché case jammed with NKVD top secret documents identifying and detailing the arrests, brutal interrogations and executions of 468 professors, authors, artists, journalists and intellectuals from Kyiv in the late spring of 1937. The nature and scope of the clandestine operation shocked the professor to his core. The files showed that the accused, seen as potential dissenters who might challenge Stalin's totalitarian regime, were rounded up in a four day sweep and taken to the Lukiyanivka Prison. One by one, they faced two or three of the Stalin's henchmen who leveled a stream of charges. There was no trial or due process. There was no lawyer-assisted defense and the accused were not allowed to speak. All were found guilty, photographed and summarily executed with a single bullet to the back of the head. Their bodies were piled onto large trucks, and under the cover of darkness, taken to the Bykivnia forest next to the Chernihiv Highway several kilometers northeast of Kyiv. The dead were dumped into a pit and covered with lime, rendering their remains unidentifiable. In the files was a map indicating where these particular victims of Stalin's atrocity had been secretly buried. It was in "sector 19." Spruce saplings had been planted on the gravesite and over the decades, the trees had matured into a fully-grown forest where families flocked for picnics and to escape the oppressive summer heat of the city.

Dr. Yashan shelled out another $50,000 for the package and immediately headed home to Edmonton. Soon after, the colonel mysteriously disappeared, never to be seen or heard from again. The professor heard whispers that the former agent had been taken into custody by the NKVD, interrogated, viciously tortured, and then murdered for leaking State secrets. His mutilated body was purportedly dumped in an unmarked grave.

A year later, the professor released his second scholarly tome entitled: Intellectual Purges. It received instant international acclaim in academic circles and blistering criticism from the Ukrainian and Russian governments. At a hastily called press conference, the President of Ukraine and Russia's Foreign Minister took sharp aim at Dr. Yashan accusing him of falsifying the documents while at the same time declaring him persona non-grata in both countries. The political uproar catapulted the professor once again onto the world stage.

The professor never revealed the source of the files nor the fact that he had paid for them. He reveled in the thought that it drove so many of his envious colleagues to the brink of distraction trying to figure out how he managed to get his hands on classified, top secret NKVD documents. It was a secret he would take to his grave having shredded all traces of the bank transactions. In his entire adult and academic life, they were the only papers he'd ever destroyed.

Mykola vividly remembered the publication of *Intellectual Purges*. The pomp and circumstance as his father strutted around the house, the phone ringing off the hook with requests for speaking engagements and media interviews worldwide. For the better part of two years, Professor Yashan was on the road basking in the limelight. As a result, his family tumbled into virtual obscurity. His wife Iryna took her husband's long and frequent absences in stride. She had long carved out a fulfilling life of her own. Not so with Mykola. He took his father's absences hard. He was just a child – too young to understand why the man was so distant and worse, so indifferent toward him.

"Your father loves you in his own way," Iryna would assure him after yet another no-show at what should have been a family event. "He's just busy with work. You know that. But I'm here," she'd add with a beaming smile and a hug.

Iryna was the polar opposite of her husband. She was a warm, engaging woman with never a mean word to say about anyone. Everyone adored her. All of Mykola's friends thought the world of her. She was the ultimate super mom, quintessential hostess and featured musician. Whenever people dropped by unexpectedly, which was often, she made them feel right at home. Her fridge was always well stocked. She enjoyed entertaining, even the self-important stuffed suits her husband occasionally invited for dinner. She especially loved it when Mykola's wide coterie of friends dropped by.

Throughout his teenage years, the basement family room was packed with guys from his high school football and hockey teams, or dancers from his Ukrainian dance troupe. The jocks gathered for two reasons. The first was to watch the Grey Cup football final and the Stanley Cup hockey play-offs on the 52-inch wide-screen, high-definition television. The second was for Iryna's homemade perogy smothered in caramelized onions and topped with cold sour cream. The dancers gathered to party and chat about past and upcoming performances.

Mykola was the center of his mother's universe. She doted on him, and more importantly, she made certain his roots were firmly planted in Ukrainian culture. She spoke only Ukrainian to him at home and signed him up for Saturday school where he learned to read and write the language. When he was three, Iryna enrolled the boy in Ukrainian dance school, and by sixteen, he had worked his way up to lead male dancer in the celebrated Edmonton Ukrainian Dance Company.

Iryna Yashan was steeped in things Ukrainian. In her spare time, she painted pysanky – Ukrainian Easter eggs. The intricate detail of her work was the envy of the community. Several of her works were featured in the Ukrainian Easter Egg Exhibition at the Canadian Museum of Civilization, as well as Ukrainian cultural centers in Edmonton, Winnipeg, Toronto, Chicago and Philadelphia. She loved art and had an impressive collection of paintings and sculptures by Canadian-Ukrainian and Ukrainian artists. She was also heavily involved in the community as president of the Canadian Ukrainian Women's League and vice-president of the Alberta Ukrainian Congress. And she was devoutly religious. The family attended church every Sunday. Iryna and the professor were on the board of the Ukrainian Catholic Cathedral in Edmonton.

One of Mykola's favorite pastimes was listening to his mother play the bandura. It was as if she'd been born with the instrument in her delicate hands. She would close her eyes and her long, fine fingers would float across the strings like butterflies. Mykola could see it gave her immense joy. Iryna produced two CDs of original compositions and was a featured soloist at numerous Ukrainian and multicultural events. Her concerts were packed and always ended with standing ovations. The haunting sound of the bandura struck a deep chord with Mykola. His mother saw it in him at a very early age and began teaching him to play when he was just four. By the time he was 12 he was a brilliant musician.

When Mykola was 14, curiosity pushed him to pick up a copy of *Blind Defiance*. He wanted to learn about the minstrels of old who played the instrument that he and his mother loved. The book, which had a black and white illustration of an old man gently cradling a bandura on the cover, had sat unopened on the bookshelf in his bedroom for more than a decade. He had refused to read it out of spite. Cracking it open, he found that the professor had inscribed it for him when he was just a toddler. It read: "For Mykola from your father, Dr. Stepan Yashan." Mykola grimaced. He remembered the man sitting him down when he was five and exhorting the boy to call him "father". He was no longer to call him "daddy" or "tato." The boy was confused. The only time he'd heard the term "father" was when addressing Father Ihor, the parish priest. That night as he lay in bed, he heard his mother chastising her husband.

"How could you be so cold-hearted? He's just a boy who craves his father's love and attention. Is that too much to ask?"

The professor did not respond.

Hesitantly, Mykola turned to Chapter One: The History of the Kobzari. He figured he'd be bored silly by the second paragraph. Instead, he was completely drawn in. While the writing was academic and somewhat pedantic, he found the subject matter riveting. He never knew that the Kobzari were members of a clandestine brotherhood with its own secret traditions, rites and rules. The church was at their center where they gathered on certain holy days to attend a requiem mass for deceased brothers and to settle urgent issues. Every spring, they secretly gathered in the forests outside Kyiv to elect their pan otets (leader), to decide the territory individual minstrels could play, and to initiate new members in a secret ritual. To become a member, a kobzari had to be blind and study the bandura with a master for at least two years before obtaining permission to perform independently. Any member who violated the kobzari's strict code was tried in a brotherhood's court. The most serious punishment was banishment. Lesser punishments included whipping and fines. The brotherhood made it known that the kobzari were not beggars but professional artists, and instilled a strong sense of pride among its members. They were forbidden to fall to their knees.

Spellbound by the chapter dealing with the roundup of the bards, Mykola wondered how he would have reacted if his precious bandura had been ripped from his hands and smashed. Looking at the photographs of the minstrels' moments before they were executed, he felt a profound sadness in his heart for these proud men. He also felt a rare surge of pride well up in his chest for his father. When he finished the book, he went to the professor's study in hopes of engaging him in a discussion.

Knocking on the open door, Dr. Yashan turned from his desk, casting an annoyed glare at his son. He hated being disturbed. "What is it?" he snapped.

"Father, I just finished reading your book. It was really good," he said standing at the doorway, not daring to cross the threshold without permission.

The professor scoffed. "Really good! I'll make sure my publisher puts your scholarly critique on the back jacket when it goes in for the next reprint."

The boy's stomach went sour. The professor turned and went back to what he'd been working on. Mykola went back to loathing his father.

In his early teenage years, Mykola would often stare at his mother and father at the dinner table and wonder what possessed her to marry such a pompous man. He could never summon the courage to ask her, and he knew that despite her husband's snooty nature, she would defend him.

While she was a loving mom, for better and for worse she was fiercely loyal to her man. Her parents had died when she was in her early teens – her mother from ovarian cancer, her father five months later from booze and a broken heart. The professor's parents also died when he was in his teens. Tuberculosis killed them. The tragedy of their parents' deaths was what drew the couple together when they met in their first year at university. They were all they had, neither having any siblings. Then Mykola came along and the Yashan clan became a family of three.

When Mykola graduated high school with honors and was accepted to university, there was no slap on the back or words of congratulations or encouragement from his father. Worse yet, the announcement that he was going to major in civil engineering triggered a tasteless response from his father.

"I could have expected that. A blue collar fits you well."

Mykola could feel every fiber in his body tense up. "Sorry I'm not a chip off the old block."

"You're not even a chip," the professor shot back without looking up from the dinner table.

"Stepan!" Iryna screamed. It was the cry of panic.

Mykola got up and left the table, cowered yet again by his domineering father.

Iryna was livid. "How dare you! I can't believe you could you be so cruel? Don't you ever make a comment like that again! Do you understand?"

As was his way whenever Iryna rebuked him, the professor shut down and said nothing.

"Why can't you show him a little support? Why can't you be proud of his achievements instead of always ignoring him or putting him down with your snide comments?"

It was like talking to a wall. Iryna turned and left. A moment later, she was at her son's bedroom door.

"May I come in?"

"Yes."

Sitting down on the edge of his bed, Iryna tried to play down the incident. "Your father meant nothing. It's just that ..."

"He's a jerk," Mykola offered with a scowl.

"Mykola! I'll not have you talking about your father like that."

"What did he mean by I wasn't even a chip?"

"It was just a silly off-handed remark. He meant nothing by it."

"He means everything he says. That's the one thing I know about him."

"Well, you know I am always in your corner."

"Trouble is you're trapped in two corners. His and mine! He's your husband and I'm your son. You love him and you love me and he hates me."

"He doesn't hate you."

"Oh yes he does. I just wish I knew what I ever did in my life for him to hate me so much."

"You did nothing wrong. He is the way he is. He doesn't hate you. Please erase that thought from your mind. Do it for me. Please?" Iryna pleaded.

"For you," Mykola said. But he never did and never would.

At breakfast the next morning, Professor Yashan laid down an edict. At the very least, Mykola was to enroll in the introductory course in Slavic Studies 101. His son calmly pointed out that his major was civil engineering and that he had no interest in minoring in Slavic Studies. But there was no arguing or debating the issue. It was a matter of family pride, or more to the point, Dr. Yashan's pride. Mykola wanted nothing more than to ignore his father's directive but his mother, the ever-present calm in the eye of the storm, urged him to acquiesce. It didn't take much. She merely pointed out that he could breeze the subject and be assured of scoring an A.

Mykola relented but held off for as long as he could, finally enrolling in the class in his third year. He figured he'd rarely have to set foot in the classroom. He figured wrong. He drew the short end of the straw and got saddled with the loquacious and mind-numbing Professor Vasyl Romaniuk. Turned out that the professor viewed a sparsely filled classroom as a personal affront. He felt that if he took the time to prepare a lecture, then the forest had better be filled with living, breathing creatures to hear it. His sure-fire method of ensuring a robust turnout was to award 25 per cent of the final mark for attendance.

On the chilly Tuesday afternoon, as Professor Romaniuk lectured on the Ukrainian genocide, Mykola sat in his normal spot at the very back of the auditorium out of the instructor's immediate sightline. He pulled out his IPhone and began texting his longtime girlfriend. He had known Lesia

Kordan all his life. The two grew up together and hardly a day went by that they didn't see, talk or text each other. When he was five and Lesia was four, Mykola scrawled a note to her in orange crayon: "*I like you a lot. I want to merry you.*" Lesia kept it neatly folded under lock and key in her diary, occasionally reminding her boyfriend that she had a legally binding document in her possession, which she expected him to honor.

Mykola would often tease her, saying that: "I wrote 'merry' as in to make you happy."

Lesia's mother, Sonia Kordan, was Mykola's godmother, Iryna's best friend and the closest person Iryna had to a family member, apart from her husband and son. From what the two women could determine while climbing up a family tree of many disparate branches, they were distant fourth cousins, but they considered themselves to be no less than sisters. They absolutely adored each other and did everything together. They were each other's confidant, support network, therapist and greatest fan. Sonia had happy, brown eyes and was a bit on the heavy side. She was a gourmet cook and like Iryna, she loved to sing and dance.

The two moms often teased Mykola, saying that it was up to him to keep the family tree alive with a not-too-subtle wink and nod towards Lesia who would blush with embarrassment.

Sonia's husband, Orest, was a high school gym teacher, a salt-of-the-earth guy who loved to laugh, sing and joke. He could never keep his hands off Sonia and was forever hugging her. He was also the father Mykola wished he'd had. Orest loved Mykola like a son and the boy loved him. The Kordan couple had four girls and no boys so Orest did all the things a dad was supposed to do with a son with Mykola. He took him camping, fishing and to sporting events. He drove him to football and hockey practice, and was in the stands cheering him on at all his games. When Mykola turned 16, he gave the boy his first beer. Orest talked to him only once about girls. The subject dealt with condoms. It was a very short and awkward conversation considering the boy was dating his eldest daughter. Little did Orest know that over the past year, Mykola had been taking precautionary measures.

While Sonia often joined the Yashan family at formal dinners, mostly to help out in the kitchen, Orest steadfastly refused to go over to the house and break bread if the professor was at the dining room table. The two men intensely despised each other. Orest thought the man was a condescending, arrogant ass. Dr. Yashan viewed the lowly gym teacher as nothing short of a knuckle-dragging Neanderthal with the IQ of a chimp. The professor was obsessive about anyone who identified himself or herself as Ukrainian but did not speak, read or write the language. As far as he was concerned, they had no right to call themselves Ukrainian. A third generation, hyphenated Canadian-Ukrainian, Orest knew a smattering of Ukie phrases and could not read or write a word. Still, he was proud of his Ukrainian roots, and didn't give a damn what the purist doctor thought.

Mykola felt a vibration in his pocket. He reached for his IPhone. It was a text message from Lesia.

"r u going to dance practice 2nite?" she asked.

"Wouldn't miss it. U?"

"4 sure." And then: "Miss u!"

Mykola smiled. "Miss U 2. Maybe after practice we cud go 2 my place," he offered. "Parents r out of town."

Expecting a snappy response, there was nothing. After a few minutes, he wrote back.

"Hey! Was it something I said?"

No response.

"Was it something I did?"

Still nothing. Mykola leaned back, slightly annoyed, and tried to refocus on the boring lecture.

Twenty minutes later, a female student tiptoed into the auditorium through the side door and approached Professor Romaniuk with a note. He glanced at it and scanned the room. His eyes landed on Mykola.

"Mr. Yashan! Can you accompany this young woman to the Dean's office, please?"

Rising slowly from his seat, Mykola felt a knot in his stomach. Something was wrong. He could sense it.

Sitting in front of the Dean's desk were two women: Sonia Kordan and a grim-faced, female officer with the Royal Canadian Mounted Police. Sonia had been crying. Her eyes were red. He had never seen her so pale.

"What's wrong? What's happened?" Mykola asked, rushing over to give his godmother a hug. Her embrace was limp.

Mykola felt a hand on his shoulder. It was the police officer, nudging him to sit down.

"What's going on?" he asked, his pulse now racing.

"I have bad news, Mr. Yashan. Please, sit," the officer said.

Mykola felt his knees start to buckle. He obeyed.

"I'm very sorry to tell you this. There was an accident ..."

"Lesia!" Mykola's head began to reel. "Was she driving? I didn't know she was driving when we were …"

"No," his godmother interjected. "It's not Lesia."

Mykola felt a flood of relief. He closed his eyes, took a deep breath and exhaled slowly, trying to get his nerves under control.

"It's your parents," Sonia said, slumping in her chair. Her body began to shake uncontrollably.

The police officer took over. "I'm so sorry to tell you this. Your mother and father were killed this morning in a traffic accident on the Trans-Canada Highway near Red Deer," she said in a soft but firm voice.

Mykola looked up at the officer in disbelief. He closed his eyes and felt the room start to spin. The officer's words echoed in his brain. He could hear them get louder and louder. His eyes opened in a fright and let out a loud moan.

"Mama!"

CHAPTER THREE

Sonia tiptoed down the stairs to the basement family room where Mykola had been holed up since being told of his parents' death. He was sitting in the dark, not moving, just staring blindly into nothingness. On the coffee table sat his dinner, untouched.

"Mykola, I need to speak to you," she began in a soft tone.

He didn't respond.

Sonia sat down beside him and took his hand. "Mykola, I know this has been extremely hard on you. It's been hard on all of us. I can understand why you didn't go to the panakhyda on Thursday and this evening. The services at the funeral home are one thing but you must go to the church for the funeral tomorrow. Father Ihor says you must. They are your parents, Mykola," she pleaded.

"I don't give a damn what Father Ihor says. I'm not going."

"I know you're hurting terribly and I know you're angry right now but just know that your mother and father are in the arms of God."

"There is no God. I no longer believe in God, and I will never set foot in church again. You can tell that to Father Ihor."

"Mykola, you need to say goodbye to your parents. You have to say goodbye to them or you will never find peace in your life. You need closure. This is not a good thing, sitting alone in the dark like this."

"Teta, I've made up my mind. I'm not going. I want to be left alone. Please Teta, I need to be alone."

Sonia made her way up the stairs, meeting Orest at the top. He had been listening.

"Should I go down and talk with him? Maybe he'll listen to me," he whispered to his wife.

"No. He wants to be left alone. This is all so tragic. I'm worried about Mykola. He's not eating."

"He's not eating. He's not talking to anyone and Lesia's up in her room crying. She wants to see Mykola. She wants to be with him and he won't let her near him," Orest said with a trace of anger in his voice.

"This is a difficult time for him and for Lesia. I'm sure they'll get through it. They just need a little time," Sonia said.

It was a few minutes past 10 pm when the doorbell rang. Mykola could hear the chimes from the basement. He heard Orest's heavy footsteps bound across the living room floor overhead and pull the door open. The voice was unmistakable, a booming baritone. It was Father Ihor. Mykola winced. There was a brief muffled conversation and a moment later, the priest was lumbering down the basement stairs.

"May I come in?" Father Ihor asked politely. He was wearing a black robe. A large gold cross dangled from a thick chain around his neck.

"You're already in," Mykola said, not looking up.

"You have my sincerest condolences, my son. This is a very sad and tragic time for you and indeed for the entire community," the priest said, stretching out his hand.

Mykola ignored it.

"Mykola, I spoke with your godmother earlier this evening after the panakhyda for your parents at the funeral home. She is worried about you. She said you have lost your faith in God. This is understandable but you must ..."

"I'm not going to the church," Mykola interjected sharply.

"I understand your anger. I know you are deeply hurt. It's to be expected. But you must go to church to say goodbye to your mama and papa. It is proper for you to do so. You will never forgive yourself if you don't. The service begins at 10 am tomorrow. I expect to see you there," he said in a calm, but firm voice.

Again, Father Ihor held out his hand. Mykola didn't take it.

"Can I assume then that you will be at the church tomorrow?"

Mykola didn't respond.

Shaking his head in dismay, the priest left.

The funeral was a must attend event. The cathedral was packed to standing room only with the who's who of the Ukrainian community from around the globe. The Ukrainian Minister of Foreign Affairs and the Minister of Justice flew in from Kyiv. Also in attendance: the Ukrainian Ambassador to Canada and his counterparts from Britain and The United States. There were several Members of Canada's Parliament including four federal Cabinet Ministers; a dozen members of the Alberta Provincial Legislature, including the Premier, as well as the Mayor of Edmonton, most of the city counselors; a large entourage of professors from several universities; and the entire executive of the Alberta and Canadian Ukrainian Congress.

Scores of mourners stood outside the church chatting quietly as they waited for the hearses from the nearby funeral home. At precisely 10 am, a solitary church bell pealed a mournful tone announcing the arrival of the long and winding cortege. The crowd suddenly went silent as a police motorcycle escort rounded the corner. Several of the women held onto each other as sixteen pallbearers – eight for each coffin – marched down the church steps, took their places at the back of the hearses and removed the identical oak caskets. As they approached the entrance, Father Ihor, dressed in a white robe with gold trim and wearing a red and gold crown, offered a prayer, blessed the coffins with holy water and led the solemn procession into the church. As the closest living relatives, Sonia, Orest, Lesia Kordan and her three sisters followed the coffins. Many of the women began sobbing, some uncontrollably, and many of the men struggled to hold the tears as the caskets were placed on wreath-laden piers in front of the sanctuary. The Kordan family took their place in the front pew reserved for immediate family members. One space remained conspicuously empty.

A stillness settled over the congregation as the funeral director opened the lids to expose the bodies of Stepan and Iryna Yashan. While reciting a prayer from the Requiem Divine Liturgy, Father Ihor placed an icon of Saint Joseph on the chest of Stepan Yashan and an icon of the Blessed Virgin Mary on Iryna's chest. He then turned, faced the altar and a choir of 50 men and women on the balcony at the back of the church began a haunting dirge. Over and over, they sang: "Hospody pomylui! (Lord, have mercy)" as Father Ihor, an incense burner in one hand and a gold crucifix in the other, circled each coffin three times chanting a prayer. He then circled the caskets another three times blessing the bodies with holy water.

A half-hour into the service, during a moment of silent reflection, the church door creaked loudly as it was pulled open. Standing in the blazing sunlight was Mykola, dressed entirely in black. Those in the back rows turned and started to whisper frantically. Within seconds, the entire room was filled with muffled conversation. All eyes were riveted on Mykola. Father Ihor raised his hand for silence and gestured to Sonia. She quickly walked down the aisle to accompany her godson. She looked up at him, nodded her approval and took his arm. When Mykola's eyes focused on the coffins, he tumbled to the floor. There was a collective gasp as two pallbearers rushed to help him up. Lesia buried her face in her father's chest and cried. Mykola was led to the front pew and sat down between Sonia and Orest. An altar boy brought him a glass of water. Father Ihor raised both his hands to put an immediate end to the chatter.

With trepidation, Mykola slowly lifted his head and peered at the coffins. His eyes focused first on his father's casket. It was the nearest to him. He could see his father's nose and his salt and pepper goatee. He could also make out that he was dressed in his $2,800 navy blue Canali suit. Iryna had cajoled him into buying it six months earlier. She teased him about how handsome and distinguished he looked when he had tried it on at the Harry Rosen men's clothing store in the Edmonton Mall. But he never got to wear it. He argued that he was saving it for a special occasion.

Mykola felt strange looking at his father's lifeless body; strange in that he felt nothing. There was no sadness, no regret and certainly no tears. He was completely disconnected. It was as if he was at a funeral for a total stranger.

Then the dread set in. His heart started to pound fiercely in his chest as he fearfully turned his gaze over to his mother's coffin. He could see the outline of her face and her fine blond hair. He could make out the intricate, burgundy and black embroidery of her favorite Ukrainian blouse and he could see her gold cross and chain wrapped gently around her pale wrists. His eyes filled with tears as he bowed his head in prayer, pleading over and over for God to give him back his mother. But she lay there, still.

Mykola glanced up at the altar adorned with the hand-painted icons of a dozen saints staring down at him with their holy eyes. Once again, he felt his sadness begin to turn to anger. God, Jesus, Mary, Joseph and all the saints were not to responding his prayers. He closed his eyes. His mind began to float in a dense, black void. The melodic chanting of the choir reverberated in his ears. It felt like it was coming from a distant land. His nose was filled with the acrid aroma of burning incense. Then one by one, the icons suddenly came to life, the saints circling around him in a bizarre, pagan dance. The dancers swirled faster and faster around him, chanting "Hospody pomylui". As the human chain tightened around him, Mykola's eyes shot open. He screamed: "No!" at the top of his lungs.

The cathedral had become eerily quiet. Mykola was breathing hard, desperately trying to catch his breath. He looked over at his mother and knew the most difficult moment in the service had arrived. The end was at hand. Father Ihor looked up at the balcony, nodded and the choir began singing:

"Vichnaja Pamjat" (Memory Eternal). The heartrending lyrics wafted through the rafters and pierced Mykola's soul. When the lament ended, the priest invited the congregation to come forward to say their final farewells. They kissed the gold crucifix he held in his right hand as they filed by the coffins. Many of the men touched Stepan's hand. Most of the women, holding each other for support, sobbed openly and gently kissed Iryna on the forehead.

Sonia gripped her godson's hand as Father Ihor approached. He held the crucifix up to Mykola's face.

"Kiss the cross," she whispered.

Mykola turned his head away.

"My son, it is time for you to say a last farewell to your mama and papa," the priest said softly.

"I can't. I can't do it," Mykola said turning to his godmother.

"You have to," she whispered. "You have to." With that she got up and, holding hands with Orest and Lesia, went over to Stepan's coffin. Their other daughters followed. Sonia touched his hand and said a short prayer. There was no outward display of emotion. She then walked over to her best friend's casket and began shaking uncontrollably.

"Goodbye, Iryna. I love you. I will miss you so much," Sonia said, placing her favorite photo of the two of them beside the icon.

"Goodbye, teta," was all Lesia could get out before grabbing onto her father for support.

Slowly Mykola rose from his seat and approached his father's coffin. He looked down at the lifeless body. He didn't reach in to touch his hand or lean in to give him a last kiss. He didn't say a prayer.

"Goodbye," was the only word he uttered.

He then turned and went to his mother's coffin. He gazed down at her face. She looked like she was sleeping but he knew she was dead. The tears began to flow. He fell to his knees in prayer. "Why did you have to die? Why did you have to die?" he moaned.

Orest placed his hand on Mykola's shoulder and helped him up. "It's time. Say your goodbye. It's time."

"Mama, I love you. I will always love you." Mykola leaned in to kiss her and recoiled in horror when his lips touched her ice-cold forehead. He could taste the thick, pancake makeup on his mouth.

The room went black. A church attendant was sprinkling cool water on Mykola's face. Sonia was propping up his head. Lesia stood behind her, crying.

Mykola could hear the bell tolling and turned to see the coffins being carried out of the church. He scrambled to his feet and watched in silence as the caskets were placed in the hearses. Funeral workers were busy placing the mountain of floral tributes in the backs of a dozen flower cars. Most of the people were rushing to their vehicles to line up for the procession to the cemetery.

"Come with us," Orest said, pointing to a black stretch limousine, parked directly behind the hearse carrying Iryna's remains.

Mykola stood frozen in his tracks. "I'm not going to the cemetery. I can't."

"I understand," Sonia said, giving her godson a hug. She wasn't going to push the issue any further. "You came to say goodbye and that is a good thing."

"Where are you going?" Lesia asked, running over to Mykola as he made his way down the church steps.

"I don't know."

She reached out and grabbed his hand. "I'm here for you. Please stop shutting me out, Mykola. I love you."

He didn't respond.

As Father Ihor got into the limo with the Kordan family, he shook his head in dismay as Mykola disappeared down the street.

CHAPTER FOUR

More than 400 people packed the church hall after the burial for the tryzna, the traditional meal after the funeral. Mykola was a no show although a setting was placed at the head table for him. On each side was a setting for the departed. The ladies church auxiliary spent the past two days preparing the food – borscht, perogy, cabbage rolls, patychky (meat on a stick) and a sweet table filled to overflowing with a variety of cakes, cookies and pudding. Dozens of collapsible tables were set up in neat rows decorated with embroidered tablecloth. Sonia was ushered to the head table along with a score of dignitaries from the Canadian Ukrainian Congress, the Shevchenko Foundation and the University of Alberta. All the politicians of Ukrainian background attended knowing it wouldn't look good if they didn't show. The non-Ukrainians sent their regrets.

Father Ihor began with a short prayer for the departed, followed by grace.

For an hour, the mourners ate, drank and regaled each other with stories about Stephan and Iryna, or chatted about their own recently deceased loved ones. As coffee was being served, Andrew Pinchuk, chairman of the Shevchenko Foundation, stepped up to the microphone.

"Your eminence, ladies and gentlemen," he began. "On this most sad of occasions, we have gathered here in the centuries old Ukrainian tradition to honor the memory of the dearly departed; Dr. Stepan Yashan and his dear wife, Iryna. I ask you all to stand."

Everyone rose.

"Dear Stepan and Iryna, you will forever be in our thoughts. May you find peace in the arms of our Lord Jesus Christ. Amen."

Spontaneously, the mourners began singing: Vichnaja Pamjat.

Pinchuk continued. "Professor Vasyl Romaniuk has been asked to give the eulogy honoring his colleague and longtime friend. He will be followed by Sonia Kordan who will pay tribute to her dearest friend Iryna. At this time I call on Professor Romaniuk to say a few words about the life and times of a very great man."

Pinchuk stressed "a few words," knowing full well that Romaniuk was not one taken to saying "a few words" on any subject. And the loquacious professor was not one to be muzzled. He spoke for more than an hour describing in laborious detail the historical and political contributions made by Dr. Yashan over his lifetime. He cited every article, paper, thesis and all six books penned by his eminent colleague. It was like attending Slavic Studies 101 through to 414. While much of what Romaniuk had to say fell on bored ears, it was his closing comments that moved everyone to the edge of their seats.

"Dr. Yashan made international headlines with his seminal work; *Blind Defiance* in which he documented the brutal executions by Stalin's henchmen of our beloved Kobzari. In the book, he revealed the resting place of those tragic, lost souls and with that revelation Dr. Yashan had repeatedly implored several Presidents of Ukraine over the past two decades to have their remains exhumed so that they can be given a hero's funeral and a proper Christian burial. This was the singular passion of Dr. Yashan; to see to it that the kobzari received a proper funeral, and that a memorial be placed on the soccer field under which their remains rest to this very day. Yet year after year, the various Presidents of Ukraine have ignored this simple, Christian request."

Rumbles of outrage reverberated through the hall with most guests shaking their heads in disgust and disbelief. Many shot an angry glare at the Ukrainian ambassador to Canada who nervously stared down at his cup of coffee. Then suddenly, as if on cue, everyone rose and broke out in a chorus of Vichnaja Pamjat, followed by Shche ne vmerla Ukraina, the Ukrainian national anthem, which was sung by the defiant kobzari as they were led out, one by one, into a courtyard and shot.

In his long-winded homily, there was not a word about Stepan, the friend, or Stepan the husband or Stepan the father. It was all about the academic works of Dr. Yashan, the acclaimed historian and writer. In Yashan's world, one thing was abundantly clear: there was little time for family and no time for friendship.

As Romaniuk began citing yet another of Yashan's myriad papers, Andrew Pinchuk sidled over to the podium and stood behind him, tapping his foot. After several minutes, the professor got the hint and wrapped up.

Vera Moroz, first vice-president of the Canadian Ukrainian Congress, then took to the podium to introduce Sonia Kordan.

"Sonia has been a good friend, a loyal friend, and like a sister to Iryna Yashan since they were children. She will share with us some of her cherished moments. Sonia?"

Sonia stood for a moment at the podium trying to gather her thoughts and steel her emotions. "Anyone who ever met Iryna was touched by her incredible warmth. Her love of life was contagious. She was always so happy. She possessed a vibrant energy. Iryna was a wonderful and giving woman but mostly, she was an amazing mother to her only child, Mykola. "

Sonia was suddenly hit with an overwhelming wave of grief. Staring up at the ceiling, she gasped for air in a vain attempt to regain her composure. "All I can say is that I miss you so much, Iryna. I loved you like a sister. I'm sorry." She rushed off the stage.

Orest and the girls intercepted her at the door and left the church hall holding each other for support, as one by one, a dozen women walked up to the podium to share their memories about the life and times of their dear friend, Iryna. It was a tender outpouring of love for a remarkable woman.

No one else got up to say another word about Stepan Yashan.

On the drive home, Lesia felt her IPhone vibrating. Frantically, she tore into her purse, hoping it was Mykola. It was a text message.

"Sitting on our bench by the river at William Hawrelak Park," he wrote. It was their favorite spot. It was where they shared their first kiss under a full, golden harvest moon when they were fourteen. It was where they fell deeply in love.

Lesia could hardly contain herself. It was his first real communication since the accident. When the family arrived home, Orest gave his daughter the car keys.

"Don't speed. Drive carefully," he warned. "Mykola isn't going anywhere."

"I won't speed, daddy," she promised, giving him a peck on the cheek.

When she arrived at the park, she sat quietly beside Mykola and took his hand. For the longest time they said nothing. They just watched chunks of ice float down the river.

"I'm sorry that I shut you out," Mykola began.

"You have nothing to be sorry about."

"Everything is so messed up. Nothing makes any sense to me anymore."

"You lost your mother and father. I've been trying to think of what to say and I can't find the words. I don't know what I would do if mama and tato were killed. I pray to God that never happens. It would destroy me."

"Don't bring God into this."

"Mykola, you can't lose your faith. You need it now more than ever. Don't allow yourself to lose your faith in God."

"Where was He that day? If there is a God, why did He allow this to happen? What reason could there possibly be to kill Mama?"

Lesia paused. "I don't know.

No more words were spoken. Each wrapped in their thoughts, they sat holding hands looking down at the river.

CHAPTER FIVE

Sonia came down to the basement carrying a large cardboard box. Mykola was sitting on the sofa watching a mindless chick-flick with Lesia. It had been a week since the funeral and he had yet to go out. He was in no mood for any more outpourings of pity or prolonged condolences. He just wanted to be left alone. Lesia intercepted all his calls, voice mail and texts. She simply told everyone: "Mykola needs his space. He'll call when he's ready. I'm sure you understand."

Mykola looked up as Sonia placed the box gently on the coffee table. He could tell from the look on her face that something was amiss.

"The police dropped this off earlier today," she said.

"What is it?" Mykola asked.

"It's your mama and tato's personal effects from the accident."

Lesia drew a sharp breath and grabbed Mykola's hand.

"When will this nightmare end?" he wondered aloud, rubbing his temples.

"Do you want me to open the box?" Sonia asked.

"I guess."

At the very top were two large envelopes, one containing his father's wallet, gold Rolex watch, wedding band and a ring of keys. Mykola picked up the watch, stared at it for a moment and then said flatly: "I don't want it. Do you think Orest would like it?"

"You should think about this. After all, the watch is a keepsake, a memento," Lesia said.

"A keepsake of what? I don't want anything that reminds me of that man. Anyway, Orest will look cool with a Rolex on his wrist!"

"I'll put it away for now and when you decide you want it back…" Sonia began.

"I'll never want it. I'll never wear it and if Orest doesn't want it, then I'll sell it and give the money to charity."

Sonia looked at her daughter and shrugged her shoulders as she placed the watch back in the envelope.

The second envelope contained his mother's wedding and engagement rings, a diamond encrusted, gold Cartier watch and a gold chain and locket. Mykola's eyes began to well as he opened the locket to find her mother's favorite picture of him taken when he was three-years-old. Lesia threw her arms around Mykola and held tight. He closed the locket and stared hard at the ceiling.

"I'll put these in a safe place for you," Sonia said.

"Teta, I want you to have the watch. Mama would have wanted you to have it."

Sonia didn't respond. She was remembering how much Iryna cherished the watch. Stepan had given it to her on their 25th wedding anniversary.

At the bottom of the box was the professor's beloved Toshiba laptop computer. The doctor never ventured anywhere without it. It was his baby, more precious to him than the family bible. It went to the washroom, to the university and to his bedside table. The two were joined at the hip. It contained his entire life works.

Mykola pulled it out of the box, flipped it open and pushed the 'on' button. In an instant if flashed: Vitayemo (Welcome in Ukrainian) against the yellow and gold flag of Ukraine fluttering in a computer animated breeze. Then it demanded a password.

"It's locked," Lesia noted. "You'd have to know the password."

A wry smile appeared on Mykola's lips as he typed in: Doctor. The computer suddenly came alive.

"Your father told you his password?" Lesia asked incredulously.

"Are you kidding? He'd never do that."

"Then how did you know it?" Sonia inquired.

"I just asked myself what was the most important thing to him? The answer was simple; the fact he insisted on being called 'Doctor'. The man was an egomaniac."

"Mykola, I will not have you talking about your father like that," Sonia admonished.

As the computer threw open the doors to the professor's private domain, Mykola's mind was suddenly beset with morbid curiosity. He began scrolling through the various folders. Every single one dealt with Ukrainian issues – historical, political, economic, cultural and religious. There were numerous papers written by the doctor on the 1932-33 Ukrainian Famine, Josef Stalin's purges of Ukrainian Intellectuals, and the resistance groups that rose up to fight Russian oppression of Ukraine. There were several papers dealing with Ukraine since its independence from the former USSR – the economic hardships, the political corruption and excesses of the oligarchs, the moves to bring Ukraine into the European Union, and the rampant voter fraud perpetrated by political parties and their leaders during Ukrainian elections. There was a long treatise on the schism between the Ukrainian Catholic and Orthodox Church, as well as a paper on moves by the Ukrainian Orthodox Church to break away from the Russian Orthodox Archdiocese. There was also a searing letter to Sig Gissler, the administrator of the Pulitzer Prize Board, demanding that Walter Duranty, a long deceased reporter with the New York Times, be stripped of the prestigious Pulitzer he garnered in 1934.

The letter captured the attention of both Mykola and Lesia.

It began: "Walter Duranty was a Stalinist sympathizer, Soviet propagandist and a blatant liar. While millions of Ukrainian peasants were being starved to death in the forced famine of 1932-33, Duranty wrote of bumper crops and full stomachs. Scholars worldwide have long discredited his reporting. Moreover, in 2003 the New York Times hired Mark von Hagen, a professor of Russian History at Columbia University to review Duranty's work. Von Hagen found Duranty's reports to be unbalanced and uncritical, and that they far too often gave voice to Stalinist propaganda. He suggested that 'for the sake of the New York Times' honor, they should take the prize away'. In a letter accompanying von Hagen's report, Times publisher Arthur Ochs Sulzberger, Jr. called Duranty's work 'slovenly' and said it "should have been recognized for what it was by his editors and by his Pulitzer judges seven decades ago. As well, scholars worldwide had long discredited Duranty's so-called reporting."

Professor Yashan pointed out that "even The New York Times hall honoring all its Pulitzer winners over the decades has placed a caveat under its photograph of Walter Duranty stating: Other writers at The Times and elsewhere have discredited this coverage. So it escapes me as to why the Pulitzer Committee steadfastly refuses to rescind Duranty's award stating 'there was no clear and convincing evidence of deliberate deception'. I am astounded by this nonsensical conclusion. It is time that the Pulitzer board does the right thing. It must revoke the award."

Mykola was forced to concede that if anything, his father was a prolific writer. He was the personification of an academic. He had to give the man that much credit at least.

"I never knew any of this," Lesia said as Mykola moved the cursor over to another file folder.

"I used to hear him rant about it with other professors at the dinner table. This was one issue that really pissed him off. Given all that has been exposed about Walter Duranty, I don't understand why the Pulitzer Board continues to refuse to revoke the prize."

Mykola then opened the picture file. It contained scores of photographs of the doctor standing at podiums giving lectures and receiving rewards. There were reams of photos of Ukrainian politicians, professors and noted writers, as well as the requisite picture of Ukraine's poet laureate Taras Shevchenko. As he scanned the photo library and document files, he felt his pulse begin to pound in his temples. To his disappointment, he realized there was not a single reference in the professor's precious laptop about his wife or his son. There was not even a single photograph in the computer's picture folder of the woman who so devoted her life to him. Dr. Yashan's life was all business and all about himself. Wife and child were not given entry into his cerebral world.

"Why the angry frown?" Sonia asked.

"I know tato didn't love me but what I don't get is why he didn't even have one picture of Mama in his laptop?"

Sonia didn't respond.

"What do I do with this?" Mykola asked, tossing the laptop to a corner of the sofa.

"Knowing your father, I'm sure he left specific instructions in his will where all his papers should go. Do you know Roman Walchuk?" Sonia asked.

"The fat guy?"

Lesia laughed.

Sonia grimaced. "He's your parents' lawyer. He drew up their will. Roman called me this morning to set up an appointment for tomorrow afternoon to read the will. I'm the executor."

"And I guess I have to be there," Mykola said with a tone of exasperation.

"Yes," Sonia said.

Mykola and Sonia were escorted to the glassed-in boardroom of the downtown Edmonton law firm of Foster, Mitchell, Schwartz, and Walchuk. A dozen high-back, black leather swivel chairs surrounded a large, gleaming, oval, smoked glass conference table. Sonia sat. Mykola stared out the 32nd floor window at the city skyline. His mind was totally blank. He just wanted the day to be over with as quickly and painlessly as possible.

A few minutes later, Roman Walchuk shuffled in. He was a classic, walking advertisement for high cholesterol, diabetes, hardening of the arteries, and heart attack. The man was obese. His breathing was labored, his

flesh pallid and his beet-red face was beaded with perspiration. He held out
a limp, clammy palm and shook Mykola's hand.

"My condolences. Your father was a great man. His death is a great
loss to the community," he said, dropping a thin file on the table. It was
labeled: Yashan.

"And my mother?"

The lawyer looked quizzically at Mykola.

"My mother's death was also great loss."

"Yes. It was. I'm sorry." The lawyer looked over at Sonia who shot back a
stone cold glare. She loathed the way so many men in the community acted
as if only one person of consequence had died in the tragic accident that
killed her best friend.

"So, we are here to read the last will and testament of Stepan Yashan and
Iryna Yashan," Walchuk said as he eased his ample girth between the arm-
rests of the chair. He opened the file and began reading the standard script,
which was anything but standard.

With the passing of his parents, Mykola was the sole beneficiary of what
amounted to more than $14-million in property, investments and cash. He
was stunned when he heard the figure. He knew his parents were well off but
had no idea they were so wealthy. From the stunned expression on Sonia's
face, it was obvious she had no idea as well. Her best friend never discussed
money and certainly did not live the lifestyle of the rich and privileged. But
as Sonia thought back, Iryna had spent a small fortune on her art collection.
It alone had to be worth more than a million dollars.

"Much of your parents' wealth came from their parents," Walchuk
explained. "Long ago, your grandfather – your mother's father - wisely
bought up huge tracts of land in and around Edmonton. Your parents sold
most of the properties in the last real estate boom but there are two large
industrial lots that are leased out near the airport. They must be worth
several million. In addition, there are two $1-million life insurance poli-
cies – one in your father's name, the other in your mother's name, as well as
a $500,000 life insurance policy that your father had with the university.
Again, you are the sole beneficiary."

Mykola could not believe his ears. His mother was frugal and his father
was plain cheap. They rarely went on vacations and whenever they did travel,
which was extensively, it was usually on an invitation for a speaking engagement, which was paid for by some university or international institute.

"Now, unless you specify otherwise, I will draw up the necessary papers to
transfer their assets and bank accounts to your name," the lawyer continued.
"But before I can do that, I will require the originals of the death certificates."

Mykola looked over at Sonia.

"I have them here with me," she said, retrieving an envelope from her purse.

Flipping to another page in his file, Walchuk added: "There is one specific clause in Dr. Yashan's will that is of the utmost importance, and that is his papers. He has instructed that they be donated to the Canadian-Ukrainian Shevchenko Foundation. This includes all documents, files, papers, his entire library, and all materials relating to research contained in his computer. He has provided me with the secret password to the computer which I will pass on to the Foundation."

"Doctor," Mykola said.

"What?" the lawyer asked.

"The password. It's Doctor. Uppercase D and the rest lowercase."

"Yes. Well, I can't discuss that. It's solicitor/client privilege. I will contact the chairman of the Shevchenko Foundation and we will make the necessary arrangements to retrieve Dr. Yashan's materials from his university office and your home at your earliest convenience."

Mykola nodded his agreement.

"Before the archivists from the foundation attend to your father's home office, I suggest you go through his papers to see if there is anything of a personal nature that should not be included and taken away," Walchuk suggested.

"I can't think of anything my father would have of a personal nature in his office. He was all about his work," Mykola said in a snide tone.

"Well, you never know. I just want to save him from any potential embarrassment," the lawyer noted stuffing a sheaf of documents back into the file folder. He then looked at Mykola. Clearing his throat, he began: "I've been your parents' lawyer for 32 years. If there is anything you need, I'm a phone call away."

With immense effort and a labored groan, Walchuk pushed himself up from the chair and waddled down the hallway to his office.

CHAPTER SIX

Mykola sat in the darkened, formal living room staring apprehensively at the locked door across the hallway leading to his father's study. It was the first time he had set foot in the family home since the funeral two weeks earlier. His stomach was churning acid. He had haphazardly ventured into the professor's sanctuary only once in his life and never forgot it. He was four. His father had gone to the kitchen to get a mug of coffee. Racing about the hallway pushing a red, toy fire truck, the boy zoomed through the open door and into the hallowed chamber. In a flash, he was mesmerized by the plaques adorning the walls. As he gazed around the room, he was drawn to a bookcase housing a treasure trove of shiny trophies and gold medals. He grabbed at a bronze wheat sheaf perched on a second shelf. Unaware that it was quite heavy, the award slipped from his tiny fingers and crashed to the wooden floor with a thunderous thud. A moment later, he heard the pounding of footsteps rapidly approaching. His father charged in. He hauled Mykola to his feet by the back of his tee shirt and hurled him into the hallway.

"Don't you ever come into this office!" he shouted, his face red with rage. A thick, blue vein popped out like an enormous earthworm on his forehead. "You hear me, you little cretin? Never, ever come into this office."

Iryna dashed into the hallway. "Stepan, please don't talk to the boy like that!"

"I don't ever want him in my study," the professor bellowed.

"Oh for God sake, Stepan, the boy made a mistake. You don't need to act like an ogre."

"He is to stay out of my study!" he yelled as he slammed the door shut.

Mykola was sheet white and trembling. His mother pulled him up from the floor and carried the sobbing youngster to his bedroom.

"Mama, I didn't mean to make tato angry."

"I know, Mykola. I know," she said, holding him close.

As she gently laid him down on his bed, Mykola asked: "Mama, what is a cretin?"

"It's nothing. Forget about that. Your father didn't mean it," she said in a calm whisper while stroking his head. "His office is his own special place just like the secret hideout in your closet is your special place."

Mykola could never erase the event from his mind. It was branded into his memory banks. It was the day that whatever love the boy had for the man he called tato evaporated forever. For the rest of his childhood, he dreaded doing anything that might ignite his father's wrath. He stayed clear of the study and the man never yelled at him again. He also never apologized for his vile outburst.

At the age of twelve, while rummaging through a box of old toys, Mykola found the fire truck and the memory of that infamous day struck like a bolt of lightning. The word "cretin" echoed in his head. He sat down at his computer, logged onto Google and typed "cretin". His heart sank as he read the definition: "a stupid, obtuse or mentally defective person." He felt like he had been kicked in the stomach. He couldn't believe his father thought of him in this way, or that no matter how angry he was that he could think of his four year old son as a "mentally defective person." His loathing toward his father intensified.

Now, Mykola held the keys to the inner sanctum tightly in his right hand, the brass teeth carving groves into his palm. He was overwhelmed by a powerful sense of trepidation. Taking a deep breath, he pushed himself up from the family room sofa and forced himself to walk to the study door. His hand shook as he fumbled with the key. With a click, the lock snapped. He turned the crystal doorknob and pushed the door open. For the longest moment, he stood frozen surveying his father's righteous realm. Then his gaze landed on the bronze wheat sheaf statue perched on the top shelf on the doctor's trophy case. His mind flashed back to the day his father tossed him out of the room like a piece of trash. He could hear his father's angry voice pounding in his ears: "Don't you ever come into this office! You hear me, you little cretin? Never, ever come into this office."

As he crossed the threshold, he was hit by the musty smell of old books and moldy paper. Manuscripts were stacked three feet high on an antique oak desk Iryna had purchased for him on their 10th anniversary. Bookshelves, jammed with academic tomes on Ukraine, Russia, Poland and the Union of Soviet Socialist Republics, flanked an entire wall from floor to ceiling. A computer workstation faced the window that was blacked out by a thick indigo velvet curtain. On it sat a Dell computer with a flat screen monitor and a high-speed laser printer. Underneath was a black computer tower. The unit was shut down. The only activity was a red blinking light from the Internet modem.

Mykola couldn't bring himself to sit in his father's weathered, leather chair. Instead, he shoved it out of the way and pulled open the top left drawer of the desk. It was filled with pens, paper clips, yellow, red and blue Post-Its and blank index cards. Nothing out of the ordinary. The top right drawer was jammed with envelopes, stamps, Scotch tape and printing paper. When he tried to yank open the large lower drawer, he discovered it was locked. Mykola hunted through the key ring, trying out several keys before hitting on the right one. He turned the lock and pulled open the heavy drawer. There were at least half a dozen large, sealed manila envelopes stacked one top of the other. Pulling them out one at a time, Mykola immediately recognized their importance. On each was printed, in Ukrainian, the contents. The first were the original documents containing orders from Stalin to execute the kobzari. The second envelope detailed the plan to lure the minstrels to Kharkiv on the pretext of a National Assembly of kobzari to be followed by a concert. A thick, third and fourth package contained the identities and particulars of each musician, including place and date of birth, and date of execution. Inside the fifth envelope, instructions of where the bodies were to be disposed of and a map of the burial site. The sixth envelope held photos of the doomed men. Mykola slowly thumbed through the black and white mug shots. An icy shiver shot up his spine as he looked at the faces of the men. He was particularly seized by the face of a proud, white haired minstrel with a long drooping Cossack moustache. The man, identified only as KZ158, knew he was about to meet his Maker and yet he showed no fear. His unseeing eyes flamed with defiance and pride. Mykola had seen the photograph years before when reading his father's book. It was also the centerpiece in his father's travelling exhibition with the release of *Blind Defiance*. But it was a photocopy blow up. Now Mykola was holding the original, taken seconds before the man was dragged into a courtyard and shot. It was clear and chilling. As he flipped through a few dozen more photographs, he began to wonder how he would have reacted, knowing he was about to be executed for the crime of being a proud nationalist. Would he stand tall and defiant, or would he cave and fall to his knees like a coward, pleading for his life to be spared? And what would his father have done? Looking up at the ceiling, Mykola muttered: "Cowered, no doubt about that." He wondered too about the cold-blooded agents who pulled the triggers. What must have gone through the mind of those executioners? What kind of person would hold a gun to the heads of those honorable bards? The men were old and blind. What possible threat could they pose? Filled with a deep sense of reverence, Mykola carefully placed the photos back in the envelope and laid it on the desk.

He then retrieved the remaining file folder. His eyes focused on the name inscribed in black marker on the large, yellowed envelope. It read: Mykola Danylo Yashan. He thought it odd that his father would have a file on him. He stared at the envelope for quite some time. He felt an uneasiness. His hands started to shake as he tore it open. Inside were two smaller envelopes; one was very thin with no writing on it. The second bore his name and was one inch thick. He placed it on the desk and ripped open the first. It contained receipts for two money transfers from Western Union. One was dated July 28, 1993, the other August 9th of the same year. Each was for $10,000 in U.S funds. There was no explanation for the payments. They were made out to a woman named Natalka Matlinsky.

CHAPTER SEVEN

Mykola turned his attention to the second, thicker envelope. It contained a six-page, legal sized document written in Ukrainian with an official government seal at the bottom of the last page. The document began: "This is to certify the legal adoption by Stepan Yashan and Iryna Yashan of Edmonton, Alberta, Canada, of a two-week-old orphan boy hence forth to be known as Mykola Danylo Yashan. It was dated August 26, 1993. It was signed by his father, mother, Vitaly Assimovich, the deputy minister of Families and Children, and Natalka Matlinsky, director of Orphanage 41, Lviv, Ukraine.

Mykola's eyes froze. His mind was spinning. His breathing was out of control. Desperate to get out of the study, he grabbed the documents and retreated to the family room. For what seemed like hours, he sat staring blankly at the papers he'd strewn across the coffee table. He couldn't bring himself to read the contents in their entirety. He was in shock and while nothing made sense, strangely tiny missing pieces of the jigsaw puzzle that had been his life slowly began to fall into place. For as long as he could remember, he'd never felt the slightest connection to his father. The man treated him as an afterthought. He was distant and much of the time acted as if the boy didn't exist. And while Mykola knew in his heart that his mother loved him more than life itself, he could never understand why his father treated him with absolute indifference. Ironically, he had often fantasized in his childhood daydreams that he was adopted and as he got older he sometimes caught himself wondering why he possessed absolutely no physical resemblance to either his mother or his father. His mother was blond, fine boned and blue-eyed with marble white skin. His father was thin as a rail, with frizzy black hair, a long narrow face, ice green eyes and a pointed chin. Ruggedly handsome, Mykola had the sleek build of an athlete, flowing brown hair, a chiseled Slavic face, and deep brown, brooding eyes that betrayed his every mood. When grandmothers and grandfathers in the Ukrainian community saw him, they would gush, likening him to a Hutzul – the mystical mountain people who inhabit the Carpathian Mountains of Ukraine.

Mykola was 14 when he summoned the courage to ask his mother why he didn't look anything like her or his father. He'd pointed out that all his friends were often told how much they looked like either their mother or father or a combination of both. He'd never once heard that comparison about himself. Iryna explained that he resembled her side of the family, in particular his maternal grandfather. The boy had pored over old, faded black and white photographs of both sets of grandparents but couldn't find the slightest resemblance even though his mother insisted that he and her father shared the same square jaw and eye color.

Yet to all who saw mother and son, there was no doubt that Mykola was a mama's boy. He possessed a lot of his mother's mannerisms and idiosyncrasies. Iryna Yashan was infused with the joy of being alive and she infused that happiness into the very core of her son as a child. They were both very expressive and had the gift of gab. They waved their arms when they talked. They loved to dance and sing. They teared up at sad movies. They always took time to smile at the simple pleasures of life. They loved the peasant food of Ukraine – Borscht, cabbage rolls and perogies lathered with sour cream and golden sauté onions, and could not wait to wolf down their favorite dessert: wild Saskatoon berry pie.

Yet whether he liked to admit it or not, Mykola also shared some of his father's traits. He possessed a sharp, inquisitive, critical mind. Over the years, he would sit at the dinner table listening to the professor and his colleagues discuss and debate political, historical and social issues. It matured him beyond his years. And like his father, he possessed a stubborn streak. Once he latched onto an issue, he wouldn't let go until all the loose ends were tied. He could hold his own in a debate, and beneath the surface, there was a hint of the Yashan arrogance.

As he got into his mid-teens, he became more and more moody. He would often retreat into the dark recesses of his mind. He didn't know what triggered these bizarre, bleak episodes of depression that sometimes lasted weeks. He'd be overwhelmed with an inexplicable sense of loss and yearning, and an overpowering feeling of emptiness. He had a hard time with emotion and kept it bottled up, another trait he'd likely picked up through osmosis from his father.

Mykola flung the documents onto the floor. Breathing heavy, he scanned the family room. It was his mother's sanctuary, her refuge from the insanity of the world outside. She had filled it with the things she cherished. The walls were adorned with the works of famous, and a few not so well known, Ukrainian-Canadian and Ukrainian artists. Her favorites were three paintings by Alberta-born, Manitoba-raised artist William Kurelek. His works depicted bucolic reminiscences of a simpler and timeless past on the Canadian prairies for newcomers from Ukraine in the early 1900s. From various established and budding artists in Ukraine, she'd purchased four sweeping canvasses of the idyllic landscapes of the Steppes and the Carpathian Mountains with women dressed in traditional embroidered blouses and skirts, and men in baggy trousers and black boots. There was a stunning woodcut portrait of Ukraine's poet laureate Taras Shevchenko, an embroidered sash respectfully draped over the oak frame. Several bronze and marble sculptures dotted the room, and on each end of a long, antique, black lacquer hutch two huge cognac-shaped tumblers were filled to overflowing with dozens of intricately, hand-painted pysanky (Ukrainian Easter eggs); each one gifted to Iryna from friends and admirers. Perched lovingly on the mantel above a log burning, fieldstone fireplace was a cluster of framed family photographs. Pictures of Mykola's entire life: his jubilant mother lovingly cradling him in her arms when he was a week old; his mother posing with her son on his first birthday with a single candle on a homemade strawberry shortcake; Iryna pulling him on a blue wagon at three; Mama posing happily with him on his first bike at five; her arm wrapped around a beaming seven-year-old dressed in the dance costume of a proud Cossack. Every single year of his life, up to the age of 18 with burgundy cap and gown when he graduated from high school, was represented on that mantle and two coffee tables at either side of the sofa, and beside him in every picture was his mother. His father, omnipresent in community life, was conspicuously absent from all the photos.

Mykola began to cry, quietly at first and then he began to wail, purging two weeks of unrelenting torment from his soul. He slumped down on the sofa and buried his head into a pillow. Slowly he drifted into a deep sleep. He came to three hours later, his mind tangled in a maze of cobwebs. Through a blur, his eyes focused on a photograph of his parents in a silver frame sitting on a walnut end table against the wall beside the fireplace. He had seen the photo a million times but something about it suddenly seemed odd. It was a snapshot of his father and mother posing in front of the opulent Opera House in Lviv; his father ever the intellectual poseur, his mother overjoyed to be in the land of her parents' birth. He couldn't put his finger on it but something in his gut propelled him off the sofa. He rushed over to the table, picked up the frame and unfastened the backboard. On the reverse side of the photo, in his mother's swirling penmanship, was written: Lviv Opera House – August 6, 1993. The date was three days before Mykola was born! He flipped the photo over and stared at his mother's thin, flat waistline. She wasn't pregnant. In a sudden burst of anger, he whipped the frame across the room, the glass smashing into shards on the stone fireplace.

"My life is one big fucking lie," he shouted. "My whole fucking life is a fucking lie!"

At that moment, the doorbell rang. Mykola didn't want to answer but whoever it was, didn't go away. The bell kept chiming.

"Okay … okay … I'm coming! Just lay off the damn bell!" he yelled.

It was Sonia.

"I was worried about you. I knew this would be your first day home since the accident. I thought you might want someone around."

Mykola stared coldly at her.

Sonia began to feel uneasy. "Is something wrong?"

"You knew all along, didn't you?"

"Knew what?" Sonia asked, taken aback by Mykola's tone. She had no idea what he meant but she knew something was terribly wrong.

"That I was adopted. That my mother and father are not my real parents."

Sonia felt her knees go weak. She drew a deep breath and walked over to the family room. Her eyes shot wide open when she saw a sheaf of documents strewn on the floor. She stooped down and picked up the adoption record.

"Oh my God," she whispered. "Where did you find these?"

"In tato's desk."

"That man swore to your mother that he destroyed them," she said angrily.

"So you knew all along."

"Yes."

"Who else knew?" Mykola demanded.

"No one. Just me and your parents."

"Does Lesia know?"

"No. No one else. Not even Orest. I swear. Your mother was my best friend. She was like my sister. I swore to her I would never tell anyone her secret."

"Her secret! I can't believe this. Why didn't my parents ever tell me?"

"They wanted to protect you."

"Protect me from what?"

"There are a lot of backward people in the community who have this belief that an adopted child is someone who is defective. For them, the question is, why else would a mother abandon her child? They believe that if you adopt a child, you are taking on someone else's problem. No good can ever come of that child, only heartache and trouble. Your parents didn't want these ignorant fools whispering behind their backs or your back. People can be very cruel. They can say some very nasty things. Iryna and Stepan believed it was better this way. Iryna loved you as her own whether she gave birth to you or not. She loved you as her son. You were her everything. You know that. You know that in your heart."

"Now I get why my father hated me."

"He didn't hate you."

"He didn't much care for me, and you know that."

"Stepan was what he was."

"Yeah, an arrogant prick."

"Mykola, please don't speak ill of the dead. I won't stand for it."

"I guess I must have reminded him every day of his life that he wasn't a man."

"What do you mean by that?"

"The acclaimed professor couldn't father a child. It must have driven him mad."

Sonia shook her head. "No, Mykola. It was your mother. She couldn't have children. That's why she wanted you. She fell in love with you the moment she held you in her arms. You made her life whole."

"Yeah, and I made tato's life hell. Now I understand everything. I guess he thought there was something wrong with me. I guess he belongs to the gang that believes adopted babies are defective."

"Stop talking like that! There is nothing wrong with you."

"You know, when I told him I was enrolling in civil engineering at university, he insulted me, saying that blue collar was all he ever expected I would amount to. When I apologized for not being a chip off the old block, do you know what he said?"

Sonia didn't respond.

"He said I wasn't even a chip! Now I finally know what he meant." Mykola looked over at the mantle. "Were they ever going to tell me?"

"I don't know. Your mother and I never discussed it. You were her son. There was nothing to discuss because no one else knew."

Then it hit him like a lightning bolt. If Iryna Yashan wasn't his biological mother, then who was? Did the woman die while giving birth? Did she abandon him because she was too poor to take care of him? Was she an unwed mother? Why was he given up? And who was his father? Mykola's mind was swirling with questions.

"Do you know anything about my real mother? Did mama ever say anything about her?"

"Iryna was your real mother and don't you ever forget that. I will not have you saying otherwise. Do you understand that?" Sonia said firmly.

"I know she's my mama and it tears at my soul that she is no longer here." Sonia reached out to her godson.

Mykola pressed on. "I need to know. Did mama ever tell you anything about the woman who brought me into the world?"

Sonia was worried. She knew her godson. He was headstrong like Stepan and would not let go until he got the answers to all of his questions. The trouble was she couldn't give him the answers he needed because she didn't have them.

"Iryna told me that several months before you were born, your mother would often visit an orphanage in Lviv. She became friends with the director. There were so many abandoned and unwanted babies. Your mother's heart broke seeing them in their cribs reaching out to her. She was such a loving, giving person. The director asked your mother why she didn't have children of her own and when Iryna told her she couldn't conceive, the director suggested adoption. Your father wasn't enthusiastic about the idea. But as you know, your mother can be persuasive. After a few months, Stepan gave in, and the orphanage director promised Iryna that she would find her a healthy orphan baby. And she did. She found you after your biological mother died giving birth to you."

"So it's a dead end. My real mother died. There's no doubt."

"No doubt. Iryna told me she died."

"Nice friend," Mykola said.

"What? Who?" Sonia asked.

"The orphanage director."

"Why would you say that?"

"From what I can gather from these documents, my parents gave the woman $20,000 U.S. Why did they pay her $20,000?"

Sonia shook her head. It was obvious she hadn't been apprised of the financial aspect of the adoption.

"My mother didn't tell you that? It's all here in these documents that Tato forgot to shred."

"Mykola, I know this is very hard for you."

"It's so messed up, Teta. First mama and tato are killed, and now this."

"I know. I know," she said, reaching for his hand. "But I want you to know I will always be here for you. You must believe that. I'm your godmother."

"I know that Teta."

"Why don't you come home with me? It's not good staying alone in this house."

Mykola thought about it for a moment and decided against it. "No. I'll stay here tonight. I feel like I've got to be here tonight."

Sonia gazed at her godson with sadness in her eyes. "I'm worried about you. Lesia is worried about you. You shouldn't be alone. This is not a time to be alone."

"Teta, I'll be okay. It's just that my mind is in a jumble. I need to be alone. I need to sort out of few things."

"Then promise you'll call if you need me. I'll come and pick you up right away."

"I promise." Mykola said, kissing his godmother on the cheek as she left.

Try as he might, Mykola couldn't fall asleep. His mind was careening out of control. He felt like the silver ball in a pinball machine. The discoveries of the day had ignited every synapse in his brain. He tried staring at a spot on the ceiling to push his mind into neutral. It didn't work. He plugged his IPod headphones into his ears and cranked up the tunes. It didn't help. He kept tossing, turning, and rocking back and forth. Finally somewhere around 4 am, he tumbled into the land of nightmares.

A ghostly curtain of blue smoke from an incense burner wafted over the room. His nostrils filled with the intoxicating scent of burning beeswax candles. In the distance, a male choir chanted 'Hospody pomylui' in a somber funeral rite. A priest cloaked in a black shroud circled a coffin blessing it with holy water. A crush of stone-faced mourners stood vigil around the oak casket resting on a gold plated pyre before an icon festooned altar. Several easels placed around the coffin were adorned with awards, medals and plaques. Mykola pushed his way through the crowd. In the coffin with an icon of Jesus on his chest, his father laid stoic dressed in a steel blue suit. An arrogant sneer was plastered on his thin lips. He seemed proud to be on display. For Stepan Yashan, it was his penultimate moment of glory to have so many dignitaries and men of substance paying homage to his lifeless body. As he stared down his father, Mykola felt a sudden surge of panic in his chest. He turned and anxiously began scanning the church in search of his mother. His blood rose to a boil as he spied her casket. It had been relegated to a darkened recess of the sanctuary. She was alone, ignored by the mass of the self-important who came to bask in the memory of the man who was once Dr. Yashan. Mykola ran over to his mother and knelt before her coffin.

In fervent prayer, he promised to cherish her memory and love her forever. He stood, gazed at her sleeping face and kissed her ice-cold forehead. His father's scornful laughter echoed in the rafters.

Mykola tumbled deeper. He saw himself as a small boy, chasing after his father, seeking a little attention, a nod of approval, a hug. Out of breath, he kept running, his tiny legs carrying him as fast as they could. At the top of his lungs, he was yelling "Tato … tato … tato!" But his father pretended not to hear. He never once stopped to look back. He continued at a brisk, deliberate pace ignoring the plaintive cries of a four-year-old who could never catch up to him no matter how hard he tried.

Mykola was now in free fall. He was back in the family room staring at the family photographs on the mantle. His eyes focused on a picture of his mother with her arms wrapped around a happy eight year old in his Ukrainian scout's uniform. He remembered that day so clearly. It was another no-show by his father but it no longer mattered. Mama was there. She was always there. Then strangely, as he was admiring the photo, her image faded into a thick, white mist. Mykola's eyes darted from one frame to the next. In each, his mother began to disappear. Panic stricken, he leapt up from the sofa and charged over to the mantle in a desperate effort to save the few photographs where his mother still held him. He was too late. Mama was gone. He was totally alone, abandoned. He felt an evil presence lurking in the shadows. He turned and saw his father, his lips curled in an icy, malevolent sneer, an eraser in his left hand. He was erasing the last photo of the pair taken at his high school graduation.

Mykola shot bolt upright drenched in a cold sweat. He was gasping for air and screaming. "Mama, don't leave me!"

CHAPTER EIGHT

Mykola spent an entire day combing through his father's papers and scouring his laptop computer in search of anything that had to do with his adoption. He found nothing more. Not a single clue. Running his fingers through his hair, he cursed the man who, even in death, continued to make his life a living hell. He was now firmly convinced that his father had deliberately left the papers in his desk. A meticulous man, Dr. Yashan never did anything without thinking through any and all possible outcomes and consequences.

As Mykola headed for the kitchen, he stopped at the door to his mother's studio. Hesitantly, he walked in. He could almost feel her presence. The scent of her perfume still lingered in the air. He looked over at two beautifully hand-carved banduras perched on chrome stands against the back wall. They were magnificent instruments. On an easel by the window, Iryna's last watercolor – a field of daisies, her favorite flower.

Mykola went over to her desk and opened the bottom drawer. He felt a twinge of guilt as he rifled through his mother's private files. But he was on a mission. For more than three hours, he pored over reams of papers – contracts with a recording company, invitations to play at concerts, royalty statements for CD sales– and then he came across an envelope with copies of wire transfers – one a year for 20 years. They were made out to Natalka Matlinsky - $1,000 for each year and sent by Western Union on August 6th, his birthday. A note in his mother's handwriting was attached to each transfer. It simply read: For the children.

Mykola went to his bedroom and grabbed his laptop. He sat down at the kitchen table and typed in Natalka Matlinsky. Within seconds a website popped up about Matlinsky, director of Orphanage 41 in Lviv, Ukraine. It was a high gloss, hard sell presentation. The opening page featured a photograph of Matlinsky receiving the Award of Merit from Viktor Yurkovich, the President of Ukraine. She was grinning but Mykola saw something in her eyes as she gazed up at the nation's leader. It was an odd look. The next page was awash with photos of wide-eyed orphan babies and toddlers craving love and affection. He breezed through the site noting that it offered a tour to all out-of-town guests and a final page asking for donations with instructions on how and where to send money. Mykola clicked onto another page that dealt with procedures for foreign families wishing to adopt orphans from Ukraine. The key contact: Natalka Matlinsky. He went back to the opening page and stared hard at the woman's face. He knew she had the answers. He made up his mind to go to Ukraine.

Sonia wasn't happy about her godson's decision.

"Why do you need to do this?" she asked before Mykola revealed his travel plans to Lesia and Orest.

"You wouldn't understand."

"Then make me understand," his godmother pressed.

"I spend hours looking into the mirror asking myself: Who am I? Who is my real mother? Who is my real father? Because everything I've been told, all I've ever known, has turned out to be a big lie."

"That's not true. Everything you have lived is what has made you into who you are today, and that is not a lie."

"Then who am I?"

"You are Mykola Danylo Yashan!"

"That's the name my mother and father gave me."

"Yes. Remember that. Your mother and father," Sonia said firmly.

"But before all that, before they adopted me. Who was I?"

"A baby in an orphanage. You were placed there because your biological mother had died."

"But who was she?"

"I don't know."

"And I don't know either," Mykola said, his voice straining with frustration. "That's why I need to go to Ukraine."

"You need to get yourself back to university and finish your degree."

"I can't. My mind won't let me. When I'm awake, I can't concentrate. All I do is think about my real mother. When I'm asleep, my dreams are haunted by a strange woman lurking in the shadows."

"Mykola, you're letting your mind wander. There is no woman in the shadows," Sonia said. "You have to stop torturing yourself."

"I know it's her. I need to find out about her. I'm going to the orphanage in Lviv. I want to find out her name and where she came from. I want to visit her grave. And who knows, I might find an uncle or an aunt who could tell me something about her."

"Mykola, I say this because I love you. You should leave well enough alone. No good can come from this," Sonia warned.

"What do you mean by that? Do you know something you're not telling me?"

"I've told you everything I know, but if you go out on this quest, who knows what you might find. I know that you're hurting inside and that you're confused. But there is always the chance you may not like what you discover, and then what? Sometimes searching for answers can often lead to more pain and confusion."

"Damn right I'm confused. I've just found out that my entire history is a lie."

"Your mother and father were no lie," Sonia shot back sharply.

"The stories they told me about my grandparents are a lie. I look at their pictures in the family album and I now know they have nothing to do with me. They have no connection to me. Their history has nothing to do with my history. Their blood, their genes, their DNA doesn't run in my veins. I don't know whose blood runs in my veins and it's driving me crazy. I need to find some answers."

Sonia was at a loss for words. She was afraid for her godson, but she understood his anguish.

"Do you want me to come with you?"

"No. I need to do this alone."

"Mykola, I don't think this is the time to be alone."

"I need to do this by myself."

"I care for you."

"I know that, Teta, and whatever happens, mama will never stop being my mother. I will always love her. You know that."

"Mykola, I wish you would include your father."

"I can't. The closest I've ever had to a real father is Orest. My so-called father never wanted me. He made that clear all my life. You know that, and now I know why."

Sonia shook her head in dismay as she wiped tears from her eyes. "You're a good boy, Mykola. You've turned out to be a fine young man. Your mama was so proud of you."

"I know that, teta. I love you."

"I love you too. Remember that. Now, what are you going to tell Orest and Lesia?"

"I'll tell them I need a bit of time away on my own and Ukraine is as good a place to escape to as any."

"Lesia will want to go with you."

"I'll just have to convince her that I need this time to figure a few things out. I just hope she'll understand."

"She'll be very upset but I'm sure she'll understand."

Sonia was right. Lesia was upset. And she was wrong. Lesia didn't understand.

"I don't want you to go," Lesia argued. "I don't understand all this need to figure things out stuff."

"Look, I just need some space. Anyway, it's only for a couple of weeks."

"There's a ton of space all over Alberta. Find a retreat in the mountains for God's sake! You don't have to go all the way to Ukraine to find space."

"I've made up my mind. I need to go."

"Is there something you're not telling me?" Lesia asked.

"No! Why?" Mykola stared up at the ceiling to avoid eye contact. He knew that Lesia could read his eyes. They always gave him away.

"I don't know. I get this feeling there is more to this need for space thing than you're telling me."

"Lesia, I'll be back in a couple of weeks. I just need some time to sort things out."

"Then I'll go with you."

"I'm going alone," Mykola interjected firmly, and with those final words, Lesia stormed out of the room.

Orest simply shrugged his shoulders and said nothing. What did he know? If Mykola wanted space and needed to get away, then it was fine with him. His tacit support did not go over well with his daughter.

CHAPTER NINE

Mykola was on edge as the Aerosvit Airlines jet landed on the tarmac of Lviv airport. It was a cool, rainy May afternoon. The 84 passengers were directed into an antiquated arrivals lounge and herded into a long, slow weaving queue. Only two uniformed customs officers manned the passport control booths and they were being annoyingly officious examining every travel document and questioning everyone about their reason for coming to Ukraine. The absurd adherence to red tape left most visitors muttering aloud that the communism of the former USSR was obviously still entrenched in the psyche of Ukrainian bureaucrats even though the nation had been free for more than two decades.

While waiting in line, a balding, heavy-set retiree from Regina standing behind Mykola struck up a conversation. "It's my sixth time coming here. I visit my cousins every second summer," he said.

"This is my first visit," Mykola offered.

"Then let me warn you. They may try to get money from you when you get by the passport officials. "

"What do you mean?"

"Someone may pull you over and try to hit you up for medical insurance. It's a scam, pure and simple. Refuse," the man explained.

Mykola laughed. "Thanks for the heads up."

The passport officer thumbed through Mykola's passport with a look of suspicion. It was brand new. There were no stamps in it from trips to any other country. He also recognized that the family name was of Ukrainian origin. With a wry smile, he figured he had hooked a neophyte, another young man of Ukrainian heritage visiting the motherland in search of his roots. The officer turned and rapped on the glass booth with his pen. A woman wearing a white lab coat and holding a clipboard a few meters down the hallway nodded. Mykola picked up on the signal. He sensed something was up.

After the officer stamped the passport, Mykola strolled down the hallway toward the baggage area but was quickly intercepted by the woman with the clipboard.

"May I see your passport?" she asked in an authoritative voice.

"Why?"

"Regulations!"

Mykola reached into his jacket and handed her the document. She gave it a cursory glance and handed it back.

"You are Canadian. You will need medical insurance while you are in Ukraine. How long do you intend to stay?"

"I'll probably be here a week or two at the most."

"Then you will have to pay 1,500 hryvna. That will be in cash, of course," she said as she primed an application form. "Can you spell me your family name?"

"I don't need medical insurance. I'm fully covered in Canada and I already have medical coverage with my travel insurance," Mykola pointed out.

"We require all visitors to get medical insurance in Ukraine. It is the law," she stated with an officious tone.

"Really? Then why didn't you stop the four people who were ahead of me?"

"They have the insurance."

"Sure they do. Well, you show me the law that states all visitors to Ukraine must buy medical insurance and I'll buy it. If you can't, then please allow me to pass."

"It is here on this application form," she noted, pointing to a document written entirely in Ukrainian.

"Exactly where? Show me the paragraph."

"Right here," she said, indicating a line of fine print at the bottom of the form.

Mykola looked down at the document and smiled. "I read Ukrainian fluently and I see nothing about a law or a regulation requiring visitors to buy medical insurance. All it says here is that the purchaser agrees to the terms and conditions. Show me the section that says there is a law or regulation that all visitors must buy medical insurance."

The woman glared at Mykola and shot a flustered glance toward the passport control booth. The officer simply shrugged his shoulders.

"I will allow you to pass but I must warn you that if anything occurs in which you require medical attention, you will be required to pay the full sum in cash and it will be very expensive."

"Thanks for the warning. And have a good day."

Outside the airport, the parking area was chaotic with gypsy cab drivers besieging the arrivals area as visitors emerged from the building. The fare into the city varied from the year and make of the car, to how well dressed and clean-shaven the driver was. A one-way trip was touted as costing anywhere from 100 to 1,000 hryvna. Mykola scanned the faces of the men who surrounded him like ravenous vultures and settled on a barrel-chested, mustached man with a friendly twinkle in his eyes. There was something about him that struck Mykola intuitively, something that radiated goodness and honesty.

"Where to young man?" he bellowed as he tossed Mykola's backpack into the trunk.

"What's a good hotel?"

"The Grand is the best. It's expensive but it is in the center of the city on the main square near the Opera House and close to the girls. Ukraine has the most beautiful girls in the entire world," the driver said with a wink.

"I'm not interested in the girls," Mykola interjected.

"We also have good looking young men."

Mykola rolled his eyes. "I have a girlfriend back home. I'm here on business. Just take me to the Grand."

"Then the Grand it is."

As the cab wove its way through the narrow streets of the city, Mykola began to feel a faint connection to Ukraine. He had planned to visit after graduation, a gift from his mother. In fact, Mykola had organized a month long tour with five of his dance troupe buddies. It was to be a guys' only Ukrainian beer fest, vodka-swilling blow out with jaunts to Kyiv, Odessa, Poltava, Kharkiv, Ivano-Frankivsk, Ternopil and Lviv. He couldn't wait and made only one request of his buddies: never to discuss the proposed trek in the presence of his girlfriend. Lesia wasn't thrilled with the thought of her ruggedly handsome boyfriend trekking through a nation teeming with young, gorgeous, long-legged, marriage-minded women on the prowl for foreign husbands.

The death of his parents changed everything.

"First time in Lviv?" the driver asked.

"Yes."

"This is the City of Lions. It is a very old and very beautiful city. If you wish, I can give you a guided tour."

"It's a possibility."

"And if I may, where does a young man who is obviously not from Ukraine, learn to speak Ukrainian so beautifully?"

"Saturday Ukie school in Edmonton. That's in Canada."

"I know where is Edmonton and where is Canada."

"Lots of Ukes in Edmonton. Anyway, my parents insisted I speak Ukrainian in the house. That's all we ever spoke at home, well … most of the time."

"You speak very well."

"By the way, what do you charge for a full day?" Mykola asked.

"It all depends where I will go. We charge by the kilometer. I can give you a special rate."

"Good. Give me your phone number and I'll be in touch."

The driver gave his young passenger a skeptical glance through the rear-view mirror.

"I promise," Mykola said. "I'm definitely going to need a driver."

At a red light, the driver scrawled his name and cell phone number on a scrap of paper and handed it to Mykola.

"Alex Boychuk is my name. Good to meet you."

"My name is Mykola Yashan." The two shook hands. "I was wondering, do you know where Solnechnaya Street is? I need to go there tomorrow morning."

"Yes. It's not too far from the center of town. Maybe twenty minutes away. What is the address?"

"41 Solnechnaya."

"No problem. I will pick you up at 8 a.m. in front of the hotel if you wish."

"I wish," Mykola said with a smile as the cab pulled up at the hotel.

The Grand dripped with the faded elegance of a bygone era. Built during the Austro-Hungarian Empire, it was impressive from the outside with its ornate facade. Inside, the lobby was adorned with paintings by renowned Ukrainian artists. A sweeping staircase led to meeting rooms and offices on the second floor. However, that's where the four-star rating came to a screeching halt. The accommodations while comfortable were austere. Mykola's room was tiny with two single cots on opposite walls. The mattresses were rock hard. There was a small mahogany desk on which sat an ancient color television set. Next to the door was a closet-sized washroom with a cramped shower stall equipped with a heavily calcified, hand-held, dripping showerhead. Two white towels that felt like sandpaper to the touch were hanging from a chrome rod attached to the side of a tiny, rust-stained porcelain sink.

Mykola unpacked his clothes and headed for the hotel dining room. After an uninspiring dinner of meat that had the texture of shoe leather, boiled potatoes and over cooked Brussels sprouts, he decided to go for a walk along the tree-lined walkway dividing the boulevard.

Directly across from the hotel was a magnificent, towering bronze statue of Taras Shevchenko, Ukraine's poet laureate. Mykola watched as several elderly women and men laid floral tributes at the base, make the sign of the cross and bow their heads in a moment of silent prayer. On both sides of the boulevard, the sidewalk cafes, bars and restaurants were humming with locals and tourists alike: families out on a stroll with their children, young lovers holding hands, men playing chess, and pockets of aging veterans with Soviet medals pinned to their suit jackets sitting on benches on the central walkway, and looking forlorn.

As Mykola ambled along the sidewalk, his eyes locked onto the Opera House. Built in the 19th Century, it was a Renaissance and Baroque architectural marvel. As he took in the statues representing the allegorical figures of Comedy and Tragedy standing on either side of the main entrance, his thoughts flashed back to the photo of his mother and father posing in front of the theatre just days before he was born; his mother's abdomen flat as an ironing board. He felt a mix of anger and sadness sweep over his him. Mykola turned and headed back to the Grand.

CHAPTER TEN

A dozen boisterous retirees - eight women and four men of Ukrainian descent from Winnipeg - sat together in the Grand Hotel restaurant having breakfast. Mykola was sipping a double cream, double sugar American coffee, trying to fight off jetlag when he heard one of the women gush about visiting "the orphans". On the floor beside the group were a dozen tote bags filled with stuffed animals. A five-kilogram bag of individually wrapped candies rested on a nearby chair.

"What an honor it will be to meet Natalka Matlinsky," one of the women chimed.

Mykola's ears perked up instantly.

"She is almost a saint," the woman added with a tone of reverence. "I read recently that she received the highest civil award for her charitable work from the president himself."

"I can hardly wait to see the little ones," another woman gushed.

It was the opening he needed. Mykola got up from his table and approached the group.

"Hi. My name is Mykola. I'm from Edmonton," he said with a warm smile.

"Hello from Winnipeg!" a few of women rejoined gleefully. "What brings you to Ukraine?"

"I'm going to visit the village where my grandparents came from. It's kind of a roots thing."

"That is so wonderful," one of the men said. "I wish more young Ukrainian Canadians would make an effort to find out about their heritage."

"I couldn't help but overhear you say that you're going to visit an orphanage," Mykola said.

"Yes. We read about Orphanage 41 on the Internet. The pictures of the children touched our hearts. They're such beautiful little angels," a grandmotherly woman said, her eyes tearing up. "It broke my heart to see so many sad faces. We thought it would be a nice to visit and bring a little cheer into their lives."

"That is so nice of you. I was wondering if I could tag along. I'd love to see the children. Maybe there might be something I could do to help out at the orphanage."

"What a fine gesture! We'd love to have you to join us," she said.

"I've got a cab driver picking me up in a few minutes. I could meet you in the front of the orphanage."

Alex was punctual. He was sitting in his vehicle outside the Grand reading a newspaper when Mykola emerged into the daylight. During the fifteen-minute ride, Mykola was tense. He sat silent, wondering how he would broach the subject of his adoption. His biggest fear was that this Matlinsky woman would refuse to offer up the information he wanted and needed. Then what? He had no idea how he would handle an outright refusal.

As the cab pulled up in front of the orphanage, Mykola rolled down the window and looked up at the dilapidated building. In the more than two decades since Matlinsky took charge, it had not changed one bit on the outside. The yellow stucco structure was stained with the soot of diesel fumes spewed over several decades by the never-ending caravan of passing trucks and buses.

For a moment, Mykola thought the driver might have driven to the wrong address. "Are you sure you got the right place?"

"Yes. This is 41 Solnechnaya."

"It looks like an abandoned warehouse."

"Do you know what this place is?" the cab driver asked.

"I was told it was an orphanage."

"That it is." Turning in his seat, Alex asked, "May I ask why you are coming here?"

"My mother has been donating money to this place for years. She died recently and I wanted to see what this place was all about. I was thinking of carrying on her legacy."

For 25 years, Alex Boychuk had been observing mankind through the rear view mirror of his taxi. He'd heard it all, and he knew instantly the young man wasn't being straight. But whatever the reason for the visit, Alex didn't press the issue. It wasn't his business.

"Should I wait here for you?" he asked.

"I'd appreciate if you would. I might be here for a while."

"No problem. The meter keeps ticking," he said, retrieving the newspaper from the driver's side pocket.

Mykola stepped onto the sidewalk still milling over the approach he would take with Matlinsky. Playing various scenarios in his head, he decided it would be best to let the situation unfold. Taking a deep breath, he pulled open the wooden door and walked in.

The cry of babies echoed through the empty, cavernous corridor. To the right, he noticed a sign on a door that said: Office of the Director. Assistant Maria Demianenko suddenly emerged from a doorway down the hall carrying a tray of teacups. She was startled at the sight of a lone, male stranger in the corridor.

"I'm sorry. I didn't mean to scare you," Mykola said.

"It's okay. I didn't expect anyone at this hour in the morning. How may I help you?"

"I'm with a group from Winnipeg coming to visit the orphanage. Not enough room in the van for all of us so I took a taxi. I got here a little ahead of them. We're all hoping to meet the director. "

"Director Matlinsky is expecting the group and is looking forward to meeting everyone. She should be arriving shortly."

"I can see you have a bit of work to do. I'll just go back outside and wait for the group. Sorry I startled you."

As he stepped back outside, Natalka Matlinsky burst through the door. Mykola immediately recognized her from the photos on Google Images.

"Good morning," he offered with a smile.

Barely paying him any notice, she nodded without breaking stride.

In that split second, Mykola decided he didn't like her. There was something about her brisk manner that rubbed him the wrong way. She exuded an air of supreme arrogance. She didn't walk, she swaggered, and the overpowering scent of her pungent Parisian perfume made him gag.

Minutes later, the mini-bus ferrying the Winnipeg contingent pulled up. One of the women rang the bell at the side of the main entrance. Maria, a welcoming smile on her face, greeted the cheerful group and ushered them into the corridor.

"It is so very nice of you to visit. Director Matlinsky is in her office. She is expecting you. She will be so happy to greet you," Maria said, rapping lightly on the office door.

Mykola could feel his pulse quicken as he entered the room. It was large and Spartan; furnished with the barest necessities – a utilitarian, green metal desk, eight wooden chairs surrounding a battered conference table and a threadbare rug covering a creaky floor. As he scanned the room, he noticed there were no filing cabinets. If there was information on his adoption, he figured, it definitely would be stored in a filing cabinet. While wondering where the cabinets might be kept, his gaze landed on the wall above the director's desk. On it was an 8x10 glossy, color photograph in a gold-gilt frame of the President of Ukraine presenting Matlinsky with the Order of Merit. Mykola's eyes focused on the shadowy impressions protruding from the middle of the four sides of the frame, bestowing a somewhat ethereal aura on the blessed event. It looked like the imprint of a cross.

"Kind guests, I would like to introduce Director Matlinsky," Maria announced once everyone was in the room.

The visitors broke out in joyful applause. Placing himself inconspicuously at the back of the room, Mykola kept his hands at his side.

"Vitayemo. Welcome," the director chirped exuberantly. She smiled and in an instant Mykola felt a frigid Artic blast shoot through his body. The first thing he noticed was Matlinsky's eyes. They were black, coal pits, blocking any entry to the soul. Her demeanor was odd. She exuded a kind of rehearsed congeniality, and it worked wonders on the good natured and well intentioned.

After a short meet-and-greet and the pre-requisite round of cookies and tea, Matlinsky got down to business, proposing a tour of the institution.

"I know you all must want to see the children," she said. "It will be my pleasure to show you our humble home," she added, leading the eager band into the corridor.

As they exited the office, Maria glanced at Mykola. She sensed there was something about him that was both puzzling and disquieting. It was as if he didn't belong with the group. Suspicion rippled through her thin frame.

The first stop was the baby ward. Pausing for a moment outside a wooden door, the director gave a short briefing.

"We have two baby units. Each one has 22 newborns and toddlers. They don't have much but as you will see, the women who care for them are very loving and attentive. They treat the babies as if they are their own."

Matlinsky tapped on the door with the ring on her key chain and was respectfully greeted by two matronly women in white, nurse uniforms cradling infants in their arms. As the visitors filed into the massive room, they were hit by the smell of urine, baby formula and baby powder. The room was crammed with cribs, two large change tables and four wooden playpens. Several babies were crying. A few were asleep in their cribs, oblivious to the commotion while most sat passively in rockers, high chairs and playpens.

As the visitors huddled together in the nursery, Matlinsky mentally ran through her script. With a practiced, thoughtful smile, she subtly placed her right hand on her chest and gently caressed a small, gold cross dangling on a chain around her neck. It didn't go unnoticed. The believers nodded their approbation. The director had observed long ago that most of the visiting outsiders had a thing for Jesus. The cross was merely a prop in her arsenal to play to their evangelical zeal.

Drawing the nurses to her side, Matlinsky launched into her presentation. "These two little angels were left on our doorsteps last week. It breaks our hearts to see so many mothers abandoning their babies. But sadly, this is the reality of Ukraine today with so much poverty and unemployment."

The visitors shook their heads in dismay. Mykola kept his eyes focused on the director.

Matlinsky motioned the group to a nearby crib. "This baby suffers from seizures," she lamented, pointing to a sleeping infant wrapped tightly in a blue blanket. "The State gives us so little money for each child. We don't have enough to buy medicine for him. It's awful watching him when the attacks hit …" she said, her voice breaking with emotion.

Approaching a seven-month-old sitting wide-eyed in a playpen, she continued: "This poor child's father died in a traffic accident. He was drunk and the mother was severely disabled in the collision. She had no choice but to give up her baby. She died a month ago. It is a very sad and emotional situation. We hope this lovely little girl will be adopted soon by a loving family."

The director then led the entourage to an isolated crib in the far corner of the ward.

"This poor child's mother is a prostitute, a drug addict who has AIDS. She simply abandoned her baby at the hospital after giving birth. We are monitoring the child very carefully. Sadly, her future is bleak. We pray for her every day."

Leading the group to another playpen, Matlinsky noted: "We don't know who the parents of these two babies are. They are twins and were abandoned at the hospital in the darkness of night. It is all so sad, so sad. But as you no doubt can see we do the best we can with what we have."

The director plucked the twin girls from the playpen and placed them in the eager, outstretched arms of two dewy-eyed grandmothers. They stood cooing and awing until the director nudged them towards the door. The nurses then retrieved the babies and placed them back into the playpen.

The visitors appeared immensely impressed with Matlinsky's knowledge of the circumstances of each baby in her care. That is everyone except Mykola. His instincts were on full alert.

The director was ushering the group back into the corridor when she finally noticed Mykola. She caught the look of skepticism in his eyes, and in an instant, her guard was up. She wondered what a young man was doing with a bunch of old folks, and then figured he was probably the grandson of one of the visitors forced to tag along. Still, she had an uneasy feeling about him.

The second stop on the circuit was the chapel: a placid, spacious corner room at the far end of the main floor. At the makeshift altar, draped with a beautifully embroidered linen tablecloth, stood a plain brass crucifix, flanked by two, hand painted icons – one of the Blessed Virgin Mary, the other of Saint Joseph. As the group filed reverently into the room, they bowed and crossed themselves three times. Matlinsky saw that Mykola did not cross himself.

"The older children love coming here on Sunday or when it's raining to reflect and pray. But they must sit on this dirty wooden floor. It would be so nice if we could afford to buy a simple carpet." she suggested ever so subtly. "They would be so happy, and we could bring them here more often. We wouldn't have to worry about them catching a cold."

Mykola began to wonder what his mother's annual donation of $1,000 was spent on. For $250, Matlinsky could easily purchase an inexpensive machine made rug from India that would cover the entire floor. The director noticed a cynical sneer on the edges of the young man's lips. Now she was even more suspicious of him, but she carried on.

The tour took a sharp but brief detour, descending into the bowels of the institution. The basement was a labyrinth of rancid utility rooms, each lined with clapboard storage closets and cupboards. A spider web of clotheslines wove throughout the maze of dank corridors and largely empty rooms, all leading to the far south end where the laundry facility was located. Urine soaked bedding, cloth diapers and pajamas were piled three-feet high in front of four ancient washing machines and two deep cement tubs. Three women wearing blue overalls, their sleeves rolled up to their elbows washed each load by hand in sinks.

"The washing machines no longer work. They broke down months ago and the Ministry has no money to replace them. We have to wash every-thing by hand. We do not have enough laundry detergent; one box for a whole month is what we get. So we make our own with bars of soap and a cheese grater."

Matlinsky walked over to one of the workers and pulled her hands out of the sink. "Their knuckles, as you can see, are perpetually raw. The work is hard and it is takes away the time these loving women can spend caring for the children."

At the far north end of the basement, a mammoth, antiquated oil furnace dominated the grease-smeared, concrete cell. It clanged, clunked and hissed incessantly as it pumped hot water into rusting radiators throughout the building. As they were being led back to the main floor, Mykola noticed that three of the rooms near the furnace area had doors: on one was an ominous dead-bolt lock. The other two were shut tight. He wondered what lay behind them. Matlinsky did not include them in the tour.

The show-and-tell culminated at a ramshackle unit on the second floor, which accommodated 21 four- and five-year-olds. The children squealed with delight as the visitors entered with treats and toys in hand. Like a swarm of happy bees, they rushed the adults, grabbing at legs and raising their arms for a hug.

"Children, sit down here on the floor. I will introduce our wonderful guests. They have come all the way from Canada especially to see you and they have brought you some gifts," Matlinsky said.

The children giggled and clapped.

The Winnipeg contingent gleefully dug into the bags and pulled out stuffed polar bears, beavers, moose, puppies and kittens. The director called the children forward one at a time to receive a gift and one piece of candy. Each visitor was rewarded with a hug and a polite thank you.

While the children sat happily clutching their gifts and eagerly unwrapping candies, Matlinsky led the group through the unit. She explained that the entire top floor of the institution contained a series of eight identical units - each home to 21 children age two to seven. The units were divided into two main sections – a dormitory jammed tight with sagging cots three abreast and seven deep, and a sprawling kitchen/living/recreation/school area. Small wooden desks facing the kitchen served as tables during mealtimes. Behind the kitchen, a door draped with an orange plastic shower curtain, led to the washroom. Six sinks lined one wall and three porcelain toilets with no seats hung on the opposite wall. There was a large, gray-tiled shower stall with a black, rubber hose attached to a single dripping, cold water faucet. There was no hot water tap.

In this particular unit, the common area had no sofas, just two wooden chairs for the staff. Lined neatly against a wall on the worn linoleum clad floor were a few battered toys, ratty stuffed animals and dog-eared children's books. There were no arts and crafts materials, and no television, just an AM clock radio that constantly crackled with static.

"As you can see, this place is in such disrepair. We need money for renovations but the government keeps cutting back and cutting back. We started some painting, patching some of the cracks in the walls and fixing holes in the floors. Then the money for this work stopped."

As they headed back into the main room, Mykola decided to throw a few questions at the director.

"Can I ask, what happens to the children who are not adopted?"

Matlinsky eyed him suspiciously but answered. "Very few are the fortunate ones who get adopted by loving families abroad," she began. "Most of the children you see here are not orphans in the true sense of the word. I would say that 95 per cent of the 100,000 children in orphanages throughout Ukraine today are what we call social orphans. They have a living parent somewhere. Often the mother is too poor to take care of the child. In most cases, the father has long disappeared. This is the sad reality of Ukraine today. It is all so very tragic."

The visitors let out a collective sigh.

"And the children we see here who don't get adopted, where do they go when they get older?" Mykola continued.

"At the age of seven, they are sent to various state-run institutions we call internats where they stay until they graduate at 18. But their placement all depends on the assessment," the director noted.

"What do you mean by assessment?" Mykola asked.

"At the age of four, they are assessed by a psychologist. Those who are diagnosed as imbecily are transferred to an institution for these types," Matlinsky explained.

Myola could not believe what he had just heard. "Imbecily? What the heck is that?"

"The mentally retarded," Matlinsky said.

Mykola cringed. "We don't use that terminology back home. We say developmentally challenged."

"What is the difference?" the director asked tersely.

"Political correctness," he replied calmly, looking at the children around the room.

"I don't see any children with physical handicaps," he added.

"Defective children are sent to a different internat," the director said in a matter of fact tone.

"Defective?" The very word grated his ears. He heard his father's voice echoing in his brain, calling him a cretin. Definition: a defective person.

"The blind, the deaf and dumb, and the crippled children," Matlinsky explained.

Mykola could hardly contain his disgust. "Back home they are called physically disabled."

The director fixed him with a cold stare. He was derailing her tour and her instincts were telling her to move on. Moreover, the visitors were getting visibly annoyed with their young tagalong's seemingly impolite and challenging demeanor.

Matlinsky turned her attention to the children. Gently pulling two girls to her side, she began. "The children must wear hand-me-downs. We have no choice. We have no money to buy new clothes. But as you can see, they are well cared for and happy. That is the most important thing."

The director then shot a glance at one of the workers, giving her a knowing nod. It was time for the grand finale.

"Children come here and sing a song for the nice people from Canada," the worker exhorted with a smile.

Obediently, and excitedly, the children rushed over, lined up in two pre-rehearsed, neat rows – girls in the front, boys in the back - and joyously belted out a children's folk song about a randy rooster in a barnyard, and closed with a tribute to "Mama – always there, always ready with a hug and a kiss … so blessed to have a Mama like you." It was a song that most visitors knew well – their children and grandchildren having sung it at Mother's Day concerts at Ukrainian halls back home in Winnipeg.

It was the coup de grace! Except for Mykola, there was not a dry eye in the room. Handkerchiefs and Kleenex were pulled from purses and pockets. Matlinsky had accomplished her task. Moments later in her office, she was stuffing wads of Hryvna into her desk drawer, profusely thanking each bene-factor while doling out the blessings of Jesus, Mary and Joseph. Mykola was now totally convinced that Matlinsky's entire presentation was a staged dog and pony show aimed at the heartstrings and targeting the purse strings of foreign Good Samaritans. She was nothing more than a two-bit con artist peddling snake oil.

CHAPTER ELEVEN

Matlinsky was surprised and more than a little irritated to find Mykola sitting in the chair facing her desk when she returned to her office after biding farewell to the Winnipeg contingent. She shot an inquisitive look at Maria who shrugged her shoulders.

"Your group just left in the van," the director said curtly.

"I'm not really with them. I just happened to join up with them for the tour."

From the moment she had laid eyes on the young man she had an uncomfortable feeling. There was something disconcerting about the way he looked at her.

"And what may I ask is it that you want?" she asked guardedly.

"My name is Mykola Yashan," he began, pausing momentarily for the director to react.

She didn't.

"You knew my mother. Iryna Yashan."

Matlinsky sat at her desk stone-faced.

"I'm sure you knew her. She's been sending you $1,000 every year on my birthday since I was born. Nineteen checks to date to be exact."

Matlinsky broke her silence with a wary half smile. "Iryna Yashan. Yes, I remember her. She is a fine Christian woman."

"My mother and father were killed recently in a car accident."

"Please accept my deepest condolences," Matlinsky offered with no show of emotion.

"I'm so sorry. This is such a tragedy," Maria added in barely audible whisper.

"As you know, my mother has been sending money as a kind of thank you gesture for helping her with my adoption," Mykola continued.

"Yes," the director said with a trace of hesitation in her voice.

"I was thinking of continuing her charitable works as a kind of memorial to her."

Matlinsky's ears perked up. "That would be very kind, very kind."

Now that he had captured the director's attention, Mykola revealed the true purpose of his visit. "After my parents were killed, I found the papers regarding my adoption in my father's office. I never knew I was adopted so you could imagine the shock."

Matlinsky didn't react.

Mykola continued. "Anyway, I was told by my god-mother the reason I was adopted was because my biological mother died giving me life."

"Yes. That is true," the director confirmed.

"I was hoping you could tell me about her. For starters, her name, where she came from."

Matlinsky's radar was now flashing on red alert. She studied Mykola's face and sensed a determined young man who could spell trouble. She began slowly and carefully choosing her words.

"If I recall, and you must appreciate it was some time ago, your biological mother died in childbirth."

"I know that. I just want to know who she is and where she came from."

"Whatever for?" the director interjected.

"I was thinking maybe I could to go to her town or village and see if I could find a relative, or someone who could tell me something about her. It would be nice if I could find her grave and put some flowers on it," he said, noticing that Matlinsky's forehead was beginning to crease with thick tension lines.

"I don't understand why you would want this. Your parents adopted you. By the looks of you, they gave you a wonderful and privileged life. You should be grateful to them for that. I do not think you should dishonor their memory by going on this wild goose chase," she offered in a tone laden with condescension.

Mykola couldn't understand the seemingly antagonistic response. To his thinking, his request was nothing short of benign. He sensed she was trying to derail him. The director had erected a brick wall. Her coal black unblinking eyes emitted no sign of truth or deception.

"Wild goose chase? I don't get what is so unusual about wanting to know where I came from."

"Where you are from is a woman who died giving birth to you. She is long gone. What your parents gave you is a good life, a life far better than you would have received here, and for that, I keep repeating, you should be grateful."

Mykola bit his lower lip. He shifted in his chair, glancing over at the director's assistant. Maria's head was bowed and her eyes were closed as if in prayer. She had said nothing the entire time, but it was obvious from her body language, legs crossed and arms folded tightly against her chest, that she was distressed. She definitely knew something and Mykola knew it.

Looking back at the director, he said: "I am grateful. Believe me. I will always be grateful. I just need to know about my biological mother. I need to know about my past."

"Your past began the day of your adoption. You were a day old. There was nothing before that," Matlinsky replied tersely.

Leaning forward in his chair, he searched for another approach: "Can I see my adoption file?"

"No, it is confidential," the director said firmly.

"But it is about me. I think I have a right to see it," he noted, his voice tightening.

"It has to do with the confidentiality agreement we signed with your parents."

"And they're both dead and I am the sole survivor. So I would think the confidentiality agreement is moot."

"There is also the confidentiality of the biological mother," Matlinsky pointed out.

"And she too is dead. So again, I don't see the problem."

Keeping her tone calm and even, the director continued: "Not having seen the file in years, I am not sure whether your biological mother had family or not. But if she did, think for one moment of their surprise, their anguish, and the possible wounds that can reopen if you suddenly show up on their doorstep. They may not have even been aware that she was pregnant. She was after all, and I'm not saying this to be unkind, an unwed mother, and that would have marked her for life. I am sorry. The file is confidential. You cannot see it."

Mykola could feel the rage building and he was fighting to keep it bottled.

"What is so wrong with giving me that bit of information? I came all this way because I need to know. It's been driving me crazy ever since I found out I was adopted. Surely you of all people can understand that."

"We are going round in circles, Mr. Yashan. As I have already informed you our records are confidential. The matter is closed."

His shoulders knotted with tension, Mykola glared at the woman with intense loathing. She didn't flinch.

"Now, if there is nothing more, I have much work to do. I want to thank you for your visit and I sincerely hope you will consider carrying on your mother's good work. It would be much appreciated. As you saw with your own eyes, our children have so little."

With white knuckles, Mykola pushed himself out of the chair.

"We are always open to visitors," Matlinsky called out as he opened the door. "And we are always appreciative of any help we can get."

Mykola felt like telling her to drop dead but kept his mouth clamped shut. Not for a second did he buy her line about confidentiality. He left with the distinct feeling there was something more to his adoption. Throughout the short meeting, the director was on the defensive, constantly throwing up roadblocks. But more strange was the demeanor of her assistant. She looked like she was about to unravel, nervously rubbing the cross dangling on a fine gold chain around her neck. It didn't take much to see the woman was deeply conflicted about something.

Mykola left the office without another word. But in the corridor, he drove his fist into the concrete wall out of frustration. A sharp pain shot up his arm. He shook his hand trying to calm the throbbing. As he turned to leave, he noticed a short, medium-built man with a Slavic oval face staring at him with concern. He looked to be in his early thirties.

"Is everything okay?" the man asked with a meek smile.

"No. But thanks for asking."

"My name is Petro Bidniak. I am the caretaker," he said proudly, offering his hand.

Mykola wondered where the man had come from. He was nowhere to be seen during the entire tour. Carrying a plunger, it was obvious he was on his way to unblock a clogged toilet.

Favoring his stinging right hand, Mykola shook Petro's outstretched hand with his left. "Sorry about that."

"I think the wall will always win if you punch it," Petro offered.

Mykola smiled. He could sense there was something odd about him. He just couldn't put his finger on it.

Suddenly, the office door flew open.

"What did I tell you about talking to visitors? Don't you have a toilet to fix? Get to work!" Matlinsky shouted.

Turning pale with fear, Petro scurried down the corridor and disappeared in the stairwell.

"I thought you were leaving," she said sharply.

Mykola stormed out of the building like a wounded young buck. He climbed into the taxi and slammed the door.

"The locks work fine. You don't have to slam the door," Alex said in an annoyed tone.

"Sorry."

"I gather things did not go well during your visit."

"No they didn't."

"Where to?"

"The hotel."

For a good part of the journey, Mykola's mind was racing, trying desperately to formulate a new approach, a new plan to get the information he so needed. Then an idea hit him.

As the car pulled up at the Grand, Mykola asked Alex, "What are you doing tomorrow?"

"What I've been doing almost every day for the past 25 years. I drive a taxi."

"Good. Can you pick me up at 8 a.m.?"

Like a pesky horse fly, Mykola was standing at the orphanage door early the next morning. Maria brushed by trying her best to ignore him. Mykola followed her into the building.

"Good morning," he offered in a cheery voice.

"I don't think I should be talking to you," she replied nervously.

"Why? Did the director order you not to?"

"No. However, she was very angry with you. You upset her."

"Well, I'm here to make amends."

"What do you mean?" Maria asked cautiously.

"Amends, like saying I'm sorry and to see if there is any way I can help out at the orphanage while I'm in the city."

Every word was a lie. Mykola was on a reconnaissance mission and his target was Maria. He recognized that she was a weak link and he was certain if anyone knew all the dirty little secrets of the institution, it would be her. All he had to do was win her over. His problem was how. The woman was a petrified lap dog.

"When do you expect the director?"

"She should be here in an hour."

"I guess I'll just stand out here in the hallway and wait."

Thinking that Mykola may have come around, Maria let down her guard, feeling it was safe enough to engage in small talk. "Last evening, I looked up your father on the internet. He was a very famous man."

"He certainly was famous, I'll give him that."

"You do not sound like a proud son."

"Let's just say that as an academic, he was a colossal success. As a father, he was a colossal dud. His orbit spun around the school of higher learning. He lived for the intelligentsia. My mother and I were mere appendages."

"Some people see their work as their true calling in life."

"Well, some people should also learn that there is more to life than standing on a stage trying to show the world how smart they are."

There was a sudden bang of metal at the far end of the corridor. Petro was hoisting a 12-foot aluminum ladder under a burned out light bulb dangling from the ceiling on a black wire. Mykola waved. Hesitantly, Petro waved back.

"What's his story?" Mykola inquired, pointing to Petro.

"His story?"

"Yeah."

"Petro is the caretaker."

"What's he all about?"

"Petro came to us several years ago as the caretaker."

"He seems nice."

"Petro is a very kind man. He is always happy and very helpful. The children adore him."

"What about his family?"

"He has none. He is an orphan. He has lived most of his life in an internat for the imbecily."

Mykola shook his head. "I can't believe in this day and age anyone would ever refer to another human being an imbecile."

"It is how it is done. All children in the orphanages are assessed at the age of four and diagnosed as normal, defective or imbecily," she explained.

"What happens to the children labeled imbeciles and defectives?"

"When they are seven, they leave the orphanages and are sent to internats for these types where they must live for the rest of their lives."

"Where are they?"

"The internats for these types?"

Mykola nodded.

"In towns and villages away from the cities."

"Out of sight, out of mind."

"Yes, I guess that is the case."

"I didn't see the man on the tour yesterday. Does he live on the premises?"

"He has a room in the basement."

"And what's your story?"

"I am a graduate of child care work. I've always wanted to work with children. This is my first and only job."

"You love children."

"I absolutely adore them," Maria said with a warm smile. "I enjoy helping out in the nursery. I just love the little ones."

"It shows on your face. Do you ever get frustrated?"

"Frustrated? I don't know what you mean."

"I mean working for someone as tough as your director must be a challenge."

It was not a subject Maria wanted to discuss. "The director has a very difficult position. It is not an easy task running an orphanage."

At that very moment, Matlinsky walked in and leered angrily at Mykola. Maria froze and started to tremble.

"I told you I had nothing more to say to you. Now I want you to leave." She nodded at Maria and the two women disappeared into the office.

Mykola looked up at Petro, smiled and waved goodbye. In his mind, he knew they would soon meet again.

CHAPTER TWELVE

Mykola was pacing anxiously outside the hotel at 6:25 am when Alex pulled up.

"Where to my young Canadian friend?" he asked stifling a yawn.

"Back to the orphanage."

"I don't think the place is open for visitors at this hour."

"I know. That's why I need to get there. There's someone I need to talk to."

Mykola was somewhat surprised when he found the main door unlocked. Then again, from what he'd seen during the tour, there was nothing of any value in the place worth pilfering, and there was always someone on duty around clock in the nurseries and dormitories. He made a beeline for the basement where he found Petro in his room brewing his morning tea.

"Good morning, Petro," Mykola said with a smile. "Remember me? The guy who fought the wall and the wall won."

Startled, Petro jumped up from his chair, sweeping breadcrumbs off his shirt. "Yes. I do. How is your hand?"

"Still a little sore."

"It will probably hurt for some time. You must put ice on it"

"I'll do that."

"You would like some tea?" Petro asked.

"No thanks. I had two cups of coffee at the hotel before I left."

Mykola looked around the room and shook his head in total disbelief. He'd seen photographs and videos of prison cells in maximum-security penitentiaries across Canada and the U.S. that, compared to this dump, would merit a four star rating. The caretaker's room was nothing short of a dank dungeon with cold grey cement walls and no windows, a sunken cot, a beat up chest of drawers and a vintage, portable black and white TV with a twisted coat hanger for an antenna. On the wall above his bed was a simple wooden crucifix. It was how Mykola had always imagined what solitary confinement would look like in a third world jail, minus the television set.

"How come you are here?" Petro asked. "The director will be angry if she sees me talking to you."

"I came to see how you are. I felt bad that I got you in trouble the other day."

"I'm fine. The director tells me I must never to speak to the visitors I forgot. She has told me I must stay in my room with the door closed and say nothing when the visitors come."

"I was wondering what was behind the closed door when I was down here on the tour."

Petro pointed at himself, a sheepish grin on his face.

The man was a curious addition to the orphanage. Abandoned as a baby, Petro was a product of the Soviet-era "internat" system. Like all four-year-old children in the care of the state, he was assessed by a government appointed psychologist. During the one-hour session, the shy, reclusive boy cowered in fear as the stern-faced, bespectacled stranger administered a series of rapid-fire tests. At the end of it, he was diagnosed and labeled an "imbecily". It meant a life sentence to institutionalization, never to experience a normal life in society. At seven, he was transferred from the orphanage system to a children's internat for the mentally challenged. When he turned 18, he was shipped to an internat for the elderly and infirmed. It was a veritable cuckoo's nest brimming with the walking wounded – men and women suffering from a myriad of psychiatric illnesses, and elderly people afflicted with dementia and Alzheimer's disease. There were men and women who were severely mentally challenged, as well as the physically disabled and visually impaired.

While at the internat, Petro developed an uncanny aptitude for fixing things – motors, pumps, furnaces, and virtually anything to do with electrical and plumbing. The director of the institution took pity on the so-called "imbecile." He knew full well the man was in no way mentally challenged. But there was little he could do about it. Once labeled, the classification stuck for life.

Petro had been at the internat for almost a decade, when the director contacted the Ministry of Social Policy, asking if there was a place for someone as skilled and abled as Petro. A month later, he got his walking papers. At the age of 27, he was dispatched to Orphanage 41 as its caretaker. It was a moment of incredible pride for the man. He was not paid a salary but received a small stipend, enough to buy cigarettes, toiletries and the occasional bottle of horilka. He got three meals a day and the luxury of an ancient television to keep him occupied in the evenings.

Petro reveled in his work and dove into it with zeal. He was constantly on call repairing the furnace, plugging leaky pipes, forever unblocking overflowing toilets and sinks, mopping floors and trapping the colony of sewer rats that thrived in the countless nooks and crannies of the basement. The children absolutely adored Petro, especially the boys. He was the only man in the entire complex. The older boys would sit in a semi-circle and observe while he made repairs to stoves, refrigerators and washing machines, taking the time to meticulously explain what he was doing. Yet while the children followed the friendly caretaker like a flock of lambs, the director forbid him to play with them. Matlinsky could not stand the sight of Petro. As far as she was concerned, the man was a janitor at best and an imbecile at worst. Petro knew his place. He never crossed the director. He dreaded all contact with her and did his best to stay out of her way. She held his fate in her hands, and his biggest fear was that she would return him to the internat.

"How long have you been here?" Mykola asked.

"Going on six years."

"Before you came here, where did you live?"

"I was in an internat for old people. I lived there a long time."

"Why on earth were you put in an old age home?"

"That is where I was sent when I turned 18."

"What was it like?"

"It was a terrible place. There were many young people in there. Some were in wheel chairs because they could not walk. Their bodies were twisted up. Some were imbecily like me except they were very much more imbecily. I was in a room with five old people, three men and two women. Every day it seemed someone was dying in that place and the strong ones like me had to carry the bodies from the rooms. There was no priest to give them the last rites. There was no funeral. It was so sad. No one came to say goodbye. We would put the body in a car and take it to the cemetery where we must first dig the grave. It was not marked. I would always say a prayer before I would fill the grave with dirt. I think in the years I was there I must have buried 300 people."

Mykola squeezed his eyes shut unable to imagine the unbelievable nightmares Petro must have suffered in his young life. Shaking his head, he asked: "You ever get beaten?"

"Only one time by another imbecily. He wanted my cigarettes. I said no and he hit me over and over on the head with his shoe. He was a crazy man who was hearing voices in his head. The assistant director punished him very badly with a leather belt. Most of the people who worked there were very mean. Everyone feared them. They beat anyone who would not listen or got in their way. Sometimes they would put them in the punishment cells in the basement for many weeks. It was a horrible, evil place. I could not believe such a place could exist."

"Were you ever told why you were sent there?"

"It is because I am imbecily."

"Petro, I want to tell you something. From what I see, you definitely are not an imbecily. You are as normal as I am. In fact, in many ways, you are so much smarter than I am."

"No. You are smart," Petro said with a shy grin.

"Petro, I couldn't repair a furnace, plug a leaky pipe, or do even the simplest electrical job if my life depended on it. I can't do anything that you can do without making a complete mess of it. I'd probably electrocute myself screwing in a light bulb."

Petro laughed. "Surely you are joking."

"No, I'm not. You are an amazing handy man, and I can tell you without a word of a lie, if you were in Canada, you would have a good paying job as a superintendent for an apartment complex."

Petro beamed.

Looking at his watch, Petro's face turned ashen. "The director will be arriving very soon. You should not be here. The director does not allow me to talk to the visitors."

"Don't worry. I'll be long gone before she gets here," Mykola said, as he got up and wandered into the corridor with Petro tagging close behind.

Mykola pulled open the other closed door and could not believe his eyes. The room, the size of a large walk-in closet, was jam-packed from floor to ceiling with stuffed animals, dolls and toys.

"What the ..." he whistled. "I don't get this."

Petro shrugged. "So many foreign visitors come every week. They always bring gifts for the children. But there are only so many children and the visitors keep bringing gifts. After they leave, Maria collects them and puts them in this room."

"Why doesn't she just send them to another orphanage or donate them to poor families with children?"

Petro didn't have an answer.

Mykola walked over to the next door and rattled the lock. "And what may I ask is behind door number 3, the one with this ominous lock on it?"

"The file room. The director keeps all the files in there for safe keeping."

Mykola's eyes were riveted on the lock, realizing that behind that door, a filing cabinet might contain a folder with his name on.

"I gather only she has the key?" he asked hesitantly, while anxiously eying a ring of keys dangling from Petro's belt.

"Yes."

Mykola's heart sank.

His voice reduced to a whisper, Petro then added. "But one time she lost her key. She was very upset and she yelled at me as if it was my fault because I did not have a spare. She had both keys. I had to remove the lock with bolt cutters. She sent me to buy a new lock and again she took both keys. But this time I made sure the director would not have the same problem if she ever lost them," he said with a proud grin.

"How's that?" Mykola asked.

Petro pointed to the ring on his belt. "I made a spare key."

Mykola's pulse quickened. "Ever go inside the room?"

"No. The director would be very angry."

"How would she ever know?"

Petro shrugged.

"Can I see what it looks like? I hear the director is very organized."

"I don't know. I'm afraid."

"There's nothing to be afraid about. I won't ever tell. And some time later this week, I'd like to come by and take you out for dinner to a restaurant," Mykola offered with a false smile and a pang of guilt.

"I would like that," Petro said. "You are sure director Matlinsky will never know?" he asked as he fumbled with the dozen or so keys on the steel ring.

"Not a chance. I mean how could she? I'll never tell. I swear, and there is no one else around. It's just for a peak."

Petro knew exactly which key on his bulbous ring fit into the lock. A moment later it snapped open.

Mykola pulled the door open and scanned the eight, four-drawer, metal filing cabinets lined up against the walls on both sides of the room. All the drawers were labeled by subject and date - budgets and expenses; children in care; adoptions; and a newer, cream-colored two-drawer cabinet that simply read: Cooper. Mykola honed in on the filing cabinets labeled: Adoptions. The faded tag on the bottom drawer of the cabinet at the far end of the room read: 1993-1996. He walked over and yanked it open.

Petro panicked. "No. You must not do that. The director will be very angry."

Mykola ignored the caretaker's plea. His was staring straight at the very first file. It read: Yashan Adoption. Mykola's hands were shaking as he pulled it out and quickly examined the documents. On the last page of the formal adoption record was an illegible scrawl, a signature. Below it was typed:

Kateryna Chumak, mother. Village: Stornovitzi, Zakarpats'ka Oblast. It was an agreement stating that she willingly agreed to give up her baby boy for adoption.

"That's odd," Mykola thought. "Maybe she knew she was dying."

Petro grabbed Mykola's arm firmly in an attempt to get his attention. "Please, you must put this back. We must leave the room. I don't want to get in trouble. The director will send me back to the internat if she knows what I have done."

Seeing the fear in the caretaker's eyes, Mykola returned the file, patted Petro on the back and said reassuringly. "She'll never find out. I will never breathe a word. I promise."

"You promise?"

"I swear to God," Mykola said, looking at his watch. "I have to go but I also promise I will come by soon and we'll go out for dinner."

Mykola darted up the stairs and headed out of the building. Committed to memory was a crucial piece of information: the name of his biological mother and the village she came from.

"You look as if you have seen a ghost. Is everything okay?" Alex asked as Mykola jumped into the front passenger seat of the cab.

"Yeah, I think so. Do you know of a town or a village called: Stornovitzi?"

Alex scratched his head. "No, never heard of it."

"It's in Zakarpats'ka oblast."

Reaching into his glove compartment, Alex retrieved a tattered road map of Ukraine. Running his finger down the index on the flip side, he found the coordinates. A second later, he pointed to a tiny blip on the map. "It's right here. I would say 320 kilometers southeast of Lviv. It is at the foot of the Carpathian Mountains where the Hutzuls live."

"How long would it take to get there?"

"Given the state of our roads and the manner in which many fools drive, I would say maybe four or five hours."

"You've got to be kidding."

"Do you wish that I drive you there today?"

"No. I need some time to think. I have to figure out a few things. Can you take me there tomorrow?"

"No problem."

"Pick me up at 6:00 a.m. then."

Alex laughed. "You are like a rooster, always up at the break of dawn."

CHAPTER THIRTEEN

In Soviet times, with far less cars on the road, the drive normally took three hours. But with the advent of freedom from the hammer and sickle, the traffic had more than tripled, and the driving time increased to no less than five hours. Large stretches of road had been reduced to an obstacle course of cavernous potholes and loose rocks. Cars, trucks and buses moved along at a snail's pace, creating a snaking line of vehicles several kilometers long. Road rage reigned supreme. Drivers steamed and leaned on their horns while angrily gesturing at each other with closed fists and middle finger salutes. Fender benders and fist fights were a regular occurrence.

"Those bastard politicians in Kyiv line their pockets instead of paving the roads," Alex cursed as his eased his car across a strip of roadway that had been carved into a pockmarked moonscape. "This is killing my suspension."

"Not to mention what it's doing to my stomach," Mykola added.

At the three-hour mark, Alex turned onto a back road.

"This is more like it. I would bet a member of our Parliament lives nearby."

"Why's that?" Mykola asked.

"The road is freshly paved. It is a good thing to have power and influence."

With the traffic insanity in the dust, Mykola relaxed and took in the countryside. It was dotted with small, family-owned farms, the occasional dairy cow grazing in a field, a downtrodden nag, small herds of goats butting heads, and gaggles of domesticated ducks and geese waddling in muddied puddles of rain water.

"This is all a man needs in this world," Alex began. "An acre to grow wheat, another acre to grow potatoes, and a cow for butter and sour cream! All the ingredients for perogy! Give a Ukrainian man a plate of perogy and he is happy. What more can he want for?"

Mykola laughed. "I have to admit it's my absolute favorite food in the world. But I don't think I'm going to get into farming when I can buy perogy in a grocery store!"

"That is the problem with young people today. You want instant, frozen food! I spit on pre-packaged food! It has the taste of cardboard."

"Actually, some of it is pretty good!"

"Cardboard is only good when you put American red stuff on it."

"You mean ketchup?" Mykola asked with a laugh.

"I will never eat it. A real Ukrainian eats only homemade perogy!" With that, Alex launched into a Ukrainian folk song close to his heart and stomach.

> *One day I was out walking*
> *In a meadow full of thorns,*
> *And suddenly - a vision:*
> *Perogy carried by a girl!*

Mykola had learned the ballad as a young teenager at Ukrainian scout camp and joined in the second verse.

> *I said to her, "My darling"*
> *"Do you know my hopes and dreams?"*
> *"I must confess my love -*
> *for perogy ... and for you!"*

The duo belted out several more verses as the car wove through the pastoral countryside. An hour later, Alex veered off onto a gravel road and slowly approached the tiny selo of Stornovitzi nestled in a bucolic valley at the foot of the Carpathian Mountains. Mykola stared in disbelief at the sight of a dozen men, their shirt sleeves rolled up, their backs soaked with sweat, pulling the reins of ploughshares like spent oxen, while bedraggled women took up the rear guiding the single blade through the rich, black soil. On another nearby section, a sunburned farmer and his wife fared slightly better with one-horse-power at their disposal. But they spent as much energy yelling at their exhausted nag to pull. As far as the eye could see, there was not a single operational farm vehicle on any of the fields.

"I don't believe what I'm seeing," Mykola said.

"This is the life on many of the farms throughout the country," Alex said.

"Why? I don't get it."

"When Ukraine got its independence, the Russians stole all the farm machinery and left. There was nothing these farmers could do about it and this is why most of the farmland lies fallow."

As the car reached the crest of a hill, Alex slowed down. "That is what the Russians left behind," he said, pointing to four cannibalized, Soviet-made grain harvesters and two rusting tractors perched at the edge of a steep gully. "The Russians wanted to make sure we could not stand on our feet. They wanted us to crawl."

From the hilltop, Mykola spied three gleaming, copper-clad onion domes topping a church in the distance. From its spotless white stucco exterior, it was obvious it had been recently built. He wondered how these desperately impoverished farmers could find the money to erect such an impressive monument to God.

"These people can't afford a tractor yet they somehow manage to scrape up the cash to build an opulent church," Mykola said, brushing his hair away from his forehead.

"The fields may give them a broken back and send them to an early grave with empty stomachs but the church guarantees them a place in heaven for eternity," Alex replied, a wry smile cracking his lips. "That's what the priests tell them, and if you can't believe men of the cloth, then who can you believe?"

"You're quite the cynic," Mykola offered.

"I like to think of myself as a philosopher, observing my corner of the world through the windshield of this taxi. Take yourself, for example."

"What about me?"

"You are on a quest."

"Not hard to figure that one out."

"What I find interesting is how much you look like these mountain people. Dark hair, dark brooding eyes. You definitely have Hutzul blood in you. No doubt about that!" Alex said with a laugh.

Mykola gazed quietly out the window. There was something mystical about the mist-shrouded mountains that played on the strings of his soul.

The driver continued along the dirt road toward the center of the village, cautiously avoiding gaping water-filled potholes. He came to a stop in front of a dilapidated, clapboard shack that served as the local convenience store. Outside, a motley crew of ruddy-faced, elderly men sat quietly on wooden benches puffing on hand-carved pipes and smoking hand-rolled cigarettes. As Mykola leapt out of the car, he was hit by an overpowering wave of body odor, made only slightly bearable by the pungent aroma of the raw tobacco that literally smelled like cow dung. The old men stared at the visitor with a glint of humor and disbelief in their eyes. His big city appearance triggered a group grin and a communal nod. A six-foot, tanned young man sporting Serengeti aviator sunglasses, a Hugo Boss canary yellow tee shirt, designer jeans and black leather loafers was a rare sight in their humble village.

"Dobre ranok," Mykola said respectfully as he approached the tiny gathering.

"Dobre ranok," the men replied in unison.

Parched from the grueling drive, Mykola headed into the store.

"Bottled water?" he asked a plump woman behind the counter.

"Bottled water? We don't sell water. Our water is from the well," she said curtly. "We sell beer in a bottle and vodka in a bottle. Only a fool would pay for water in a bottle. Maybe you would like some beer."

"No thanks. It's a little too early for that."

Mykola scanned the interior. It was filled with local produce - whole milk, cottage cheese, sour cream, root vegetables, eggs, freshly baked black bread and wooden barrels filled with pickled cabbage, beets and pickles. Various cuts of raw meat from recently slaughtered chickens, goats and pigs hung from metal hooks attached to the ceiling rafters at the back of the store. On the counter were two large jars containing individually wrapped candy and chocolates, and on unpainted, plywood shelves against the back wall were packs of Ukrainian cigarettes and large tins of shredded tobacco, as well as a half dozen liter bottles of horilka (homemade vodka) and several jars of locally produced wild flower honey.

Mykola left the store empty handed. He was thirsty but firm in his resolve not to risk drinking well water!

"Do any of you know a family by the name of Chumak?" he asked the men outside.

"Why is it you want to know?" a grizzle-faced man asked.

"I'm from Canada. I was told my family might be related to them."

"Canada! When I was a very young boy I remember some families leaving the village for America. That was sixty, maybe seventy years ago," the old man offered.

"And do you know the Chumak family?" Mykola repeated.

The old man and his cronies laughed. "Which Chumak family? There are a dozen Chumak families in this village. I'm a Chumak. He's a Chumak," he added, pointing to a leathery, weathered man across from him. "The woman in the shop is a Chumak."

Alex burst out laughing. "You must pick out a relative."

"I think my mother told me that the family had a daughter," Mykola noted.

"All of them have daughters and sons and grandchildren," the old man said.

"I think the daughter's name was Kateryna."

There was an instant chill in the air. The men looked at each other in stone silence. Mykola had struck a nerve. Alex immediately sensed it.

The old man drew on his pipe, exhaled slowly and measured his response.

"The family Chumak you seek lives in the white, thatch-roofed cottage at the south end of the village. It is 500 meters past the church. You cannot miss it," he said pointing his pipe in the direction of a mud-filled road. "Maybe old lady Ulyanna will know your kin. She lives with her oldest son Bohdan."

"Thank you for that. I appreciate it." Mykola then turned to his driver. "You might as well wait here. I'll walk."

Alex nodded as his fare headed down the road.

Mykola's heart began to pound like a jackhammer as he caught sight of the cottage. As he approached, he tried to figure out how he would confront the family. He was anxious about what he might find. Recalling Matlinsky's warning about upsetting family members and opening old wounds, he decided it would be wise to tread lightly. The last thing he needed was a silly misstep to blow up in his face.

The Chumak homestead was a humble structure, recently white washed and topped with a corrugated tin roof. It was obvious there was pride of ownership. A white picket fence fronted the property. There was a flower garden teaming with roses, chrysanthemums of all colors and blankets of buttercups in full bloom. On the left side of the cottage was a carefully tended vegetable patch with long rows of tomatoes, peas, beans, carrots, turnips, beets, cabbage and corn. Surrounding the entire plot was a line of giant golden sunflowers. On the right side porch, a black hose attached to an outdoor spigot brought water into the house. A few meters down a small incline toward the back stood a weathered, wooden outhouse. The low drone of hordes of black flies emanated from its interior. The sweeping backyard was a mini orchard of apple, cherry, peach and plum trees. A mottled brown horse, reins hanging loose from its neck, chomped on a clump of hay in a nearby paddock. Throughout the property a dozen, free-range chickens, ducks and geese, and scores of newly hatched chicks hunted and pecked the ground for food.

Mykola's attention turned to the barn where a burly man in blue jeans and a black tee shirt was sharpening a scythe with a double-cut flat file. He looked to be in his mid-40s, muscular and swarthy with a thick, black drooping Cossack moustache. His hands were massive, the palms callused and coarse. His ferocious attack on the scythe showed he was not a man to be trifled with.

"Hello, I'm looking for the Chumak family," Mykola said, standing hesitantly at the entrance to the barn.

"How may I be of assistance? I am Bohdan Chumak," he said in a firm but polite tone.

"My name is Mykola Yashan. I'm from Canada. My mother told me that our family, that is my grandparents on my mother's side, originally came from this village. Her mother was a Chumak," he said, feeling his face flush once the lie left his lips.

"I'm not aware of any member of our family having gone to Canada. When would that have been?"

"Oh, I'm talking the 1940s. Way before you or I were even born," Mykola said with a smile.

"I'm not certain but mama might know. Come into the house. We'll have some tea. Mama is making lunch and soon my brother Markian and his wife Ruslana will be in from the fields."

They headed for the cottage.

"Mama! We have a guest from Canada," Bohdan called out as he ushered Mykola across the threshold. "He says he might be related to us."

The woman, dressed in a wash-worn, black smock turned from the stove and stared at the visitor. There was distrust in her eyes. Mykola instantly felt the coldness.

"This is Mama," Bohdan said.

Ulyanna Ivannova Chumak was short, standing four feet, ten inches, if that. She was stooped and no doubt in her mid-60s although she looked much older. Her skin was wrinkled and weathered like cracked leather from decades of working in the fields.

Mykola was suddenly struck by the realization that he could be standing in the presence of his maternal grandmother. He wanted to tell her who he really was but he knew it was the wrong thing to do. The woman had a bleak aura.

"Vitayemo," she offered up in an insincere, raspy whisper.

"Nice to meet you."

"Sit, sit," she said, pointing to one of four wooden chairs around the kitchen table. "You would like chai?"

"Tea would be nice. Thank you."

Ulyanna placed a kettle on the wood burning stove and turned to Mykola.

"Tell me, how is it you feel you are related to us?"

"Through conversations with my mother. She died recently and I became interested in finding out more about where the family came from. She was born in Canada and so was my father. But their parents came from Ukraine, in fact from this village."

"When was that?"

"I think the early 1940s."

"I don't know if I can help you. I was not born until 1947 and I do not recall any talk in my family of a relative going to Canada," the woman said flatly.

"Your sons don't know either."

"If I don't, then they don't," she snapped.

"Your other son is working?"

"Markian will be here soon," Bohdan interjected.

"Is he one of the men in the fields pulling those plows?" Mykola asked.

"We own two horses," Ulyanna shot back.

Mykola took a sip of the tea and scanned the small room that functioned as a kitchen, dining area and family room. On the back wall above a frayed, floral sofa, he spied several family photographs. A framed black and white picture of a young man shot a cool shiver down his spine. He bore an uncanny resemblance to Mykola.

"Who is that?" Mykola asked, getting up from the chair and pointing to the photo.

"Markian," Bohdan said. "I think he was about 20 when it was taken. He is 38 now."

Bohdan turned and looked into Mykola's face. "You two look a bit alike. You could almost be brothers or father and son. Don't you think so, Mama?"

"I see no resemblance," Ulyanna replied tersely without bothering to look.

Mykola's eyes landed next on a family photo of an older man and Ulyanna sitting on wooden chairs, flanked by two young boys. What struck him as odd, aside from the fact no one was smiling, was that the woman was cradling a bundle on her lap that was blacked out with an indelible marker.

"Is this the family?" he asked.

"Tak. Mama and tato. Tato died many years ago in a farm accident," Bohdan said.

"And that's you and your brother?"

"Tak."

"What's that on your mother's lap?"

"That is nothing," the woman shouted angrily from the kitchen. "It is none of your business!"

"Mama, please. He is our guest," Bohdan pleaded.

"He is not related to us," Ulyanna barked.

Mykola took a deep breath and exhaled slowly before daring to wade into obviously troubled and murky waters. "I heard someone in the village say that you had a daughter."

Ulyanna's eyes narrowed into piercing, hate-filled slits. "Who told you that? What person told you that?" she demanded, storming into the room, her face inches from Mykola's face.

"Some old man. I don't know his name."

"He should mind his business. I no longer have a daughter. She is dead to us. You ask too many questions. I want you to leave my house at once. Get out."

"Mama, the boy meant no harm," her son offered meekly.

"I want him out of my house," the woman shrieked.

Bohdan, the ever-obedient son, scrambled to his feet and grabbed Mykola roughly by the arm. "You heard Mama. Get out of here!"

"Look I'm sorry I upset your mother. I didn't mean to."

Mykola's apology fell on deaf ears as Bohdan jostled him to the roadside. He stood for a moment on the other side of the fence, his mind reeling over the suddenness and depth of rage he had triggered in the old woman. He wondered what he had said that could possibly spark such a visceral reaction. He was also confused by her choice of words. He didn't know if he had translated them correctly. His knowledge of Ukrainian, while fairly strong, was not the same as in this part of Ukraine. He wasn't familiar with the dialect, which bore little likeness to what he had been taught at Saturday Ukrainian school in Edmonton. Still, her words had rattled him.

As he walked slowly back toward the village center, he kept repeating the phrase in his head: "She is dead to us. I'm sure those were her exact words."

Mykola paused for a moment in front of the church and looked up at the newly installed copper copulas reflecting the blazing afternoon sun. He was thinking about going in and having a word with the priest when the holy man suddenly exited a side door. He was short, balding and looked to be in his mid-fifties. His bloated belly pushed tight against his black robe. Thick, mud brown moles dotted his fleshy face. Heavy lids drooped over his faded eyes giving him a tired appearance. He had the nose of a boozer, swollen and crisscrossed with tiny, purple veins. His red lips protruded out over a pointed, graying goatee. When he smiled, his teeth flashed four gold fillings. He gave off the air of a man full of petty pride and superiority. After all, he was a man of God.

"Good day, my young visitor. I am Father Zenon," the priest said, extending his right hand.

"Mykola Yashan," he said, shaking the outstretched, beefy paw.

"I see you were admiring our new church."

"Truth be told, I was actually wondering how the people in this village could afford to build a new church when they don't even have a tractor to plow the field. Yet you drive across this entire Oblast and brand new churches are popping up like mushrooms after a summer rain."

"Poetic!"

"I wasn't trying to be."

"God moves people in mysterious ways."

"I don't think God is the one doing the moving."

"You don't?"

"No. I think it has everything to do with the promise of life after death if they build it and the threat of eternal damnation if they don't."

"And where do these threats you speak of come from?" Father Zenon asked.

"Priests who want their castles in the clouds."

"Ah, the simplistic cynicism of youth."

"The people here are barely making a living and you push them to give so that you can build."

"I don't push. They give from the heart."

"They give from the fear of burning in hell."

"And where does such a learned young man come from?" the priest asked with sardonic grin.

"Canada."

"What brings you to Stornovitzi?"

"I was hoping to locate some long lost family members."

"You have family here?"

"I thought I might. I was told my grandmother on my mother's side immigrated to Canada from here in the early 1940s. She was a Chumak." Mykola may have forsaken religion but lying to a man of the cloth in front of a church made him feel a little twitchy.

"There are many Chumak families in the village," the priest noted.

"I was told it was the family in the white cottage at the end of the road."

"I know the family. If you would like, I could introduce you to them."

"I met them a few minutes ago. To say the least, it was a strange meeting."

"How is that?"

"The old woman went into hysterics when I asked about her daughter. She started yelling at me to get out of her house. She said something that sounded like 'she is dead to me.' I didn't mean to upset her."

"Sometimes one must walk lightly on muddy ground," the priest said, looking intently at Mykola.

"Now who's being poetic?"

"You opened an old and very sensitive wound."

"I didn't mean to do that," Mykola said, wondering what the priest meant by an old wound.

"I am curious, how did you know of her daughter?"

"Someone in the village mentioned her to me." Mykola could sense the priest was not buying the line he was shoveling. "Can I ask you where Kateryna Chumak is buried?"

"Why on earth would you want to know that?"

"I would like to put flowers on her grave."

The priest's eyes bore into Mykola's face. "Kateryna Chumak is not buried here."

"Then can you tell me where she is buried?"

"She is not buried anywhere because she is not dead."

Mykola could feel the blood rush to his face. "She's alive?"

"She was when last I caught a fleeting glimpse of her. That was maybe a year ago."

Staring intently at Mykola, he asked: "Why are you so interested in Kateryna?"

"Just that I thought my family might be related."

The priest knew full well Mykola was lying.

"Do you know where she lives?" Mykola asked hesitantly.

Father Zenon began to worry that perhaps he had already offered up too much.

"Do you know where she lives?" Mykola repeated.

Pinching the bridge of his nose, he replied: "I do not think this is a good idea."

"I don't know what you mean by that. I just want to know where Kateryna lives. I gather you know so why don't you just tell me. I need to see her."

"For what reason would you possibly need to see her?"

"It's a private matter but it's very important. I'd really appreciate it if you would just tell me where she is."

Father Zenon stared hard at the ground. He looked troubled.

"I have a good idea why you want to meet Kateryna," the priest began hesitantly. "I think this is not wise on your part. It would be better if you leave well enough alone."

"And why is that?"

"It is not for me to say. But I feel I should not tell you her whereabouts."

Mykola took a deep breath and exhaled slowly. "I'm sure if I start asking around this village I'll find out where she is."

"That would not be wise."

"Well, you leave me no choice. I'm not going to give up until I find her."

The priest stared nervously down the dirt road leading to the Chumak farm. "If you do what you are threatening to do, your actions will stir a lot of trouble in the village. You have no idea how much. You also have no idea what you are stepping into. I advise you in the strongest way possible to consider ending here and now whatever it is you are doing. Again, I say this for your own good."

"I need to see this through. I have to see this through. So please tell me where Kateryna is."

Father Zenon gazed up at the sky, a look of resignation on his face. "You did not hear this from me. Kateryna lives in the town of Dobrody near the Polish border. It's about five hours from here by car. If memory serves me correctly, she works at a bar near the bus station off Zaluky Square. The bar owner is a man called Yuri Mazurenko. He is neither a good man nor a nice man."

"Can I ask you one more thing?"

Father Zenon shrugged.

"Why would Kateryna's mother tell me that her daughter is dead when she is alive?"

"That is not for me to say."

"More riddles. Anyway, I want to thank you for your assistance." With that, Mykola turned and at a clip headed for the waiting taxi.

CHAPTER FOURTEEN

It was late afternoon the next day when the taxi pulled into Dobrody. With the nose of a bloodhound, Alex found Zaluky Square within minutes. The place had a distressed feel to it. Standing prominently in the center was a pigeon-stained brass statue of Taras Shevchenko perched on a concrete podium. It was surrounded by rambling, unkempt rose bushes. They were not in bloom. Dozens of discarded vodka bottles and beer cans lay strewn on the grounds. Aside from a pack of stray, flea infested mongrels, not a soul was in the square.

Mykola instructed Alex to wait. As he got out of the cab, he heard the wail of a cat in heat reverberating loudly from a nearby alleyway.

"Depending on how things go, we might be staying the night" he said before shutting the door.

Alex glanced up at Mykola with a look of consternation. He hadn't planned on an overnight trip and had been hoping to get back to Lviv for a home cooked meal and his own cozy bed. Small town Ukrainian hotels were not known for comfort. They smelled of cigarette smoke and Lysol detergent. The mattresses were stained with urine, sweat and semen, and the walls were paper thin, offering up a cacophony of disturbing and disruptive noises: quarrels and arguments; the moans and groans of lovers; loud snoring; the incessant hacking of chronic smokers; and the bodily explosions of gassed-up men.

"Don't worry I'll pay for your hotel and your time," Mykola offered as he scanned the surroundings.

Six narrow, cobble-stoned streets radiated from the square. Mykola decided to walk no more than a block down each in search of the bar. He was halfway down the fourth when he spotted a hand-painted wooden sign that simply read: "Bar." It was on the street level of a two-story, stucco build-ing painted light grey. He hesitated for a moment and then walked in.

Coming in from the blinding afternoon sunlight, Mykola squinted as he tried to adjust to the dark interior. His nose had far more difficulty adjusting to the rank smell of body odor, raw tobacco smoke and sour beer permeating the room. He sat down on a stool at a bar. The counter top was encrusted with squashed flies and peppered with cigarette burns. A dozen unlabeled, liter-size bottles of homemade horilka lined a shelf along the back wall. A tray of streaked, green, plastic beer tumblers sat atop the far end of the bar. Cases of beer were piled on the floor: only one brand, Lvivsky. Large tin cans, filled with gobs of spit and cigarette butts, were strategically placed around the cramped room. There were six plywood tables, each surrounded by four mismatched, wooden chairs. A faded calendar, dated 2006 with a picture of a beaming Viktor Yushchenko, the former president of Ukraine, was the sole piece of décor on the walls.

Aside from the barman, there was one other person in the place. A woman was sitting at a table at the far end of the room. She was nursing a tall glass of what was probably water. At least Mykola assumed it was water. He could see she had long brown, braided hair pulled back in a ponytail and appeared to be in her late-30s. She glanced over at Mykola. Her eyes were like shards of shattered crystal that sliced through him like a razor forcing him to look away.

The bartender was a heavy-set man with a scowl on his pockmarked face. His nose was swollen and purple, and his blood shot eyes had the puffy look of someone who had consumed a great deal of booze over his lifetime. With his thinning black, greased back hair, he looked like an aging biker with a mean and abusive streak.

Mykola understood immediately why the bar was virtually deserted. Only a low-life would frequent a wretched, uninviting establishment such as this. The place was a rancid pigsty.

"What do you want?" the bartender growled. His teeth were rotten and stained brownish-yellow from nicotine. He smoked roll your own cigarettes and the raw tobacco he used smelled like cow manure.

"Pevo (beer)," Mykola said.

The bartender placed a large bottle on the counter and flicked off the cap with his thumb. No glass. Not that Mykola would have dared use one. The beer was room temperature. He took a swig and would have spit it out had he had a glass. It tasted like it had been filtered through soiled socks. He forced the amber liquid down his throat.

Shaking off an overwhelming urge to gag, Mykola turned to the bartender.

"Can I ask you a question?"

"Depends."

"I'm looking for a woman."

"There is one in the corner. She will cost you 200 hryvna for one hour. She has the room upstairs," the oaf grunted.

"No, not that kind of woman. Her name is Kateryna Chumak. I was told she might work in a bar around here."

"Not here," declared the bartender.

"Maybe she works at another bar near here?"

"I am the only bar."

Mykola pressed on. "The woman comes from a village called Stornovitzi. It's in Zakarpas'ka Oblast."

"Vera! Vera!" the barman barked at the woman sitting at the back table. "You come from Stornovitzi. This young man is looking for a woman from there." He turned to Mykola. "Name! What was her name?"

"Kateryna Chumak."

"Kateryna Chumak!" he bellowed.

In a flash, the woman called Vera was on her feet barreling over to the bar. Her eyes were hot red with fury. Mykola jumped up fearing she was about to attack him physically.

"What is your business with Kateryna Chumak?" she demanded, moving threatening close.

Mykola backed up. "I need to talk to her about something."

"How do you know about her?"

"I was told we might be related."

Vera's eyes registered instant distrust. She took in the young man's clean-cut appearance and his seemingly earnest expression.

"Liar! Who told you she was in Dobrody?" she challenged, inches from his face.

Mykola was beginning to wish Alex had come into the bar with him. He needed someone to watch his back, and this woman was obviously crazy.

"The priest in Stornovitzi."

"He is a fat pig who should learn to mind his business. Now I ask you one more time, what is your business with Kateryna?"

"Like I told you, I think we may be related."

"You are not related. Get out!" she yelled.

Watching the drama unfold, the bartender angrily intervened. "Whore! I own this bar. You tell no one to leave. He is a customer. Go sit down before I kick your ass."

The barman's gruff tone stunned Mykola. He didn't want the woman to be in harm's way because of his actions.

Defiant, Vera wasn't about to retreat. She stood her ground.

"I'm sorry if I upset you," Mykola said. "I didn't mean to. If you know where Kateryna Chumak is, I would appreciate it if you would tell me."

The woman continued to glare menacingly into the young man's face, distrust and suspicion swirling in her dark eyes. She said nothing. Mykola wondered why she was so enraged.

Accosted by two crazy women in as many days.

Taking a step back, he looked at Vera's face. There was something very familiar about her. What was it? Had he seen her somewhere before? Then it struck him like a thunderbolt; the family photo on the wall of the Chumak homestead in Stornovitzi. She was a carbon copy of Markian. He knew in an instant.

"You are Kateryna," he blurted out.

His words seemed to steal her thunder. The woman called Vera stared at Mykola for what seemed an eternity and then she asked firmly. "What do you want?"

Mykola couldn't speak at first. He just stared at the woman.

"Well, what is it you want with me?' she pressed.

"Maybe he wants sex," the bar owner suggested. "It will cost you 200 hryvna!"

It was the second time he made the comment but this time it caught Mykola completely off guard. "What did you say?" he sputtered.

"200 hryvna. You can take her upstairs and have sex. Why do you think she is here?"

"Go to hell." Mykola shot back, reality washing over him like a tidal wave. The woman standing before him was a prostitute.

"Watch how you talk to me!" the bar owner warned. "I can break you like a twig."

Grabbing Mykola by his shirtsleeve, the woman asked a third time: "What do you want with me?"

Mykola was in shock. He couldn't breathe. He wanted to run away, but something kept his shoes nailed to the floorboards. In a rundown bar in some God-forsaken town half way around the world, he stood face to face with the woman who gave him life, and she was a despicable prostitute! The very thought sickened him. He felt his legs weaken. He reached for the bar stool to steady himself. Suddenly, Mykola understood what his godmother meant when she warned him that it was better to leave well enough alone. Her words were now echoing loudly in his ears.

Vera, or Kateryna, looked like she was about to pounce and tear him to shreds. Mykola would have been wise to run but somehow he managed to reach deep down and summon a scrap of courage to press on.

"August 9, 1993," he began in a hoarse whisper.

Kateryna's eyes widened. She loosened her grip on his shirt.

Mykola knew the date had registered with her. He continued. "I was born on August 9, 1993 in Lviv."

"So were a lot of babies," she said tersely.

"I was told my mother died while giving birth to me."

"If she died then what business do you have with me?"

"Right after I was born, I was adopted by a family from Canada. They were killed recently in a car accident. It was shortly after their funeral that I learned I was adopted and that my real mother died giving me life. I came here to see if she had family. The other day I learned her name and yesterday when I was in Stornovitzi I found out that she did not die. The name of my birth mother is Kateryna Chumak. It was on the records of the orphanage in Lviv."

The bar owner broke out in loud laughter. "Well, if this doesn't beat all. Vera, you have a bastard son!"

Ignoring the vulgar boor, Mykola kept his eyes fixed on the woman. She began to shake uncontrollably.

"That is not possible. There is confusion. On that day in question, I gave birth to a baby boy but he died. I know this to be true. I held him in my arms. He was dead."

Mykola was taken aback. Running his hand nervously through his hair, his mind was totally fried. For half a day, he was under the assumption that his biological mother was alive and for a few anxious minutes in this loathsome bar he thought he'd found her. Now, nothing was making sense. Kateryna Chumak's name was clearly and unmistakably on his adoption file. He saw it there, and here she was standing in front of him telling him her baby had died, that she held a dead baby in her arms. Was she lying? If so, why would she offer up such a macabre story? It was all too much for him to process. He needed space and time to figure out what was going on. He needed to breathe fresh air. He turned and left the bar without saying another word.

Alex watched in the rearview mirror as Mykola crossed the road on wobbly legs. He could see something had gone seriously sideways.

"We should head back to Lviv," was all Mykola said as he got into the car.

"It is getting late. I don't want to risk the roads at night, too many potholes and too many drunks. I am told there is a decent enough hotel at the edge of town. We will stay the night."

Mykola didn't respond. His mind was consumed with one unsettling thought. Like a broken record, it kept playing over and over in his head. If the woman in the bar was his biological mother, then no doubt he was the by-product of a sordid one-night stand. There was no way he could handle the thought that he was the bastard son of a prostitute. There was just no way. He tried to force his mind to accept the woman's version of events, but something kept telling him that Kateryna Chumak was his biological mother.

CHAPTER FIFTEEN

The hotel clerk had a mischievous grin plastered on his pasty face as Mykola walked into the lobby of the Grand Hotel after the four hour drive from Dobrody.

"Good morning Mr. Yashan, I trust you had a good night," he said.

Mykola was in no mood for pleasantries. It was 11 a.m. and he'd hardly slept the night before. The rancid hovel in Dobrody was called Hotel Impressa. It did not live up to its name. The septic tank was backed up and the place reeked of human excrement. But far more annoying were the droves of bloodthirsty mosquitoes buzzing around his head throughout the night.

"You have had many, many, many phone calls over this past evening and this morning," the clerk called out as the young guest headed for the elevator. "I would say one precisely every half hour since 10 pm.

Mykola stopped dead in his tracks. "What do you mean?"

"Same young woman. She was becoming more and more agitated as the night wore on. Her name is Lesia. She is from Canada."

"Oh, shit," Mykola knew he was in big trouble.

Lesia was jealous and extremely possessive. No matter how many times he tried to reassure her that she was his one and only, she had an insane insecurity streak when it came to him. Mykola couldn't figure out why. Her mother was such a together woman, and her father was as faithful as a Golden retriever. True a lot of her girlfriends in the dance troupe suffered the indiscretions of their various boyfriends, but Mykola wasn't like them. He only had eyes for Lesia. She owned his heart. The thought of losing her over some one-night flirtation kept him on the straight and narrow. Yet she was always suspicious and always checking up on his whereabouts. It drove him crazy and led to many arguments.

With a wry smile and a wink, the clerk handed him a small sheaf of phone messages, all timed and all stating: Lesia called. Mykola dreaded the thought of what awaited him on the other end of the line when he called home. As he turned to head to the elevator, the phone on the front desk rang.

"Good morning. Grand Hotel. This is the front desk. How may I be of service?" the clerk chirped. "Ah, you are in luck. He just at this very minute walked through the door."

The clerk waved at Mykola, holding the receiver in his right hand.

"What a prick!" Mykola muttered under his breath. "Tell her I will call her in a minute from my room."

As he dialed the long distance code, he knew he was in for an Artic blast. He was tired and in no mood for a grilling. His dilemma now was coming up with a plausible explanation for his overnight absence. The phone barely completed one ring when Lesia answered.

"Where have you been? Where were you all night?" she shouted. "I've been calling you on your cell phone and at the hotel every half hour since last night."

"Calm down. There was no cell phone coverage where I was. I ended up staying in some town because it got too dark and my driver didn't want to risk the craziness of the drunks on the roads at night."

"What town?"

Mykola felt the interrogation shifting into high gear.

"Dobrody. It's near the Polish border."

"Why on earth did you go there?"

"We went first to a village called Stornovitzi and then to Dobrody but like I said, it got dark and…"

"Who is this we? Who did you go with?"

"My taxi driver, Alex."

"Why did you go to these places?"

"Look Lesia, I didn't call you back to get the third degree. I'll tell you all about my trip when I get home. Just calm down."

"When are you coming home?"

"I'm not sure just yet. Maybe in a week."

"I don't see why you have to be away."

"Like I told you before I left. I need some time to sort things out in my head. How are your mom and dad?"

"Don't try to change the subject. You always do that when you don't want to tell me what's going on."

"I always do that to get you off my case. Listen, Lesia, I'm really tired and I need some sleep."

"I bet you're tired. You've been out all night."

"Okay. I've got to go. I'll call you later in the week. Say hi to your mom and dad." With that, he hung up.

Not 30 seconds later, the phone rang. Mykola didn't pick up. He left the room and went out for a walk to clear his head. He was distraught and confused over his trip to Stornovitzi and Dobrody. He couldn't figure out why the adoption file at the orphanage listed Kateryna Chumak as his biological mother, and yet the woman in the bar was adamant that her baby died at birth. Surely she wouldn't lie about that, especially when she told him she had held her dead child. Still, his gut kept telling him that something didn't add up. He was certain the answers lay in the orphanage but he knew he would never get any straight answers from Natalka Matlinsky. There was one person, however, if pressed, might offer up some clues.

CHAPTER SIXTEEN

As morning light was edging over the grey horizon, Alex eased his taxi onto the sidewalk of a narrow side street a block away from Orphanage 41 and turned off the engine. Pulling his cap over his face, he slumped back into the seat. Mykola stared out the rain-soaked windshield hoping to catch Maria Demianenko on her way to work. Not 20 minutes later a bus came to a stop at the far end of the road. A single passenger disembarked. Mykola could make out the silhouette of a slightly built woman, her head protected from the sheets of fine drizzle under a flowery umbrella. It was Maria. When she got within striking distance, he leapt from the vehicle. The woman froze, fearing it might be a mugger, or worse. Then her eyes focused on the young man's face. Recognition came instantly, as did panic.

"What are you doing here?" she stammered as Mykola approached.

"I went to see Kateryna Chumak yesterday."

Maria blanched. She felt her knees go weak. "Oh God! Oh God! We cannot talk here. There is a café around the corner."

Mykola motioned to Alex, signaling him to wait. The driver nodded.

Maria headed for a table at the rear of the café. Mykola ordered mint tea for her and a large, black Americano coffee. He needed a jolt of caffeine. The barista, a thirty-something woman with spiked black hair and tattoos covering her arms, chest and legs, took the order with a sneer of contempt. To her, Mykola was a hyphenated American-Ukrainian tourist, and she loathed what she felt was their Western sense of privilege and superiority. Anxious to get back to Maria, Mykola was getting more and more steamed at the barista who dawdled while preparing the order.

"Ten hryvna," she said as she placed the mugs on the counter.

Mykola pulled out a ten note and dropped it on the counter. There was no way he was about to leave her a tip. As he walked away, he could hear her mutter an obscenity under her breath.

Maria was staring intently at Mykola as he sat down. The fear in her eyes was palpable. "How did you find her name?"

The question caught him off guard. He had half expected and fully hoped she would say he had the wrong name. He looked at her inquisitively, and replied in a matter of fact tone: "My secret."

"If the director finds out you discovered her name, she will suspect it was me who gave it to you. No one else could have this information. She will fire me."

"Why would she think you told me?"

"I am the only other person who has seen your adoption file. I have never forgotten the woman's name. It was burned into my memory. I will never forget that day."

"There are other ways I could have gotten Kateryna's name," he said, fighting to keep his nerves and voice steady.

"There is no other way you could have learned her name."

"If you help me out," Mykola said, "I'll tell you, and when I meet up with Matlinsky, I'll tell her as well. There's no way she'll think you're responsible."

"Please tell me that you are not going to see Director Matlinsky. She will explode with anger."

"I have to confront her about this. I need to get some answers."

"I know she will blame me."

"You won't be implicated in any way but I need you to verify a few things for me."

Staring down at her cup, Maria knew she was caught between a rock and hard place. Guardedly, she nodded her agreement.

"It wasn't difficult to get the information. I know the date I was born. I figured it was in Lviv. I must have been delivered in a hospital. So I went to the main hospital. It's amazing what information a clerk can find in the archives when you flash a 100 hryvna bill."

Maria bought the explanation. It sounded totally plausible. Ukraine was a nation of rampant corruption, sleaze and greasy, outstretched palms.

"Tell me. What happened when you met her?" she asked cautiously.

"Something very strange and very disturbing," Mykola said, his eyes never leaving her face.

Maria shifted nervously in her chair.

"Kateryna told me it was impossible that I was her son. Do you have any idea why?"

Maria didn't' respond.

"She told me that her baby died in childbirth. She said she held her dead baby. She kept insisting that there was no way I could be her son. I have to admit the visit really messed with my mind, and now what I'm getting from you is that she is in fact my biological mother. Now it's your turn. Tell me, what's going on here?"

Maria began to pick anxiously at her fingernails. Her forehead was dotted with beads of perspiration. She fumbled for the cross around her neck as she flashed back to Dr. Kowalchuk's office almost 20 years earlier. She could hear the heart-stopping scream and then the doctor's explanation: *A grieving mother. Her baby was stillborn. She demanded that she see him. I sent a nurse to the morgue to get the baby so she could hold him for a moment."*

The sheer horror and utter depravity of that day hit her like a bullet to the chest. She now realized that the woman sobbing in the hospital ward was Mykola's biological mother, and the dead baby she was holding belonged to someone else. The full extent of the deception Director Matlinsky and Dr. Kowalchuk had committed sickened her beyond words. Her breathing quickened and she went dangerously pale.

Mykola rushed over to her. "What's wrong with you? "

"I feel sick. I feel very sick."

"Do you need to go to the hospital? I can take you."

"It's not that kind of sick." Maria's hands were shaking uncontrollably. She reached for the cup to steady her nerves. "You will hate me for what I am about to tell you."

Mykola's was apprehensive as he sat back down. "Tell me what?"

Maria gripped the cup tightly. "You need to know that Kateryna Chumak is definitely your mother. You are her son. I know this as fact."

Mykola slammed his hand on the table. The barista looked over and gave him a disapproving nod.

"What in hell is happening here? Every time I try to get answers, I get hit by another insane twist. What's going on?" he shouted.

"You must keep your voice down," the barista warned.

"What is going on?" Mykola repeated through clenched teeth.

Maria could sense Mykola's anguish. She closed her eyes for a moment of prayer, searching for strength and some divine guidance. She realized the time had come to lay bare the truth as she knew it. There was no turning back. The words poured from her trembling lips.

"Director Matlinsky met your mother, the woman who adopted you, several months before you were born. I met her briefly at the orphanage shortly after your birth when she and your father came to pick you up. The director had told me that your mother could not conceive and that she so much wanted a child. Director Matlinsky promised she would find her a healthy baby. And she did. She found you. Your mother wanted to make it appear that she had given birth. We understood her concerns. She didn't want you to be looked upon as a pariah by people back home in Canada. People can be cruel. There are those who believe that nothing good can come from adopting someone else's child. They believe there must be something wrong with the child. Why else would a mother give up their child?"

"Yeah, yeah. I get it. My parents didn't want anyone thinking I was a defective bastard. I heard all about that crap." He wanted her to get to the point.

Maria hesitated, gathering her thoughts. "Director Matlinsky knows the doctors who deliver babies at all the hospitals in and around Lviv. The doctor who was treating your biological mother called the director two days before you were born. He told her he would soon have a healthy baby for her. He assured her that the expectant mother," Maria paused, "that Kateryna Chumak was not an alcohol drinker or a drug addict, that she was a healthy woman who had taken care of herself throughout her pregnancy."

She paused again. The hard part was coming. "You will hate me for what I am about to tell you but you must believe me, I'm only aware of this now because of what you have just told me. I knew nothing of this until this moment. You must believe me."

Mykola was at the edge of his seat.

"When we went to the hospital to pick you up, there was a woman in one of the wards who was screaming. The doctor told me she was crying because her baby was stillborn. She had demanded to see her child. The doctor ordered a nurse to bring a baby up from the hospital morgue. I swear to you I am only now finding out about this evil deception from you. May God have mercy! The distraught woman was your mother. I cannot believe that the doctor did this to her. I am so ashamed and so sorry that I was ever involved in any of this."

Mykola's mind was spinning wildly as he tried to come to grips with the stunning and macabre revelation. "Oh, God! This is sick. This is really sick," he said, running his hands roughly through his hair.

Maria sat rigid as an ironing board. "You must believe me. Director Matlinsky told me that the woman, your biological woman, would not be able to care for you given her situation. She was a teenager and she was not married."

"Stop making excuses for her! That despicable bitch knew all along what she was doing."

Maria's eyes were fixed on her cup. She said nothing.

Mykola squeezed his eyes shut, desperately trying to sort out the jumble battering his brain. "I don't believe this. It's too sick to believe anyone could do this."

Maria began to panic. "You can never tell the director of this conversation. You cannot confront her about this."

"The woman is evil. What she did is illegal."

"She will simply deny your allegations. She will say Kateryna Chumak willingly gave you up for adoption. The public will believe the director. They see her as a saint, and you will be revealed as the bastard son of a woman with loose morals. You cannot win."

"Did my mother know about this?" Mykola asked.

"I'm confused. Are you asking about your biological mother or adopting mother?"

"Jesus, the woman who adopted me! Did she know about this?"

"I can tell you without a lie your parents knew nothing of any of this. Director Matlinsky informed them that your birth mother died of complications while in labor."

"But you knew this was an outright lie."

"Director Matlinsky felt it was better your parents were told that the biological mother had died. She was worried that your parents might not take you if they knew Kateryna was alive and there might be a possibility she could demand to take you back some time later."

"So she lied to my parents."

"After we took you from the hospital, Director Matlinsky went to the hotel to get your parents. Your mother was so happy. She wept such tears of joy as she held you for the first time in her arms."

"Ironic."

"What is ironic?"

"Mama is crying tears of joy and the woman who brought me into this world is in some hospital ward crying tears of loss. And my father, what was he doing?"

Maria thought back for a moment. "If I can recall, he seemed somewhat distant."

"That's him wrapped up in a word. Distant. Maybe he knew I was the spawn of a prostitute."

Maria sat bolt upright. "A prostitute?"

"Yeah. That's what she does for a living. You didn't know that?"

"I never knew this. I swear it, and I am certain Director Matlinsky was never aware of this."

"God, when will the lies end?" Mykola asked. "Matlinsky hatched this entire scheme, and you went along with it."

"I am ashamed of what I did, but I was young. I was afraid. You wouldn't understand."

"You're right. I don't understand. I can't understand. I'll never understand how anyone could stand by and allow something as depraved as this to happen."

"I understand your anger but you must also understand that Director Matlinsky believed she was doing a good thing. She wanted to save you from a terrible life."

"Oh save me the social worker crap!"

"If you had stayed with your birth mother, your life would have been a certain tragedy. Wherever your biological mother would have gone, you would have been treated with scorn and derision. I would hate to think what you would have become."

"Well, thank you so much for saving me. I'll be sure to go to church on Sunday and light a candle for you and Saint Matlinsky."

Mykola closed his eyes, trying to absorb all that he'd been told. Then he asked an odd question, seemingly coming out of nowhere: "The picture of Matlinsky with the president of Ukraine, the one on the wall behind her desk, what's that all about?"

Maria looked at him curiously. "She is receiving the Order of Merit."

"Yeah, I know all about that. It's just that I thought maybe I was having a religious moment when I was in her office the other day looking up at it. There are four shadowy protrusions coming out from four sides like a cross."

"There used to be a large crucifix on the wall."

Mykola scoffed. "Let me guess, Matlinsky replaced it."

Maria nodded.

"Unreal. Saint Matlinsky and her award of merit trump Jesus Christ on the cross. That really says it all about that woman, doesn't it?"

Maria didn't respond.

"So how many other babies did Matlinsky save?"

Maria didn't answer.

"I should have asked: how many babies has she ripped from their mother's arms?"

"You are the only one. I am sure of it. Every adoption since then has been done through proper and legal government channels. I know what she did to Kateryna is unconscionable but you must see that it was in your best interest. You must know that."

Mykola remained silent.

"What will you do now?" Maria asked hesitantly.

"Damned if I know. My head feels like it's about to explode. I come here all along thinking my biological mother is dead. All I wanted to do was to find her grave and put flowers on it, and maybe meet a family member or two. Now I find out she's alive and far worse, that she's a prostitute. I don't need this in my life. I should never have come to Ukraine. I should have listened to my godmother."

Maria sat quietly, wishing she could say something to help ease Mykola's anguish but she drew a blank.

"Do you think you will go back to see Kateryna?" she asked.

"It messes me up to even think about it."

Without saying another word, Mykola got up and left the café.

Staring blankly out the window of the cab in the morning rush hour traffic, Mykola caught sight of a familiar figure behind the wheel of a brand new, refrigerator white 328i BMW drive by in the opposite direction.

"Alex, make a U-turn," he shouted. "Follow that white BMW!"

"Whatever for?"

"I'm sure that was the director of the orphanage behind the wheel."

"You are seeing things. The woman runs an orphanage. She cannot possibly afford such a vehicle."

"Turn!"

"You're the boss," Alex said, swerving into oncoming traffic and causing several drivers to break and blast their horns in anger.

"I didn't mean for you to risk killing us," Mykola admonished.

Alex was more than two blocks behind with no hope of catching up to the car in the tight wedge of traffic. But the good thing was the BMW stood out like a shiny beacon among a sea of faded and rusted wrecks. The car then made a sudden right turn and disappeared into a garage. It was a block away and around the corner from the orphanage.

"See I told you. It is not possible to be this woman. She works in an orphanage. It is impossible for her to own such a vehicle," Alex reiterated.

"I'm sure she was driving the car," Mykola insisted.

A moment later, as the taxi slowly passed the garage, Matlinsky emerged from a side door. Mykola ducked, not wanting to be spotted.

"Well I am damned," Alex whistled. "You have the eyes of an eagle."

"I knew I saw her. Now you tell me what the hell a woman who runs an orphanage is doing driving around in a 2014 BMW. That car costs at least 40 grand if not more."

Alex knew the answer. She was on the take. What he couldn't understand is how she could scrape together enough money to afford a luxury German vehicle. The donations from foreign visitors to the orphanage would never yield that much cash! Of that he was fairly certain.

"The woman's up to no good," Mykola said. "I knew it the moment I laid eyes on her. I'll bet you she parks a block away from the orphanage so the people who come for her tours and give her donations don't see it. What a sleaze bucket!"

When they pulled up at the hotel, Mykola handed Alex his fare and got out of the taxi.

"Will you be requiring my services tomorrow?"

"I'm going to find out if I can get a flight out of here first thing. I've had it with this place. I'll call you later to let you know when my flight leaves so you can pick me up and take me to the airport."

"I will await your call."

"My mother is a prostitute," Mykola cried out into the darkness. "My mother is a prostitute!"

Dropping down on his bed, he stared hard at the ceiling. Hot adrenalin coursed through his veins, blood whistled in his ears. His mind spinning, he couldn't sleep. He kept admonishing himself for not listening to his god-mother. She'd warned him. She told him to leave well enough alone, and she was right. But he was too stubborn to listen and now he was paying a huge price.

"God, why did she have to be a prostitute?"

Mykola felt nauseated. He loathed the woman he had encountered in the bar. To him all prostitutes were social pariahs who sold their bodies to men for cash. "Why did you have to be alive? Why couldn't you have been dead? Of all things, why did you have to be a prostitute?"

Closing his eyes, he prayed to his mama. He missed her terribly. She had been the anchor in his life; a gentle, loving soul who always rushed to his side whenever he was sad or depressed.

"I miss you Mama. I'm sorry I went looking. You will always be my Mama. I will always love you. God, why did you have to die? Why is all this happening to me?"

Mykola longed for the night to end. As soon as daylight hit, he swore he would head to the nearest travel agency to book the next flight home. He wanted out of Ukraine. It had become his worst nightmare. He turned onto his side, pulled the pillow to his face and wept uncontrollably.

A loud backfire from a garbage truck in the laneway behind the hotel jolted Mykola from his sleep. He looked down at his feet. He'd dozed off on the bed. His shoes were still on. Rubbing the sleep from his eyes, he stripped off his clothes, dragged himself into the shower and turned on the cold water to clear his head. While he was drying off, he heard a couple engaged in a wild sexual romp in the room next door. The headboard was slamming up against the wall and the woman was squealing in ecstasy. Thankfully, the passionate tryst was over in less than 90 seconds.

As he left his room, the romantic couple emerged in the hallway. The last of the red-hot lovers was a short, balding, pork ball. Dressed in an ill-fitting suit, the grinning buffoon was old enough to be the woman's grandfather. The woman was a tall, lean, dark-haired, dark-eyed, 20-something beauty. Her dress code – a black leather mini-skirt and tight, black halter – gave away her profession. From the sour expression on her face, Mykola knew full well that the moans and groans at the height of passion were faked. As she brushed by him, the reality of that brief encounter slammed into his consciousness like a train wreck. This was how Kateryna made her living.

Mykola headed down to the outdoor café of the Grand, ordered a large, black Americano coffee and sipped it slowly while he waited impatiently for the start of the business day. All he wanted was to change his return airline ticket to Canada and get the hell out of Ukraine for good. He stared up at the imposing statue of Taras Shevchenko in the park across from the hotel. Ukraine's poet laureate gazed down like a kindly grandfather. In-Memoriam, he offered no solace. Mykola desperately wanted someone to talk to. He felt alone and confused. His mind was totally rattled. As his eyes dropped to the base of the statute, he noticed a shrouded figure staring at him. It was Maria. She scurried over to a nearby bench behind the base of a huge chestnut tree.

Mykola leapt up from his chair and rushed across the street.

"What are you doing here?" he asked.

"I did not sleep a wink last night."

"Guilt has a way of doing that," Mykola said coldly.

"I have enough guilt to last my lifetime and beyond."

"Well, there's a Catholic church up the street. Maybe the priest will give you absolution and you can get on with your pathetic life."

"There is no need to be rude."

"You think? My world has been turned inside out and upside down, and you don't think I need to be rude. I find out the woman who brought me into this world is a prostitute and now that I've found the missing pieces of my life, I should just ride off into the sunset."

"Is this what you intend to do?"

"What?"

"Ride off into the sunset."

"As soon as the travel agency opens I'm changing my ticket and flying home on the next plane out of here."

"Are you certain this is what you want?"

"What else can I possibly want? I got all the answers I'll ever need."

"Maybe you owe it to yourself to speak to Kateryna."

"Are you kidding? Whatever for?"

"Closure."

"I hate that word. Anyway, I've got all the closure I'll ever need. My biological mother is a prostitute and I'm her bastard son. Case closed."

"I know you hate me and there is nothing I can ever do to change that. But I came here not out of guilt but to see if there is anything I could do to help. I spent the entire night wondering what you will do. How you will handle this."

"I just told you how I'm going to handle this. I'm leaving on the next plane out of here."

"I think that would not be a good thing for you to do."

"Well maybe you should have thought about that when you and your boss did what you did."

"You've come this far. You can't allow yourself to walk away. You need to speak to Kateryna. You need to hear her side of the story."

"I know her side. She's a prostitute."

"Before you judge her so harshly, maybe you should find out her circumstance."

"Her circumstance? Let's see. She doesn't want to work at a real job. She's happy making money the easy way, on her back. That's her circumstance."

"Maybe she has no choice."

"We all have choices. You chose to say nothing when I was stolen from Kateryna. Matlinsky chose to be a con artist and a thief. Kateryna chose to become a prostitute. And I choose to get as far away from here as possible."

Maria pressed on. "There are many reasons why we make choices as you call them. If you want to fit the missing pieces into your puzzle, it might be wise for you to see your biological mother and hear her side of the story. It may help you to get on with your life. Otherwise, this situation will remain unresolved in your head and cause you to become a bitter, angry man."

"Thank you Dr. Maria."

"I understand your anger with me and Director Matlinsky. But you must also understand that what she did was a good thing for you. Maybe you should take some time to visit an internat for the older children and see for yourself what you would have faced. There is such a place several streets up the road from your hotel. It is Internat 72. We send most our children there when they reach seven years of age."

"You don't give up, do you? You just keep making excuses for that evil woman you work for. What she did was unconscionable. She committed a crime, and you were complicit in it."

Mykola got up and returned to his hotel room. He sat on his bed still trying but unable to make sense of the revelations that had become his wretched autobiography. He hated Kateryna and he now hated his life.

Totally spent, physically and emotionally, he closed his eyes. As he drifted off, he called out: "Mama." She didn't respond. Instead, his father appeared with a smirk on his face. Mykola awoke with a start. He had been asleep for two hours. It was 11 a.m. He rushed down the stairwell and raced over to the travel agency. He came to a stop at the entrance and stared in. Two agents sat behind their desks painting their fingernails. There were no clients.

In the back of his mind, he kept hearing Maria's refrain. *"Before you judge her, you should find out her circumstance."* Mykola flipped open his cell phone and called Alex.

"Alex, what are you doing tomorrow morning?"

"I gather I'm taking you to the airport?"

"I changed my mind. I need you to drive me to Dobrody."

There was silence on the other end.

"Can you drive me there?"

"If this is what you must do, then I will drive you."

"Hey Alex, thanks for not passing judgment."

"No problem my young friend. I am simply worried for you. I will see you tomorrow at 7 am."

It was overcast and Mykola had an entire day to kill. He knew how he would to spend it.

CHAPTER SEVENTEEN

Swarmed by a pack of giggling, giddy seven-, eight- and nine-year-old boys and girls, Mykola suddenly understood what it must have felt like to be the Pied Piper. No matter which way he turned, there they were dozens of abandoned, lonely children craving attention. They squealed with delight as he placed a chocolate bar in each out-stretched hand. The director of the orphanage, a stern-faced man in his late 50s, tried in vain to restore a semblance of decorum.

"Children! Children! Calm down! Calm down! You will each receive a treat," he called out, but to no avail.

"It's okay," Mykola said with a smile. "They're just excited."

On this dismal day, the institution, known as Internat 72, housed 184 boys and girls aged seven to 17, all alumni of baby orphanages. It was a stark and oppressive, four-story structure within walking distance of the downtown core. Yet it was virtually ignored by the foreign visitors who preferred to steer their goodwill toward the baby orphanages. Older children were not as cute and cuddly as babies and toddlers.

Mykola dropped by the internat unannounced and the director, a frustrated, low-level bureaucrat, offered an impromptu tour. Mykola assumed he was about to be led on yet another guided sideshow. It was nothing like that. The entire institution was open for inspection, warts and all. There was no sugar coating or planned deception. The director was not a man prone to playing games for a handout. He had his hands full trying to keep order in a place where mayhem ruled supreme.

The duo headed up the stairwell to the junior dormitory on the second floor. It housed 62 children aged seven to nine; boys in the west wing, girls in the east. At the entrance to each unit was a barred, steel door that was locked at 9 p.m. when the children went to bed. The prison-like gates were installed on every floor as a security measure, the director explained, mostly to prevent nighttime raids by older kids on the younger children, and also to keep randy teenage boys and girls from crawling into each other's beds.

The labyrinth of rooms was jammed with sagging cots and clothes were scattered helter-skelter. There were no lockers or dressers. The washroom consisted of an open, white-tiled stall with four showerheads jutting out of the ceiling, a row of four sinks and two porcelain toilets with no seats. Only the cold-water taps worked. There was never hot water. It was too costly to heat.

On the south side were two spacious classrooms. They were occupied with children who had little to keep their eager minds stimulated. The teachers, who looked harried, spent most of their time attempting to teach reading, writing and basic math skills on a chalkboard.

"We have no money for school supplies," the director said flatly.

"I can see that."

The third floor housed the intermediate dormitories: 64 children aged 10 to 13; the senior fourth floor contained 58 teenagers from 14 to 17. They were mirror images of the two floors below with one exception. The classrooms on the fourth were totally empty. There was not a single student or teacher in the rooms. It was obvious the older kids had virtually given up on school and any future it might offer.

"It is simply too difficult to keep the older ones in class," the director said.

"Where are they?"

"On the street, in the park across the road, drifting around the downtown. As long as they stay out of trouble and return for dinner and lights out, it's all I can hope for. Sadly, so many 16 and 17 year olds don't come back. They simply leave and run away."

"Where do they go when they take off?"

"They stay in abandoned buildings or underground in the sewer system."

"Do you report the runaways to the authorities?"

"I used to but they don't care. If the police happen to find them and they are under-age, they bring them back, and the next day, they're off again. I have enough to deal with trying to run this place. If they decide to run, they run."

Mykola shook his head, troubled by the depth of the man's indifference towards his charges. He looked totally beaten down and running on empty.

"What happens to these kids when they can no longer stay here?"

"They age out at 18. Then they must leave. The sad reality is that most of the boys end up in prison not long after they leave, and a lot of the girls end up being forced into prostitution. The children here have no prospects. They are doomed once they enter these doors."

"That's a pretty grim statement."

"True," the director said with sigh of resignation. "But as you can see, we can do next to nothing to prepare them for life. We give them a roof and bed. That is all. We do not have the facilities to train them for anything. Most of the girls don't even know how to boil water, and the government keeps cutting our funding. We get barely enough money to feed and clothe the children in our care."

It was an odd word choice Mykola thought. "Care" wasn't how he would describe what these children were getting.

Their next stop was the kitchen and dining area on the main floor. Two matronly women, wearing stained aprons and drenched in sweat, were boiling two huge caldrons of whole chickens and another three filled with potatoes, carrots and onions. It smelled unappetizing.

"This will be dinner for tonight," the director said lifting the lid off one pot.

Mykola's stomach turned when he peered in and spied a chicken head floating atop a thick layer of yellow sludge. He hoped the director wouldn't invite him to stay for a bite.

"What's for dessert?" Mykola wondered aloud.

The director laughed. "We rarely have money to buy sweets. Sometimes we get in a dozen watermelons or a few bushels of apples or plums donated to us from farmers when they are in season. Most of the time, this is it, just the main course."

With the tour over, the director told Mykola he could wander around the premises for as long as he wanted. He held out his hand, but only to shake hands. He was not looking for a hand out. His shoulders slumped in defeat, the man returned to his office.

Mykola headed out the back door to a sprawling fenced-in, dirt yard. It was a rambling minefield of rusted swing sets and monkey bars, collapsed slides and broken seesaws. Sitting under a tree at the far end, Mykola noticed a seven-year-old boy sobbing. He looked like a tragic Dickensian waif, dressed in a tattered sweater and pants that were two sizes too large. Mykola approached him holding out a Mars candy bar. The boy took it without looking up and stared at the colorful wrapper.

"Why are you crying?" Mykola asked

"I don't like this place. I want to go back to the orphanage. The older boys pick on me."

"How long have you been here?"

"Two weeks."

"What do the older boys do?"

"When I got here, they took all my new clothes and ripped the head off my teddy bear. They try to force me to go into the street to pick up cigarette butts. I don't want to do that and when I say no, they hit me and push me," he said, finally looking up.

Mykola was taken aback. In that fleeting moment, he saw himself in the boy; the same dark brooding eyes, the same fiercely independent nature. The only difference was this boy's future was likely very bleak. His dire situation virtually programed him for failure.

"Where is your family?"

"Mama died. Tato left."

"You have no aunts or uncles?"

"They didn't want me," he said, his eyes darting in fear to a dark corner of the building.

"What's your name?"

"Mykola."

Mykola's began to tear up. "We have something in common. That's my name too."

The boy said nothing. The fear on his face was growing more and more evident. Mykola followed the boy's terror-stricken stare. Several feet away, a 16-year-old was leaning against a back wall, leering menacingly at the boy. His fists were curled into tight balls.

"Who's he?"

"Lubomyr. He is the one who is always picking on me. I will have to give him my candy or he will beat me. He's mean. I wish I was big because I would beat him up good."

"You go ahead and eat your chocolate bar," Mykola said, as he ambled over to the bully.

"What's your name?" he asked in a friendly tone.

The boy didn't respond. He glared defiantly into Mykola's face.

"When I was in school, I came across a few boys who went around picking on little kids. You know why they picked on little kids?"

The teenager ignored the question.

"Because they're bullies, and the one thing I learned about bullies is they're all cowards. Why else would they pick on smaller kids who can't defend themselves? What you should do instead of being a bully is to try and be a big brother to the little kids that are sent here. That is what will make you a man. What do you say?"

"Drop dead!" With those two words, the bully called Lubomyr swaggered off.

Mykola returned to the young boy who was devouring the chocolate bar.

"Here's a couple more. Don't let anyone see them. Hide them under your pillow."

"Thank you." The boy said in a barely audible whisper.

"Would you like it if I visited you?" Mykola inwardly cringed the second the question left his lips. He knew the offer was disingenuous.

The boy stared up at Mykola and shrugged his shoulders. The look on his face said it all. He had heard those words countless times by visitors to the baby orphanage and never once did any of them come back for a second visit. They had done their Christian duty, assuaged their conscience by doling out gifts and candies, and returned home feeling fuzzy with loads of photographs to show family and friends of them posing with the orphans.

As Mykola turned to leave, he looked one more time at the forlorn face of this lonely boy, and grudgingly conceded that Matlinsky was right about one thing – this could have been his life.

Later that afternoon, while strolling through the backstreets of Lviv, Mykola was hit by a tantalizing aroma wafting from a nearby bakery. Feeling peck-ish, he walked in to buy a rogaliki: an almond crescent. His eyes lit on several large, flat cardboard boxes on steel racks at the back of the bakery – each brimming with 120 freshly baked cookies. Grinning ear to ear, he ordered up a dozen cases – four boxes of chocolate chip, four of oatmeal-raisin and four of chocolate fudge. The jovial, curvy baker wondered why the young foreigner wanted so many cookies and smiled when he gave her the address for the special delivery. Mykola then headed to the city market where he purchased 200 storybooks and novels for children and teens, 300 pens, 500 notebooks, and several Ukrainian language, math and general knowledge textbooks. He also bought a wide selection of art supplies – watercolors, crayons, markers, brushes, craft paper in assorted colors, glue and scissors, and had them delivered to Internat 72. It was a noble gesture and as he left the market, there was a bounce to his step. A block later, the bounce was gone. In his heart he felt like a 10-carat hypocrite. He got to go home. These kids had no home and a bleak future.

CHAPTER EIGHTEEN

It was a few minutes before 10 am when the cab lumbered into Zaluky Square.

"I hope you know what it is you are doing," Alex counseled.

"If I knew I probably wouldn't do it."

"Then that, my young friend, should tell you something. I have always lived by what my gut tells me, and right now it appears that your gut is saying this is a bad idea. You should listen to it."

"Yeah but I'm a stubborn guy," Mykola said with a forced smile.

"Where I come from stubborn can get you into more trouble than it is worth," Alex pointed out, his face grim with concern.

"It can also get you the answers you're looking for."

Mykola took a deep breath and headed for the bar. It was closed. No one was in sight. The church bells began to peal, reminding him that it was Sunday. The faithful, and those in need of absolution for recent sins, were attending mass. Taking a couple of steps back into the middle of the deserted street, he peered up at the apartment on the second floor. He recalled the bar owner saying Kateryna lived there, or at the very least did her business there. There was a sliver of light peeking out from behind a thick, burgundy velvet curtain. He took a chance and rapped on the door below. There was no answer. After knocking several times, he decided to hammer on it. A moment later, he heard the maddened footsteps of a woman clacking down the flight of stairs. It was Kateryna. She had just gotten out of bed. The look on her face could freeze water.

"You! Get away from here or I will call Yuri and he will give you the beating of your life," she shouted when she saw who was on the other side of the door.

"I need to talk to you."

"I don't want to talk to you. Now leave. You have caused me enough trouble."

"All I need is a few minutes," Mykola said calmly.

"Go away." Kateryna ordered, slamming the door.

"I won't leave here until you give me a chance to talk to you."

"Go away!" she screamed from behind the door.

Two men walked by and shot the young man a knowing glance and a wink.

"What are you two assholes looking at?" Mykola challenged angrily.

It was a big mistake. The moment the words left his mouth he knew he was in big trouble. The duo stopped dead in their tracks. The larger of the two approached Mykola, grabbed him by his jacket and slammed him up against the stone wall.

"I would be very careful how you talk to me," he threatened. His breath, heavy with garlic sausage and sour beer, made Mykola turn his face away in disgust.

"Oleh, let the boy go. Can't you see he needs to get laid?"

Ignoring the entreaty, Oleh shoved Mykola once again against the wall. "No, I think he needs that I teach him a lesson in respect."

In a flash Alex was behind the two men. "If anyone is to teach respect it will be me," he said, seizing Oleh by the scruff of his neck and tossing him bodily into the street. "Now get on your way or I'll beat you two bastards to a pulp."

The men took one look at Alex's powerful build and knew instantly that he was not a man to be trifled with. They turned and high-tailed it, giving him the middle finger salute once they were at a safe distance.

"We should leave," Alex suggested. "The woman wishes to be left alone."

Mykola ignored him, turning his attention back to the bolted door. He knew Kateryna was still there waiting … listening.

"On August 9, 1993, you gave birth to a baby boy at the hospital in Lviv! I need to talk to you about that," he said in a loud, measured tone.

There was dead silence. Alex returned to the car.

"I need to speak to you about that," Mykola repeated.

"Why are you doing this to me? Why are you persecuting me?" the woman pleaded.

"I'm not persecuting you. I'm just looking for some answers."

"I told you the last time, you have the wrong person. My baby died at birth. You are confused. Leave me alone."

Mykola gathered his thoughts, trying to find the right words to say.

"Your baby didn't die," he said softly. "The baby they brought you at the hospital wasn't your baby. I know this for a fact. I also know for a fact that

. . ." Mykola hesitated, "I am your son," his voice trailing off in an embarrassed whisper.

There was no response. Mykola put his ear to the door. He could hear the muffled sound of sobbing. He sat on the stoop and waited. He was not about to leave. Alex stared at him from the car and shook his head in disbelief. An observer of the world, he'd thought he'd heard it all, until this very moment.

The church bells began to chime, signaling the end of the service. It was 11. Moments later, Mykola noticed a portly, middle-aged man dressed in his natty Sunday best hovering pensively near the corner. After a few minutes, he waddled by gazing expectantly up at Kateryna's window with eyes that seemed to be bulging out of a skull so huge it looked deformed. In an instant, Mykola realized he was a customer. He looked the man over and noticed a silver cross dangling from his neck and thick gold wedding band on his left hand.

"What the hell," Mykola charged, his blood at a boil. "You come straight from church to cheat on your wife. You're one piece of work!"

"Go to hell," the man shouted as he scurried away.

Alex shook his head. As far as he was concerned, the man was simply partaking of a service offered by a whore. It was a simple business transaction. Why attack him for it?

Kateryna sat hunched over in agony on the stairwell reliving a tragic and horrifying episode she had long since put behind her – the day she gave birth. She was told her baby had died. She held a dead baby and with an outpouring of tears, she had mourned the infant's passing. She was long over it, and now, almost 20 years later, a young man was on the other side of the door professing to be her son. Why was he doing this? Was it a cruel joke? Did someone put him up to this?

Another hour passed before Mykola heard the latch rattle. The door suddenly flung open. Kateryna's face burning hot with rage.

"You are a liar. Get away from here!"

"I am not lying. Why would I come all this way if I were lying? I swear I'm telling you the truth."

Kateryna's eyes caught Alex staring at her from across the road. "Who is that? Why is he staring at me?"

"He's my driver."

Turning her attention back to Mykola, she demanded in a hard tone: "I want to know who told you this crazy story."

"A woman who works at the orphanage. She told me the whole story about my birth and how I was taken away from you right after I was born and adopted by my mother and father and taken to Canada."

As Mykola blurted out the circumstances of his adoption, Kateryna stared hard at his face, taking in his eyes, nose and lips. It was something she hadn't done in their first encounter. Then she noticed the dimple in the middle of his chin. It reminded her of someone from her distant past. She knew right then, Mykola was her son. Tears streamed down her face. Her breathing became erratic. She began to sob uncontrollably and then suddenly collapsed onto the pavement.

Alex rushed over. They carried the woman up the narrow stairwell to her tiny apartment and laid her down on an unmade double bed in the middle of the room. The apartment was dark and reeked of flesh. It was a smell Alex recognized instantly. During his five-year stint in the Soviet Army he and his buddies had frequented many brothels.

Beside the bed were a worn, flower print sofa and a tea-stained nightstand. On the cracked plaster ceiling, a single light bulb dangled on a wire. An eight by 10 black and white photograph turned sepia with age was attached to a far wall with a single thumbtack. Mykola walked over to it. Hand-printed across the bottom was a faded, single word: Tato. He instantly recognized the man. He had seen an image of the same man on the living room wall in the farmhouse in Stornovitzi. It was Kateryna's father, and his maternal grandfather.

Alex motioned to Mykola suggesting they go to the kitchen to get a cool, damp cloth to place on Kateryna's forehead. They couldn't believe the mess. The room was cramped and filthy. Unwashed cups and plates were piled high in a grimy sink. There was a grease-stained hot plate and an ancient refrigerator that clunked loudly when it started up or shut down. The cupboards were cobbled together with cheap, unpainted plywood. Yanking open a counter drawer in search of a clean cloth, Mykola jumped back, startled at the sight of dozens of cockroaches scurrying for cover.

"Damn, I hate cockroaches!"

Alex laughed. "A big boy like you is afraid of little bugs."

"It's so bloody disgusting. I can't believe this place. It's a pigsty. How could anyone live like this?" he said in a muffled whisper.

"This is no worse, no better than in what so many live."

"It doesn't make it right."

Kateryna moaned.

"It sounds like she is coming to. I think it is better I not be here when she wakes up," Alex said, making his way to the staircase. "I will wait in the car for you."

Mykola placed the cool compress on Kateryna's forehead and sat down on a chair by the bed, looking intently at her.

"How long have I been here?" she asked, trying to shake the cobwebs from her mind.

"Maybe ten minutes."

"How did I get here?"

"Alex and I carried you up."

"Alex?"

"My driver."

Kateryna focused on Mykola's eyes. They were dark and brooding, like her eyes, and the eyes of her brothers. Then she looked down again at his chin. She drew a deep breath and exhaled slowly.

"What's your name?" she asked in a soft whisper.

"Mykola. Mykola Yashan."

"Mykola. It's a nice name."

"What would you have called me?"

"Danylo, after my father," she said calmly, her eyes not leaving his face.

"That's my middle name."

Kateryna was awestruck by the coincidence. "Tato died in a farm accident when I was eight," she said, pulling herself up to sit facing Mykola.

"I know."

"How could you know that?" she snapped.

"Your brother Bohdan told me."

"That big oaf is a mama's boy. He never got married. No woman he brought home was ever good enough for mama."

"But he is one strong oaf with a hair-trigger temper."

"Strong, yes. But he never protected me. My father was my protector. I was his girl. I loved him so much. When he died I felt my world come to an end. My mother never much cared for me. The sun rose and set on her Bohdan. She used me like a dishrag, ordering me to pick up and clean up after her precious Bohdan. She was always yelling at me and calling me names in front of people. I hate that woman."

"She told me you are dead to her," Mykola offered.

Kateryna grimaced. "Because I brought shame on the family."

"By doing what you're doing?" Mykola asked. The tone of disdain was not lost on the woman.

"This life was never of my choosing."

A sudden loud banging on the door caused Mykola to jump up. Kateryna looked toward the stairwell, hoping whoever it was would give up and go away. The hammering continued, growing more and more insistent. From the annoyed and somewhat flustered expression on Kateryna's face, Mykola realized it was a client, probably the same man he'd seen pacing the street earlier. His stomach clenched with the cold confirmation that this woman, his biological mother, was a prostitute.

"I'll be back in a moment," she said, as she scurried down the stairs.

There was muffled conversation. The man sounded irritated. He argued that it was his regular Sunday appointment. Kateryna said she was ill. He didn't care. He had an appointment and wanted to be serviced. Kateryna refused. He stormed off vowing to tell Yuri. The door slammed shut, Kateryna returned. Looking frazzled, she went to the kitchen and put a kettle of water on the hot plate.

"You would like chai?" she called out.

"No thanks. I don't really like tea," Mykola replied. Truth was he didn't want to partake of anything in the apartment, especially anything prepared in that cockroach-infested kitchen.

When she returned, Kateryna could tell from Mykola's demeanor that he was agitated. Staring down at the floor, he couldn't bring himself to look at her. She sat down in front of him and waited for him to raise his head.

"You are ashamed of me," she said with detached coolness.

He didn't respond.

"You have no idea of the fate that has befallen me. Yet you pass judgment on me."

Again, Mykola said nothing.

Kateryna closed her eyes to gather her thoughts. After a few minutes of dead silence, she decided she would tell him about the circumstances that brought her into the sordid world of prostitution. But she would spare him the horrific details. She would give the young man a sanitized account.

"When I was 17, the priest's sister came to the village," she began slowly, setting her cup on an end table. "She was driving a fancy car and wore a fur coat. Everyone in the village was so impressed. The priest introduced her with such pride and joy in his voice. In church during mass, I noticed she kept looking at me and at my girlfriend, Anya. Later outside, she approached us. She told us she could get a job for us in Germany cleaning hotel rooms. We would each be paid 450 Euros a month. It was a small fortune back then. She assured us it was legitimate work. Anya wanted to help out her mother. I was desperate to get out of the village. So the next day we left with her for Lviv."

Mykola's eyes were fixed on a knothole in the floorboards.

"The woman took us across the Polish border and passed us to this Polish bastard. The man yelled at us to get in the back of his van. Anya turned to run. He grabbed her by the hair, slapped her in the face and threw her in the back of his van. She was screaming for help. The man jumped into the van and beat her. I pleaded with the priest's sister to take us back to Ukraine but she turned her back on us. She got into her car and drove away. I was crying and begged the man not to hit me. I got into the van and he drove to Germany. It was the middle of the night when we arrived and that was when we learned our fate."

"Your fate?" Mykola asked. "What do you mean?"

Kateryna's face darkened, her eyes flashed with terror as her mind tumbled back to the events that followed; events that would remain locked in her memory forever. She would never reveal the full horror of what she had suffered to anyone.

It was pitch black when the van came to a stop outside what looked like an abandoned warehouse on the outskirts of Hamburg. When the rear doors flung open, three men with flash lights shone their beams on the petrified cargo huddled together, their faces streaked with tears.

"Get out!" the driver yelled.

The girls didn't move.

"Get out now!"

Kateryna crawled to the exit and was hauled out by the hair by one of the men and thrown to the ground. Shaking uncontrollably, Anya was frozen. She couldn't move. The driver leapt into the van and grabbed her legs, dragging her to the door and tossing her to the ground. She curled into a fetal position.

"Get up!" he shouted.

Kateryna obeyed. Anya squeezed her eyes shut, hoping it was all a bad dream. Kicking her twice in the backside, the driver yanked her up by her neck. The other two men laughed as they examined the girls before taking them into the building. They grabbed at their breasts and buttocks.

The two were locked in a concrete room with bars on the windows. There were at least 30 young women in that massive, holding cell. They were from Russia, Moldova, Romania, Ukraine and Latvia. Several were sobbing. Most of them sat on stained mattresses on the cement floor huddled together in abject fear. No one spoke. The new arrivals had no idea of the unbelievable horrors they were about to endure. The place was a breaking ground where the captives were seasoned for the international sex trade.

An hour later, six men stormed into the basement. They viciously attacked Kateryna and Anya, raping them repeatedly. They were yelled at constantly and threatened that if they did not submit and do as they were ordered they would suffer the consequence. With each attack, they were instructed on how to act and perform sexually.

Anya was a virgin. She refused to submit and paid dearly for it. She was brutally tortured and humiliated repeatedly by the attackers. They burned the backs of her arms and legs with cigarette butts to get her to comply. They tore out her hair, whipped her with a belt and sodomized her. It was executed in front of all the young women as a warning. They were all crying, begging the men to stop, and pleading with the stubborn victim to give in. She didn't. Anya went limp and retreated into a catatonic state. She would not speak. She simply stared into space. It was as if her soul had left her body.

Witnessing the horrific violence inflicted on her childhood friend, Kateryna gave in. She was no hero. She was afraid of being tortured and even more afraid of being killed. She did as she was told and was spared from torture.

A week later, the women were paraded naked before several pimps and brothel owners, and sold at auction like cattle to the highest bidder. Kateryna was bought for 15,000 Euros by an Albanian thug named Attar. He smuggled her into Italy to work the streets of Milan along with two other purchases from Moldova. Anya went to a Greek brothel owner for a paltry 4,000 Euros. A year later, she was re-sold for 2,000 Euros to a Bosnian pimp and smuggled into Tuzla to service randy peacekeepers with the United Nations.

Attar was a nasty pimp with a violent streak. He laid down the law and the six women in his harem lived in fear of crossing him. They were required to work the streets every night no matter their health or inclement weather. Their night would end once they had each earned 500 Euros. They were promised 100 Euros as their cut, which he said he would set aside for "safe keeping." But he had no intention of ever paying them. The women were housed in a two bedroom, flophouse walk-up with mattresses on the floor while Attar partied in the lap of luxury at his upscale condo in another part of the city. Often, he would summon his girls to private soirees where they were required to service his friends and passing acquaintances for free.

Kateryna would never share all these details with anyone, especially Mykola.

"What do you mean by your fate?" Mykola repeated, snapping Kateryna out of her trance.

She fixed her eyes on her teacup. "We were forced to become prostitutes. I was sold to an Albanian pimp named Attar who took me to work in Milan."

"And your friend?"

She looked up at Mykola's face for a moment, her brow creased in thought. "Anya was first taken to Athens and then about a year later, I heard she was sold to a brothel in Bosnia to be used by UN peacekeepers. No one has heard from her for almost 20 years. I'm sure she is dead."

Mykola sat in numbed silence, riveted by Kateryna's story and clueless that she had deliberately left out the most violent and depraved parts of her gruesome initiation into the flesh trade.

"How did you end up here?"

"I became pregnant. My pimp went insane. He told me he was going to do an abortion. I ran out of the apartment and into the street begging for someone to help me. No one came to my assistance. They could see what I was and didn't want to dirty their hands. I ran into a nearby church begging the priest for help. He ordered me to leave his holy sanctuary. Then an elderly nun suddenly appeared from the shadows. She put her arm around me and fell to her knees in prayer. It was the strangest thing. When she got up, she told me I was to come with her. Attar was outside the door lying in wait. He rushed up and grabbed me by the arm but this little nun stepped between us and commanded that he let me go. He knew better than to hit a nun in Italy. The mafia would find him and kill him. He stormed away saying one day he would find me and kill me," Kateryna recounted.

"What happened then?"

"The nun took me to a convent. I stayed there for four months while the sisters got my travel documents in order. They raised money to buy me an airplane ticket and I came home. It was like a small miracle. I will be forever grateful to the sister. She was such a caring soul," Kateryna recalled. "She never once judged me."

Her last comment was not lost on Mykola. "What was the nun's name?"

"Sister Eugenia Benedicta. She was with the Consolata Order. If she is still alive, she would be close to 90 by now."

"When you got back, did you go back home to Stornovitzi?"

Kateryna gritted her teeth as she recounted the family reunion. "When my mother saw I was pregnant, she spit in my face and called me a whore. She told Bohdan to put me in the barn to sleep with the chickens and the pigs. He forbade me to walk around the village. He said it would kill mama. It made no difference to her or to Bohdan that I was forced into this life. I know that Markian and his wife Ruslana felt terrible for me but there was nothing they could do. Sometimes Markian came to see me with Ruslana but only when Mama was away in the fields or in church lighting candles for her dead parents. They brought me cookies and sat with me for a while."

"Did anyone ever ask about your friend?"

"One afternoon, Anya's mother came to see me. She was crying, begging me for news of her daughter. She said she had gone to Lviv to see the priest's sister a month earlier. She hadn't heard a word from her daughter since she had left the village. That woman sat there and lied. She told her Anya was living the good life and probably wanted to forget her past life. I couldn't bring myself to tell her what had happened to her daughter. The following Sunday I sneaked out of the barn and went to the church. I ran up to the altar and screamed at Father Zenon in front of everyone, denouncing him as a hypocrite and telling everyone what his sister had done to me and to Anya. I had no idea Anya's mother was in the church. Bohdan ran up to the altar, grabbed me by the hair and dragged me to the shed at the back of the house. He locked me in there for a week."

Kateryna paused, her eyes glistening with tears. "The day I was let out of the shed, I could hear the church bell tolling. It was the ring of death. Bohdan told me Anya's mother had committed suicide. He said it was my fault for the blasphemy I committed in church. I felt so guilty, so horrible. He said I should have kept my mouth shut. When it came time to give birth, Bohdan drove me to a hospital in Lviv and you know what happened there."

"Do you remember who the doctor was?" Mykola interjected.

"I don't remember his name. But I can recall I did not like him. He examined me. He seemed so interested in me. He kept asking me questions about my health. He wanted to know if I drank, if I used drugs, if I had any diseases. At the time, I thought it was odd. I had grown accustomed to everyone treating me like dirt and this doctor seemed so interested in me. The following day, he came to tell me he had bad news. He said the tests revealed that my unborn baby had congenital defects. He said I should give the baby up the moment it is born, that it would be very difficult for me with a baby with serious health problems."

"What did you do?"

"I did not trust the look in his eyes. I told him I would keep the baby and he became very upset with me. I could not understand his behavior. One day he is so nice, the next so mean. When I went into labor he refused to give me any drugs to ease the pain. When I could take it no more, he said he would give me something but first I had to sign a medical form giving him permission."

"Do you remember what it said?"

"I was in no shape to read it. I just wanted to stop the pain. You were a big baby and as you can see, I'm not a big woman. I signed it and he gave me a needle."

Kateryna paused for a moment, thinking back to that morning. "When I gave birth, I could have sworn I heard the baby cry. I know I heard the baby cry. I heard you cry. Then suddenly I went unconscious. I think I was given another needle. When I came to many hours later, the doctor told me my baby was stillborn. I had no reason to distrust him. I asked to see the baby. I wanted to hold him and say a prayer. He was such a sweet little boy with a perfect face. My heart broke when I held him. I begged God to bring him back to life. I begged God to take me instead but he lay there still in my arms."

Tears rolled down Mykola's face.

"The next day, Bohdan took me back home. My mother screamed at me. She said God had punished me for my sins by making certain my bastard child was born dead. I spit in her face. Bohdan beat me. The next morning, he came into the barn and told me to get into his car. He drove me to this town and told me I was never to return to Stornovitzi. He gave me 100 hryvna, barely enough to get by for a month and left me in the square with just the clothes on my back. When I ran out of money, I ended up at the bar."

Mykola closed his eyes. He was having difficulty absorbing the total insanity of Kateryna's story. "I can't believe your family wouldn't understand what you'd been put through and not be there to support you."

Kateryna managed a forlorn smile.

"Why are you smiling?" Mykola asked hesitantly.

"When you first saw me, you immediately passed judgment and dismissed me as a worthless whore."

Mykola felt his face flush with embarrassment. "I am so sorry."

"It's okay. You have an excuse. You're young. You have no idea of the horrors that go on in this world."

There was a long silence. Mykola sat quietly.

"What are you thinking?" Kateryna finally asked.

"All my life I wondered who I looked like. I found it strange that I bore no resemblance whatsoever to my mother or father. Now I look at you and I see so much of me."

Kateryna said nothing.

"Can I ask you, do you have any idea who my father was?"

"Of course I do," she said curtly. "He was Italian. He was such a handsome man. His name was Antonio Rinaldo. He was in university studying to become a civil engineer."

Kateryna's mind drifted back to the night she first encountered Antonio. It was on a particularly brisk evening in late November. She noticed a small, blue Fiat circle the street at least four times. On the fifth drive by, she stepped in front of the car. Looking somewhat sheepish, the driver rolled down the window and fumbled as he tried to find the right words.

"I was noticing you might be cold. Would you like to go for a coffee to warm up?" he asked.

Kateryna laughed. "I'm not here to have coffee. I have to work and if you haven't a better offer, then keep driving."

"I'll pay you. What do you ask?"

"It depends what you want."

"An Espresso."

"I said I don't do coffee."

"I will pay you 20 Euros to have coffee with me."

It was the going price for oral sex.

Kateryna eyed the young man with amusement. She waved to one of the women on the other side of the street, motioning her to take down the license place and make of car. Feeling she had little to fear, she got in.

The man introduced himself. He was a year older than Kateryna. He admitted that he had first noticed her two weeks earlier and was instantly smitten by her Slavic beauty. He understood what she was but he also felt in his heart that she was not on the street of her own free will. He could see it in her eyes and felt it in his soul. He also caught sight of Attar depositing his harem at various intersections along the roadway. He could sense they were all terrified of him.

On their third encounter, Antonio and Kateryna made love for the first time. He paid but convinced himself that he had to give her cash so that her pimp would not punish her. In a few short weeks, their romance blossomed. Antonio suggested that she runaway with him. She agreed but on the night they were to flee, Attar got wind of the plan. He and two other Albanian pimps waited for Antonio to pull up in a cul de sac where Kateryna was positioned. She was unaware of what was to happen. As soon as the Fiat turned onto the street, two black SUVs followed closely behind and blocked the escape route. Antonio was pulled out of his car, beaten and left unconscious in a pool on blood. Kateryna begged the men to stop. Attar turned and smashed her in the face with his closed fist. She fell to the street unconscious. It was the last time Kateryna ever saw Antonio.

"How do you know he is my father?" Mykola asked.

"He is the only man I slept with who did not use protection. We were in love and despite all the men who had used me, I was always very careful. I knew I was safe. And now, when I look at you, there is no doubt in my mind. You look so much like him. You have his chin, the same dimple and you are built like him."

Mykola rubbed his temples, trying to process the startling revelation that his biological father was Italian and a john.

Kateryna waited a moment and then asked: "What did you expect to find when you came here?"

"To Ukraine?"

"Yes."

"I don't know," he said, feeling uncomfortable and wondering where she was going with the questions.

"No. Tell me."

"I thought you were dead, that I was adopted because you had died."

"And?"

"And maybe I'd find an aunt or an uncle, and your grave. I was going to put flowers on it."

"And now?"

"And now what?" Mykola asked.

"Do you wish you had found a grave?"

Mykola didn't respond but the look in his eyes said it all.

Kateryna nodded knowingly. "Easier to find the grave of a dead mother than a mother who is alive and who is a prostitute."

In his heart, Mykola knew she'd read him right. He was wishing she would change the subject. She did. But it didn't make the situation any easier.

"The people who took you, what did they do?"

"My father was a professor and I guess you can say mama was an artist, a musician and a community volunteer."

A frosty glare flashed in Kateryna's eyes.

"What?" Mykola asked.

"Nothing," she replied tersely.

"No, what? Obviously I must have said something that offended you."

"You called the woman, mama."

Mykola was not about to lie or make apologies. "In my heart she will always be my mama. She loved me. She brought me up. I will always love her."

"Then why do you bother me?"

"I needed to know."

Kateryna said nothing. She glanced at a framed picture of a landscape from a travel magazine taped to the wall across from her bed. It was a National Geographic photograph of the Great Wall of China.

Breaking the disquiet, Mykola asked: "What are you thinking?"

"I look at you and I see a healthy, handsome, educated young man and I wonder what would have become of you had you remained with me."

"I guess we'll never know."

"It scared me to think of it when I was pregnant. My family would never have accepted you. The people in the village would never have accepted you."

"I'd have been the village bastard," he said with a shameless grin.

"That is not so funny. It is precisely what you would have been."

Mykola then asked guardedly. "What should I call you?"

"What do you want to call me?"

"I don't know."

Kateryna could feel his unease. "Call me Kateryna," she replied in a matter of fact tone.

"Can I ask why that pig of a bar owner calls you Vera?"

"It is who I am in what I do. It is not who I am in real life. Vera is who I must be to survive. She is who I must be to get me through each day, to do what I must do. She is this body, and that is all that she is. Kateryna is my soul and no one will ever have my soul. It is the only thing that truly belongs to me."

"Why do you continue to do this?" Mykola asked hesitantly.

"I have no choice."

"We all have choices. You could have chosen to do something else when you got back here."

Kateryna's eyes narrowed. "Spoken like a man, or from the looks of you, a man raised with a silver spoon in his mouth. As I have told you, my situation was not of my choosing. I was forced into this life. Do you think any woman wants to do this? Do you think any woman wants to have strange men invading her body night after night? Do you really believe that?"

"You can always get other work."

"You're not listening. No one will give me other work."

"Ask the bar owner to let you waitress."

"Yuri owns me. He tells me what to do."

"What do you mean he owns you? How can he own you?"

"He just does. That is the way of the world in which I am trapped."

"Then leave. Run away!"

"All of this is so easy for you to say."

"Isn't there something else you could do instead of this?"

Kateryna could sense Mykola's disapproval, and more importantly, his shame. "There is nothing else. Everyone knows what I am. In this town I am a whore. In the village, I am a whore. Wherever I go I am known as a whore. No man wants to marry a prostitute although ironically most of the men I see are married. And if I try to run away, Yuri will hunt me down and when he finds me, he will bring me back here and beat me. Yuri is an evil and dangerous man. He has no soul. He often boasts he is the spawn of Satan. All he cares about is money."

"Why don't you go to the police? Tell them what's happening to you."

"Ha! Many of the police are customers. Yuri makes me service them for free so they will leave him alone."

"You have to leave this life," Mykola urged, his voice breaking.

"I have already told you I can't. Yuri won't let me. He owns me."

"Nobody owns anybody. This isn't the Middle Ages."

"The only way he will let me go is if somebody buys me."

"Then I'll speak to him."

"And do what?"

Mykola's mind was racing, trying to formulate some kind of plan. He felt he had an obligation to get her out of this untenable situation for her sake and for his own peace of mind. He couldn't live with the knowledge that the woman who brought him into the world was a prostitute. Every fiber in his being screamed he had to free her from her bond. The problem was how.

The words came out of his mouth before he had time to think them through.

"I'll buy your freedom!"

"And then what?"

"I'll bring you back home with me to Canada."

"How will you do that?"

"You're my mother. I'll go to the Canadian Embassy in Kyiv and tell them that I am going to sponsor you. I have all the money I will ever need. You'll be safe, and I promise you, no one will ever know about your past."

Kateryna said nothing, but her expression said it all. She didn't believe him.

"What time does that piece of garbage open the bar?"

"I would be very careful how you talk to him. He will stomp you like a bug if you cross him. He runs the underworld in this town," Kateryna warned.

"I'll be nice and polite. What time does he open?"

"In an hour."

"Could you not come down until after I've spoken to him? I just need maybe 15 minutes."

Kateryna nodded.

"I promise you that I will take you away from all this," Mykola said as he got up and left. "I swear."

As he reached the stairwell, he turned and looked at Kateryna. "Can I ask you for a big favor?"

"What is it?"

"Can I take a picture of you?"

"I must look terrible."

"Believe me, you look just fine. Please. I want to capture this moment. It's really important to me."

"Let me fix my hair," Kateryna said, rushing off to the washroom.

When she returned, Mykola snapped three photographs in a row on his IPhone.

"Let me see them." She approved two and asked Mykola to delete one in which she felt she looked dark and sorrowful.

As he was heading down the stairs, Kateryna called out. "Mykola, when you come back, I have something else I must tell you."

Mykola looked warily up at Kateryna. "What is it? Can you tell me now?"

"No, it can wait. You have more than enough on your mind to deal with. I will tell you on your next visit. It is something important that you need to know."

"Now you know I'll be coming back," Mykola said with a hesitant smile. "I will see you soon."

Alex studied Mykola's face as he got into the passenger seat. He could see that his young friend's brain was fried after five hours in the apartment.

"First my parents were killed, and then this. I am so messed up. I can't believe what that woman has been put through," Mykola said, his head slumped back against the headrest.

Alex said nothing.

"I don't know where to go with all this. I made a promise to Kateryna but I don't know if I will be able to keep it."

"What promise?"

"I promised to buy her freedom and take her to Canada."

Pursing his lips, Alex looked down at the steering wheel. "What do you want to do?"

"Get as far away from here as possible and somehow try to forget that this ever happened, but I made a promise. The bar owner is supposed to be here at 6 pm."

"Well, he must be early. That's him coming up the street."

Yuri looked the worse for wear after a night of heavy drinking. It was obvious he was not a church going man. He was unshaven and wearing dark sun glasses even though the sky was heavily overcast. Three men walking in his direction darted across the street when they realized who he was.

"Holy crap! What do I do?"

Alex didn't respond. He was not about to wade into the turgid waters of Mykola Yashan's thought process with any advice. It was not his issue. But he knew if he had a choice in the matter, he would be happy to see the town of Dobrody and all its misery disappear in the dust from his rearview mirror.

His eyes filled with trepidation, Mykola asked, "Could you come with me?"

Alex nodded. Despite his reticence, there was no way he was going to allow a neophyte to venture into the lion's den alone. In the short time he had chauffeured his young passenger from one place to another he had gotten to like him. He understood Mykola's quest, even though he came from the school of leaving stones unturned. Still, he respected the young man's drive, passion and stubborn will. But he also knew that Mykola was a stranger in a foreign land, and without someone watching out for him, he could land in a pile of trouble, especially when dealing with the likes of Yuri. If Mykola didn't tread carefully, he'd leave the bar on a stretcher, or worse, in a body bag.

"A warning before we go in there. While you were up in the apartment, I spoke to a man who told me all about this bar owner. This Yuri chap is a very dangerous man. He runs the crime syndicate in this town. Even the police are afraid of him. You must be very careful not to cross him. Watch your words. Pick them carefully."

Mykola squeezed the bridge of his nose. He had no idea what he was getting into or how to get out of it. Once again, he found himself quietly wishing he'd listened to his godmother and stayed put in the safety of his home in Edmonton.

"He owns that mansion on the hill just outside the town," Alex noted as they headed for the bar.

"That god awful monstrosity we saw on the way in?"

"That is the one."

"I bet the prick built it with the money he made off Kateryna's back."

"People like him need to have a lesson taught. Trouble is people like him rarely ever get what should be coming to them," Alex pointed out.

Mykola nodded in agreement, not that he knew a thing about people like Yuri.

"I will watch your back, my young friend. But I want you to understand that when I say we must leave. We leave right away. Do you understand?"

"Yes."

"There must be no hesitation. I know this kind of man. We leave right away."

"I got it."

The two men entered the bar.

Looking up, Yuri's instincts zapped on high alert. He recognized Mykola. He posed no problem, but Alex was another story. His street sense told him the man was a formidable force. Yuri fished his cell phone out of his pocket and placed it within hand's reach on the counter, just in case there was trouble. The move did not escape Alex.

"What is your pleasure?" Yuri asked with a gruffly.

"I want to talk to you about Kateryna. I mean Vera," Mykola began, trying to keep his voice firm.

"She will cost you 200 hryvna. She is upstairs," he said glibly.

"I'm not interested in her for that."

"Then what is your interest in the whore?" Yuri asked, his bloodshot eyes boring like a power drill into Mykola's face.

"Humanitarian," Mykola said, trying to keep from spitting in the man's face.

Yuri burst out laughing. "What is this humanitarian horse shit? I asked you, what is your interest? I warn you not to fuck with me."

"I found out she's my aunt. I want to bring her back to her village."

Yuri didn't buy the explanation. "She is my property. I cannot just give her to you," he said smugly. "There is a price to be paid."

Alex sat quietly at the bar, staring coldly at the owner. Yuri returned the look and scoffed: "You are nobody here. Do not think for a moment I fear you. I run this town." His fingers inched closer to his cell phone.

Alex didn't respond. He knew he could snap the man in two but he also understood the consequences. He probably wouldn't make it out of town alive.

Turning to Mykola, Yuri laid out the terms of Kateryna's freedom. "You want her then you must buy her."

"How much?"

Yuri sized up the young man. "She is like a used car. Many have driven her."

Alex interjected. His tone was decisive. "He asked you how much to free her?"

Drumming his hands in mock pensiveness on the bar, Yuri shot back, "At her age, she is worth 25,000 hryvna. I can let you have the whore for 25,000."

Mykola wished he'd brought a baseball bat to the meeting. All he could think about was crushing the man's skull.

"I will bring you the cash in a couple of days. I need to get a wire transfer from Western Union."

"In the meantime, Vera will be here, working hard earning her keep," Yuri noted with a daring smirk.

When Mykola exited the bar, he felt like he was drowning in a raging torrent of emotions. His soul was overwhelmed by a deep empathy and sadness for Kateryna, while at the same time churning with an intense loathing towards the bar owner. The very thought of the other cast of players who played a role in Kateryna's wretched saga – Matlinsky, Maria, the village priest, the holy man's sister, Kateryna's mother and Bohdan - sickened and disgusted him. He could not understand why no one, other than an elderly nun in a far off country, would offer a helping hand to the woman.

On the drive back to Lviv, Mykola sat quiet thinking about the untold pain and humiliation Kateryna had endured over the years. He was now firm in his resolve to save her, to rescue her from the horrific world in which she was ensnared – held prisoner since she was a mere teenager. His mind also percolated with thoughts of revenge. He wanted to expose Matlinsky for what she really was – an amoral fraud artist. He wanted to destroy the bar owner for the evil he had forced onto Kateryna. How dare he demand 25,000 hryvna for her purchase! She was not his property. She was not a slave. Mykola wished he'd studied martial arts instead of dancing. He would have relished pounding Yuri into the dirt. But Alex had warned him that the man was not one to be trifled with. The trouble for Mykola was that he was ill prepared and ill-equipped to deal with the violence and depravity of Kateryna's world. He knew it. He would simply get the cash and bring Kateryna to his home in Edmonton where she could live out the rest of her life in peace, where she would no longer have to work as a prostitute, and where no one would ever know about her past. That was his plan.

Then his mind fixated on Kateryna's last words. What was it, he wondered, that she needed to tell him.

CHAPTER NINETEEN

Lying down on his bed, Mykola closed his eyes, trying to clear his head and figure out his next move. The visit with Kateryna had completely messed up his mind. He was having a difficult time dealing with all that she had told him. It was a world he had never known and in his wildest imagination could never comprehend. He felt disgusted with himself for having judged the woman so harshly without knowing her truth. Yet he was still sickened with the unspeakable reality that he was the son of a prostitute. His once protected little world had imploded and he was in free fall.

He stared up at ceiling trying to force his brain to focus. He now had a mission. He had to rescue Kateryna, of that he was sure. He couldn't believe that she was a slave and that he would have to buy her freedom. The very thought rattled him to his core. His first step: he would phone his godmother later in the day and ask her to wire the money he needed to pay off the bar owner. He knew Sonia would ask him why he wanted the cash. He'd simply lie and tell her it was for an extraordinary piece of artwork.

"What have I gotten myself into," Mykola said aloud, feeling he may have acted too hastily in promising to bring Kateryna to Canada. He should have thought it out. But he had no time. Now, he found himself wishing he hadn't made the offer. Despite his best intentions, he had no idea who this woman was. Kateryna was a total stranger with a ton of baggage that could easily spell serious trouble down the road. Still, she was his biological mother and she desperately needed his help. Mykola was torn. How, he wondered, would he explain Kateryna's sudden appearance to Lesia, her parents and his friends? He knew he could never reveal her past. At all costs, it had to remain a secret. His mind was made up. He decided to fly to Kyiv and talk to someone at the Canadian Embassy to start the paperwork. But there was something he needed to do and before he could logically and calmly think it through, he pushed himself off the bed and was on his way.

Twenty minutes later, Mykola was in Natalka Matlinsky's office. He was in no mood for any more deceit, deception or dancing around. Steadfast in his resolve to get at the truth, he fully grasped that he was up against a formidable foe, one who knew how to skate and obfuscate. Yet while he kept telling himself to play it cool, his fuse was lit.

"I need to talk to you," he began.

The director was clearly irritated by his unscheduled arrival. The very sight of him grated on her nerves.

"As I have already told you Mr. Yashan, I cannot give you the name of your biological mother. It is against regulation. The issue is one of strict confidentiality and there is no way I will breach that."

"I have her name."

With a look of disbelief, Matlinsky wondered if he was bluffing. "I don't believe you," she said dismissively.

"Her name in Kateryna Chumak."

The director's eyes narrowed. Leaning forward on her desk, she asked: "How did you get her name?"

"It doesn't matter."

"I demand to know."

"I have my ways."

Shooting an accusatory glare at Maria, she asked: "Did you have anything to do with this?"

Her face flushed, Maria sputtered nervously, "I had nothing to do with this."

"If I find you had anything to do with this, I will fire you on the spot!"

"I swear. I did not give him her name. As God is my witness, I did not give him her name."

Mykola jumped to Maria's rescue. "Just because you won't share the information with me, doesn't mean there aren't other ways to get it."

"I don't believe you," the director countered.

"It didn't take much digging," he said smugly. "I figured I was born in a hospital here in Lviv, and guess what? The record of my birth is contained in the archives of the Lviv Regional Hospital, as is the name of my biological mother, Kateryna Chumak."

"Well, aren't you the clever little detective!" she fired back. "So what is it you want from me then?"

"You told me and you told my parents that Kateryna had died."

Matlinsky did not respond. Her mind was consumed with the troubling realization that the young man had become an ever-present danger.

"Now I find out she's alive. In fact, I met Kateryna in a bar in a town called Dobrody, and I'm willing to bet you know the story she told me about my birth?"

Looking down at an open file on her desk, the director attempted feigned disinterest.

"Kateryna said the doctor told her that her baby was stillborn and when she asked to see the child, a nurse brought her a dead baby. She was told it was her baby."

Sitting stone-faced behind her desk, Matlinsky said nothing. She offered no response.

The powder keg ignited. Mykola jumped up from the chair and slammed his fist on the director's desk. "You stole my life!"

"I stole your life?" Matlinsky countered defiantly. "Ha! I gave you a life you ungrateful fool. Tell me, what would you have done if I had told you the day you walked in here wanting answers that your biological mother was a prostitute? I would venture you would have immediately abandoned your silly quest and run back home."

Maria stirred nervously in her chair stunned by yet another piece of information that her boss had not bothered to disclose. All she had ever said about Kateryna was that she was an unwed pregnant teenager. Never did she mention that the young woman was a prostitute.

Matlinsky continued. "Just think for a moment what your life would have been like being the son of the village whore?"

"Don't you dare call her that," Mykola shouted.

"She was what she was, and I assume she still is. These women never change. You met her. Tell me, am I wrong?"

"You have no idea the hell she's been through. She never wanted that life. She was forced into it."

"Oh, save me the sob stories. I've heard them all. Innocent village girl goes to Germany or Italy or Greece to work in a restaurant or cleaning rooms in a hotel, and suddenly she is forced into prostitution. I have no time for the naiveté of fools. They get what they deserve for being so stupid," Matlinsky said, staring coldly into Mykola's face.

"Whatever her circumstances, you had no right to do what you did to her. What you did was illegal, let alone immoral and unethical."

The seemingly unflappable director was unmoved. "You sit there so angry and so self-righteous. Why don't you go and see for yourself what you would have become had I not taken you away from that woman? Visit any prison in Ukraine and you will see firsthand. They are filled with young men who never got the opportunity I gave you! Fortune did not smile on them when they came into this world. They were simply abandoned by their mothers and left at the doorstep of orphanages across Ukraine. They were branded for failure the moment they entered the doors of the internats. You would have been branded for failure had you remained with that whore. That is a fact."

"That's not the point!"

"Then you tell me what the point is? Go ahead. Enlighten me."

"You stole me from my real mother. You had no right to do that. Holy fuck, you people gave her a dead baby to hold and told her it was her baby. That is so messed up. It's way beyond depraved."

"Are you quite through?" Matlinsky interjected, obviously bored with the exchange. "I have more important things to do with my time."

Mykola was not about to back off. "I have one more question. My parents gave you $20,000 in U.S. funds. I don't get that. Why would they give you so much money?"

The question, which carried the tenor of an allegation, caught Matlinsky completely off guard.

"You are speaking nonsense. I do not think it was that much. I am certain you are mistaken," she said flatly.

"No, I'm not mistaken. One thing about my father, he was a meticulous man. He kept every scrap of paper. Along with the adoption papers I found two receipts from Western Union for money transfers to a Natalka Matlinsky in Lviv, and unless there is another Natalka Matlinsky, then …"

"There is no reason for sarcasm. It may have been that much. I'm not sure. It was a long time ago."

"A $20,000 cash payment is not something the memory forgets."

Matlinsky said nothing.

Maria sat in silence. She distinctly remembered her boss telling her that the Yashan family had donated 5,000 hryvna to the orphanage for facilitating the adoption. On the international exchange, that would have amounted to a little more than $500 U.S. There was never any mention of a $20,000 payout. Of that she was certain.

"What was that money for?" Mykola asked.

"Fees for your adoption. There is legal paperwork. There are lawyer's fees. There is also government paperwork."

"You have a baby. You have two people who want a child. You have an eight-page adoption document. At least that's what my parents got. I'm at a loss how something so straight forward as that could cost $20,000."

A defiant look in her eyes, the director replied: "I do not have to explain myself to you. You should be grateful that you were given such a life of privilege. This meeting is over."

It wasn't over for Mykola. He pressed on. "How many other babies have you stolen over the years?"

"Get out!"

"This was never about rescuing me. It was about money. It was about lining your pockets with cash. I saw that the minute you took those people from Winnipeg on your bogus dog and pony tour. You're nothing but a money grubbing cheat."

"Get out or I will call the police."

Mykola knew he had her on the ropes. Pushing himself up from the chair, he went for the jugular. "There's no doubt in my mind you probably have the police on your payroll. But let me tell you this. I'm not done with you. Not by a long shot. I've got a lot of money. A hell of a lot more than you have, and I swear I'm going to make it my life's mission to expose you. What you did to Kateryna is way beyond unconscionable. It's criminal. You'll go to jail for that when it comes out, and mark my words, it will come out."

Matlinsky looked up from the file. Her right eyelid began to twitch. "Get out, now!" she shrieked at the top of her lungs. "And if you ever set foot in this building again, I will have you arrested for trespassing. Then you will learn first-hand what prison is all about and what your life would have been like had you not been adopted, you thankless little fool."

"Mark my words, I'm not going to let this rest. When Kateryna's story comes out, you'll be finished. I'd be very worried if I were you." With that Mykola stormed out the office, slamming the door, triggering reverberations down the hallway.

Several of the staff poked their heads out of the nurseries wondering what the commotion was about. Petro was standing at the entranceway to the stairwell as Mykola brushed by.

"At least this time you did not punch the wall," he said with a meek smile.

Mykola paused, not wanting to take out his frustration on the caretaker. "You taught me an important lesson the last time, Petro. The wall always wins."

As the caretaker made his way to the stairwell, Mykola was snagged by a twinge of remorse.

"Petro, wait. What are you doing this evening?"

"The same as always, waiting for a toilet to unplug."

"I want to take you out to dinner. I'll pick you up outside at 6 sharp."

Petro's face lit up. "I would like that very much. I will be there," he said, cringing when he heard the director screaming Maria to get out of her office.

Her face a mask of panic, the ever-obedient assistant scurried into the corridor.

Sitting at her desk, Matlinsky was in a state. She now realized that Mykola posed a serious problem, one that could land her in a cauldron of boiling water. She picked up the phone and punched in a familiar number.

"I have a matter that must be dealt with. We need to meet. Tonight!"

CHAPTER TWENTY

Petro stared down at the sidewalk as the taxi pulled up in front of the orphanage. He was definitely upset.

"What's wrong?" Mykola asked as he got out of the cab.

"I cannot go."

"Why? Is it Matlinsky?"

"No. She does not know of this."

"Then what is it? Tell me."

"Look at me. All I have are these old work clothes. I feel ashamed to go out."

Mykola smiled. "Listen, I've got a really nice sweater and a pair of new jeans over at my hotel. They should fit you just right. All you'll have to do is roll up the pant legs. You'll look great. Come on."

When Petro emerged from the washroom, he was beaming in his new outfit. Alex and Mykola whistled their approval.

"Wow, you're going to have to fight to keep the women off you," Mykola joked.

Petro blushed.

When the trio entered Lviv's best restaurant, Petro was like a kid at the zoo, staring at all the patrons in total wonderment. In his entire 33 years, he had never been out in public, let alone break bread in a fancy eatery. The place was a hive of activity. In one corner of the sweeping establishment, a wedding celebration was taking place. In another, a raucous birthday fete for a young man who had just turned 21. There were couples on romantic dates holding hands and sitting across from each other at tables clad with white linen and candles. Businessmen and bureaucrats in muted conversation occupied a bank of burgundy leather booths lining a back wall.

Decked out in a black suit, starched white shirt and a bowtie, the waiter handed Mykola, Alex and Petro menus. Petro's face went red.

"Is something wrong?" Mykola asked.

"I cannot read," he replied, embarrassed by his admission.

"Don't worry about it. I'll order us a grand dinner. What do you think of the place?"

"I would never in my life believe such a place exists or that I would be here."

"Have you ever had chicken Kyiv?"

"No. Does the chicken taste different when it comes from Kyiv?"

Alex laughed. "No. Chicken is chicken no matter where it comes from. They all cluck the same. Chicken Kyiv is a kind of recipe for cooking it. It's quite delicious."

"You're in for a gastronomical treat," Mykola added.

The waiter re-appeared. "Would you like to order a bottle of wine or some other spirit?"

"Yes. Do you have Lex?" Mykola asked.

"But of course. We only carry the best vodka."

"From the freezer?"

"It is the only way we serve our vodka."

"Then bring us a bottle to start with. And for our appetizers, I'd like to start with mushroom Ushka and Baklazhan rolls. For the main, we'll both have Chicken Kyiv. Alex what do you want for your entrée?"

"Beef Stroganoff!"

"A fine choice. I will be back with the vodka," the waiter said.

With the frosted, triangular bottle on the table, Mykola proposed the first toast. "We should drink to our new friendship," he said, gingerly pouring an ounce shot into three glasses.

Grabbing the bottle from Mykola's hands, Alex chided: "This is how we do it in Ukraine. I would think you would know this by now!"

He filled each glass to the brim – a full six ounces! Mykola knew he was in trouble.

"To friendship!" Alex shouted as he stood up.

Both Alex and Petro downed the contents in three non-stop gulps. Mykola managed two meager sips before giving up.

Turning to Petro, Alex teased: "These Canadian-Ukrainian men drink like women."

Petro laughed.

"I need something to eat or I'll be too drunk to do anything," Mykola offered in his defense.

Petro then picked up the bottle. He topped off Mykola's glass with a mocking giggle and filled the other two.

"To the children!" Petro said with a gleeful smile.

"To the children," Alex and Mykola repeated.

Mykola stuck to a sip.

As Alex poured a third full glass, he noted: "You know Petro, the third toast is always to the women. Should we drink to the women?"

"Of course! To the women!" he cheered.

After watching the two men each down 18-ounces of 80-proof vodka like it was mountain spring water, Mykola wondered how they managed to sit upright. The large quantity of booze didn't seem to be affecting Petro or Alex in the slightest. He'd only sipped a total of three ounces and was feeling tipsy. He was relieved when the appetizers arrived and he could get some solid food into his stomach.

Half way through the main course, the entire liter bottle of Lex had evaporated. Mykola ordered a second one. But before any more toasts, he told Petro he had something important he needed to get off his chest.

"I want to apologize to you," he began.

"For what do you have to apologize?" Petro asked.

"For taking advantage of you. When you told me you had a key to the file room, I talked you into opening it because I needed to find out if there was information about me in there."

"I do not understand. Why would that be?"

"Not too long ago, my mother and father were killed in a car crash."

"I am very sorry to hear that," Petro offered.

"Then not long after the funeral I was going through my father's papers and discovered I was adopted. I never knew that. When I started looking into my adoption, I was told that shortly after I was born, my biological mother died and I was taken to Orphanage 41. Natalka Matlinsky sold me to my parents and I was taken to Canada. Anyway, I decided to come to Ukraine in the hope of finding out some information about the woman who gave me life and maybe even find a living relative. But Matlinsky absolutely refused to give me any information."

"Is that why you punched the wall?"

"Yeah. I was really frustrated. Then when you told me about the file room in the basement and you said you had the key, I knew I just had to get inside. I tricked you into opening the room. I'm truly sorry for using you like that," Mykola confessed.

"It is nothing."

"Well, in fact, it's a lot. Remember when I pulled open that filing cabinet drawer and you panicked?"

"Yes."

"Well, I found my file. It was the very first one in the drawer. My biological mother's name was on one of the documents and so was the village she was from. I went there with Alex a few days ago basically to find her grave and to find out if I had any relatives. To my surprise, I learned that she in fact didn't die. She is alive. As you can well imagine it came as quite the shock. I met with her the other day."

"This is like a miracle," Petro said with a smile. "It must have been like a dream come true."

"It was more like a nightmare. I found out that just moments after I was born, the doctor told my biological mother that I had died and gave her a dead baby to hold. It's all so sick."

Petro's jaw dropped.

"Anyway, I feel terrible for having tricked you and I want to apologize."

"You have no need to apologize. You are my friend. I am happy that I helped you."

"You're a good man, Petro, and I'm glad I met you."

Petro stared down at his glass in silence. When he looked up his eyes were burning with rage. "I do not like that woman," he began. "She has always been very mean to me. She calls me names in front to the staff and the children. She calls me imbecily. Sometimes the children laugh and they start chanting imbecily when I come into their units. I don't blame them. They are young and do not know better. I blame the director."

"Why don't you leave the place?" Mykola asked.

"I love working at the orphanage. I love the children. When I hear them laugh, when I hear them playing, when I hear them sing, I feel very happy inside. It is only the director who makes my life miserable. I am afraid of her. She has the power to return me to the internat so I try as much as I can to stay out of her way. But she is always using me."

"What do you mean by using you?"

"Four years ago, the director ordered me to do work on her new apartment in the old part of the city. I could not refuse. I worked there every day for more than three months. The director would pick me up in the early morning and send me back by bus late at night. She bought two apartments side by side and converted them into one. I did all the plumbing, electrical work, plastering and painting. It was hard work drilling into stone and plaster walls to run the wires and pipes. For all my work, she paid me not one hryvna. Not once did she even say thank you. All she did was constantly yell at me. 'Do this. Do that. What is taking so long?' She was very mean to me."

Leaning forward in his chair, Mykola said, "Tell me about the apartment. What's it like?"

"It is grand. The kitchen is very modern with black stone counter tops and there are so many modern appliances, all of stainless steel. They were imported from Germany. There is even a washer for dishes. Can you imagine that, a machine that washes dishes? When I was making all the electrical and plumbing connections, I was wondering why she would need such a lavish kitchen. She cooks for no one. Maybe in the morning and evening she boils water for tea."

Petro closed his eyes trying to recall the décor. "There is a large living room with beautiful rugs on the marble floor and many paintings on the walls, and you should see her bedroom, the bed is the size for a king and on it is a fur blanket."

"Sounds like she spared no expense," Mykola whispered to Alex.

"There is a closet next to her bedroom that is so much bigger than my room in the basement at the orphanage and it is filled with clothes: lots of coats and dresses and so many, many shoes. I do not know why anyone would need so many shoes. She also had me install a safe in the back wall behind one of the clothes racks. But what upset me were the washrooms. The one that connects to her bedroom is very large with marble tile on the walls and floor. There is another smaller one near the entrance to the apartment. She has two toilets and they have seats," Petro noted incredulously. "The children in the orphanage have no seats on their toilet bowls. They must sit on the cold porcelain."

Petro looked over at Alex and suddenly asked: "What is this thing that looks like a toilet but shoots up water like a fountain?"

Alex and Mykola burst out laughing.

"It is what is called a bidet," Alex said once he caught his breath.

"What is this bidet?"

"It is for women to sit on and wash their private parts," Alex explained pointing to his crotch.

Petro eyes widened. His face turned bright red.

"You have such amazing skills, Petro. Why don't you just leave the orphanage? You could easily get a job in the city," Mykola said.

Petro didn't respond.

"He cannot leave," Alex explained.

"Why?"

"He has no papers. All those found to be incapacitated or imbecily are sent to internats where they must stay for the rest of their lives. It is an official classification and because of this, they are stripped of all rights. Petro is one of the very few lucky ones. He has managed to get out but he is still trapped by the classification."

"You call him lucky. He's being used by Matlinsky and the orphanage as slave labor."

"But I am no longer in the internat for the imbecily," Petro offered.

"Petro, please quit calling yourself that," Mykola pleaded. "There is absolutely nothing wrong with you."

"He has been diagnosed and once that label is on, it is on for life," Alex reiterated.

"This is bullshit," Mykola shouted.

Several patrons glanced over at the table, giving Mykola a look of disapproval.

"It is what it is," Alex pointed out in a matter of fact tone.

"Well, let's undo it. We have to find a way to undo it."

Alex grimaced. "I do not know how or if it can be undone. But one thing that is certain in Ukraine these days and that is most things can be done, or as you put it *undone* if you have the money."

"Then one way or another we'll get it undone," Mykola vowed.

Staring wide-eyed at the two men, Petro looked confused and scared. He had never known life outside of an institution and the very thought terrified him.

Mykola grabbed his glass and stood up. "Let's drink a toast to Petro's new life, and this time I'm going to down the entire glass."

Alex nudged Petro with a laugh. This was something they had to see.

CHAPTER TWENTY-ONE

"Do you have an appointment?" a security guard barked from the other side of an electronic iron gate.

"I'm Canadian," Mykola replied calmly, somewhat taken aback by the surly attitude.

"So?"

"So does a Canadian citizen need an appointment to speak to an official at a Canadian Embassy?" he asked, waving his passport.

"Everyone must have an appointment," the guard responded flatly.

"Well, this is an emergency and I need to speak to someone in charge."

The guard sized up Mykola. He could readily see he was no terrorist or nut bar hell bent on causing an incident. "Your passport," he demanded, picking up the phone.

The guard spelled out Mykola's name, recited his passport number and hung up. Several minutes later, the phone beeped. The guard handed Mykola his passport and buzzed him through the gate.

"Someone will greet you at the door."

A fashionably dressed receptionist was there with a cheery smile on her face. "Vitayemo. Welcome to our humble home away from home. My name is Lindsay Fields."

"Mykola Yashan," Mykola responded with a smile. Based on her Anglicized pronunciation, he was certain "vitayemo" was probably one of only two words she knew in Ukrainian, the other being "dobre."

"Come on in. Where are you from?" she asked.

"Edmonton."

"Oh, just up the road from me. I'm from Calgary. What brings you to Ukraine?" she asked as she led him into a spacious waiting area.

"A family matter, in fact, it's a very serious family matter. I need to talk to someone about immigration."

"I'll see if Robert Fraser is free. He's our senior counselor in charge of all immigration matters. Please sit. I'll be back in a jiffy."

Mykola found it curious that in the middle of the afternoon on a normal workweek, no one was in the waiting room. He sat down and scanned the posters, prints and portraits on the walls. On the main wall was a large, framed print of the Canadian Coat of Arms, surrounded by the Coat of Arms of the individual provinces and territories. It was flanked on one side by a portrait of Prime Minister Stephen Harper and on the other of Queen Elizabeth II celebrating her diamond jubilee. On another wall were several colorful posters depicting the breath and beauty of Canada's mountains, lakes, prairies and rugged ocean shorelines. But Mykola's eyes were drawn to one particular poster on a third wall. It was of a battered and terrified woman. She was crouched down, curled up in a fetal position in a cement cell. The caption in bold black letters stated: "I'm not for Sale."

Mykola got up from the sofa and went over to read the wording at the bottom right hand corner. It stated:

> Have you seen someone: Who is being controlled by threats, however subtle? Who fears for their safety or that of loved ones? Who has bruises, or shows other signs of abuse? Who has been tattooed or branded by someone? Who is being deprived of any of life's necessities? Whose freedom of movement seems to be restricted? Who is working under unreasonable conditions? If you think someone is the victim of human trafficking, call your local police.

For more information, it suggested visiting the RCMP website.

Mykola's thoughts drifted to Kateryna's situation. She clearly exhibited the telltale signs of a victim of trafficking noted in the poster. Yet no one, except for a caring nun, ever bothered to stop and ask her if she needed help. No one ever called the police to voice their concerns. Worse yet, there was no way the police in Italy, who surely must have seen her working the side streets of Milan, could not have realized that Kateryna was a victim of sex trafficking. She was just 17, an obvious foreigner in a strange land who was under the tight control of a vicious Albanian pimp. How could the authorities not see that unless they were willfully blind or on the take? And certainly the police in the Ukrainian town of Dobrody knew Kateryna was a sex slave. Yet they too chose to turn a blind eye while every so often partaking of Yuri's bribe: a free go at Kateryna whenever the primal urge struck.

Mykola snapped back to reality with the arrival of Robert Fraser. The man had short, cropped red hair and a razor thin beard. He wore designer, tortoise shell glasses, a blue blazer, white shirt, red and blue tie, grey pants and sensible Oxford shoes. He looked to be in his mid-40s and talked in a loud, officious voice.

"Pretty scary stuff that," the officer began, offering his hand and pressing a strong, deliberate grip on Mykola's right.

"What?"

"The poster. Every year tens of thousands of young Ukrainian woman are being trafficked around the world and sold as sex slaves. It's hard to believe that this is happening in this day and age."

"What's being done about it?" Mykola asked.

"Here, in Ukraine, as in Russia, next to nothing. On the world stage there are lots of endless conferences and papers written about this issue. But little is happening in the way of real, meaningful action to put an end to it. This is a very difficult and complex problem to deal with. The trafficking of young women into the global sex market is a multi-billion industry. It is controlled by organized crime and the corruption is staggering. The tragedy is that these poor girls, and I call them girls because most are teenagers, are just beginning their lives as young women when they suddenly find themselves trapped in what I call the anteroom of hell."

"Do any of them ever get rescued or manage to escape?" Mykola asked, nodding toward the poster.

"Some. Most are simply abandoned to the streets of foreign cities after they've been used up and no longer useful to their pimps. As you might imagine, they're in terrible shape, both physically and psychologically. A lot of them are infected with HIV and AIDS. They end up being deported back home penniless where their families and locals treat them like vermin instead of victims. It's all very tragic."

Mykola turned and looked at the poster one more time. He could see Kateryna's face on the victim.

"I'm sorry. I sometimes get carried away. It's just that this issue really makes my blood boil," Fraser said apologetically. "How may I be of assistance?"

Mykola hesitated. Choosing his words carefully, he began. "I need to talk to someone about getting my biological mother to come to Canada."

Fraser looked somewhat perplexed. It was as though he had never heard the phrase. "Your biological mother?"

"Yes. I recently found her and she's in a bad situation. I want to bring her to Canada."

"Follow me to my office. We'll talk there," he said.

Fraser's office was a standard eight by ten with a modern, module maple desk and wall unit. The room was immaculate, not even a paperclip was out of place. There was a framed professional portrait of a woman and two prim and proper teen-aged daughters on his otherwise clear desk.

"As a visitor or permanent resident?"

"I want her to come permanently."

"I see but I'm a little confused here. What do you mean by your biological mother?"

Mykola offered a bare bones explanation of his birth and adoption, and finally locating Kateryna.

"I will give you the necessary forms. Fill them out once you get home. Then you can FedEx them directly to my attention. This woman, your so-called biological mother, will have to fill out another set. Once we get them in, we can start the process," he explained, while hurriedly typing a text message into his Blackberry cell phone.

"I was hoping we could get things started right away," Mykola insisted. "As I told you she is in a dire situation. I need to get her out of Ukraine."

"Is there a health problem? Because I have to tell you that if she has a serious health issue she will not be granted approval to come to Canada whatsoever. We do not admit anyone who will be a burden on our health system."

"It's nothing like that. She's dirt poor and has no one. I just want her to have a good and decent life. How long will this process take?"

"We have a heavy backlog. I figure at the very earliest a year."

"A year? You've got to be joking? Why would it take a year?"

"As you no doubt are aware, there is a substantial Ukrainian population in Canada and a lot of Ukrainians want to come to Canada," the visa counselor explained.

Fraser's Blackberry suddenly vibrated across his desk. He grabbed it, read the message and typed in a quick reply. "The ambassador would like to meet with you. Follow me."

Mykola sensed something was up.

The ambassador's office was at the far end of the corridor. The door was ajar. Frazer knocked and walked in.

"Ambassador Keith Simpson, this is Mykola Yashan."

Simpson, a stocky, balding man in a pale grey suit, rose and offered a limp handshake "A pleasure to meet you. Please, sit down."

With an inquisitive smile, the diplomat inquired: "Yashan. Are you related to Dr. Stephan Yashan?"

"Yes. He was my father."

"I figured as much. Robbie ran your name through the Google search engine and made the connection. May I offer my sincerest condolences? The loss of such a remarkable man is absolutely tragic, and at such a young age," the ambassador said, waving his subordinate out of the room.

Mykola didn't respond. His mind was still trying to come to terms with one-year wait time to bring Kateryna to Canada.

"I had the honor of meeting Dr. Yashan on several occasions" Simpson continued. He then lowered his voice and leaned over his desk. "Just between you and me, we, that is the embassy, helped Dr. Yashan get a number of documents out of Ukraine through our diplomatic pouch. I don't think he could have ever gotten them out otherwise," he revealed with a satisfied grin.

The dowdy diplomat then droned on for twenty interminable minutes about the myriad accomplishments of the late, great Dr. Yashan.

Glancing down impatiently at the Omega wristwatch his mother had given him on his high school graduation, Mykola figured it was time to dam the babbling brook.

"I need to get my birth mother into Canada," he interjected with a tone of desperation.

Ever the political sycophant, the ambassador smiled a syrupy smile. "I see."

"Mr. Fraser said it could take a year and possibly longer."

"Unfortunately he's right. There is a huge immigration backlog in the pipeline."

Mykola could feel the frustration seize his chest like a vice grip. "But a year! You've got to be joking. She's my biological mother. I'm Canadian and therefore I would think she's entitled to come to Canada."

Simpson looked perplexed. "I don't understand. I am under the impression that Dr. Yashan and his wife are, or I should say, were your parents."

"His wife has a name. It's Iryna," Mykola snapped. He took a deep breath and stared up at the ceiling, trying to regain his composure. "They adopted me from an orphanage in Lviv right after I was born. I only learned this shortly after their death. I came here with the hope of finding a relative because I was told my biological mother died while giving birth. Instead, I found her alive and well. She's had a rotten life and I want her to come to Canada to live with me."

"I see. I see. Well, I can assure you we will do everything we can to assist you but as Mr. Fraser informed you, it will take time. Once the paperwork is in place and she is provisionally approved, she will have to undergo a medical and a criminal check. I trust she's in good health?"

Mykola nodded but his brain had fixated on two words: *criminal check*. There was no doubt in his mind that the police in Italy and in Ukraine had a record that Kateryna was a prostitute. He would be astounded if they didn't. He also wondered what she would put down on the immigration form as her profession. Waitress? It suddenly sunk in that her chances of getting a green light to come to Canada were in serious jeopardy.

"Is everything okay?" the ambassador asked. "You look troubled."

"While we're waiting for all this paperwork to go through, can you at least give her a visitor's visa?" Mykola asked.

"That might be difficult given the circumstances. She has to prove she has gainful employment and that she will return to Ukraine once the visa expires. She cannot remain in Canada to wait for her permanent status, and given our experience in matters like this, the probability of her returning to Ukraine after the visa expires are very, very slim."

"I need to help her," Mykola pleaded.

"I know you do and I can sense your frustration. However, we have a process in place. I'll have Mr. Fraser give you have all the necessary applications. Fill them out and send them directly to my attention. I'll do my best to rush them through."

"How long are we looking at?"

"It's difficult to say. Again, provided she has no health issues and passes the criminal check, it won't be sooner than nine months."

"It's just that she's been through so much. I don't want to leave her here."

"Believe me, I understand your predicament. I promise I'll personally handle the application when it hits my desk."

Mykola left the embassy feeling crushed. He was certain Kateryna would never clear a criminal check. On the flight back to Lviv, he racked his brain trying to come up with a way to pull the woman out of her dire straits. Then it hit him. The solution was relatively simple. He would buy an apartment for her in Lviv and provide her with a monthly allowance. After all, he had a ton of money. She would be safe and would no longer have to live the sordid life of a prostitute. He gazed out the window at the pastoral countryside below but just couldn't appreciate its beauty. The unbearable thought of Kateryna selling her body to strange men kept gnawing at his insides.

"Why did she have to be a prostitute?" he whispered angrily under his breath. "Why?"

CHAPTER TWENTY-TWO

Kateryna was jolted out of a sleepy haze by Yuri's loathsome snarl ripping through the floorboards under her bed like a saw-toothed blade. He was yelling at a couple of stragglers to finish their beer and get their drunken butts out of his bar. It was 3:20 a.m. He'd had it with their interminable griping about their miserable lives. He wanted to close up shop and go home.

Kateryna prayed he would not send up another customer. She had serviced six clients that evening and she was spent. She had no more energy to put on another affected act of lust to make some inebriated fool think he was the last of the red hot lovers. All she wanted was to take a long, hot shower and scrub away the sweat and filth of the evening's demands.

Ever since her encounter with Mykola two days earlier, her mind had been reeling over the stunning revelation that her baby did not die at birth . . . that for almost 20 years, her son was alive and well, and living in Canada. There was no happiness or serenity in her soul. Her moods swung wildly from detached wonder to unholy rage. In her calmer moments, she wondered what it would have been like mothering Mykola, rocking him to sleep, hearing his first words, seeing him take his first steps. When she was pregnant, she constantly sang to him, danced with him and recited fairy tales. She'd spent hours daydreaming about what the baby might look like. She knew whether it was a boy or a girl, it would be a beautiful mix of both parents. Antonio Rinaldo was a striking young man, and back then she was a dark-eyed beauty. She thought about how handsome Mykola was and how much he reminded her of her one and only true love. And although she had long ago lost her faith, she thanked God for Mykola's good fortune in life, something she knew she could never have given him. She knew full well what his life would have been like had she been allowed to keep him. He would have been branded the village bastard. His grandmother and uncles would have spurned him. The village folk would have treated him with contempt.

The children would have mocked and tormented him incessantly, calling him the son of a whore. His life would have been intolerable, and who knows what he would have turned out to be: most probably a low life loser dulling his pain and misery in a noxious mix of alcohol and drugs. There was also no doubt in Kateryna's mind that her son would have despised her for bringing him into the world.

Her pulse began to race when she thought about Mykola's promise to take her away from all the misery and suffering. In her soul, or what little was left of it, she prayed he wasn't putting her on. Yet every time she closed her eyes, her mind was haunted by the look of revulsion on his face when he first set eyes on her in the bar and realized what she was. True he came back, and after listening to her story, it appeared as though he cared and sympathized. But when he left her flat, she could sense he was deeply conflicted. Kateryna was firmly convinced that once the blunt reality hit – that she was a prostitute – he'd rush to the nearest airport and she would never see or hear from him again. Who would blame him? After all, he was a young man with absolutely no idea, no clue of the dark side of life. And there was one thing about his visit that clawed at her insides, reinforcing her belief that she had seen the last of Mykola Yashan. As he headed for the door, after he had taken her photograph, he didn't approach her for an embrace or even a handshake. He just turned and never looked back.

"Why did he have to come?" she whispered aloud. "Why did he have to find me? Why couldn't he have left well enough alone?"

Kateryna's thoughts flashed back to the hospital ward. She was suffering the excruciating pain of labor. A dark, sinister image struck her like a lightning bolt. As she screamed out, she glimpsed her older brother, Bohdan, standing stone-faced in the doorway of the hospital ward.

"You rotten, evil coward!" Kateryna yelled, her eyes popping wide open as the horrifying realization sunk in. "You knew my baby didn't' die. You knew, you rotten, evil coward! Why would you let them do this to me? Why would you allow them to bring me a dead baby? I hope when you die you rot in hell for what you did to me. I pray God sends you to burn in hell!"

The sound of the bar door slamming shut snapped Kateryna back to reality. She heard Yuri's heavy footsteps pounding along the cobblestones. A moment later, his car roared to a start and faded into the night. She breathed a sigh of relief. There would be no more customers.

She was wrong.

Not ten minutes later, there was sharp rap on the door below. She rolled her eyes and muttered a curse. She knew she couldn't ignore it. If Yuri found out, he would beat her senseless. He had beaten her for turning away the customer that Sunday afternoon when Mykola was over. Her left eye was still black and swollen.

From the moment he took control of her body 19 years earlier, Yuri's orders were clear. She was on call 24/7. It didn't matter if she was on her period, suffering from a blistering migraine or down with the flu. If a client was so inclined and had the cash, she was never to refuse. The first time she did, she paid dearly. Yuri whipped her with a leather belt, leaving her entire backside black and blue.

Yet despite his violent bent, the bar owner protected her from the seemingly endless bands of knuckle-draggers he sent up to her flat. All understood that Kateryna, or Vera as she was known, was there for their sexual predilections. There was to be no violence and the clients were instructed to use a condom.

"I don't want the bitch to get pregnant!" Yuri would warn with a threatening scowl. "She is of no use to me if she is pregnant."

In all her years at the bar, Kateryna had been viciously assaulted only once by a client. It happened soon after she arrived. The customer was a nasty drunk who harbored a pathological loathing for women. Once up in her flat, he immediately demanded sex without a condom and refused to take no for an answer. He paid his money and as far as he was concerned, he got to call the tune and she had to dance to it. Realizing the situation was spiraling out of control, Kateryna made a dash for the stairwell. She didn't make it. He grabbed her by the hair and threw her onto the bed. He then ripped off her robe and panties. When Kateryna tried to scream for help, the man, veins in his neck popping blue with rage, broke her jaw with a devastating blow with his elbow. His victim knocked unconscious, he had his way with her and then left.

When Yuri went up to the flat a couple of hours later to find out why she was not answering the door, he exploded. Storming down to the bar, he dispatched two of his goons to find the assailant and bring him to a wheat field on the outskirts of town.

Now sober and trembling with fear, the attacker's pathetic pleadings for mercy fell on deaf ears. Yuri was hell bent on revenge. His objective was to send a very clear and unequivocal message to every man in town.

"Mess with my property and you pay the price."

No one was to do harm to Kateryna. It wasn't because he harbored any feelings for her. The bar owner's sole concern was that she stay healthy so he could continue making money off her back. She was his cash cow. She was of no use to him if she was out of commission, and now, because of her grievous injuries, she was in hospital and would be incapacitated for several weeks.

With his confederates holding the terrified rapist on the ground, Yuri took pleasure in breaking the man's legs and arms. Then removing a pair of hedge cutters from a potato sack, he castrated him. The message was sent, reverberating loudly throughout the town and beyond.

The rapping on the door grew more insistent. Kateryna forced herself off the bed. Throwing a flimsy, hot pink Chinese-made, silk robe over her shoulders, she headed down the stairwell.

CHAPTER TWENTY-THREE

Alex kept two cars back while Mykola slumped down in the rear seat.

"She is turning into the Historic Quarter," Alex said. "She just drove into a private garage. I cannot stop here. The street is too narrow. I will block traffic."

"I'll get out," Mykola said, popping his head up to survey the surroundings.

"She went in there," Alex said, pointing to a dark alleyway.

"You may as well go home. I'm just a couple of blocks from the hotel. I'll see you in the morning. We'll head off to Dobrody at 7 a.m."

"Fine. But be careful," he cautioned.

"What could possibly go wrong?" Mykola said as he got out of the car.

"In your case, everything and anything," Alex shouted as he drove away.

Mykola caught sight of Natalka Matlinsky as she exited the alleyway and entered a swank, three-story condominium across the road. On the outside wall was an historic brass plaque indicating that the structure was more than 200 years old. A moment later, the lights flickered through slits in the curtains on the second floor. As he approached to take a closer look, a curtain parted ever so slightly. Mykola didn't notice.

Matlinsky had a feeling she was being followed. Her eyes flashed with venom when she spied her annoying nemesis hovering in the shadows on the street below. She flipped open her cell phone and punched in a number.

"I'll teach that little bastard to toy with me."

Minutes later, two police cars, blue lights flashing, came to a screeching stop in front of Mykola. With Glocks drawn, the officers ordered him to lie face down on the ground with his hands behind his head. He was handcuffed, hauled to his feet and thrown into the back of one of the cruisers. The cops gave no reason for his arrest but it didn't take him long to figure out who was behind it. Looking up at the orphanage director's apartment window from the back seat, he could make out her silhouette behind the curtain.

At the police station, he was escorted to a large room and strip-searched while nine officers, including two women, looked on in amusement. It was the most humiliating experience of his life, especially when he was ordered to bend over and forced to undergo a cavity search. His valuables – watch, silver link bracelet and high school ring – were removed along with his belt and a wallet containing 1,250 hryvna. He was thankful he'd left his passport, credit cards and 12,000 hryvna in the hotel safe. He was then told to dress and escorted to a huge holding cell, awash with drunks, vagrants, and an assortment of low-life criminals. The cell reeked of urine, vomit and feces. There was nowhere to sit except the floor, which was sopping with urine. He made for the wall and nervously stood with his back against it. Menacing eyes glared at him. A bedraggled, bearded man frantically paced around the cell ranting incoherently. He was obviously suffering from schizophrenia and battling demons in his head. He charged up to Mykola, screaming inches from his face about God's wrath and some impending doom about to befall the world. For the first time in his life, Mykola feared for his physical safety. Ten minutes into the non-stop verbal diatribe, a burly officer with a shaved head clanged a black, wooden baton on the bars of the cell door and shouted out: "Yashan!"

To the sound of laughter and mock kissing noises, Mykola rushed to the steel gate. The officer grabbed him under one arm and led him to an interrogation room. He sat there for two hours before the lock rattled and a detective in an ill-fitting, brown suit entered. A dark man with slanting eyes and a peach-shaped face, there was no doubt in Mykola's mind that this muscular behemoth was a distant descendent of the invading Mongols from a bygone century. He didn't offer a handshake, nor did he identify himself. The ice-faced officer was assigned to the case to get answers. Intimidation was his strong suit.

Sitting at a table, he retrieved a ballpoint pen from inside his jacket and took his time jotting down indecipherable scribbles onto a large, yellow notepad. Mykola figured it was a pressure tactic designed to intimidate. After what seemed like ten long minutes, the officer looked up and glared into Mykola's eyes. Whatever he was hoping to do didn't work. Mykola held his ground. He'd seen enough cop shows on television and understood the drill. He did not avert his eyes.

"Now, Mr. Mykola Yashan," he began in a threatening tone. "You will tell me what you were doing outside the apartment of Natalka Matlinsky. You will tell me why you are stalking this woman."

"Well, first of all, I wasn't stalking the woman. Why in heaven's name would I stalk her?" he asked, his voice edging on attitude.

"You will not fuck with me. Do you understand?" the interrogator warned pointing a thick, index finger an inch from Mykola's face.

"I'm not, as you so aptly put it, fucking with you. I wasn't stalking the woman."

"You were outside Miss Matlinsky's apartment."

"If so, then it was by sheer coincidence. I was taking an evening stroll through the city's historic quarter. I'm staying at the Grand Hotel. It's two blocks away."

"Miss Matlinsky accuses you of stalking her."

"Miss Matlinsky is wrong, and no doubt suffering from paranoia."

"Once again, what were you doing outside her apartment?

"I'm from Canada. I'm a tourist. Like hundreds of tourists, I was out taking a walk in the historic quarter of Lviv. I don't think you can describe that in any way as strange or even criminal behavior, and if Miss Matlinsky says she saw me outside her apartment then again, I repeat, it was by sheer coincidence. I don't even know which building she lives in."

"Miss Matlinsky accuses you of harassment."

"Then again Miss Matlinsky is either mistaken or paranoid, or both. I met with her briefly at the orphanage where she's the director. We talked. I offered to make a donation, and that was that. I left. I don't understand where she gets the idea that I was stalking or harassing her. Maybe you should bring her in and ask her why she thinks that."

The detective scrawled a half page of notes and then abruptly left without saying another word. It was well after midnight when a young police officer came in carrying a brown paper bag containing Mykola's valuables.

"You are free to go."

Mykola was relieved and somewhat surprised but figured the investigator had decided he had no grounds to hold him. After slipping on his belt and putting on his watch, he went through his wallet.

"For the record I would like you to know that 500 hryvna are missing," he informed the police officer.

"Are you making a complaint?" the cop asked.

"No, just making an observation," he responded, thinking it wise to leave well enough alone. All he wanted was to get out of the place, return to his hotel room and take a long, hot shower. He smelled like sewage.

As Mykola crawled into the passenger seat early the next morning, Alex gave him a curious glance.

"Pardon me for sounding rude but you look like shit." he offered with a grimace.

"The result of a close encounter with the people meant to serve and protect," Mykola replied.

"What is this serve and protect?"

"The cops."

"I do not understand what this phrase 'serve and protect' has to do with the police in Ukraine. They do not do this. Here the police take and intimidate."

"Well, they certainly lived up to that motto."

On the drive to Dobrody, Alex listened attentively as Mykola recounted the hair-raising details of his first ever arrest, incarceration and interrogation.

"Man, they don't even tell you why you're being arrested. I had guns pointed in my face. I almost crapped my pants. Then to be strip-searched in front of a bunch of cops including a couple of women cops, and get a finger shoved up my butt. My ass still hurts," he noted, squirming in his seat.

"Ah, so that is what you meant by 'close encounter,'" Alex said with a laugh. "I hope he was wearing protection."

"It's not funny. To add insult to injury, they stuck me in a cell that stunk of excrement with all these disgusting low-life losers who have absolutely no idea what a bar of soap is for, let alone deodorant. I was never so bloody scared in my entire life. I thought this one psycho was going to kill me."

"You are very fortunate the police let you go. They could have held you for a week or maybe longer without charge, and simply not inform anyone where you are."

"Then they'd have to answer some pretty tough questions when I got out because I sure as hell would have gone straight to the Canadian Embassy and demanded that something be done."

"Did the police say why they let you go?"

"I guess they bought my story."

Alex rubbed his chin. "This director woman is obviously connected. This is definitely a very clear message."

"Yeah, I got it. And now it's my turn. She's going to pay for this."

"I have said this before. You are a stubborn young man. Sometimes it is better to know when to leave well enough alone. Maybe this is the time."

Closing in on Zaluky Square, Alex was waved off by a police officer manning a roadblock. Mykola noticed several police cars, blue lights flashing, and an ambulance in front of the bar where Kateryna worked.

"Ask him what's going on," Mykola said.

Alex rolled down the window. "Officer, what is the problem?"

"There has been a murder. No one important, just some prostitute."

Flinging open the car door, Mykola bolted up to the police barricade just as the ambulance driver and an assistant were placing a shroud covered body onto a gurney.

Alex caught up and grabbed Mykola by the arm. "We must leave this place. It is big trouble. Listen to me, you must not get involved."

"No. I need to know what happened," Mykola insisted as he spotted the bar owner talking with an investigator.

"Yes, she worked in my bar. She was a whore."

"Do you know of any family she might have?" the investigator asked.

"No."

"No one to claim the body?"

"You can stick her in the dump for all I care," Yuri suggested.

Hearing those words, Mykola leapt over the barrier and tackled the bar owner.

"You rotten piece of shit!" he yelled.

Mykola was no match for the bar owner. Yuri twisted him to the pavement and punched him on the side of the head before two uniformed officers rushed in and pulled them apart. Alex paced anxiously behind the barricade worried that Mykola had just plunged himself into a very deep vat of trouble. One of the officers restrained Mykola, pinning him up against a wall.

His nostrils flaring, the bar owner yelled: "You little shit! You attack me? I will make you pay for this. You put your hands on the wrong guy."

The chief investigator, a no-nonsense looking cop with an inch-long scar on his forehead, approached Mykola. "What is your name?"

"Mykola Yashan," he said, trying to clear the cobwebs from the hammering right hook he took to the head.

"You are not from Ukraine," the plain-clothed detective said, picking up on Mykola's accent.

"I'm Canadian."

"What is this all about?" he asked, pointing to the bar owner who was glaring at Mykola.

"He makes me sick, that's all. He's a disgusting pimp. But something tells me you probably know that."

"He is what he is."

"And he should be in jail where he belongs."

The investigator noticed that Mykola kept looking over at the gurney.

"You know the victim?" the investigator asked as he calmly pulled back the black tarp, revealing Kateryna's bruised face.

"Oh, my God. Oh my God!" Mykola cried out at the sight of her.

"You know this woman?" the detective asked again.

"Yes, only slightly. She is a relation." Once the words were uttered, Mykola felt a wave of shame sweep over his entire body. He could not bring himself to say the dead woman was his mother.

"A relation?" the investigator inquired.

"I learned only recently that we might be related."

"I see. You had no relations with her?"

"What? No! I was told she might be a . . . a cousin."

Yuri broke out in a loud cackle. "Cousin, my ass. She's the bastard's mother. I heard this with my own ears."

"Is this correct?" the investigator asked.

Mykola turned, looked toward the police barricade and spotted Alex. His driver shook his headed slowly telling him to say no.

"The man is a liar. I met this woman the other day in his bar. That is where I determined she is a cousin. My parents in Canada are connected to her family. That is all."

Once again, Mykola couldn't help himself. Shame kept him from revealing his true connection. He closed his eyes and in his mind asked Kateryna for her forgiveness.

Looking back at the gurney, he asked: "What happened to her?"

"She was stabbed. We have no idea who did it. Probably a customer who hates prostitutes," the investigator surmised.

"Please don't call her that."

"It is what she was. There is, however, something strange about this killing. There is nothing sexual in the attack. There was no struggle. It appears she merely came to the door and was stabbed once in the abdomen. It was as if she was a target. This was very precise and very deliberate."

A chill ripped through Mykola's body. His thought back to the confrontation with Natalka Matlinsky, and it hit him like a thunderbolt. Could she be behind the murder of Kateryna?

Mykola turned pale. His breathing became erratic.

"Are you going to be ill?" the detective asked, stepping back.

"No. No, I'll be okay," he said, forcing himself to catch his breath.

He heard the sound of the attendants loading the gurney into the ambulance.

"What will happen to her?" he asked as the vehicle pulled away.

"I doubt anyone will claim her body. She will be buried in a pauper's grave," the officer said.

"Someone will claim her body. I will inform her family in Stornovitzi."

"Then you must come to the police precinct to make certain her body is held for removal by next of kin. I will take you there to sign the necessary papers."

It was late evening when Mykola emerged from the police station. Alex was waiting in his car outside.

"You could have made much trouble for yourself," Alex said sternly.

Mykola said nothing. He was emotionally drained.

"It is very late. We will stay the night at the hotel and leave for Lviv early tomorrow," he continued. "We just have to watch out for the bar owner. I don't trust him. He is very angry with you. That was a stupid thing you did."

"We need to talk," Mykola said, getting into the car.

As they drove to the Hotel Impressa, Mykola offered up his theory on why he believed Kateryna had been killed. "Do you think Matlinsky is capable of something like that?"

"I've learned that evil people are capable of anything when their world comes under threat. But I do not know this woman. I do not know her connections. She may be behind this and she may not. Remember, and I do not say this to upset you, but you must understand that Kateryna was a prostitute, and the world of prostitution is a very dangerous one. These women never know when a psychopath will enter the room and beat them or kill them. In this country the bodies of prostitutes litter the side streets, and no one pays them any notice. They are carted away and buried in unmarked graves. It is as if they never existed."

"Do you think the bar owner could have done it? He's one mean S.O.B."

"No. He's the kind of garbage who beats up women and forces them to do his bidding. You must keep in mind that she was his meal ticket. Remember, you were bringing him a lot of cash to free her. A snake like him worships at the altar of money. He may have no soul but he is no fool. He did not kill her. Of this I am certain."

Mykola desperately wanted and needed to believe Alex's hypothesis: the killer was a man who harbored a psychotic hate for prostitutes. He couldn't bear the thought that he was the catalyst in Kateryna's murder; that his confrontation with Matlinsky pushed the woman to arrange the killing. Yet try as he might to convince himself that he was in no way responsible, in his mind he firmly believed he was.

"I have a room for us at the hotel. We will leave here first thing in the morning. You need to get some sleep," Alex said.

Once in the room, Alex went back to his car and retrieved a flask of Georgian cognac from the glove compartment. He poured a full glass for Mykola and himself.

"Drink this. It will steady your nerves," he instructed.

An hour later, Mykola lay passed out on the bed, his mind careening into the murky underworld of nightmares.

Both his mothers came to him: Iryna and Kateryna arms outstretched. Mykola struggled to grab hold of their hands as he tumbled farther and farther into a jet black void. Something was preventing the women from reaching him. From the shadows his father emerged, an odious smirk on his face, his skeletal grey fingers gripping their ankles like steel leg irons.

Mykola woke up with a start. He was drenched in sweat and shaking with fear. He had never felt more scared in his entire life. He wanted to run away. Every fiber of his being was screaming at him to run. Someone had murdered Kateryna and it was possible his life was now in jeopardy. He had waded into dangerous waters. Of that, he was convinced. What he couldn't understand was why Kateryna had to pay for it with her life. If Matlinsky was behind it, what possibly could push her to resort to murder for hire. His abduction as a baby? Surely not. It was a despicable and illegal act but Mykola never really believed there would be much in the way of consequences. His threats were more bluster than action, and he'd more or less resolved never to make his story public. It would be too embarrassing ... for him.

Sitting on the edge of the bed, Mykola forced himself to concentrate. He needed to gather his wits and figure out his next move. Closing his eyes, he thought back to the day in his father's office when he came across the photographs of the kobzari and the image of the white haired, blind minstrel. Facing death, the old man stared down his executioners. No one would ever know his name. Photo number KZ158 accepted his fate with dignity. He would not drop to his knees and beg for mercy. He stood tall and defiant.

Mykola knew he didn't possess the courage of the kobzari. He wanted to run as far away from Ukraine as he could possibly go. But Kateryna haunted him and guilt overpowered him. He could not live with the torment, and he knew it was wrong to run. He had to confront his fears, whatever the outcome. He was convinced something pushed Natalka Matlinsky to resort to murder. Clenching his fists, he swore he would find out what it was.

Mykola fell into a deep sleep and awoke hours later with a start. There was wild commotion outside the door. He turned to wake Alex but discovered he was not in his bed. He was not in the room. Mykola stumbled outside.

Several men and women had gathered in the parking lot. They were staring up at the night sky to the west of the town. An eerie orange glow danced on the horizon. Mykola looked down at his watch. It was 2:40 am, when he spotted Alex ambling towards him.

"What's going on? What is that?" Mykola asked pointing up at the sky.

"It appears to be a rather big fire."

"What in hell can burn like that?"

"I would think the only thing in this town would be a very big mansion!" Alex suggested with a crafty grin.

Mykola looked at the cab driver in disbelief. "The bar owner's place?"

"I am informed that this may be the case."

"You didn't …"

"Surely you do not think of me as a person capable of such criminal activity," Alex replied, feigning insult.

Gazing up at the fiery glow, Alex noted matter-of-factly: "What is interesting about people like this bar owner is they do not trust the banks of Ukraine. And who can blame them? Instead, they prefer to hide their money in their homes. By the look of those flames, there must be a small fortune in hryvna under the mattresses and floorboards to feed such a blaze. I would venture that his plan for an early retirement has just gone up in smoke."

"That's a lot of hryvna."

"I think maybe it is best we leave for Lviv," Alex suggested. "I don't want this mobster to start adding one plus one and coming up with our number."

"We won't be going to Lviv. We'll be going to Stornovitzi."

"Whatever for?"

"I need to tell the family that Kateryna is dead, and I want to make arrangements for her to have a proper funeral."

Alex stared straight ahead, and said nothing.

CHAPTER TWENTY-FOUR

Father Zenon looked surprised to see Mykola back in the village. He approached him with a tentative smile. Seeing the stern expression on the young man's face, he knew in an instant something was wrong and dropped his outstretched hand.

"To what do we owe this unexpected visit?" the priest asked.

"Kateryna Chumak."

"Yes," he said, his lips pursed with tension.

"She was murdered last night outside her flat in Dobrody."

"May God have mercy on her soul," Father Zenon said, crossing himself three times.

"I want her body brought back to the village. I want to have her funeral at this church, and I want her buried in the cemetery close to her father."

"You demand a lot. What gives you the authority?" the priest asked in a dismissive tone.

"You know what gives me the right. You figured it out when we first met."

His brow creased with worry, Father Zenon stared into Mykola's face. He knew he would be wading into choppy waters if he acceded to Mykola's demands. He was worried about the reaction of his tiny congregation. In their eyes, Kateryna was a whore and a sinner who had no place in their blessed church or in their hallowed graveyard. But more importantly, he, like most others in the village, was afraid of Bohdan Chumak. The man had a hair trigger temper and would not think twice about roughing up a man of the cloth.

"I do not think this is a wise decision," the priest said firmly.

"Well, it's my decision, and my mind is made up."

"I cannot bury her. She is no longer of this parish."

"She grew up here. She was baptized in your church and she'll have her funeral here."

"And if I refuse?"

Mykola's eyes narrowed. "You'll bury her or I swear I'll make certain everyone in this country and beyond finds out about your complicity in what happened to her and that missing girl, Anya ..."

"And what is my complicity?" the priest challenged.

"Your sister sold them into prostitution. You knew it and you did nothing to stop it. You did nothing to hold your sister the pimp responsible for what she did."

"That is a vile accusation!"

"Really? Well, you're a so-called man of the cloth. Put your hand on the cross around your neck and tell me I'm wrong. Swear to God that what I just told you isn't the truth."

"How dare you! I will do no such thing. I resent ..."

"I am not asking you to perform the funeral service. I'm telling you, or as I said, I will make certain everyone outside this village knows what happened to Kateryna and her friend Anya, and I'll bet they weren't the only two girls your sister sold into prostitution. You bury Kateryna or I swear I will spread this story all over the Internet, and I guarantee it will go viral."

"You cannot come into this village and threaten me."

"I'm doing precisely that. I'm threatening to expose you for the hypocrite you are. I want Kateryna to be buried in the village that turned its back on her."

Father Zenon knew he was backed into a corner. He feared that if the Russian Orthodox archdiocese in Moscow got wind of his sister's activities and more importantly his deliberate failure to act, it would put his position in serious jeopardy. He had one final card to play.

"Her family will be outraged. They will not stand for it."

"Look at my face. Does it look like I give a damn?"

"If I were you, I would be very worried. Bohdan Chumak is not a man to be taken lightly."

"You worry about the funeral. I'll worry about Bohdan."

"No one will attend the funeral," the priest pointed out.

"I will, and that's all that matters."

Father Zenon stared up at the overcast afternoon sky. He knew prayer was not going to extricate him from this situation.

"Looking for divine intervention?" Mykola asked.

"There is no need for sarcasm."

"I want you to make all the arrangements to have her body transferred here from the morgue in Dobrody, and don't worry, I'll pay for everything.

Your church will receive a sizeable donation. I want her buried in a proper grave with a headstone."

"What do you wish to be inscribed on the headstone?" the priest asked in a tone conceding defeat.

"I want it to say 'Kateryna, beloved mother of Mykola.' That's all."

"It may take a few days. I will need to go to Dobrody to make the proper identification and have the body released to the church. How will I contact you when all is set for the funeral?"

"Here's my cell phone number," he said, handing the priest a piece of paper. "Call me soon as all the arrangements have been made."

With that Mykola turned and headed for the taxi. A proud grin was plastered on Alex's face.

"What's so amusing?" Mykola asked as he got into the car.

"You, my young friend, have balls of brass. To talk to a man of God like that, you are risking a reservation in hell."

"I'm already in hell."

"Where to now?" Alex asked.

"Down the road to the Chumak farm. I want to inform the family that Kateryna is dead."

"I do not think that is a wise move," Alex warned.

"Right now, I don't care what anyone thinks. Are you going to take me there or do I walk?"

"Whoa, my young friend. No need to use that tone with me. Remember, I'm on your side." With that, Alex hit the gas pedal and a moment later pulled to a stop outside the cottage.

At the gate, Mykola was greeted by Markian, Kateryna's younger brother. Mykola recognized him from the photo he had seen in the cottage on his first visit. He had thick brown hair and a drooping moustache like his brother. His wife, Ruslana, was nearby tossing handfuls of grain to a flock of ravenous chickens, ducks and geese.

"How may I help you?" Markian asked.

"My name is Mykola Yashan."

"Ah, the young man from Canada. Bohdan told me about you. You upset my mother. You are lucky Bohdan didn't beat you senseless. He has a bad temper."

"So I've been told."

At that very moment, the man with the temper barreled out of the house, his face burning white-hot with rage. His mother scurried close behind, a broom in her right hand.

"What are you doing here? I told you never to come back," Bohdan shouted.

Mykola realized he had better keep his wits about him. He knew if Bohdan clocked him with one of his ham hock fists, he'd be seeing stars for a week.

"I came back because I have sad news."

"Get away from here," the old woman yelled.

"What news?" Markian asked, Ruslana rushing to his side.

There was no other way to say it, so Mykola said bluntly but softly. "Kateryna was murdered last night …"

Before he could utter another word, Bohdan's powerful hand seized Mykola by the throat and in one thrust heaved him bodily over the gate. Markian leapt on top of his brother trying to release the vice-like grip. Mykola could feel himself losing consciousness.

"Let him go! Bohdan, let him go!" Markian yelled. "You're killing him!"

Alex tore out of the taxi, charged over the fence and tackled Bohdan to the ground. It was sheer mayhem with all four men wrestling in the dirt. The old woman was swatting Alex with her broom. Ruslana was desperately trying to stop her. With his grip broken, Bohdan directed his wrath at the barrel-chested intruder. It was a mistake. What the man didn't know, and what Alex hadn't even told Mykola, was that he had been a commando in the former Soviet Army trained in martial arts. With one well-placed side kick to the solar plexus, he rendered his opponent helpless. As Alex hauled a gasping Mykola to his feet, Markian tended to his brother who was writhing on the ground gasping for air.

"What gives you the right to come here and upset our family?" Markian asked as he stood between his brother and Mykola. "Kateryna is no longer part of this family."

Mykola brushed the dust from his jeans, keeping a wary eye on Bohdan. He was having trouble catching his breath. "I have the right because Kateryna was my biological mother."

There was a moment of stone silence and then the old woman's knees buckled. She collapsed to the ground. Ruslana rushed to her. Bohdan stood speechless. Markian broke the spell.

"What the hell are you saying?"

"Your sister gave birth to me at a hospital in Lviv on August 9, 1993," Mykola shouted loud enough for the entire village to hear.

"You're a liar. Her baby was born dead. I was there," Bohdan yelled.

The interjection caught Markian by surprise. "You never said anything of this," he said, turning to his brother.

"You knew all along your sister's baby didn't die," Mykola charged. "You son of a bitch! You knew all along. I can see it in your lying eyes."

"What is this all about?" Markian demanded. He was inches from Bohdan's face.

"The family! Mama! That is what this is all about," he fired back in his defense. "We did not need a whore running around the village with her bastard son tugging at her apron strings."

"Well the bastard son is finally here!" Mykola shouted.

"You must calm down," Alex interjected, putting his hand on Mykola's shoulder.

"Don't tell me what to do," Mykola shot back, swiping the cab driver's hand away.

Raising his hands in mock surrender, Alex retreated to the car. Leaning against the hood, he watched the insanity continue to unfold.

"I don't understand this about the baby dying," Markian continued.

"Your sister was told I had died, that I was stillborn," Mykola explained. "A nurse brought Kateryna a dead baby to hold and told her it was her baby. Isn't that right, uncle Bohdan?" he noted caustically.

Bohdan lunged at Mykola. "You little …"

This time Mykola was ready. He stepped quickly out of the way as Markian grabbed the back of his brother's shirt.

"Bastard! Isn't that what you were going to say? Yeah, I'm your bastard nephew!" Mykola said defiantly.

"My God," Ruslana screamed as she crossed herself. "May God have mercy on Kateryna."

"She is a whore. She will go to the devil," the mother screamed.

"This is insane," Markian said, rubbing his temples. "This is totally insane."

Alex shook his head in disbelief at the exchange between Mykola and his birth mother's bizarre family.

"I was taken away from Kateryna and sold to a family in Canada. I found out I was adopted by my parents shortly after they died in a car accident. I found the adoption papers in my father's desk. I was told that my real mother died giving birth to me. I decided to come to Ukraine to find her grave and maybe even find a relative who could tell me a bit about her. I went to the orphanage in Lviv where I was taken the day after I was born and learned the truth about what had happened 20 years ago."

There was a long silence. Then Markian asked quietly: "What do you want with us?"

Mykola shook his head. "Nothing. Absolutely nothing at all. I don't want anything from this family. All I want you to know is that your sister, your daughter, my birth mother was a victim in so many ways. I met Kateryna ever so briefly and the one thing I learned is that her situation was never of her making. She never chose the life of a prostitute. She was tricked and forced into the trade by the sister of your holy priest. Both Kateryna and her friend, Anya, were victims. Then again, you all know that. Everyone in this village knows that but rather than seeing it, you've all judged, convicted and condemned Kateryna as a whore. Kateryna told me how all of you and all the people in Stornovitzi treated her when she came back home. No one came to her defense. No one went after the real criminal in this entire disgusting tragedy, and again I'm talking about the sister of your hypocrite priest."

Mykola paused, looking at both Markian and Bohdan square in their eyes.

"What kills me is that all of you know what the priest's sister did to Kateryna and her friend Anya, yet you did nothing about it. Worse yet, the priest did nothing. That is one thing I will never understand."

Mykola stared up at the sky, trying to steady his nerves. "Anyway, I came here to let you know that I am having Kateryna's body returned to the village for a funeral and burial in the cemetery here."

"You have no right!" the old woman shouted. "I will not allow it. You have no right!"

"You're wrong about that. I have every right. I'm her son and let me just say one more thing. Before she died, she told me about her father. She told me he loved her dearly and she loved him with all her heart. She believed that had he been alive, none of this would have ever happened. He would have protected her. She deserves to be buried near him. She deserves respect and a proper funeral. Most of all she deserves an apology."

"Father Zenon will not allow this. She is a whore!" the old woman screamed. "She will burn in hell!"

"Mama, please. Kateryna is dead. Please don't speak of her in that way," her daughter-in-law pleaded.

"The priest has already agreed to perform the service. So if any of you wish to pay your respects, the funeral will be in a few days." With that, Mykola turned and nodded to Alex. They got into the car and drove off.

"You are lucky that big oaf didn't break your neck," Alex said.

"This place makes me sick."

"Where to now?"

"Lviv. Can you drive me back here for the funeral?"

Alex nodded.

During the drive, Mykola stared intently out the window, but he wasn't taking in the bucolic scenery. His mind was trying to figure out what would push Matlinsky to murder for hire. Why would the fact that he was stolen from his mother at birth trigger such a lethal response? There had to be something more to it.

"You looked very troubled, my young friend," Alex said.

"I just can't seem to figure out why Matlinsky would want Kateryna killed. I mean, so what? She stole me at birth from my mother. I don't get it."

"Kateryna may have been the key," Alex suggested.

"The key to what?"

"Pandora's Box. Sometimes one thing that may seem innocuous can lead to something much bigger and trigger an avalanche."

"What though?"

"I have no idea."

"Alex, I'm sorry I got you involved in all this."

"No problem. It will make an interesting chapter in my autobiography which I intend to write one day."

They both laughed.

CHAPTER TWENTY-FIVE

Alex dropped Mykola at the Grand Hotel with a few words of advice. "Be very careful my young friend. This has become a dangerous situation, and if there is anything you need, if there is any sign of trouble, you call me immediately. Do you understand?"

"I will."

"And try to stay out of jail."

"I will."

As Mykola entered the lobby, the clerk anxiously waved him to the front desk.

"Mr. Yashan, two men came by early this morning asking for you. I told them you were away. I noticed they sat on a bench in the park across the street for hours watching the door. The doorman told me they finally left around 8 p.m. I do not like the look of these men. My great fear is that they will be back."

"Thank you for that," Mykola said. He wisely dug into his pocket and pulled out a 100-hryvna note and handed it to the grateful clerk.

"Listen, I'm going to check out. Can you suggest another place to stay?"

"If this is trouble, I do not think you would be safe in any hotel. People like that have connections to all the hotels. They will find you quickly."

Mykola bolted up to his room, grabbed his knapsack and headed back down to the lobby to pay his bill. Before leaving, he asked the clerk to check the area for any sign of the duo. Once he got the thumbs up, he darted across the street and wove his way through the narrow alleyways to a square in the old quarter. Sitting down on a bench, he punched in Alex's number on his cell phone.

"I need your help. Two men were at the hotel looking for me. Can you pick me up? I need to find a safe place to stay."

"I knew there might be trouble. I will speak to my wife. You can stay at my apartment. We have a sofa you can sleep on."

"Thanks. I really appreciate that."

"I am leaving at this very moment. You must be very careful. I will pick you up outside the Opera House in 20 minutes."

Alex's apartment was on the fourth floor of a 22-storey building amid a depressing grove of nine identical structures. Sitting smack in the heart of a tree-less, concrete oasis at the edge of the city, it was a barren, soulless place coated in spray-painted graffiti and peeling election posters. Several children played on a nearby dusty field kicking around a soccer ball. Small gangs of teenagers, sporting red, blue or black bandanas, hung out at the entranceway to each building, staking out their turf. Most appeared lost and forlorn, a few tried to look tough and intimidating but they quickly moved out of the path of the approaching taxi driver.

"I am so glad we have an apartment on the fourth floor," Alex said, as he yanked open a steel fire door leading to a cement stairwell. "The elevators are forever breaking down and it takes weeks to get someone down her to fix them. This is one of those times when we walk. The one positive thing in taking the stairs is that it is good for the heart and the circulation."

As they headed up the stairwell, Mykola's nasal passages were assaulted by the overpowering smell of boiled cabbage, garlic and onions frying in butter.

Inhaling deeply through his nose, Alex smacked his lips. "We Ukrainians cannot live without our perogy and holopchi. Do you like this food or are you one of these Americans who eat the cardboard of McDonalds?"

"First I'm not American. I'm Canadian. And second, I die for perogy. It's my favorite, although I'm not too crazy about holopchi. Stuffed cabbage gives me a ton of gas."

"Then this is your lucky day. My wife has cooked a pot full of perogy. She makes the best perogy in the world."

Mykola laughed.

"What is so funny?" Alex asked.

"Every Ukrainian's wife or their mother or their grandmother makes the best perogy in the world!"

"This is true. But my wife makes the best. You will soon experience a culinary delight drenched in sweet onions fried in real butter and smothered in real smetanka. You like smetanka?"

"I love it. You can't eat perogy without sour cream," Mykola said, his stomach rumbling with hunger as they reached the fourth floor landing.

The apartment was a classic, Soviet-era, three room flat – a small kitchen, a living room/dining room and a bedroom. Opposite the entrance was a closet-sized washroom. On the wall in the passageway were icons of the Blessed Virgin Mary and Saint Joseph, each draped in a beautifully, hand-embroidered tapestry, and a framed portrait of Alex, his wife, their two sons and a daughter.

The floor in the cramped living room was covered wall to wall with a machine-made Persian-style rug from India. There was a small floral sofa, a flat screen TV on one side of the room, and a teak dining table on the other. On the walls were several paintings, all breathtaking landscapes of the Carpathian Mountains. They were Alex's pride and joy.

"As you can probably tell from my look, I am Hutzul. I was born and raised in the mountains of Carpathia. Soon after I was discharged from the Soviet army, I met Tamara; we got married and came to live in Lviv. One day I hope to retire to the mountains. My parents have a small house there and it will be left to me when they pass on. May they live a century!"

Alex's wife rushed out of the kitchen, rubbing her flour-caked hands on a white apron. With a welcoming smile she planted a kiss on both Mykola's cheeks. She turned to Alex and gave him a big hug.

"This is the love of my life," Alex boomed. "Tamara, this is Mykola, the young man I've been telling you about."

"I hope you boys are hungry. I have made a feast," she said, bubbling with excitement. "And I have made a special cake!"

Tamara reminded Mykola of Sonia, his godmother. She had happy eyes and a warm, infectious glow about her.

"I'm starving and I want to thank you so much for putting me up," he said.

"It is no problem. We love to have company. Alex has told me so much about you. I am very sorry about what has happened," she said, giving Mykola a motherly hug.

"We will talk more at the dinner table. Right now I must go and check on the cake," she said, rushing back into the kitchen.

"She is such a wonderful person," Mykola said. "You're a lucky man."

"Did I mention that Tamara works in a bakery? She is the pastry chef. People come from all over the city to buy her cakes and cookies," Alex boasted. "I think maybe you would like some vodka?"

"A little, and Alex, when I say a little, I don't mean a glass full. I may be Ukrainian but like you said the other night in the restaurant I have the constitution of a Canadian. And I don't want to insult you, but I hope it's not that homemade horilka. That stuff has got to rot your stomach lining!"

"I have only the best vodka. Perlova Premium. It goes down like silk. I have a bottle in the freezer."

Alex was right. It did go down like silk, and after three toasts – the third one, Alex reminded, always to the women – Mykola was feeling no pain. The tension had left his body.

At the dinner table, Mykola was apprised of the Boychuk family tree – a 22-year-old son, Yvan, was married and had a two-year-old son. He worked as a mechanic for a trucking firm in Ivano-Frankivsk. Genia, their 20-year-old daughter was also married. She had a 6-month-old girl and lived nearby. Eighteen-year-old Myron was in the Ukrainian Air Force training to be an engineer.

"What I find odd is that so many couples here get married really young and they're having babies at 18 and 19," Mykola said.

"It is the way it has always been," Tamara said. "I was married to Alex when I was 18. I had Yvan a year later. What is the way in Canada?"

"Most of the couples I know don't get married until they're in their late 20's or early 30s."

"And you? Do you have a special girl?" Tamara asked with a nudge. "Because if you don't, I have just the right one for you."

Mykola smiled. "I have a girlfriend. Her name is Lesia. We've been going out forever."

"Do you intend to marry her?"

"Sure. I love her."

"Then why not marry now?"

"Because we're too young. I still have to finish university and then get a job."

"Is she pretty?" Alex asked.

"Absolutely gorgeous!"

"Then you better marry her before some other man comes around and steals her from you," he warned.

Mykola laughed. "I don't think that will happen."

The conversation and banter continued late into the night. At one point, when Alex and Tamara were chatting about the latest antics of their grandson, Mykola sat back and thought how much they reminded him of Sonia and Orest. Even after so many years of marriage, they couldn't keep their hands off each other. It seemed they were made for each other.

Mykola looked at Alex. It was the first time he had really looked at him. What he saw was an honest man with a good heart who lived his life with honor and dignity, and most of all, with a sense of humor. True, he got riled by a lot of things: corrupt politicians, Ukraine's cesspool of thieving Oligarchs, crooked bureaucrats and dirty cops topping the list. He often flew off the handle in heated rants, but he never let the bad guys grind him down. He knew when to let go. Alex was in control of his destiny. He was comfortable in his skin. But more importantly, he owned his soul.

Mykola closed his eyes and wondered what the outcome of his trek would have been without Alex by his side. He'd probably be in the hospital recovering from a severe thumping by Uncle Bohdan, or worse, rotting in some jail cell for harassing Natalka Matlinsky.

After dessert and a shot of Georgian Saradjishvili cognac, Tamara made up the sofa and the couple bid their woozy guest a goodnight. But Mykola did not a have a good night. He tossed and turned, his mind wracked with guilt that his rash behavior may have resulted in Kateryna's murder. He kept seeing Matlinsky's face smeared with a vengeful grin. In his gut he knew she was behind the killing but realized he would never be able to prove it. His thoughts turned to revenge. He wanted to find a way to destroy the woman. Then it hit him.

Early the next morning, Mykola stood in the shadow of a shoe store near the orphanage waiting for Maria to appear. Like clockwork, he spotted her getting off a streetcar. She saw him crossing the street and turned. Both headed for the coffee shop.

As he approached the table, Maria looked at Mykola's face. "What is wrong?" she asked.

"I have horrible news."

"What is it?"

"Kateryna was murdered. Her body was discovered yesterday morning. She was stabbed to death."

"May God have mercy on her soul! I am so very sorry."

"The detective at the scene told me he didn't believe her death was a random attack but a deliberate killing. She was targeted." Mykola paused. "And I think we both know who's behind it."

Maria drew in a sharp breath. She was incredulous. "Surely, you cannot possibly believe that director Matlinsky had something to do with this!"

"I'd never be able to prove it. But I just know that woman is behind it. Kateryna was my only hope at proving what happened the day I was born. What I can't understand is why she would want Kateryna killed."

Maria stared nervously at her cup and said nothing.

"Then when I got back to Lviv last night I'm told two thugs showed up at my hotel looking for me. They spent the entire day in the park across the street watching the front door. Tell me that's coincidence."

"I don't know what to say."

"Maria, something tells me there's more to this than just one stolen baby. Matlinsky drives an expensive BMW. She lives in a luxury condo in the Old Quarter that's been renovated and decorated to the nines. You tell me, where does a lowly orphanage director get that kind of money?"

The assistant sat stone-faced, her hands curled into tight fists.

"Maria, I have this feeling you know what is going on here. I need your help. The woman you work for is no saint. She's pure evil and you know that. You've got to help me to bring Matlinsky down."

"I cannot do that."

"Nothing you tell me will be connected to you. I swear. I just need your help in proving certain things. I need to know what would push that woman to have Kateryna killed."

"I can't help you. You have no idea how far this goes. What you are asking me to do will put my life in jeopardy."

It was the first concrete sign for Mykola that he was on the trail of something.

"I will make certain you are protected. I promise you that."

"I don't know."

"Maria, by doing nothing, you will be complicit."

"I cannot. Please forgive me but I am afraid."

"You mean you're a coward."

Maria lowered her head. "It is what I am. It is what I have always been. I'm sorry," she said, getting up from the table.

"If you change your mind, here's the number to my cell phone."

Maria stuffed the piece of paper into her purse and scurried out of the café.

It was a little after 10 at night. The babies and toddlers were tucked in their cribs and cots, and the night staff was parked in front of the TV sets in their units. Holding his breath, Mykola slowly pulled open the front door of the orphanage and tiptoed cautiously down the corridor cringing at every creak in the weathered, wooden floorboards. Once at the stairwell, he exhaled and darted down to the basement.

Petro beamed when Mykola poked his head into the doorway of his room.

"Hello. It is good of you to visit with me once again."

Mykola nodded.

"But you appear troubled, my friend. What is it?"

"Kateryna, my biological mother, was killed two days ago."

Shock registered on Petro's face. "I am so sorry. How do you mean killed?"

"She was murdered, stabbed to death, and I think Matlinsky had something to do with it. In fact, I'm sure of it. When I was here last I told her that I was going to expose her for what she did to Kateryna and now Kateryna is dead. The police have no clue as to who is behind it but they believe it was a deliberate, targeted killing."

Nervously reaching under his bed, Petro retrieved a bottle of locally brewed horilka. His hands shook as he filled an empty plastic water glass to the brim. It had to measure eight ounces.

"You would like some?" he asked politely.

"No thanks. I need to keep my wits about me."

Petro polished off the contents in four, frenzied gulps.

His nerves fortified with 100-proof vodka, the caretaker repeated: "I am so very sorry. You must be sad."

"I am, and I'm very angry." Mykola hesitated. "Petro, I'm going to ask you for a favor, a very big favor, and you don't have to do it if you don't want to," he stressed. "I need you to let me back into the file room. I have this feeling that whatever pushed Matlinsky to have Kateryna killed is in those files."

"The director is a dangerous woman," Petro replied, pouring another glass of horilka.

"You should take it easy with that."

Petro ignored the entreaty and gulped down the fiery liquid.

"Listen, you don't have to do anything you don't want to. I just …"

"I have grown tired of her name-calling," Petro interjected. "I may be not a smart man like you but I am not an imbecily. I have seen so much of what she has done. She is an evil person. I have decided I will help you."

"Petro, whatever happens, I will not turn my back on you. I promise you that. You're my friend."

"And I am your friend," he said pouring a third glass of vodka.

Petro's hands were shaking as he unclipped the key chain from his belt and handed it to Mykola.

"This one is the key," he said.

Mykola offered his hand to the caretaker. Petro got up from his cot and gave Mykola a bear hug.

"Again, I am sorry for what has happened to your mother." With that, he slumped down onto the bed and faded into a totally unconscious state.

Mykola made a beeline for the file room. The lock snapped. He slowly pulled open the door trying to keep the rusted hinges from making too much noise. Switching on the overhead light, Mykola leapt back in horror as two large sewer rats scurried by his feet. Regaining his composure, he engaged his digital camera. His pulse was racing as he began sifting through the file cabinets labeled: adoptions. He selected random files and photographed the contents. He had no idea what he was looking for but he was convinced the evidence was stored in this dank room.

1 a.m. Three hours into his quest, the lights in the corridor suddenly flashed on. Mykola heard the sound of urgent footsteps clamoring down the cement stairwell at the far end. He dove for the light switch, flipped it off and held his breath, praying whoever it was hadn't seen the glow in the hallway, or worse, notice the lock was missing from the door and that it was slightly ajar.

"Petro," a woman's voice called out. "Petro, wake up! One of the toilets is backed up. We have water all over the floor. Petro! I said wake up!"

Petro didn't move. He was out, stone cold dead to the world. A powerful blast of dynamite would not raise him from his drunken slumber.

The woman spotted the bottle of horilka on his nightstand. "You're drunk," she spat. "Wait till Director Matlinsky hears about this! You will be out on your ass."

A moment later, the woman scurried back upstairs.

Mykola never intended to get Petro into trouble, and made a promise to himself to ensure his safety.

By 2 a.m., the intrepid sleuth had photographed more than 120 random files out of what he'd calculated were a total of 396 adoptions starting in May 1995 to year-end 2012. He pulled two files at random from each year to take with him, as well as his own adoption record. He then turned his attention to the cream colored cabinet labeled: Cooper. It seemed to scream: special. Meticulously arranged and tended like a well-manicured, golf putting green, it contained a total of 102 files with the first adoptions starting in April 2009 to year-end 2012. An hour and a half later, he had photographed the contents of 80 files and pulled 22 at random to take with him. Just as he was about to turn off the light, he noticed the top drawer of the cabinet closest to the entrance. Oddly, it was the only one without a label. Inside were two brown accountant's ledgers. One read: Adoptions. The other: Cooper. Mykola loosened his belt and shoved them down the front of his pants. He then switched his camera to video mode and slowly panned the interior – left to right, then right to left. Before heading out, he tiptoed over to Petro's room and clipped the key ring back on his belt. The caretaker rolled over with a contented snort.

Outside, Alex was sound asleep in his car. He was startled when Mykola rapped loudly on the driver's side window.

"What took you so long?"

"I had a lot of work to do. Don't know if anything will come of it. I'll just have to see," he said as he crawled into the car. "I've got a ton of material that I need to send to my two email accounts as back up, just in case something happens to my camera or worse yet, to me."

"We go back to my place. It's almost 4 a.m. You need some sleep and later today we will go to an Internet café."

"You don't have Internet at home?"

"No. Why should I? I don't have a computer."

"How do you stay in touch?"

"I have a cell phone."

"What about emails?"

"If someone must reach me, they can call me. I don't need a computer."

"Wow. That is so strange."

"I do not think so."

"I guess that means you don't have a copier."

"That is correct."

Mykola shook his head in total disbelief that anyone in this day and age could be so far off the grid. "I need a secure place where I can scan these files and also make hard copies of these files I photographed with my camera."

"No problem. I have a friend with a printer and a photocopy machine."

Early that afternoon, they headed to a nearby Internet café. It was Saturday and it was jam-packed with wide-eyed teenage girls huddled in small clusters around banks of computer screens admiring the latest Paris, Milan and London fashions, and pockets of spellbound boys playing video battle games. The cost for one hour of Internet use: one hryvna.

Mykola parked himself at a terminal in a far corner and got down to work. It was a dated clunker, throwing him into teeth-gnashing fits over its sluggishness. It took almost three hours to download and email all the material stored on his digital camera. At home, with his ultra-high-speed network, it would have taken 20 minutes tops. He was also put off by the nosy café owner glancing over every so often with an air of suspicion, but the man knew better than to interfere. In Ukraine, the rule of thumb was to mind your own business. With the files secure in two personal email accounts back home, Mykola transferred a copy onto a USB stick.

Back outside, Alex picked up a package containing 500 sheets of copy paper and an ink cartridge before heading to his friend's apartment. A short while later as the copies were slowly ejecting from an ancient ink-jet printer, Mykola began poring over the material. At first he had no idea what he was looking at or looking for. It was all a jumble of names, dates, figures and initials. But gradually, a pattern began to emerge.

"Holy mother of Jesus. She's operating a baby adoption business, and she's sending them all over the place. Look at this!" he shouted to Alex waving a sheaf of papers in his hand. Dropping one page after another onto the floor, he called out: "New York, Berlin, Toronto, Chicago, Rome, Philadelphia, Winnipeg, London, Miami, Buenos Aires, Paris, Vancouver, Florence … Wow, I know this family in Edmonton! Here's another to London, again New York and Winnipeg."

Alex peered over Mykola's shoulder and shook his head in wonder.

Scanning the signatures at the bottom of each document, he saw Matlinsky's signature and title, and the signature and title of Vitaly Assimovich, deputy minister of Child and Family Services. His name and official government stamp were at the bottom of the last page on every single adoption document.

"Isn't that interesting," Mykola said, pointing to signature after signature. "She's got the top Government dog in her pound facilitating this entire scam."

Alex noticed the official government stamps on each document copy but said nothing.

Mykola then turned his attention to the accountant's ledger labeled: Adoptions. Each handwritten entry was coded to a specific numbered file with the figure of $30,000 U.S. Sorting through the files he'd pilfered from the orphanage he found the corresponding coded file.

"I can't believe this. She's charging - $30,000 a baby!"

In the debit margin, beside the initials S.M./V.Y. was the figure: $9,000. V.A.: $6,000. I.K. $6,000, and N.M.: $9,000 each. N.M. had an added expenditure of $1,000 in the debit column.

As Mykola re-examined the adoption records, he was suddenly struck by a startling revelation. "Every single document has the signature of the biological mother agreeing to the adoption. These babies aren't orphans by any stretch."

"It is all very interesting but I don't see where this is illegal," Alex pointed out. "Someone wants a baby. Someone has a baby. An agreement is made to adopt the baby. There is nothing illegal about this in my books."

"Well something tells me that what Matlinsky is doing is very illegal, and I'd be willing to bet a million bucks that I'm right. The answer is in these files. You'll see."

Mykola then turned his attention to the hard copy files labeled: Cooper.

"It looks like all these babies are being adopted out through one person with the initials B.C. in Los Angeles. That's in California."

"I happen to know where Los Angeles is," Alex said indignantly

"I would guess that the C in B.C. is Cooper," he noted.

As he turned to the first page, Mykola's eyes popped. "Oh my God! I don't believe this. Alex! Look at this! These babies were sold for $100,000 each!"

Alex grabbed the ledger. He was stunned at what he was seeing. "This is simply too much to believe," he said. "There is no way someone would pay such an absurd amount for a baby. I don't understand this. It is crazy."

As he pored over the Cooper ledger, Mykola noticed that the debit column was significantly different from the other adoptions. S.M./V.Y., V.A., and I.K. continued to receive the same amounts as in the standard adoption ledger. B.C. received $40,000 from each sale, and the remainder went to N.M. However, in the debit column was a mysterious expenditure of $10,000 for each adoption.

It didn't take long for Mykola to attach names to the initials N.M. and I.K.: Natalka Matlinsky and Dr. Ihor Kowalchuk. V.A. was Vitaly Assimovich. But he had no idea as to the identity of the other three sets of initials: B.C. and S.M./V.Y.

Mykola entered all the amounts in his laptop spreadsheet program. With 396 adoptions at $30,000 U.S., Matlinsky had raked in a grand total of $11,880,000 over 18 years. Her net, after all payouts, was a cool $3,168,000!

The 62 adoptions in the designer baby scheme grossed a staggering $6.2-million in just four years! But the bookkeeping was somewhat confusing. Mykola was having difficulty trying to figure out Matlinsky's cut after all the payouts and expenditures.

Later at Alex's apartment, Mykola spent the evening at the dining room table meticulously going over each file pilfered from the Cooper cabinet. He was jotting down copious notes when his eyes hit on a scribbled entry at the bottom of one particular file.

"This is interesting," he said, turning to Alex. "This woman had twins. They were born on May 2nd of last year. There's a handwritten note here that says she had changed her mind and didn't want to give them up. Apparently she was threatening to go to the authorities if anyone tried to take away her babies. At the very bottom it says: 'situation resolved'. Looks like the adoption went through. I wonder what happened to make her change her mind."

Alex didn't hear a word of what Mykola had just said. He was wrapped in his own thoughts and worries. "I think you have to be very careful with this information. It is obvious with so much money at stake that there are bribes being paid to some very influential and powerful individuals. This kind of business cannot occur without it."

"I want to talk to this woman," Mykola said, pointing to the file on the coffee table. "It says here her name is Halya Luciuk. According to the information here she's 20 years old and lives in Lviv on Vladim Road. Do you think we have any chance of finding her?"

"I will put out the word," Alex said, flipping open his cell phone. "If she still lives in the city, it should be easy to locate her."

While Alex worked the phone, Mykola went back to his laptop. Re-opening the spreadsheet program, he began entering the reams of data from Cooper files in hopes that it would assist him in connecting the dots, and connect it did: a road map of greed and deception that beat a path from Lviv to LA!

By early evening, Alex got a good lead on Halya and left the apartment to check it out. When he returned an hour later, he found Mykola sound asleep on the sofa. He decided not to wake him up. The news could wait.

Over coffee early the next morning, Alex announced that he had located Halya. She lived in a flat above a clothing boutique. One of the sales clerks pointed her out as she was coming home. She was a student at Lviv University.

"She lives maybe two streets from the university," Alex said.

"Let's go," Mykola said, grabbing his jacket. "Maybe we can intercept her on the way to class."

Twenty minutes later, as the taxi was pulling up to the apartment building, Alex shouted: "That's her."

Halya Luciuk was easy to spot. She stood out in a crowd. The woman was absolutely stunning with long, flowing blond hair, porcelain white skin, azure blue eyes and fine bones. She was tall, at least six foot, sharply dressed and walked with the poise and determination of a high-class runway model.

"Wow, she is drop dead gorgeous," Mykola exclaimed, jumping from the cab.

As he approached the woman on the sidewalk, he was met with a warm smile.

"Excuse me, Halya. Can I speak to you for a moment?"

Surprised that the stranger knew her name, she stopped in her tracks. Turning to face Mykola, she asked: "Have we met?"

"My name is Mykola Yashan. I'm from Canada."

"It is very obvious from how you are dressed that you are not from here," Halya said switching to English.

Mykola smiled. "You speak English very well."

"It is my major at university. After I graduate I want to move to New York to work in the United Nations as a translator."

Taking a deep breath, Mykola went straight to business. "I need to talk to you about something very important and very personal."

The smile on Halya's face evaporated like a thin cloud against the searing sun. Her guard went up.

"I mean you no harm. I swear, and I promise that what we talk about will be in the utmost secrecy. "

"I do not like where this is going. Who are you?" she asked, a look of caution on her face. She glanced nervously up and down the street to see if anyone was watching them.

"I'm just a guy looking for some answers."

"Answers to what?"

"I'm looking into a situation. It involves my adoption from an orphanage here in Lviv when I was born."

Halya took a step backward. Her cheeks began to redden. "I don't think I should be talking to you."

"Just hear me out. I know you gave birth to twin girls last May and that the babies were adopted in the United States."

Halya's hands began to tremble. "I have nothing to say to you. Get away from me."

She turned and began walking away quickly, Mykola hot on her heels.

"I promise. I am not here to hurt you or get you in any trouble. I just need some answers," he pleaded.

Halya stopped. "I don't want to get into trouble. I was warned never to speak about this to anyone or I would pay dearly."

"You won't get into trouble, I swear. Whatever you tell me will not go further, I promise."

Hesitantly, she pointed to a park bench at the edge of the university grounds and the two sat down.

"I want you to understand that I didn't want to give them up," she began. "From the moment I felt them moving inside me, I wanted to keep them. When they were born and I saw their faces, my heart melted. They were so beautiful I did not want to give them up. That woman forced me to give them up."

"Natalka Matlinsky?"

"She is a treacherous person. She said if I didn't give up my babies, she would make life very difficult for me. I was frightened. Still, I refused to sign the papers and then this man, he looked like mafia, came to the hospital. He told me if I did not do as I was told, I would live out the rest of my life in a wheelchair. I did as he ordered. I signed the papers and my babies were taken away."

"Matlinsky just took your babies?"

Halya looked down at the ground. "You will make me out to be a bad person."

"No, I swear."

"She paid me for the babies," Halya admitted.

"So she finds out you're pregnant, goes to the hospital, forces you to sign over your babies and then pays you?"

"No. It was not exactly like that. I wanted so much to go to university. It was my dream, but I had no money. Then one day I am approached by a friend who says she knows of this woman who is offering a lot of money to girls willing to carry a baby and then give it up for adoption once it is born."

"When you say a lot of money, how much are you talking about?"

"$10,000!"

Mykola now understood the debit in Matlinsky's Cooper ledger.

Halya hesitated a moment, trying to maintain her composure. "When I met with the woman, she made it all sound like this was no big deal. She said she would pay me $10,000 if I gave birth to a healthy baby. I could not believe it. Never in my life could I imagine so much money. I could do so much with it. I needed money to get through my university studies and I could buy things I previously could not afford. Then when she found out I was carrying twins she was ecstatic. She promised me another $10,000."

"If I may ask, how did you get pregnant?"

"An anonymous donor. When I was ovulating I went to a doctor's office and he injected me with sperm. I learned later that several boys at the university were being paid $100 every time they donated their sperm. They were laughing about it in the cafeteria one afternoon and showing off the cell phones they purchased with the money."

"So Matlinsky was recruiting girls like you to get pregnant?"

"I personally know of nine girls who became pregnant this way," Halya said. "And I'm told there were many more."

"What I don't get is why Matlinsky is paying each of you $10,000," Mykola said.

"It was easy for me to figure that out. She specifically wanted us because we all had something in common," Halya stated in matter of fact manner.

"What was that?"

"All the girls I know that she approached were all blond with blue or green eyes. Even the boys who gave their sperm were blond."

"Wow! All of you were selected for your looks," Mykola said.

Halya nodded.

"Can I ask, do you remember the name of the doctor who delivered your babies?"

"Dr. Kowalchuk. He was a very cold man. I hated him examining and touching me."

"He's the same doctor who delivered me twenty years ago."

It was now all starting to come together. An unholy scheme. Ten thousand dollars would be a lot of money for these destitute young women but it was a drop in the bucket compared to what she was taking in. She made millions!

Halya stared apprehensively at Mykola "What are you going to do with this? As I told you I don't want to get into trouble. I am afraid of that woman."

"I promise you. I won't implicate you in anyway. I just needed to fill in some blanks and you helped me do that."

Halya gazed down at the ground, a deep sadness etched on her face. After a few moments she asked: "Can I ask you something? It is a favor."

"Sure."

"Do you think it is possible that you can locate my babies? I know I can never get them back. I just need to know they are happy and healthy."

"I'll try. I swear." And he meant it.

"I pray they have not been separated," she said. "I was promised they would be kept together."

But Mykola knew from the paper work that the babies had been adopted by different couples in California – one in San Diego, the other in Santa Barbara.

Hesitating a moment, she added: "Do you think if you find them you can somehow let the family know that if the girls want to meet me at some point in their life, I am willing for that to happen?"

"If I locate them, I'll let them know your wishes," Mykola said, wondering if the parents would in fact inform the girls at some point that they had been adopted. He was also curious whether the families were even aware that their adopted babies came into the world as one half of a matching set. He was certain they hadn't a clue.

CHAPTER TWENTY-SIX

Mykola was in a quandary. He had what he believed was an explosive cache of information. His dilemma was what to do with it. He'd contemplated setting up a blog and attaching copies of the documents. But, who would read his postings? Online surfers tripping over the blog might simply write him off as some kook teetering on the lunatic fringes of society. And he was certain that Natalka Matlinsky's dedicated acolytes would close ranks and inundate the blog with vitriolic attacks in her defense. He knew he was in way over his head and needed someone with clout to take what he'd uncovered and blow the pristine halo off the righteous Saint Matlinsky's head.

Late that night, Mykola phoned Danylo Balan, a close buddy from the Edmonton Ukrainian dance troupe. He was in third year journalism at Carleton University in Ottawa.

"Hey your girlfriend told me you're in the land of our four fathers and five mothers," Danny joked.

"Listen, I don't have a lot of time. This call is serious," Mykola said.

"What's up bro?'

"I've come across what I think might be a really huge scandal here and I need to bust it wide open. The thing is I don't know how to go about it."

"What's going on, Mykola?"

"I don't have time to explain it, Danny but I really need help. I was thinking that maybe you might be able to put me in touch with a tough investigative reporter in Ukraine. Do you know anyone in Lviv or Kyiv who might fit the bill?"

"The one thing I know about reporters in Ukraine is they've been cowed by the government. They rewrite press releases and allow politicians to blather on incessantly without so much as a single word of challenge," he explained. "They're nothing more than a bunch of toothless stenographers."

"So who can I call? I swear this is really big!"

The answer was dancing on the tip of Danylo's tongue.

"I've got just the person. He's the guy who got me all hyped up about pursuing a career in journalism. His name is Mike Petrenko. He's a Uke originally from Montreal and he's one tough ass investigative reporter. He works on a weekly national television current affairs show for CTN out of Toronto. The guy has broken a ton of scams and scandals over the years. The one thing about him is once he's on the trail of a hot story he's like a rabid dog on a bone. He makes his living nailing bad guys. Word is if he shows up on your doorstep with a camera crew, you know your day is ruined."

"What are you, his PR agent?" Mykola interjected.

"Funny."

"I need to get in touch with him now!"

"I've got his email."

"I need a phone number. Do you have his cell?"

"Yeah, but I'm under strict orders never to give it out."

"Then phone him and get him to call me ASAP. It's an emergency."

"What's going on Mykola? Maybe I can help."

"Danny, you're in J-school. This is way beyond you."

"Thanks for the vote of confidence."

"I didn't mean it as an insult. Maybe this Petrenko guy might let you help him out if he gets onto the story."

"He might. He is my mentor after all. I'll call him right now."

An hour later, Mykola's cell phone chimed. It was long distance from Toronto.

"It's Mike Petrenko. I hear you want to talk to me?"

"I've got a story that will blow you away," Mykola began.

"If I had a dollar for every time I heard that line, I'd be a freakin millionaire."

"I'm serious. It involves a baby selling scandal at an orphanage here in Lviv."

"I hate to rain on your parade, but that sounds like a story for the Ukrainian media, pathetic and gutless as those so-called reporters are over there."

"It's bigger than Ukraine," Mykola stressed. "It's international and it involves babies being sold to couples all over the world including Canada and the U.S.

"Orphan babies are sold all the time. It's not news," Petrenko said flatly.

Mykola was growing a little frustrated with the reporter's lack of fervor.

"I was told that you're a hard ass investigative reporter." Mykola said, his voice edging on annoyance.

"Yeah. So tell me something that will kick my hard ass into overdrive."

"Well, for starters these babies are not orphans. From what I've been able to figure out women are selling their babies to this one orphanage director by the name of Natalka Matlinsky."

Petrenko's ears perked up but his brain continued to idle in neutral. "You have proof?"

"I've got a ton of proof. All kinds of documentation! Names, addresses, dates. Lots of families in Canada – Toronto, Winnipeg, Saskatoon, Edmonton and Vancouver, and loads of families in the U.S. shelling out $30,000 each for a baby."

"A baby mill! Now that could turn out to be a good investigate piece especially if it has tentacles reaching into Canada and the U.S!"

"Oh, there's much more. There is also a scheme that's been set up to get young blond, blue-eyed university girls pregnant with the sperm of young, blond, blue-eyed males. Once the baby is born, the mothers are paid $10,000 to give it up for adoption. From what I can figure out from the documentation, this orphanage director and someone in L.A. with the last name of Cooper are selling those babies for $100,000 each."

"Holy fuck! Designer babies! Now that's a powerful story." Petrenko's butt was now in overdrive.

"Designer babies?"

"You got it. They're making babies to order, and if this is true, it's fucking dynamite!"

"From what I've been able to determine from the documents, we're talking millions of dollars a year passing through the hands of the director of this one orphanage in Lviv."

"Do you have any idea how long it's being going on?" the reporter asked.

Mykola could sense Petrenko salivating.

"Probably since I was born," he said, biting his tongue once the words left his mouth.

"What does that mean?"

"Nothing. From what I can figure out about 20 years."

"Have you contacted any other reporters?"

"No, just you. Well, also my friend Danylo but I didn't tell him anything. I figured this was way too big for him."

"Okay. Here's the thing. You deal only with me. Talk to anyone else and you can suck on my exhaust fumes as I drive off into the sunset. I mean it. I'll dump you in a Nano-second if I get wind you're shopping this around."

"I'll deal only with you. I promise."

"Good. Now, how can I get my hands on those documents?"

"I'll start emailing them to you right now."

"I'll read them and see where they lead." The reporter suddenly paused. "By the way, Mykola Yashan! Are you in any way related to Professor Stepan Yashan, the guy who died in the car crash a while back in Alberta?"

Mykola hesitated. "Yes. He was my father."

"Wow. Like father like son. I guess you're following in his footsteps?"

"I don't get what you mean," Mykola said, feeling his shoulders knot up.

"Well, he obviously had amazing contacts in Ukraine. I read his books. To say the least, they were a little turgid but what can you expect from an academic. Anyway, he uncovered some explosive stuff, especially about those kobzari who were slaughtered by Stalin in Kharkiv in 1932."

"It was 1933, and my situation is nothing like that of my father."

"Then how did you get involved in this?"

"That's a story for another day, and if I ever decide to tell it, you'll be the first to know."

"Okay. I'm going to give you a secure email for me," Petrenko said.

"By the way, can you read Ukrainian?"

"Hell, no! I never bothered paying attention in Saturday school and my spoken Ukrainian is the shits. That said, I have a good friend, Jurij, who runs the Ukie television program in Toronto. I'll get his scrawny butt over to my place as soon as I get the stuff and print it off. He'll do the translating."

An hour later, Mykola was firing off scores of jpeg files to the reporter. The hardcopy files were scanned and sent off as well. Totally exhausted, he slumped down on the sofa, closed his eyes, and wondered how Matlinsky would react once the full extent of her corrupt adoption scheme was exposed.

CHAPTER TWENTY-SEVEN

Father Zenon didn't post an announcement of the upcoming funeral on the church door, as is custom. He felt it wise to keep the matter low key. But it didn't take long before word spread like wildfire. In less than an hour, the entire village was a buzzing hornet's nest. Many of the women were incensed, accosting the priest on the church steps and demanding that Kateryna's body be barred from entering their sacred sanctuary.

"She's a whore," they argued. "She is filth. You cannot allow her body to defile our church. It is sacrilege!"

The priest listened, nodded and said nothing. The male parishioners stayed out of it, fearing possible repercussions from the Chumak brothers, especially the hot head Bohdan.

Three days later, when the black-lacquered, wooden coffin carrying Kateryna's remains arrived at the doors of the church, it was placed on a shroud-draped pier in front of the altar. Father Zenon contacted Mykola on his cell phone to let him know that the service would be held the following morning at precisely 10 am.

Throughout the afternoon and evening, not a single family member or villager came to pay their respects. There was no traditional panakhyda. As she was shunned in life, Kateryna was shunned in death. In the eyes of the villagers, she was a despicable sinner who deserved to burn for eternity in hell. The fact that her body rested in their beloved church was viewed by all as a desecration, and that night, the dinner tables in Stornovitzi reverberated with outrage and indignation. They could not fathom why the priest was allowing this to happen.

At the Chumak household, Kateryna's mother was fuming. Throwing pots and pans at the walls, she cursed the priest, vowing never to set foot in the church ever again. Her daughter-in-law was unable to calm or console her. Bohdan and Markian sat mute at the kitchen table numbing their minds with glass after glass of homemade horilka.

After being informed of the funeral, Mykola went out to purchase a black suit, black tie and white shirt. He didn't want to show up dressed as a tourist. He wanted to show Kateryna respect. That evening, he laid down on the sofa in Alex's apartment wrapped in a blanket of shame and sorrow. He was still having difficulty dealing with the barbs of guilt attacking his mind. He was now firmly convinced that his reckless outburst in Matlinsky's office resulted in Kateryna's death. The troubling thing for Mykola was he had no way of ever proving the director was behind the murder. All he had to go on was a raw feeling gnawing at his insides, and it was driving him crazy. He was also being swamped by waves of overwhelming sadness for the woman he had barely come to know. While he had lived a life of comfort and happiness with a mother who loved and adored him, Kateryna had suffered a life of untold and unimaginable pain, degradation and humiliation. In silent prayer, he asked for her forgiveness and then her parting words rang loud in his brain.

"When you come back, I have something else I must tell you. It is something important that you need to know."

What was it that she wanted to tell him before she died? Whatever it was, she was taking it to her grave.

A moment after the taxi pulled in front of the church, the bell in the onion-domed center steeple sounded the death toll. Father Zenon, dressed in a white funereal robe, greeted the two men on the church steps. He offered condolences and held up a gold cross. Alex bowed and kissed it. Mykola turned away when the priest raised the crucifix to his face. The three entered the tiny chapel and stood vigil over the open casket. An icon of the Blessed Virgin Mary rested on Kateryna's chest. Gazing down at her lifeless body, the tragedy of her short existence on earth swept over him like a crushing tidal wave. He knelt at her coffin and whispered a short prayer. Then he stood and looked at Kateryna's face. She seemed at peace. The pain and suffering that had been her tragic existence had faded into the ether. He leaned in and kissed her ice-cold forehead. He forced back tears as he remembered the last kiss he gave his mama in what now seemed like an eternity ago in Edmonton.

The service was the abridged version, just 20 minutes, recited by rote. There would be no high requiem mass for a lowly sinner. As the priest closed the lid of the coffin, a deep, tenor voice at the back of the church broke out in song. It was Alex singing Vichnaya Pamjat. Father Zenon did not join in.

When the church bell began to toll signaling the end of the service, four village men with heads bowed, shuffled into the church to carry out the coffin. They did not look at Mykola or the priest. They kept their eyes fixed to the floor as if ashamed at what Father Zenon had recruited them to do.

Outside, the casket was placed on a flat farm wagon drawn by a mangy, flea-bitten horse. It wasn't lost on Mykola that the cart was regularly used to move cow manure. The tiny procession followed the coffin on foot in silence to the cemetery. The pallbearers walked several meters behind, smoking and muttering in low whispers among themselves. Several of the villagers crossed themselves and uttered an anxious prayer as the cart passed them by. No doubt they were asking God to protect them from the cursed shadow of a wretched sinner. A number of women turned their backs or rushed into their homes, slamming doors loudly in a display of outrage and disgust.

At the gate to the graveyard, Mykola noticed Markian, Ruslana and a teenage girl standing to the side of a large chestnut tree. He nodded at them and they approached. The pallbearers lifted the coffin and lowered it gently into a newly dug grave. It didn't escape Mykola's attention that the gravesite was in an isolated corner of the cemetery, far from the devout and holy Christian crowd.

"I had asked that she be buried next to her father," Mykola reminded the priest.

"The family would not allow it. They own the plot. There is nothing I could do about it."

Father Zenon said a short prayer and tossed a handful of black dirt onto the coffin. He had carried out his priestly duty, even though it was under extreme duress. Before he left, Mykola handed him an envelope.

"This should more than cover everything."

The priest did not look at Mykola as he accepted the offering, tucking it securely in the belt under his robe. He left without saying another word.

As he turned to talk to Markian, Mykola noticed the teenage girl approach the grave, pick up a handful of soil and toss it onto the coffin. She showed no emotion as she stood in silent prayer staring down into the black hole.

"I'm glad you came," Mykola said, shaking Markian's hand.

Ruslana grabbed Mykola and gave him a hug. She began to sob.

"I want to introduce you to my daughter, Olenka," Markian said.

"I'm sorry we had to meet under such sad circumstances," Mykola said, offering his hand.

Olenka stared wide-eyed at Mykola and said nothing.

"Where is your father's grave?" Mykola asked Markian.

"I'll take you to it."

As they passed scores of tombstones adorned with colorful bouquets of plastic flowers and wreaths, Markian asked Mykola about his immediate plans.

"I'll probably be flying back home to Canada in the next few days. There's no reason for me to stay any longer."

"I would like to stay in touch. Is that possible?"

"I'd like that. I want to know more about Kateryna. I want to know about her childhood, the family, and my grandfather. I'd like to know more about you."

Markian stopped and pointed to his father's grave. "Tato is buried here."

Mykola knelt and offered a prayer.

"I'm sorry I never got to meet you," he said quietly to his grandfather. "Take care of Kateryna. She loved you with all her heart. She's in your arms now."

As they reached the gates of the cemetery, Mykola noticed that Markian and Ruslana stood back looking somewhat tentative.

"You must forgive my brother. Bohdan is a beaten man but he is a good man. It's just that mama ..."

"You don't have to explain. I got the picture the moment I met him and your mother."

"My mother is set in her ways. She will never change. You must realize that for her, you are ..."

"I know. Bohdan made that perfectly clear. Anyway, it doesn't matter. I'm just grateful I got to meet Kateryna. At least now I have a better understanding of who I am."

Markian paused and stared pensively at Mykola. There was something more that he wanted to say. He was trying to find the words. He cleared his throat, grabbed Ruslana's hand for support and pulled Olenka to his side.

"There is more to who you are," he offered. "Right here in front of you. "

Mykola looked at him inquisitively. "What does that mean?"

"You weren't Kateryna's only child."

Mykola's eyes widened. Markian hesitated. He looked for confirmation from his wife, then took Mykola gently by the shoulder and led him away.

"Kateryna had a baby girl 17 years ago. When she found out she was pregnant, she called me. She was in a panic. I went to Dobrody with Ruslana and we talked. Kateryna could never bring herself to have an abortion. She believed in the sanctity of life. She told us she couldn't afford to raise a child. She didn't want her baby to be marginalized and scorned, as she was, because of her unfortunate situation. She didn't want to bring a child into the world knowing that it would forever be labeled the prostitute's child."

Mykola's eyes were fixed on Markian's face, stunned at the revelation while trying to process what the man was saying.

"Ruslana and I knew what we had to do, what we wanted to do. We could not have children of our own, even though we had tried for years. The doctors had finally told us it would never happen. We had resigned ourselves to remaining a family of two. So we asked Kateryna to let us help. We offered to take the child. We assured her we would devote ourselves to raising her baby as our own, and that we would give the child our love and the best life we could. Kateryna agreed."

Mykola turned and stared in disbelief at Olenka.

"That's right," his uncle said gently. "Olenka is your sister."

Olenka offered him an uncertain smile. Mykola hadn't really looked at her before but now that he studied her features, he saw that she was the spitting image of Kateryna, and he could see tiny traces of himself. He suddenly realized what Kateryna had wanted to tell him back at her flat.

Mykola was at a loss for words. He tried to catch his breath and began to sob quietly. Ruslana reached out to take him in her arms. Olenka stood at a distance, watching them, her eyes betraying a mix of trepidation and warmth.

"Does Olenka know what Kateryna was?" Mykola asked Markian.

"Sadly, yes. She learned this at a very early age. Mama has nothing to do with Olenka and the children in the village stay away from her. At school they called her such vile names but after a while they stopped. Everyone simply ignores her when she is around. They pretend she does not exist."

Exhaling deeply as he gathered his fractured thoughts, Mykola walked over to the girl. "This has to be as strange for you as it is for me."

Olenka nodded. But at least she had been prepared. Her parents had revealed her connection to Mykola the night before.

"I have to say I am totally overwhelmed but at the same time I am so very happy to meet you, and I would very much like to get to know you."

"I would like that as well," she said shyly.

"Please come to my house and stay the night. We can talk," Markian said.

"And what would your mother have to say to that?" Mykola asked.

"We don't live with her. We live in a cottage at the other side of the village," Ruslana noted, glancing over at her daughter.

The expression on her face was not lost on Mykola. The grandmother looked at Olenka the same way she looked at him. In the old woman's eyes, they were the product of sin.

"Alex and I have to get back to Lviv. I have some unfinished business there. I'm expecting someone from Toronto … from Canada. But I promise I will come back. I want to get to know my little sister," he said with a warm smile.

As Mykola headed for the car, he nodded to Markian. "Can I speak to you in private for a moment?"

The two walked a short way up the road.

"What's the real story on Olenka? How did Kateryna get pregnant?" Mykola asked.

"Olenka does not know the real circumstances of her mother's pregnancy and I wish it to remain that way. It was a horrible situation."

"I swear, I'll never say a word to her about it. I think that was what Kateryna wanted to tell me about but never got the chance."

"Not long after Kateryna was working in that bar in Dobrody, she was raped by a man. It was a vicious attack. Two months later, Kateryna discovered she was pregnant. Even though this happened as the result of rape, she still could not bring herself to get an abortion. As I've told you, she believed in the sanctity of life."

"I can't believe the horrors that Kateryna went through. I just can't believe it," he said, glancing back in the direction of her grave.

"She was doomed the day she left the village with that woman," Markian said.

"You mean the priest's blessed sister."

"Yes."

"I can't understand why the people in this village don't kick that hypocrite out of the church."

"They are afraid."

"Afraid of what?"

"They are simple folk. They fear challenging a man of God."

"Well, believe this. He's no man of God and I'm not afraid."

"You have proven that. I don't know what you said or did to get Father Zenon to agree to perform the funeral service. But it has put him in a very difficult situation with most of the villagers, especially the women." Mykola could care less. "Look, I've got to get going but I promise I'll be back in a couple of days. I really want to get to know my sister."

As Mykola climbed into the taxi, Alex shook his head in disbelief. "This has been a most incredible journey!"

He was adjusting the rear view mirror, when he noticed a black car with tinted windows parked several meters back on the tree lined, dirt road.

"This does not look good," Alex said, tapping Mykola on the shoulder.

"Who are they?" Mykola asked, wondering if they were the same men who had been stalking him at the Grand Hotel.

"Uninvited guests to be sure. Be prepared to fly my young friend. These fools will not catch me even though they have a much superior vehicle."

At the outskirts of the village, the pursuit began. Alex maneuvered his taxi like a rally racecar driver, crisscrossing the back roads so as not to allow the chase car to pull alongside. Once on the main road, he swerved from one side to the other trying to avoid the moonscape of gaping potholes and craters.

"Jesus, they're right on our tail. They're going to ram us," Mykola yelled looking out the back window.

Alex peered into the rearview mirror and saw that the man in the passenger seat was waving a semi-automatic Glock in his right hand.

"Hang on," he shouted as he gunned the car and headed straight for a mammoth crater. The chase car was inches from his bumper.

"Holy fuck. You're going to crash into the fucking hole!" Mykola warned, grabbing hold of the dashboard.

At that very moment, Alex swerved hard to the left, throwing Mykola who wasn't wearing a seat beat right into his lap. The driver of the chase car didn't have time to react. The car careened into the crater. The front end slammed into the jagged edge at the other side, flipping the vehicle over several times.

"Man, that was way too close" Mykola said, as he pushed himself off the driver. "Now I know what it's like to be in a live video game."

"No game," Alex said.

A second later, there was a deafening explosion as the black car burst into a ball of flames.

"Oh, God! The car blew up. They're burning to death!" Mykola shouted.

"May they continue to burn in Hell," Alex intoned solemnly.

Mykola looked over at Alex. Both knew who was behind the attempt on their lives.

His voice shaking, Mykola asked: "This isn't about to stop here, is it?"

"We need to be extra careful and you need to stay undercover while I figure a way to get you safely out of the country," Alex advised.

"I'll book a ticket first thing when we get back to Lviv."

"Not from Lviv. It will be too dangerous. I am sure this woman will have her people watching the airport. You will never make it onto the tarmac."

"You can't be serious. I'm Canadian. She's not that crazy."

Alex sneered. "A Canadian tourist can have an accident like anyone else. Let me figure things out. I think it will be better if I drive you to Kyiv and you take a flight from there. We will not make any reservations in advance. You will buy the ticket at the airport."

"But I've got to meet Mike Petrenko when he gets here."

"Don't worry about that. You will stay at my apartment and I will go to the airport and pick him up. Until then, you will keep out of sight."

CHAPTER TWENTY-EIGHT

The cell phone chimed with a sense of urgency on the glass coffee table in Alex's living room jolting Mykola from a troubled sleep.

"This is dynamite stuff. How on earth did you get your hands on it?" an excited voice on the other shouted.

"Who is this?" Mykola asked, trying to shake the cobwebs from his brain.

"Mike Petrenko."

"Do you have any idea what time it is?"

"Yeah, it's 8 p.m."

"Which makes it 3 in the morning over here!"

"Your point?" the reporter asked.

"I was sleeping."

"And guess what? Now you're awake," he laughed. "Anyway, like I was saying, the stuff you sent me is dynamite. I really like the video of the filing room. It's gritty and ominous looking. Hey, smart move by you to think to shoot it. It will really help the doc. I'm looking at three, maybe four weeks before we go to air with this story and we're going for the entire show. One hour! We're putting a full court press on this one. A producer and two associate producers have been assigned. We're just starting to shake the trees and I have to tell you, a lot of people are going to go insane when the shit hits the fan."

"I told you this was big," Mykola said, sitting up on the sofa.

"I owe you big time. My buddy Jurij did a super job translating the documents for me. He couldn't believe what you got your mitts on. Come to think of it, how did you get the documents?"

"Let's just say it's a trade secret."

"Like your old man's secret!"

Mykola cringed. He loathed the thought of being likened to his father.

"Listen, I'm flying into Lviv with my camera crew and producer in about a week."

"Did you manage to line up an interview with Matlinsky?"

"No. I've got a bit more leg work to do before I ask her for an on-camera interview," Petrenko said. "I Googled her. The website on the orphanage, all those photos of fawn-eyed kids … real slick. She's one sleazy con artist if I ever met one, and let me tell you, I've met a ton over my lifetime! I can't believe people fall for this crap time and time again. And there's a link to another website urging couples to adopt her babies. Do you believe that? She calls them *her* babies. That woman is one piece of work."

"More like a piece of shit. I'm pretty sure she's behind a murder," Mykola spat.

"That's a heavy allegation. You have any proof?"

"No. But all the signs point to her."

"Tell me about it."

"No point. I can't prove a thing. I just know it."

"Then, let's stick to the facts. I don't like going off on tangents that lead to Never Neverland. Given what you've sent me, I have enough ammunition to nail her coffin shut. I don't need the network's lawyer getting sidelined over some wild allegations."

"I get what you're saying. But let me just say this. They're not wild allegations. It's just that I can't prove it 100 per cent."

"Well I deal in facts. I don't deal in anything that sounds like some paranoid whack job reading tea leaves. We'll stick to what we can prove."

Mykola didn't appreciate the admonishment and the reporter sensed it.

"I also did a Google search on Cooper, the phantom B.C. in Matlinsky's ledger. Turns out she's one Brenda Cooper and she's a lawyer. She's got a high-gloss website touting herself as a leading expert on international adoptions. She's one heck of a media slut. She's been on CNN, NBC, CBS, ABC and God knows how many stories have been written about her work in various newspapers and magazines across the States. She's even published a book on international adoptions."

"I don't get why someone like her would hook up with a slime bucket like Matlinsky," Mykola said.

"That's easy. Money. Greed. Avarice! I looked at the ledger and if my addition is correct, in the past four years at 40 per cent a pop, Cooper has raked in almost $2.5-million on the sale of 62 designer sales. I'll wager she's not declared one red cent to the IRS. And that's just the tip of the iceberg. She's got her fingers in so many different countries, so many different Third World pies. She's running a regular baby mill."

"This is really unbelievable!"

"You want unbelievable? You should see what the broad looks like. She's a virtual walking advertisement for the cosmetic surgery industry. I figure she's in her early 50s, a real California mama – blond, boob job, face-lift, tummy-tuck and lip augmentation. It's almost impossible to tell if there is anything left that is real about her. Even her smile is fucking phony. It kills me that all these asshole reporters who've interviewed her don't see through her. She's all plastic!"

"I guess she found a like-minded spirit in Matlinsky," Mykola added.

"Oh, and by the way, Jurij cracked the code on the cryptic initials in the ledgers."

"Really?"

"Yup. The guy is a political junkie when it comes to Ukraine. He figures V.Y. is probably none other than Viktor Yurkovich, Ukraine's Moscow butt-licking President. S.M. is no doubt his chief of staff, Sergei Melekov and he is one nasty bit of business from what Jurij tells me. Of course you already know that V.A. is the fat and pompous Vitaly Assimovich, the deputy in charge of the Ministry of Families and Children."

"So what you're saying is Matlinsky's baby selling scheme reaches all the way into the President's office. Incredible! I gotta say that certainly answers a lot of questions."

"It sure does and it puts you and me dancing a polka in the middle of a minefield."

"Don't I know it."

"Guess what else I figured out from Matlinsky's ledgers? It's something that is going to land her into one huge vat of pig shit," Petrenko said with a sly laugh.

"What?"

"If my reading of the Cooper ledger is correct, then little Miss Matlinsky has been ripping off her associates big time on the designer baby scam. In fact, I'll bet the perogy palace they know squat about it. She's got them convinced that every baby that goes out the door is being sold for $30,000."

"How does it work?" Mykola asked.

"Cooper gets $40,000. Matlinsky gets $60,000 but if my reading of the books is correct she is only declaring $30,000 to her confederates. The one thing I don't get is this $10,000 expenditure in the debit column," the reporter noted.

"That's the payoff to the women who agreed to have what you call the designer babies and then give them up."

"Ah! So Matlinsky then pockets a cool $20,000 per designer baby plus her $9,000 cut from the so-called $30,000 sale. So if my math is correct, she's netted almost $2.5 million for herself on the designer scam alone. I'll tell you this. I'd hate to be in Matlinsky's high heels when Melekov puts two and two together after the doc airs. That kind of double-dealing can get you killed."

"They're all a bunch of thieving rats."

"The world is full of them. What makes this all the more sickening is these bastards are using babies and orphanages for their own greed."

"Yeah. They salt away millions and the children in the orphanages live in abject squalor," Mykola added.

"Listen, I gotta go. I'll hook up with you in about a week. Until then, stay safe." With that Petrenko hung up.

CHAPTER TWENTY-NINE

Mykola and Olenka sat across from each other in her parent's kitchen, a cup of tea and a plate of homemade cookies in front of each of them. Markian and Ruslana had left to tend to farm chores. They felt it better that the new-found siblings be left alone. Biting her fingernails, Olenka stared down at the table. Mykola was trying to work out an opening line.

"Did you know Kateryna?" he asked.

"I never met her. Mama and tato rarely spoke of her. I knew if I asked it would cause tato much pain so I let it be. The only time I ever heard her name was when the old woman would explode in one of her insane melo-dramas if she caught sight of me on the road or in the fields. She is a wicked old lady. I hate her."

"She's also pretty dangerous with a broom!"

They both laughed. The ice was breaking.

"I met Kateryna only twice," Mykola said. "The first time was very brief. It was in the bar where she worked. I despised her for what she was. The second time was a few days later. We spent hours and hours talking. I ended up hating myself for having judged her. Her life was so unbelievably tragic and absolutely not of her making. I just wish I could have helped her escape."

"At least you got to see her. I don't even know what she looked like. The old woman destroyed every family picture she was in. It is as if she never existed."

Mykola smiled. "You look so much like her. Do you want to see a picture of her?"

Olenka jumped up from the chair. "You have a picture?"

"On my cell phone. I took a couple of photos when I was at her place," he said, pulling the IPhone from his jacket pocket. He watched quietly as his sister gently caressed the screen. Placing it against her heart, she closed her eyes in silent prayer.

"I'll make you a copy if you'd like."

"I would like that very much," Olenka said.

Suddenly both were overcome with emotion. Mykola put her arms around his sister and they wept.

Regaining her composure, Olenka looked up at her brother and asked: "Would you like more cookies?"

The two burst into uncontrollable laughter. They both sat down, wiping tears of sadness and joy from their eyes.

"What do you do? Do you go to school?" Mykola asked.

"I'm finishing high school this year. Every morning a bus picks up the kids from the village and takes us to the school in Rodenko."

"We drove through the town on the way here. It looks kind of interesting."

"It's boring. Everything about this place is boring."

"Can I ask you, and you don't have to answer if it's too difficult for you. How do people treat you around here?"

Olenka gripped her teacup. "When I was very small I used to cry a lot because I was never invited to birthday parties. Most of the children stayed away from me. They were never allowed to play with me. Whenever they saw me they would taunt me and call me horrible names. The adults never speak to me. They always look away when I walk past them on the road. They act like I don't exist. Even at church, Father Zenon never says a word to me."

"Do you have any friends?"

"My only friend lives up the road in the town of Rodenko. She doesn't care about what others say about me. She likes me for who I am, not what my mother was."

"You don't seem angry or bitter. I know I would be."

"I am resigned. There is no point being bitter simply because other people are ignorant."

"Very true and very mature."

"And what about you? How have you been treated in Canada? Do people behave badly toward you?"

"No," Mykola said. "They never knew about Kateryna. They never even knew I was adopted. My parents told no one except for my godmother. In fact, I had no idea I was adopted until shortly after my parents died in a car crash. I found out while going through my father's papers. That's why I came to Ukraine . . . to find out who my real mother was and hopefully find out if I had any relatives."

"Do you know who your real father is?" Olenka asked.

"No. I mean I've got a name. But that's about it. Kateryna told me he lives in Milan, Italy."

"I sometimes wish I knew who my father was. Then I wonder what I would say if I ever met him. It would be so strange because I'm certain he was a customer."

And Mykola knew he was also a rapist.

"It must have been a shock for you meeting the old woman and Bohdan!" Olenka continued.

It didn't escape Mykola's attention that she never called the old woman "Baba" or Bohdan "Uncle".

"Shock doesn't begin to describe it. This entire trip has been a journey into the fires of hell. But hey, at least there is one silver lining. I got a sister out of it."

Olenka smiled.

"Tell me, what are you going to do after you graduate from high school?"

"I guess come back here and work the fields with mama and tato."

"Don't you want to go to university?"

"It is my dream but look at us. We are poor. Mama and tato have no money to send me to university."

Mykola looked at his sister and smiled. "Listen, you don't have to give me an answer right this moment but if you want to go to university then I would you like to help you out."

"How would this be possible?"

"I would pay your way."

Olenka looked troubled. "How will I ever repay you?"

"You're my sister. It will be my gift to you."

"I would very much love to go," she said with a wide smile.

"I'll talk to Markian and Ruslana. You just make sure you've got the grades to get into university and I'll look after all the rest."

"Thank you."

"Any idea what you might want to be when you graduate?"

"I have never given more thought than to working on the farm. But when I was a child I dreamed of becoming a veterinarian. I love animals and it hurts me when they are sick or hurt. All I want is to make them feel better."

"If that's your dream, then I say go for it."

CHAPTER THIRTY

Mykola couldn't believe it.

"Matlinsky agreed to an interview? Does she know what it's about?" he asked as he sat down at a table at the back of a local bar up the road from Alex's apartment complex.

"She's clueless in Lviv," Petrenko said in his trademark gunslinger tone. "I told her I wanted to do a documentary on her work, the orphanage, and her prestigious award. I really buttered her up. I told her I'd spoken to three families in Canada who had adopted babies through her amazing graces and that they were singing her praises from the roof tops. I told her they had described her as a saint and urged me to do a documentary about her. She's salivating at the thought of having an entire hour devoted to her," the reporter said, sliding his wiry frame into the booth. "Man, is she ever in for a rude awakening."

Petrenko waved at the bartender, thrusting two fingers in the air for two bottles of beer. "Dvah pevo," he mouthed. "I just love Ukie beer! The nectar of the Gods."

Mykola's mind was on spin cycle. "You spoke to three families?"

"Yeah. They were easy to find. Their names were on the documents you sent."

"They didn't ask how you found out they had adopted babies from Ukraine?"

"They did."

Shifting nervously in his chair, Mykola asked: "What did you tell them?"

"What's the quickest way to get information out in the Ukie community?"

Mykola laughed. "The BBC! Baba babi skazala!"

"Right on. You want information on anyone in the community just tell a grandmother and she tells another grandmother, and the word gets out faster than on the Internet! By the way, did you know this Matlinsky broad speaks fluent English?"

"How did you find that out?"

"I had Jurij call her."

"Jurij?"

"My buddy, the guy I told you about who runs the Ukie television program out of Toronto. Anyway, he called her and broached the idea of a full, one-hour feature documentary on her. He told her we would focus on her humanitarian work and her big award. Then all of a sudden she breaks out in fluent English. So I grabbed the phone and chatted with her. It turns out English translation was her minor in university. What a bonus! We don't have to run subtitles under what she is saying. I hate subtitles and I absolutely hate doing interviews with an interpreter. Far too much gets lost in translation."

"How are you going to handle the interview?"

"Like I always do. I'll play good cop at first and then when she's knee deep in rat crap, I'll lower the boom!"

"Before you start the interview, have her take you on the tour. It's a classic dog and pony show."

"That's a given. I need B-reel of the orphanage. There's no way I'll get that if I slam her first in the interview."

"I'm fairly certain she's going to take you down to the basement. If she does, get your cameraman to shoot the interior of the storage room. But make sure Matlinsky isn't around."

"So what's in this storage room?"

"I don't want to spoil the surprise but I guarantee it will be a Kodak moment and it will drive your viewers absolutely nuts."

"How will I know where the storage room is?"

"It's directly across from the file room."

"And how will I know that?"

"The file room has a huge lock on the door. You can't miss it."

Petrenko grinned. He now knew precisely where Mykola had obtained the documents.

"Does Matlinsky know you gained access to this room and took the documents you sent me?" the reporter asked.

Mykola knew he was caught. "She doesn't have the slightest clue. But I can assure you, once she's aware you have them, she'll go ballistic. I suggest you tread very carefully. She's one ruthless woman. I'm sure she hired two thugs to run Alex and I off the road the other day."

"Hey, I've covered seven wars. I've gone after biker gangs, the mafia, Triads, crooked cops, drug dealers and pimps, and I'm still standing. I don't think some sleaze bag orphanage director is going to scare me off. Anyway, I'll be in and out of there before her head stops spinning and she realizes the full scope of what had just happened to her."

"Oh yes, I forgot to mention, she parks her shiny white 328i BMW in a garage up the street from the orphanage. Think about it, an orphanage director who is paid peanuts and she drives a $45,000 car. She also owns a ritzy condo in the swank Old Quarter of Lviv."

"The interview is in two days. Does your driver Alex know anyone with a van with tinted windows? I need to do some B-reel, like getting shots of the woman driving to work and the outside of her swanky condo."

"I'm sure Alex can get his hands on one."

"We'll pay him for his time and for the use of the van. Ask him to meet us in front of the Grand at 6 a.m. tomorrow."

"You don't know how much I wish I could be a fly on the wall when you do the interview," Mykola said.

"You can have a front row seat in your own living room in a few weeks when the program airs."

"Oh, one last thing. When you're in Matlinsky's office, zoom in on the framed photograph of Matlinsky and President Yurkovich on the wall above her desk. It has a very unique aura."

"What do you mean?"

"You'll know it when you see it."

CHAPTER THIRTY-ONE

As tough a reporter as Mike Petrenko was reputed to be, he couldn't help tearing up at the sight of the innocent faces looking up at him from their cribs and playpens in the nursery. The father of a five-year-old girl, he was silly putty when it came to children. His daughter was his oasis of calm and goodness in a world rife with corruption and violence. She was precious to him and he could never fathom abandoning her.

Natalka Matlinsky caught the tears and smiled inwardly. She knew she had the reporter primed, baited and hooked. Now all she had to do was reel him in and that would most definitely be achieved in the toddler unit. But the next stop on the tour was the basement. Once in the bowels of the building, Petrenko was champing at the bit to find out what was behind door number one. After that segment of the sideshow was over, the reporter explained that he needed to get some establishing shots and suggested the director head back up to her office. No need to stick around. He would catch up with her in a few minutes for the continuation of the tour. She was obliging, smiling and not the least bit suspicious.

Petrenko scurried over to the storage room door and yanked it open. His jaw dropped in stunned bewilderment when he saw the towering pile of stuffed animals and toys. Turning to his cameraman, he said: "I'll bet these are all gifts sent or dropped off by people for the children, and the bitch throws them in here like garbage. Man, will there be a lot of pissed off donors when they see this!"

The cameraman nodded and zoomed in for a close-up of a discarded Cabbage Patch doll, a stuffed white polar bear and a forlorn looking moose sporting a Royal Canadian Mounted Police hat and red tunic.

Petrenko looked across from the storage room at the door with the big lock. He knew it was the file room.

When they were done, Matlinsky joined the reporter and his crew as they made their way up to toddler unit. It made for amazing, heartwarming visuals. The kids were naturals, mugging for the camera, and their closing number was a definite heart wrencher. At Mykola's suggestion, the crew had brought along a bag of candies and passed them out before heading to the director's office to set up for the main interview.

With the lights and cameras in place, the reporter and director sat down opposite each other, Matlinsky with her plastic smile and braided bun topping her head, Petrenko with his devious grin and a fully loaded notebook. Maria sat in a corner at the back of the room.

As was his trademark, Petrenko began slow and easy, asking the director how she came to head the orphanage. She waxed eloquently lying through her teeth about how the care of its helpless children had always been her true calling and her number one priority.

"It was what I was meant to do," she said softly.

Then without any prompting, the director waded into her first misstep, citing the many kind and generous donations made by the steady stream of foreign tourists from countries like Canada and the U.S. who came to visit with the children. It was the trigger for the first semi-tough question.

"With all the visits and donations over all the years, I have to wonder why this place looks like a page straight out of a Charles Dickens novel?" he asked in a soft tone.

Matlinsky's had not anticipated the comeback, but trying not to miss a beat, she knew precisely where to shovel the blame.

"Every year, the government is cutting back on our funding. We are forced to spend the donations on the bare essentials like food, clothing and medicine for the children."

Acting like he had swallowed the explanation, Petrenko lobbed another softball question. "I read on one of your websites that you are involved as well in the adoption of orphan babies. This must bring you a lot of satisfaction . . . seeing the babies placed in loving and caring homes."

"Yes. I believe my babies deserve a good life and I am so happy when I can help couples who wish to provide my babies with a loving and caring home. I make certain that I personally meet every family wishing to adopt. I want to be certain my babies are adopted by loving families."

"And I see the President of Ukraine recently honored you with the Order of Merit for your work with orphans," he said, pointing to the photo on the wall behind her desk. The cameraman tilted upwards. "That must have been a momentous occasion."

Matlinsky beamed and relaxed, feeling the interview was back on track. "It is quite an honor but again, I must stress that what I do is for the little ones. The honor is really for all the women who care for the children in the orphanage."

Petrenko could not believe how incredibly disingenuous this woman was.

"Over the past decade, how many babies have been adopted from your orphanage?"

"I don't have the exact number at my fingertips but there have been many adopted by deserving and loving families around the globe, including I might add, Canada."

"Are we talking few hundred?"

"As I said, I don't have the exact figure but over the past 15 years or so that would sound about right."

"Are all the babies who are adopted orphans in the true sense of the definition? That is both their parents are deceased," Petrenko asked.

"They could not be adopted otherwise," the director said.

"So they're all orphans?"

"Yes."

Looking down at his notebook, the reporter continued: "The cost per adoption, I'm told is $30,000. That's one a heck of a lot of money. Could you break down the cost of an adoption for me?"

Matlinsky stirred uneasily in her chair.

"There is the government paperwork," she began, nervously clearing her throat. "The medicals for the babies, the cost of lawyers."

"That said, for the life of me, I still can't see how that could possibly work out to $30,000. Does your orphanage get a cut?"

"No." she said firmly. "We do not, as you phrase it, get a cut." Her forehead began showing creases of discomfort.

The cameraman pushed in for a tight close up. The soundman could hear her heart pounding like a jackhammer through the highly sensitive microphone he had taped on her blouse just above her left breast. It was acting like a lie detector.

"Do you personally get a cut?"

"I resent that question," she fired back, her eyes narrowing.

The interview had now moved into full accountability mode. No more Mr. Nice Guy. No more fake smiles. "Could you tell me about your relationship with Brenda Cooper and your designer baby adoption scheme?"

"I demand that you turn off your camera at this instance. This is not what I was led to believe of the interview," Matlinsky demanded.

The reporter pressed on. "Blond, blue-eyed babies at $100,000 a pop! If we talk 62 babies over the past several years, that's a hell of a lot of money. Where does it go?"

"Turn off the camera and get out."

Petrenko was not about to let up. He went for the jugular.

"You own a luxurious condo in the historic section of Lviv. That's got to set you back $500,000 easily. And you drive an awfully expensive BMW. Can I ask how you can afford to live so high on the hog on a salary of 5,000 hryvna a month? Isn't that what the government pays you to run this place?"

Matlinsky leapt up, the lapel microphone ripping from her silk blouse. "This is over. Get out now! I am insulted by your insinuations."

"Miss Matlinsky, let me assure you, I don't deal in insinuations. I deal in facts."

"Get out," she screamed as she stormed out of her office. Her assistant was hot on her heels.

A moment later, Maria, her face sheet white, re-appeared to supervise the breakdown of the lights. The cameraman was pushing in on a close up of the photo on the wall behind Matlinsky's desk.

"I can't believe she took down a cross to replace it with the photo. What an ego!" Petrenko told the cameraman. "Make sure you zoom in on the outline of the cross. Saint Matlinsky trumps Jesus Christ! I love it."

At that very moment, Maria realized Mykola was behind the interview, recalling his comment about the photograph and the faded image of the crucifix behind it. She also fully understood that once the documentary was broadcast, her boss was in big trouble. The story would go international and there would be casualties, her included. With downcast eyes, Maria escorted the camera crew to the door and returned to the office, sensing that her days as assistant director of Orphanage 41 were numbered.

CHAPTER THIRTY-TWO

Mike Petrenko tangoed into Alex's apartment with the look of a kid who had lifted a pack of gum from a candy store. He was grinning from ear to ear. In one hand he held a huge bag of popcorn. In the other he was clutching a DVD disk like it was made of gold. While it wasn't gold in the precious metal sense, it certainly was gold.

"You won't believe what I got my hands on," he began with a boyish laugh.

"What?" Mykola asked.

"After my interview with Matlinsky ..."

"Hold on. How did that go?"

"Let's just say Mike Petrenko made her day. Natalka Matlinsky left the building one very pissed off lady. I sliced and diced and she bolted out of her office screaming like a wounded banshee."

"You got her?"

"To say I got her is an understatement. I got her real good. She is toast! And this," the reporter said, waving the DVD inches from Mykola's face, "is, as they say in French, le icing on le gateau."

"What's on it?"

"After the interview, I took a cab over to the local television station and had a chat with the news director. I did a little wheeling and dealing, and I bought the rights to this video for $1,500. It's all signed, sealed and delivered. And it's mine, all mine," he said with a cackle.

"What's on it?" Mykola repeated.

"Alex, do you have a DVD player?"

"But of course."

"Well folks break out the vodka and pop the popcorn. Prepare to be thoroughly entertained. Mykola, I'm going to need you to translate."

"No problem. Will you please tell me what you have?"

"Well, let me begin with this. After Matlinsky stormed out of her office, I had my cameraman zoom in on that framed photo of her and Viktor Yurkovich. That's when it hit me. That event with her receiving such a prestigious award for the Big Kobassa had to have been covered by the local and maybe even the national news media. After all, what else do reporters here do but play - follow the leader."

Petrenko hoisted the silver disk to the ceiling. "On this DVD my friends is a compilation of the night Matlinsky got her award of merit from the President of Ukraine, and let me tell you, it is a treasure trove of moments not to be forgotten. Watch and salivate," he said, gently sliding the disk into the player.

The first shots opened with scores of Lviv's high society hob knobbing in the Grand Ballroom of the Lviv Conference Center. It was a black tie event with 350 of the who's who of Ukrainian high society in attendance. The women glided from table to table showing off their latest Paris and Italian gowns and flaunting their glitzy jewelry. The men huddled in tight circles, every so often craning their necks like expectant ganders at the entranceway. For them, the evening was a platinum opportunity to rub shoulders with all the president's men, and if fortune smiled, get a moment with the leader of the nation.

Mykola, Alex and Petrenko sat glued to the screen, in awe of the opulent spectacle unfolding before their eyes.

The ballroom was abuzz with conversation and thick lathered with anticipation. Then suddenly the main doors flew open. The cameras spun around to capture the commotion. Four teams, made up of six secret service agents, barreled into the room and fanned out like stealth fighters. Three teams wove through the crowd on the lookout for anyone or anything that emitted even the slightest whiff of suspicion. The fourth made a beeline for the kitchen to check out the help. Their faces were frozen in caricature-like expressions designed to intimidate, as were their matching outfits. The agents all wore ebony black suits, starched white shirts, black ties, dark Ray-Ban sunglasses and a radio receiver plugged into the right ear. Under their jackets, a noticeable bulge – a holstered, semi-automatic Glock pistol.

The detail commander, a behemoth of a man with a menacing sneer and an inch-long scar on his right cheek, lumbered onto the stage. With the stone cold eyes of a cobra, he scanned the room. After each team leader gave the thumbs up, he nodded at his second in command who was standing vigil by the main entrance.

The camera then cut back to the stage. The master of ceremonies, a wiry weasel of a man inflated with pomp and circumstance, marched to the podium and announced: "Ladies and gentlemen, please stand and welcome our nation's President, Viktor Anatoly Yurkovich!"

To a thunderous applause, the President, a short stocky man with a face fattened by greed and corruption, strutted with purpose down the center aisle. He walked with arms raised in triumph, boxer style, to a raucous standing ovation that lasted two whole minutes. The cameras followed him to the head table where he was warmly greeted by the guests: kisses on both cheeks from the archbishop of the Russian-Ukrainian Orthodox church and the archbishop of the Ukrainian Eastern Catholic Church, and a big hug and three kisses for the guest of honor, Natalka Matlinsky. The formalities done with, the leader waved his hands for everyone to sit, but the applause ignored him. He clearly relished it.

"You won't believe the meal," Petrenko interjected. "No Ukrainian peasant food for these people, not when you pay 500 bucks a plate for the privilege of dining with the President."

It was haute cuisine all the way, beginning with a close up shot of the appetizer: smoked wild Pacific Coho salmon and black caviar from the Caspian Sea.

"I could never understand how anyone could eat fish eggs," Petrenko offered. "It tastes like salted crap! It's freakin' disgusting."

For the main course: Duck a l'Orange with scalloped potatoes and honey-glazed baby carrots, followed by gateau blanc with strawberries and crème fraiche for dessert. The wine flowed freely - a 2006, red Bordeaux and a 2008, white Alsace, and on each table an ice-chilled bottle of Nemiroff Lex vodka.

The next cutaway zoomed in on the MC as he mounted the stage once again. He stood for a moment, like a shepherd observing his flock, before tapping the microphone with a silver Montblanc fountain pen. The crowd went silent. An electric anticipation filled the room. "Holy fathers, Mr. President, honored guests, ladies and gentlemen ... Please stand for the National Anthem."

With right hands on their hearts, the guests responded with a resounding rendition of the national hymn. A huge blue and yellow flag unfurled and slowly cascading down the wall at the rear of the stage.

The anthem over, the MC smiled proudly as he glanced down at the head table before him.

"What a portentous asslick!" Petrenko shouted, throwing a kernel of popcorn at the screen.

Clearing his throat for dramatic effect, the MC began: "It is now my extreme honor to introduce our nation's beloved leader, the President of Ukraine, Viktor Anatoly Yurkovich."

The president rose from the table and made his way to the stage to another booming standing ovation. He bowed profusely, and then raised his hands, a signal for everyone to sit. His chin square to the microphone, Yurkovich squinted into the spotlights. With the clear, crisp voice of authority, smacking of sated ego and confidence, he addressed the head table. "Holy reverend fathers and honored guests, it is my privilege to sit at your table and break bread with you."

Mykola went into translation mode.

The President then turned to the audience. "Thank you so much for such a warm and wonderful reception. I am honored and humbled. Truly, I am. However, holy fathers, honored guests, and ladies and gentlemen, this evening is not about politics or government ... And it surely is not about *me!*"

The president laughed, and the crowd quickly joined in, as it was clear that he adored being adored.

"We are gathered here to honor a remarkable woman who has served her country with dedication and resolve. A leader in the field of child-care who has taken this nation's most vulnerable, fed and clothed them, and given them respite when there was nowhere else for them to go. She has taken the disenfranchised, the abandoned, the tiniest among us, those who have no one to tuck them in bed at night, and given them more than a roof over their heads. She has given them a place to call home."

The President paused, scanning the crowd. Women were dabbing their eyes, and men looked dutifully concerned.

"This dedicated woman did all this with little fanfare, taking a once ramshackle orphanage and creating a beacon of hope, a shining example for others across this country – Orphanage 41, in this magnificent city of Lviv. It was a job nobody wanted, but this selfless woman took the assignment with commitment and a sense of duty. She embraced the daunting task of reforming this institution. When the walls were bursting at the seams with tiny mouths to feed, she did not complain. Through determined organization and efficiency, through steadfast leadership, and of course by leading by example, she has shown us all that it could be done. For not only her peers, but for me, she is an inspiration," he said, pausing for this noblest of compliments to sink in, and pleased to see the looks of approval in the sea of faces below.

Mykola could no longer reign in his disgust. "What an absolute load of crap! I can't believe these morons are buying it."

"They are not buying," Alex interjected. "They are simply playing the game."

The president concluded. "It is with great respect and admiration that I call to the podium to receive the Order of Merit of Ukraine, the highest civic award our nation has to offer, the director of Orphanage 41 -- Natalka ... Sofia ... *Matlinsky!*"

As she rose from the head table, the guests rose to their feet in vigorous applause. This was clearly her moment. It was her time to bask in the spotlight.

"Wow, take a gander at what the saint is wearing!" Petrenko pointed out.

Matlinsky was decked out in a colorful gown from Valentino. Picked up on a recent shopping trip to Rome, the dress was fitted in the right places with just the right amount of excess. In it, she walked with her head held high. Not to be outdone by the female entourage, she had taken special care to accessorize. Her neck was bedecked with a string of perfect pearls from Japan, on her right wrist she wore an 18-carat brushed gold braided bracelet, and on her left, there was a platinum Cartier watch. She wore a red garnet ring on her right hand and a blue sapphire on her left.

As she arrived at the podium, the President, his arms outstretched, a wide smile on his face, pulled her into a warm embrace, and whispered something into her ear.

Petrenko leapt up from the sofa and pushed the pause button. "Now that's the million dollar shot! I'm definitely going to use that and freeze-frame it. What dirty little secret did he whisper in her ear? I'll bet it was 'thanks for the millions. Keep the money rolling in.' I love that shot," he said with a dance before hitting the resume play button.

Matlinsky turned to face the crowd. She gazed out at the room, taking care to stand poised as the television cameras rolled and photographers snapped away. The President then presented her with a gold medal featuring the bust of Taras Shevchenko, and an engraved bronze plaque. They posed for more TV moments and photo ops, and then the President yielded the stage.

Pulling the microphone down to her level, she began.

"When I was a little girl growing up in the village of Kuchariv in Bukovina, I knew poverty first-hand. I also knew about the love of a mother. My mother worked the soil. My father was married to the bottle and drank himself into an early grave."

Matlinsky let her voice trail off. A measured pause to good effect. Men in the audience shifted uncomfortably in their seats. The women leaned forward, wanting to hear more. For this echelon of society, business was business, and personal lives were left tucked under the family rug. It was rare for someone to candidly parade their dirty laundry in public. Those who did were often ridiculed. But Matlinsky knew better. She had never been a born public speaker, but as with everything else she did, she had studied the art of communication with the diligence of a doctoral candidate. She knew where she was going with her speech.

"We were alone, Mama and I," Matlinsky continued. "She sacrificed everything so that her daughter could have a better life. She encouraged me to do well in school, as all parents do, but she also enrolled me in the youth wing of the Communist Party. She wanted me to contribute to the betterment of our people. And I wanted to, for her..." She let her eyes get teary.

"So when the party secretary called me, a little more than 20 years ago, and told me I was needed at Orphanage 41, I could not refuse. It has changed my life. What I saw was not a crumbling, decaying institution. What I saw was a ship afloat in a riotous sea with only a life preserver and a broken oar. I threw myself into the task of steering this ship until I brought it safely back to shore. We have never looked back.

"I am tremendously grateful to my party – and to the state – for helping me discover my true mission in life. Every child who enters my care, every child who finds a happy home, is forever imprinted on my soul and in my thoughts. These children are what drive me to get up every morning. They are my babies and they deserve this award, not me." She bowed.

"Oh for crying out loud, this is way over the top," Mykola shouted, leaping up from the sofa in exasperation. "I can't believe that contemptible woman actually called those children her babies."

A disquieting hush engulfed the ballroom, and then as the guests realized Matlinsky's speech had ended, there came a roar of applause. The director was astute enough to know they weren't saluting her. They were simply doing what was called for in the circumstance.

In the final sequence, the camera turned back to the president who sprang to his feet and began singing Mnohaya Lita (many happy years). The audience joined in. On cue, two six-year-olds from Orphanage 41 – a boy and girl dressed in colorful, traditional Ukrainian costume – scurried onto the stage bearing an over flowing bouquet of flowers for the director. Matlinsky graciously accepted them, giving each child a kiss on the forehead as she forced out a practiced tear.

"Well, you've got to admit, this is one hell of a show," Petrenko said as he bounded over to the DVD player and scanned back to an earlier scene. A second later, he hit pause just at the very moment the President was rising from his chair to applaud Matlinsky.

"Look behind him at the other table," the reporter exhorted with a Cheshire cat grin. "I'm talking about the surly looking guy with the buzz cut to his right. That piece of sleaze is none other than Sergei Melekov. He's the President's notorious and ruthless chief of staff. He's the S.M. in Matlinsky's ledgers. Anyone who wants to do business with Yurkovich goes through him. This is one guy you don't mess with."

His broad, square shoulders knotted with tension, Alex sat stiff in front of the television screen, glaring at the frozen image of Viktor Yurkovich. "This man . . . all these corrupt politicians, all these wealthy oligarchs, they are the ones responsible for the crisis this country finds itself in. Ukraine was once the breadbasket of Europe. Today it is a pitiful basket case because of all these thieving pigs. They should all be rounded up. Their wealth should be taken away and they should be thrown in prison to rot."

"The chances of that ever happening are as likely as finding life on Mars," Petrenko interjected. "But right now, staring us square in the face is one hell of a story that is going to make huge waves in a lot of countries, and maybe, just maybe, we might see some good come out of it."

Mykola's cell phone began vibrating in his jacket pocket. He flipped it open and noticed the number was blocked. Hesitantly he answered, hoping it wasn't Lesia. He had way too much on his mind and was in no mood for yet another grilling. It wasn't her. It was Maria and she was in a panic.

"Petro is in the hospital. She beat him with a steel pipe. This is your fault," she screamed.

"Calm down. What do you mean she beat Petro? Who beat Petro?"

"After the interview, for which I am sure you are responsible, Director Matlinsky went straight to the file room in the basement. She discovered that files are missing. She went into Petro's room and demanded to know who had been in the room. He was like a frightened boy. She kept at him, yelling and making allegations and threatening to send him back to the Internat. He was so scared that he told her about your visit and when he confessed he had made a copy of the key to the lock, she went insane. She picked up a pipe that was lying in the corner on his room and began to beat him. Everyone in the building could hear Petro's screams. After she left the orphanage, I ran down to the basement. There was blood all over his room. Petro was unconscious and bleeding from his head and face. I called an ambulance. He is in the hospital. He is in such terrible condition. This is all your doing. I hope you are proud."

"Christ, I never meant for this to happen. What hospital is he in?"

"He was taken to Central Hospital."

"What about you?"

"Me? Thanks to you, I'm finished here. I don't know where I will end up."
With that, Maria hung up.

Rubbing his throbbing temples, Mykola turned to Alex. "I need you to
take me to the hospital."

"What's going on?" Petrenko asked as he grabbed his jacket.

As they rushed down the stairwell, Mykola asked: "Did you tell Matlinsky
you had the files?"

"No. But you wouldn't have to be a brain surgeon to know from my questions that I was in possession of some pretty incriminating material. Why?"

"After you left the orphanage, Matlinsky went down to the file room and
discovered that it had been rifled. She then stormed into Petro's room. He
admitted that he let me into the room and she went berserk. She beat him
with a pipe."

As the trio raced out of the apartment, Petrenko asked: "Who the hell
is Petro?"

"He's the caretaker at the orphanage. I talked him into letting me into the
file room on the promise no one would ever find out. I told him I'd protect
him," Mykola said. "I messed up again."

Mykola stood frozen in shock as he gazed down at Petro's battered face. He
lay unconscious with an IV drip plugged into his right arm. Both his eyes
were black and blue, and puffed out like golf balls. An aluminum splint held
his re-set broken nose in place. His shaved skull was wrapped in white gauze.

Holding his hand, Mykola whispered: "I'm so sorry, Petro. I'm so very
sorry. I never meant this to happen."

Ever the journalist, Petrenko pulled out his IPhone and began shooting
video of Matlinsky's hapless victim, slowly zooming in for close-ups on each
inflicted wound. He then turned the camera on the squalid surroundings.
There were 19 other patients lying on cots in the jam-packed ward that
reeked of urine and disinfectant. Several men were moaning. There were no
doctors, nurses or orderlies in sight.

"Where the hell is the hospital staff . . . on a perpetual coffee break?"
Petrenko asked.

"This is a ward for the poor. If you have no money, you get minimum
care," Alex explained. "Lucky are the ones who have family to care for them."

A moment later, a doctor strolled by in the corridor. He stopped in his tracks when he noticed the three men standing at the foot of Petro's bed. His curiosity peaked he entered the ward.

"Are you relatives of this man?" he asked.

"I'm his friend," Mykola replied. "What is his condition?"

"He will be fine. He regained consciousness when he was wheeled into the emergency room and went into a state of panic and confusion. I gave him an injection to put him to sleep. I must say he has a hard head. There are no fractures despite the many blows to his skull. I must have put more than a hundred stitches into his head from the many lacerations he received from the attack. He did suffer a mild concussion. However I expect he will recover fully."

"I want him to get the best of help. I will pay for it."

At the sound of a cash payment, the doctor's ears perked up. "For 5,000 hryvna, I can have him moved to a private ward and I will personally see to his medical needs."

Mykola turned and held the caretaker's hand. "I swear I will make it up to you. Just get well."

Maria was sitting on a bench outside the ward when the three men came out. She looked frightened and worried.

"I'm so sorry for what has happened to Petro," Mykola began. "I never thought …"

"I have come to the conclusion that you don't think. You simply act and whatever happens simply happens. You leave a mess in your wake," Maria shouted.

"I've asked the doctor to take care of Petro. I'm going to pay for his care."

Maria was not moved by Mykola's act of kindness.

Petrenko interjected in broken Ukrainian. "You are the director's assistant. You were the one sitting at the back of her office during the interview."

"Yes."

"Mykola, you've got to translate for me. Ask her if she would come on camera and expose Matlinsky."

Maria furiously shook her head when asked. "I am afraid of that woman. As you are well aware, she has powerful friends."

"How about she gives us a road map, tells me everything she knows. It will be on a 'not for attribution' basis. She won't be identified and she doesn't have to appear on camera," the reporter suggested.

Mykola translated and added: "This is the time for you to step up. Matlinsky has made millions of dollars selling babies. She never cared about them and she certainly didn't care about the babies and children stuck in the orphanage. Look at the place. It's a dump and look at her. She lives in the lap of incredible luxury. All we need from you is a bit more information to pull all the pieces together. And as Mike told you, he will not identify you or attribute any comments directly to you."

Looking into the hospital ward, Maria's gaze froze on Petro's bandaged face. Cautiously, she nodded her agreement.

Petrenko retrieved a mini digital tape recorder from his jacket pocket and held it discreetly in the palm of his right hand. "When did this baby adoption mill begin?"

Mykola translated.

"It began in late 1993 shortly after you were adopted," Maria began. "Director Matlinsky became obsessed with finding babies for adoption to meet the demand by foreign families. But I swear to you that I never knew how much money she was making until your reporter friend questioned her earlier today. I am ashamed and disgusted. So much money and none of it went for the care and welfare of the children."

Mykola translated. "It began in the latter part of 1993," he said, faithfully completing the rest of the translation verbatim.

Maria outlined her understanding of the adoption scheme. Any baby that was healthy was immediately put up for adoption but only to foreign families. All seemed to go well until about the sixth year when the number of adoptable healthy babies began to decline. Matlinsky was beside herself.

"She would rant and rave about all the defective babies we were getting, calling the mothers who abandoned them such dreadful names," the assistant recounted.

Mykola thought back to Matlinsky's adoption ledger and remembered seeing a sharp drop in the bottom line for the years 1997 to mid-1999.

"Then in the summer of 1998 Director Matlinsky went to a farm village outside Lviv to pick up an abandoned baby. While she was there, she noticed several pregnant women who already had three, four and five children pulling at their skirts. This is when she came up with a plan to offer each of the pregnant women $1,000 U.S. if they should decide to give up their newborns for adoption. But Director Matlinsky had one clear and strict proviso; the baby must be healthy. There must be no defects."

"You knew this and went along with it?" Mykola asked incredulously.

"Yes."

"You didn't think there was something ethically or morally wrong with this scheme?" Petrenko interjected.

"At first, yes. But Director Matlinsky's explanation made proper sense. She argued that these women were destitute, that they could not afford to feed and clothe and properly care for the children they already had. When she made the offer of money, so many of them welcomed it with open arms. They saw it as an opportunity to buy things they could never afford - a television, a stove, a refrigerator, and clothes for themselves and their children. Director Matlinsky was very reassuring, telling them that their babies would be adopted by loving families who would give them a good life. In no time, the word went out to surrounding villages and towns and our nursery was filled with babies."

Turning to Mykola, Petrenko noted: "That's what that $1,000 debit was for in the adoption ledger."

Mykola nodded in agreement.

"Ask her what she knows about Brenda Cooper and the designer babies?" the reporter continued.

Maria explained that Cooper suddenly appeared on the scene in the summer of 2004. "I would see her come and go. She and Director Matlinsky got along famously. It was like they were long lost sisters. They went to dinner together, to concerts and shopping. I never knew much of what was going on between the two because they always spoke in English."

"Were you aware of the designer baby scheme?" Petrenko pushed.

"No. I swear. But there was this one occasion when an American couple staying at the Opera Hotel got the wrong baby delivered to them. I remember getting a phone call at the orphanage from a woman who was yelling that she was promised a baby with blue eyes and blond hair. She said the baby that was delivered had brown eyes and black hair. Director Matlinsky rushed into the nursery, picked up another baby and left. She came back several hours later and handed me the other baby with explicit instructions to place the child in a crib on the left side of the nursery. She said the right side was for the 'blue eyes' and the left side for the 'brown eyes.' I thought this very strange but I never made a connection to what you call designer babies."

Maria paused. "I know you were not taken there on the tour but there is a special ward for the babies that are for adoption. It is fitted with new cribs and they get the best formula and special attention by the staff."

"I definitely need to get a shot of that!" Petrenko said. "Where's the unit located?"

"It is at the far end of the hallway on the main floor. But you cannot go there with a big camera. It will cause a commotion and the staff will immediately call the director," Maria warned.

"I'll shoot it with my IPhone."

Maria stressed that while she was not aware of bribery and corruption involved in the baby trade, she had her suspicions. "Every month or so, a shiny black SUV would park in front of the orphanage and the driver, a young, well-dressed man who always wore sunglasses and a black suit, would go to the director's office. Most times, I greeted him at the door and escorted him to the office. I was never allowed into Director Matlinsky's office on these occasions."

Mykola and Petrenko shared a knowing glance.

Maria continued. "After a while we got to talking, small talk at first and one day, maybe a couple of years later, I asked the driver who he worked for. He said a man called Sergei Melekov. The name meant nothing to me and then he told me the man was the chief of staff for the President. I was in a state of shock. I wondered what business this man could possibly have with Director Matlinsky."

Both Petrenko and Mykola sat in stunned silence. It was the confirmation they needed. S.M. was definitely Sergei Melekov!

"With all the money that Matlinsky made from selling babies, you would think the orphanage would have benefitted immensely. The place looks like a run-down warehouse," the reporter noted.

Maria's forehead furrowed with tension. "I had no idea that so much money was being paid for the babies. Yes, I had my suspicions. Director Matlinsky lives very well and she takes many trips abroad to Rome, Paris, Berlin and even the United States. She once told me she inherited a sum of money and I believed her. She did place televisions in all the units but they were all gifts from foreign visitors. And she gives everyone on staff a $20 U.S. note at the end of every month. I guess it is to buy their loyalty and their silence. I feel so stupid and so ashamed."

During the ride back to the apartment, Alex could see Mykola was feeling terrible about what had happened to the caretaker. "Petro will be fine my young friend and once he is out of the hospital, I will see to it that he has a good job. I know two American men who have purchased several properties in the historic quarter. They are in need of a full time caretaker. I will recommend Petro for the position."

Mykola said nothing. He stared out the window wallowing in self-pity. Once again, his rash actions caused someone to get hurt. Petrenko sat quietly, his mind busy structuring and planning the script for his investigative blockbuster.

At the apartment, Petrenko looked down at his IPhone and let out a whoop. "I just got a text from one of my associate producers. He's lined up an interview with Brenda Cooper in L.A. for mid next week. The woman can't say no to a camera being shoved in her face."

"What if Matlinsky calls and warns her about you?" Mykola asked."

"I highly doubt she will. I would guess right about now Matlinsky is in major self-preservation mode. I'd wager she's seriously trying to figure out how she is going to dig herself out of a very deep vat of fresh rat crap. Cooper is the last thing on her mind. And if she does call her, so what! If Cooper suddenly calls it off, I'll just pay her an unscheduled interview."

"A what?"

"I'll jump the sleaze bag lawyer with cameras rolling as she arrives at her office!"

"What if Matlinsky has called her people to intercept you at the airport and they confiscate your disks?" Mykola asked.

"Two things: Firstly, I've already sent the interview via satellite last night to the network in Toronto. Secondly, I really don't think she is about to call in the big guns. Imagine their reaction when they discover she's cooked the books. No, if I read her correctly, she's into saving number one. I'll bet she's packing her bags as we speak."

"I hope you're right."

"Listen, tomorrow morning I'll drop by the orphanage to get a shot of that nursery and then I'm heading off to the airport. After I put this doc to bed, we should get together for a drink. I owe you one. Hell, I owe you dinner at a five star restaurant and a dozen drinks. So let's meet up in Toronto."

"Toronto makes my nose bleed. But if you're ever in Edmonton look me up."

"First chance I get. I'm sure I can find an environmental scandal in the oil sands worth chasing up there," the reporter said. He then turned and faced Mykola.

"You've handed me a powerful story of corruption and greed on a silver platter. People watching this doc are going to go crazy when they learn about this baby selling scheme, and the way it stands, you're not going to get any credit. Yet for some reason you don't want to come on camera and talk about how you came across this scam."

"I don't want any credit."

"You have to understand, what you've done here is nothing short of incredible. You've broken a disgusting and despicable baby selling ring that reaches right into the top echelons of power. Those bastards raked millions of dollars while the children in Orphanage 41 lived in squalor."

"Like I said, I don't want any credit. That's not why I came here," Mykola said, instantly regretting the last comment.

Petrenko had his opening. "Why did you come here?"

Mykola didn't respond.

"You know, for the record, I don't for a second believe you flew all the way to Ukraine on a vacation or whatever and just happened to trip over this story. My gut tells me you tripped over this while on a very different journey."

Again Mykola didn't respond.

"I'm right, aren't I?"

"You've got your story. Let's leave it at that."

"Cool. But I just want you to understand that when I ask someone to translate for me, the translation should be verbatim. I may not speak Ukrainian very well but I understand a heck of a lot. So don't hesitate to correct me if I'm wrong, but when you were translating for that Maria woman, I'm fairly certain she said this baby-selling scheme, and I quote, 'started in 1993 shortly after you were adopted.' Am I wrong?"

"I'm not getting into this with you or anyone else. So forget it," Mykola said firmly.

"My thinking is that maybe soon after your parents were killed, you found out you were adopted and came here on a quest to find out what happened 20 years ago. Maybe you're looking for your real mother. Tell me I'm wrong and I'll leave it alone."

"Just mind your own business and leave it alone. You have your story," Mykola said tersely.

"Well, if you ever want to tell me the real story, I'm …" Before he could finish his sentence, Mykola turned and stormed out of the apartment.

"He is a good person," Alex said. "You must respect his privacy."

"You don't have to worry about that," Petrenko said.

CHAPTER THIRTY-THREE

"You think you might ever come back to Ukraine?" Alex asked as he pushed his way through the crowded departure level at the Kyiv International Airport.

"Right now, I'd have to say no. But you never can say never," Mykola replied.

"James Bond!"

Mykola laughed. The two stood silent at the gate to the security zone searching for a way to say farewell without too much fanfare or show of emotion. They had become close. For Mykola, Alex was not just his taxi driver. He had become a big brother, his protector and a loyal friend. Into the second week of Mykola's odyssey, Alex no longer asked to be paid after each sortie. He didn't ask for any money for the week Mykola hid out at his apartment.

"I'm really grateful to you Alex," Mykola began, trying not to sound maudlin. "I don't think I could have done this without your help. You stuck by me. You had my back. You're a true friend and I want to stay in touch with you."

"That we shall. That we shall!"

"This is for you," Mykola said, handing Alex an envelope. "Don't open it until I'm gone. Promise?"

When he felt its thickness, Alex gave Mykola an inquisitive glance. He didn't know it but there was enough cash in it to purchase a new vehicle, and then some.

"I promise," he said, giving Mykola a powerful bear hug.

Once through security, the young man couldn't muster the courage to look back and wave goodbye. He was choked up.

As the jet took off, Mykola didn't once look out the window. He pulled down the shade. He didn't want look down on Ukraine. The trip had been a nightmare and he desperately wanted to put it behind him. He closed his eyes and thought about Lesia. He missed her terribly. All he wished was to hold her in his arms, to kiss her and make love to her.

At the airport in Frankfurt, he had four hours to kill before making the connection to Toronto and then on to Edmonton. Relaxing in the Lufthansa Business Lounge, he happened to glance up at the departures screen. His eyes suddenly fixed on a flight to Milan. It was the city, he recalled, where Kateryna had been held as a sex slave. It was also the city where she became pregnant. Mykola's mind wandered to thoughts about the man she'd identified as his biological father. At the time, Antonio Rinaldo was studying to be a civil engineer. How bizarre, Mykola thought, that he too was studying to be a civil engineer. The screen was flashing 90 minutes before the departure to Milan. Mykola impulsively jumped up and parked himself at a computer terminal. He hit Google.it and typed in Antonio Rinaldo and civil engineer. With the click of a mouse, Google responded with a score of direct hits. A moment later, he was reading the profile of a man who fit the age and description of Kateryna's long lost love and possibly his biological father. After a more refined search, he had the business and home address of the man. There was even a photograph on Google images. Mykola branded it in his memory. He jotted down the information and made a dash for the Lufthansa customer service desk. It was an impetuous and daring move, and no doubt insane, but something deep inside was driving him to it. Five hours later, he was checking into the Westin Palace Hotel in downtown Milan.

Early the next day, Mykola hovered nervously in the darkened alcove of an apartment building in an upscale suburb outside Milan. His eyes were glued on the entrance to a chic, four-story condominium across the street. It was a warm and sun drenched Sunday morning. He figured the man would eventually emerge, and in a little less than an hour he did, accompanied by his wife and two young children, a six-year-old boy and a four-year-old girl. The family strolled past him, taking no notice. The man adoringly held his daughter's hand. It was obvious she was his pretty little princess. His wife chased happily after her precocious boy. Mykola waited until they were a block away before he felt it was safe to follow them. From behind an ancient olive tree at a nearby park, he watched as they played on swings, teeter-totters and slides. He smiled as the children giggled while tossing chunks of day old bread into a pond that was home to two magnificent white trumpeter swans and a quacking family of mallards. At one point, he slipped behind a massive weeping willow tree when he thought he noticed the man peering over in his direction. After 45 minutes, the couple scooped up the children and hiked up a knoll toward a local trattoria for Sunday brunch.

A moment later, Mykola discreetly parked himself at a table at the far end of the outdoor restaurant. He was sipping a large cappuccino when Antonio Rinaldo approached and stood over him.

"Excuse me but I cannot help but notice that perhaps you have been following me and my family. I am noticing that you are occasionally looking over at our table," he began.

"I'm sorry, but I don't speak Italian," Mykola said.

"I speak English. I was saying I could not help but notice that you have been following my family and I. Can I ask: what is your interest in us?"

Mykola was at a loss for words. He just looked up at the man, staring into his face examining it for clues. His eyes focused on the square chin with a dimple in the middle. He had the same chin, the same dimple.

"Do I know you? Somehow you seem familiar to me," the man asked.

"Are you Antonio Rinaldo?"

"That is who I am, and you are?" he replied with a look of suspicion.

"You don't know me. My name is Mykola Yashan."

"May I ask, what is your interest in me and my family?"

"I just wanted to see you."

"For whatever reason?"

Mykola was beginning to think the planned chance encounter was another one of his bad ideas. Nothing good could come of it. Then again, he had come all this way. He drew a deep breath and began speaking in a soft, measured tone: "A long time ago, you met a woman. Her name was Kateryna …"

Antonio stared incredulously at Mykola as his mind flashed back to a long faded memory. His face ashen, he grabbed at a chair and sat down. His wife glanced over curious as to what was going on.

"Are you okay?" Mykola asked.

"Si … si." Antonio looked into the young man's face. He instantly knew the answer but nonetheless asked the question. "You know Kateryna, how?"

"She was my mother."

"You say, was."

"She died recently."

If the man was shocked, he hid it well. "I am so sorry to hear about this. How did this come about?" he asked stoically.

"A week ago. She was murdered in a town in Ukraine."

Antonio shook his head and said calmly. "That poor woman. Life was truly unkind to her. May she rest in peace."

Mykola said nothing, but his eyes never left the man's face.

There was a moment of awkward silence. Antonio cleared his throat. "I have this feeling I know who you are."

Mykola did not reply.

"Long ago, I fell deeply in love with Kateryna. We were young. I wanted to take her away from a life that she never wanted, a life she was forced into."

"I only knew her for the shortest time," Mykola interrupted. "I met her twice. A couple of days before she was killed, I spent the entire afternoon with her. She told me a bit about you. How you tried to run away with her, and how her pimp beat you up. He told her he left you for dead." He paused. "She also told me that you got her pregnant."

Antonio gazed up at a misty cloud, his thoughts awash with memories of a tragic young love. Now out of the blue, two decades later, sitting in front of him was the fruit of that forbidden tryst, a face so familiar, he knew in his heart there was no doubt. The young man was his son.

Mykola looked down at the table and noticed Antonio's cell phone. "If you'd like, I took a couple of pictures of Kateryna in her flat. They're on my IPhone. Would you like to see them?"

"Si!" he said. Antonio's hands began to tremble as he held the IPhone and the first image of his long, lost Kateryna appeared on the small screen. She was as beautiful as he remembered but the spark of life had long faded from her eyes. She looked melancholy, and there was something else. She still looked ashamed.

"Cara mia," he whispered as he stared into her face. "She was so beautiful, so radiant," he whispered, his eyes glistening with tears.

Mykola took a long sip of coffee, not knowing what to say next.

"Look, I don't want to cause you any trouble," he finally offered, placing the cup on the table. "I just wanted to see you. I want you to know that I don't want anything from you and I don't expect anything from you."

Antonio placed the phone gently on the table and took in Mykola's face. "Well, I want something from you."

"What's that?"

"I want to know about you. Who you are? What you have become?" he said, looking over his shoulder at his wife. "Wait here, I'll be back in a moment."

He rushed over to his wife. She listened patiently while he spoke. Every so often, she turned and stared inquisitively at Mykola. Then she got up and quietly left with the children.

For more than five hours that passed in flash, the two men talked.

"Are you in university?" Antonio asked.

"Fourth year."

"What is your major?"

Mykola chuckled. "You won't believe this. Civil engineering!"

Antonio laughed. "That is truly bizarre."

Throughout the long and rambling conversation, one unasked question burned in Mykola's mind. After his third Americano coffee, he finally summoned the courage to ask it. Antonio could feel it coming.

"You knew Kateryna was a prostitute when you first saw her on the street. Were you a client?" Mykola asked hesitantly, making certain not to make his question sound like an accusation or condescending judgment.

Antonio's gaze dropped to the tabletop. His face reddened with embarrassment. "When I first saw her on the street, I didn't see a prostitute. I saw a terrified girl . . . a slave in the control of a violent Albanian gangster. All the girls on that street were under the control of Albanian pimps. It was sickening to witness such vile slavery."

"Why did you go there?"

"The first time I went there, it was with a few of my university friends. We had been drinking so we went to the area where the prostitutes walk to see the sideshow, to laugh and taunt the women. We circled and yelled these terrible insults out the windows. It was such a stupid thing to do. It was on our third pass that I saw Kateryna. She held her head down in shame," Antonio recalled, closing his eyes as if reliving the moment. "I felt so guilty for what I had called her."

"And then?" Mykola asked softly.

"Something I had never before felt entered in my heart. It was very strange. After we drove away, I could not stop thinking about Kateryna. Her face, her sad eyes kept haunting my dreams. I couldn't concentrate in school. It was as if she had taken control of my soul. A few nights later, I went back to the street. I must have circled several times. I saw Kateryna but I did not have the courage to stop. This was all new to me. I did not know or understand this world."

"Yet you went back to ..." Mykola paused trying to find the right words. "You paid to have sex with her."

"No, no. It was never like that. I swear to you. It was never like that. I paid to be with her. I wanted to be with her. The first number of times, I took her to a café. We just sat and had coffee and we talked. Well, mostly I talked. I just wanted to sit next to her. She didn't trust me at first and I could well understand why. Then slowly, maybe after the fourth or fifth time we met up, she opened up and told me what had happened to her, how she ended up on the street."

"But eventually you did pay to have sex with her," Mykola pressed.

"Again, it was not like that. I gave her money because I knew if she returned with nothing that bastard pimp would beat her. I fell in love with her. It was as if we were meant to be. When she disappeared, I nearly went crazy

"Did you know she was pregnant?"

"Yes. She told me. It is the reason we planned to run away together. Then that pimp caught onto our plan. One of his girls told him. He and his friends trapped me on the street and beat me unconscious. Two days later, I woke up in a hospital bed. I had a concussion. My nose and my jaw were broken. I had four broken ribs. I was a mess. It took me months to recover. After I was released from the hospital, I spent weeks searching the streets of Milan. I even went to Rome, Florence and Naples looking for her. I drove along the highways and truck stops where these pimps put their women. But she was gone. She had simply vanished. It took me years to move on with my life."

Mykola swirled the coffee grounds at the bottom of his cup. He was overcome with emotion. He had finally come full circle. The missing pieces of the puzzle that was his life had fallen into place. But the quest had taken a tremendous toll on his soul. He began to cry, a few tears at first, and then a flood. Antonio got up from his chair and put his arm around his son.

When he regained his composure, Mykola looked up at Antonio. "It's been quite the journey. I never knew it would be so difficult and that it would turn out to be so tragic. But at least I have the answers that I need to get on with my life."

"Please permit me to offer you a little advice. Don't let all that you have discovered on this journey turn you into a bitter and angry young man. Don't let it imprison your soul. Try to understand and accept it, as difficult as that will be, and then move on. You have the rest of your life in front of you. Make it a positive journey."

Mykola nodded. "I'm glad I got to meet you. I watched you with your wife and children. You seem to be a very kind, loving and caring man."

"I too am so glad to have met you. It would be good if you would stay in Milan for a while. Yes?"

"I'm actually heading back to Canada tomorrow morning."

"You do not have to leave so quickly. I would like it if you stayed a little longer."

"I'd like that very much, but I think I need a bit of time to absorb all that has happened. It's been an insane few weeks. But I'd like to come back maybe next summer and spend some time with you and your family, if that is alright with you."

"It is totally alright. I'm sure Emma and Carlo would love to meet their big brother. We will stay in touch. Yes?"

"For sure." With that Mykola got up and offered his hand. Antonio pushed it away and hugged his son.

"Can I ask one favor?" Mykola asked.

"Of course. What is it?"

"Can I take a photo of you and me?"

"Sure, but I too must have a copy."

Antonio put his arm around Mykola. They both smiled as Mykola fired off three selfies at arm's length in rapid succession. "I do that all the time just in case one of us had our eyes closed," he explained.

"That is so funny. I do it as well. It drives my wife crazy," Antonio added with a laugh.

The two exchanged email addresses before Mykola hailed a taxi and headed for his hotel. As he was about to get out of the vehicle, something came to him.

"Driver, do you happen to know the location of a convent called the Sisters of the Consolata Order?"

"Si. It is maybe 10 minutes north of this place."

"Could you take me there?"

"Si."

The convent was an imposing, grey stone structure across from a magnificent 19th century cathedral. At the main entrance: two stately, wooden doors painted dark brown were bolted shut. In a nook just above and to one side was a high security camera. As he rang the bell, Mykola made certain to look directly into the lens. A moment later, a young nun appeared at the door.

"How may I help you?" she asked holding the heavily chained door slightly ajar.

"Good afternoon. I hope I'm not intruding but I was wondering if Sister Eugenia Benedicta was here. I would like to meet her. I need to talk to her about something."

"Sister Eugenia is in chapel. Do you have an appointment?"

"No, but if you could, please tell her that I am the son of Kateryna Chumak, maybe she might remember her."

The nun nodded. "Wait here. I will see if she will meet with you."

A few minutes later the chain rattled and the door opened. "Please come in," the nun said.

She led Mykola to a small library filled with musty, religious tomes and a wall adorned with dozens of framed images of women saints surrounding a centuries old icon of the Blessed Virgin Mary. Sister Eugenia, looking frail with old age, sat hunched over on a wooden chair. Seeing her, Mykola couldn't help but feel he was in the presence of an amazing and humble human being.

"It is an honor to meet you," she said, offering an outstretched hand.

"The honor is mine. I wanted to meet you after what you did for Kateryna."

"You informed Sister Magdalena that you are Kateryna's son," she said.

"Yes."

"Yet you do not call her mother?" the nun asked, looking deep into the young man's eyes.

The question caught him completely off guard, and as he looked at the nun's gentle face, he was suddenly hit with the realization that the time had come to acknowledge and accept the reality that Kateryna was his mother.

"I wanted to thank you for what you had done for my mother," he said softly.

"How is Kateryna?"

"I am sad to say that a week ago she was murdered."

"May God have mercy on her," Sister Eugenia said clutching the crucifix on her rosaries! "She was such a warm and loving young woman. How did this occur?"

"It happened a few days after I found her. I can't help but feel my actions had something to do with it."

Mykola went on to explain the circumstances of his adoption, how he came to find Kateryna, and the threats he'd made to expose the people who stole him from his birth mother. Sister Eugenia listened with her eyes closed, every so often nodding her head.

"When we finally met, Kateryna ... I mean my mother ... told me about what had happened to her. Well, I'm sure not everything. She told me about you and how you came to her rescue. Her face lit up when she talked about you. It was the only time in our conversation that she lit up. She called you her miracle. That's why I came here. I wanted to meet you."

Sister Eugenia opened her eyes and gently ran her fingers along her crystal rosaries. "Kateryna led me to my true mission in life. Her cries for help brought me to my calling. In the church, as I was praying before the Blessed Virgin Mary, all I could hear were the cries of this sad and frightened young woman. Her cries tore into my soul. I can remember her words, each one like a bomb exploding in the church, and I asked myself, what is it that I have been put here for? What is my mission? Is it to kneel before the sacred image of the Blessed Virgin Mary and pray? Kateryna kept pleading for someone to help her and I kept praying. Then like a miracle the message came to me. I felt the Gospel message of hope and liberation brought to us by Christ our savior pour into my soul. At that very moment I knew what I had to do. What we all must do. I discovered my true mission. It is to help this woman, and all women like her, those who have been forced into this contemptible world of sexual exploitation. It is to free them from the shackles of slavery."

Sister Eugenia said she made Kateryna's cry her own: a cry for help but also for the denunciation and condemnation of the abusers and the users of enslaved women. Her mission became the back streets and alleyways of Italian cities, night and day, in defense of women forced into sexual bondage: mere prostitutes to those who used and abused them; victims and slaves to those who knew the tragic stories of deception, terror, submission and exploitation.

Sister Eugenia and a tiny band of nuns became known as the Sisters of the Night, venturing out into the seedy side streets of Milan to rescue prostituted women who desperately wanted out of the flesh trade. They walked fearlessly into the shadow of darkness to talk with the young women, never passing judgment. They simply offered them an escape, a sanctuary of tranquility and hope where they could recover and regain their dignity. Over the next two decades, the work of the nuns spread to convents around the globe and by 2012, more than 285 nuns in scores of cities worldwide had taken up the call.

Mykola looked at the nun and saw a woman of unrelenting determination, a woman with a welcoming and merciful heart. He wondered what families out on an evening stroll must have thought watching this tiny nun walking at the side of Kateryna, a prostitute.

"I found my true vocation, my calling," Sister Eugenia continued. "It was a difficult test at first. It challenged me as a person and as a nun. I questioned my life, my vocation and my missionary motives. I had no idea where to begin, how to approach these women. Their cries and suffering told me something; that I might be the instrument of a new mission, a new frontier which had nothing to do with the classic coordinates of the missionary life of nuns, but had everything to do with the defense of human dignity and, above all, belittled, trampled, humiliated and exploited dignity. Christ put the human person with his decency at the very center. This is the foundation of our work and our service."

Sister Eugenia paused and looked at Mykola. She could see the innocence of youth in his eyes. She could sense he had no understanding, no concept of the vicious world millions of prostituted young women around the globe were forced to suffer daily. He was a lamb in a dangerous and wicked wilderness.

"There are terrible areas of darkness, invisible only to those who do not want to see. The church, all Christians, are called to do something because silence and indifference results in forms of complicity."

Those last words resonated loudly in Mykola's ears, striking an ominous chord. He thought about the priest in Stornovitzi. Father Zenon's silence and indifference no doubt led to the sexual enslavement of scores of young women. He had the power and the opportunity to shut down his sister's despicable operation when he became aware of what she was doing. Yet he chose to do nothing. And when faced with the brutal consequences, he turned his back on the victim. Like all the villagers and her family, he had shunned Kateryna. He did not inform the authorities. He did not stand at the pulpit and denounce his sister. He did not exhort his followers to have compassion for Kateryna and open their hearts to her. While officiating at her funeral service he didn't show the slightest sign of remorse or caring for the woman. His sermon was rote. It was by the book.

Mykola resolved that on his return to Edmonton, he would break his word to the priest and expose the holy hypocrite to the leaders of his diocese as well as out him publicly on the Internet. He was no man of God. He was an instrument of indifference and deserved to be defrocked.

Sensing Mykola was deeply troubled and ashamed that his mother had been involved in the flesh trade, Sister Eugenia reached out to ease his battered spirit.

"It is important for you to understand that Kateryna was not a prostitute. Your mother was a *prostituted woman*," she stressed. "Never forget that. This word prostitute is filled with prejudice and debasement. It is one of contempt and condemnation. It is one of scorn. Kateryna was forced into prostitution. It was a life she never wanted. I pray that when you think of your mother, you think of her with dignity and respect. Think of her with love in your heart."

"I will. I promise, and thank you Sister Eugenia. I am so glad we met," Mykola said. As he gazed at the elderly nun, he could feel a touch of faith begin to trickle back into his soul.

CHAPTER THIRTY-FOUR

After clearing customs and immigration in Toronto, Mykola headed to the domestic end of the cavernous airport terminal for his connection to Edmonton. On the final leg of the long flight, his thoughts focused on how he would explain all that had happened. He wondered how Lesia, Sonia and Orest would react. He agonized over whether to leave out the fact that his birth mother was a prostituted woman, and simply concoct a story that she was unwed and impoverished, and was forced to give him up because she could not afford to care for a baby. It was a clear and easy way to avoid a complicated and personally embarrassing explanation. During the four-hour flight, he tossed around several scenarios, all a combination of half-truths and outright fiction. Every one of them caused him grief. He hated being dishonest. It wasn't part of his upbringing. His mother Iryna had infused in him a strong moral code and in the short time since his parent's death, he'd committed a lifetime of lies. He was tired of it. As the plane touched down on the runway of the Edmonton International Airport, Mykola decided to be honest. It was the right thing to do. He would reveal all. Well, almost.

Lesia barreled up the arrivals ramp as Mykola emerged from the baggage area. She leapt into his arms and began to cry uncontrollably.

"Hey, what's this all about?" Mykola asked, wiping away her tears.

"I was afraid for you. I kept thinking something bad would happen to you."

"Yeah, you were afraid some young, hot Ukrainian chick would steal me away from you."

Lesia punched him affectionately on the shoulder. "Well, you know those Ukrainian women! Always on the prowl for a foreign husband!"

"But you know I'm in love with you. I have been for as long as I can remember and always will be." He leaned in to kiss her.

Later at Lesia's home, she snuggled beside him on the couch. Everyone was eager to hear about his trip. Sonia was tense, knowing the true purpose behind her godson's journey. Mykola could sense her unease.

"I owe you all an explanation," he began slowly. "What I'm going to tell you at times is going to be difficult to hear. Teta knows some of the story. She knows the real reason I went to Ukraine."

Lesia and Orest looked quizzically at Sonia. She sat quietly, fraught with anticipation.

"What happened there," Mykola paused, closing his eyes as he gathered his thoughts, "is the stuff of nightmares."

Orest moved to the edge of his seat. Lesia squeeze Mykola's hand.

"But let me begin with an amusing tidbit. You all know how much I love pasta." Mykola paused. "Well, turns out, I'm half Italian."

No one laughed. Orest and Lesia stared at Mykola in silence as they tried to process what he had just revealed.

"And there is something more. I have two half-sisters and a half-brother."

CHAPTER THIRTY-FIVE

In the week leading up to the broadcast of the full hour, investigative documentary, CTN - the Canadian Television Network - aired a series of thirty second promos showing clips of Natalka Matlinsky receiving her award from the President of Ukraine, orphan babies crying in their cribs, Brenda Cooper looking horrified as she put her hand up in a futile attempt to cover the camera lens, and a closing shot of Matlinsky screaming incoherently at Mike Petrenko as she stormed out of her office.

The background music was ominous and the voice over commentary gripping: "Orphan babies for sale. But, are they really orphans? Not satisfied with the look of these adorable newborns at $30,000 a pop? Maybe you would prefer a designer baby – a blond, blue-eyed little angel for a mere $100,000 U.S. CTN's senior investigative reporter Mike Petrenko confronts a renowned baby broker in Los Angeles and the director of an orphanage who runs a multi-million dollar baby mill in the Ukrainian city of Lviv."

Not surprisingly, the promos triggered immediate and fervent condemnation from the Ukrainian Embassy in Ottawa with the ambassador heading over to Canada's Department of Foreign Affairs with an official letter of protest. He then flew to Toronto to meet with the show's executive producer and CTN's president of news, charging that the documentary, which had yet to air, was filled with lies, distortions, innuendo and propaganda. He warned that if broadcast, the network would face a costly libel lawsuit. The executive producer politely thanked him for the visit and escorted him to his waiting stretch limo.

As excited as a kid on Christmas Eve, Petrenko called Mykola to give him a heads up. "We're on tonight at 7 p.m. Tweet everyone you know!"

"I'm already tweeting and I'll be watching."

That Sunday evening, the documentary, called: 'The Baby Mill," was broadcast to a huge viewing audience. Within minutes, the show's email box,

Twitter and Facebook accounts was deluged by viewers expressing outrage and condemnation that anyone would use newborns for greed and profit.

The next day, Petrenko's investigative report was picked up by dozens of news media outlets on both sides of the Atlantic. In Kyiv, a legion of journalists scurried to the steps of the Verkhovna Rada to get the President's reaction to the allegations contained in the documentary. In Lviv, a dozen reporters besieged Orphanage 41 demanding to speak to the director, but she wasn't there, neither was Maria. Two days earlier, Natalka Matlinsky had boarded a plane for Frankfurt. Her immediate whereabouts was unknown. Dr. Ihor Kowalchuk retreated to his cottage in the Carpathian Mountains, and Vitaly Assimovich, the deputy minister of Children and Families, was nowhere to be found. The only one in authority forced to field a stream of hostile questions and accusations hurled by opposition members in the Verkhovna Rada, was Ukraine's beleaguered president, Viktor Yurkovich. His backroom boys were in major spin control, claiming that the Canadian documentary was a vicious conspiracy mounted by disgruntled opposition forces to discredit the nation's leader. It didn't wash. Everyone knew the President's hands were dirty. His every pore oozed sleaze.

Chief of staff Sergei Melekov stayed clear of the spin. He had vengeance on his mind. Holed up in his office, he was fuming over the revelation that Matlinsky had kept the designer baby scheme a secret while pocketing a small fortune of which a good chunk should have been earmarked for his boss. Melekov unleashed his henchmen with orders to hunt down the director and bring her in. He swore he would make her pay dearly for the deception.

In the midst of the mayhem, the President was particularly enraged by the coverage of several Ukrainian television news outlets that repeatedly replayed the Order of Merit award ceremony, capturing and freeze-framing the very moment he was whispering in Matlinsky's ear. That same shot made the front pages of most major Ukrainian newspapers across the country. Now, with the "infamous whisper" broadcast around the globe, the media hounds were attempting to link him directly to the baby mill scam. The President's handlers painstakingly prepped him for the impending media assault. He was to stick to the cover story he'd been fed and was reminded not to stray, as he often did, from the mantra.

On the steps outside the Ukrainian Parliament, Yurkovich was swarmed by pack of media hounds out for blood. Standing stiff in front of a bank of television cameras and microphones, the President disavowed all knowledge of the baby selling scheme. Shrugging his shoulders, he offered no explanation for the initials 'V.Y.' found in Matlinsky's ledger. He repeatedly declared

that he never *personally* accepted money from the director of Orphanage
41. Then in a patently, politically motivated move, he vowed to tighten up
Ukraine's adoption laws, adding that for the foreseeable future all adoptions
by foreigners would be suspended.

Asked about Matlinsky's Order of Merit, Yurkovich danced a fine line.
He was fully aware that his chief of staff had warned the woman of the dire
consequences of betraying the President. But he wasn't a fool. He also knew
that, if pushed into a corner, she might just go on the offensive.

Glancing down at his talking points, the President replied: "If the allegations are proven in a court of law and director Matlinsky is found guilty, she
will be stripped of the award. However, at this moment, what we have before
us are the wild and unsubstantiated accusations of a Canadian reporter who,
I am told by my officials, has grossly distorted the facts. His documentary is
filled with inaccuracies and innuendos."

He then decided to go off script and add a touch of Yurkovich humor. "In
fact, I think the only thing this reporter got correct in his entire documentary was the name of the city of Lviv."

The President laughed alone. Every journalist in the room was aware of
Mike Petrenko's reputation as a dogged investigative journalist. Yurkovich
was clearly on spin cycle.

Halfway around the globe, a score of reporters was camped outside the
L.A. office tower where Brenda Cooper had hung her shingle. She, too, had
seemingly vanished into thin air. But she didn't get far. The day after the
documentary aired in Canada, a search warrant was issued for her home
and office. FBI agents carted away boxes of dog-eared files, and computer
equipment. That evening, Cooper was arrested while attempting to board
a flight at O'Hare International Airport in Chicago bound for London. The
following day, she was released on a $1-million bond and ordered to sur-
render her passport. A week later, the lawyer was charged with numerous
counts of wire fraud conspiracy.

Two months after the broadcast, Interpol caught up with Natalka
Matlinsky in Paris where she was arrested and deported to Ukraine. On
her arrival at Kyiv's international airport, she was met on the tarmac by two
burly men in black and taken to a secluded location to face the President's
chief of staff. Pacing the room like a madman, Sergei Melekov looked like
he was about to snap. His demands were non-negotiable. He advised her
in clear-cut terms to accept them. She was ordered to transfer $1.2-million
from her Swiss bank account to a numbered account in Lichtenstein. It was
the amount Melekov had estimated was the President's cut on the designer
baby scheme with a little interest thrown in. He also informed Matlinsky

that she would be stripped of her Order of Merit and that she would have to face charges of corruption. She would say nothing in court, but simply plead guilty to all charges. There would be no public airing of the facts of the case. She would be summarily sentenced to two years, which would be served in a comfortable, out of the way retreat outside Odessa on the Black Sea . It was all part of a deal to be worked out by the President's office and the judge. Once all the attention had died down, Melekov assured Matlinsky that she would be quietly released after serving two or three months at the most.

Matlinsky nodded her agreement.

Then Melekov lost it, his face, red with rage and inches from Matlinsky's wide fearful eyes. "You betrayed us! You lied to me. You stole from me! Didn't you?" he yelled, grabbing her by the hair.

Matlinsky gasped and replied: "Yes," in a terrified whimper.

Melekov threw her to the floor and spat on her. He kicked her repeatedly in the abdomen and chest with his steel-toed boots. His bodyguards, standing watch at the back of the room, didn't intervene. They just smirked.

"I warn you: if you ever link any aspect of what has gone on here today to me or the President's office . . . if you so much as breathe a word of this meeting to anyone, I will personally hunt you down and destroy you. There will be no prison dacha at the end of that road. You will rot in an unmarked grave. Do I make myself clear?"

Cowering in the fetal position, Matlinsky began to wail. "I will say nothing. I swear it."

Six weeks after his return, Mykola boarded a flight to L.A. He had a promise to keep. After renting a car at the airport, he drove first to Santa Barbara. His second stop was San Diego. Expecting a cool reception, he was surprised at the openness and warmth of the two families. There was an outpouring of tears and elation when both sets of parents were told that their adopted daughters came into the world as an identical set. They had no idea.

Mykola recounted his meeting with Halya Luciuk and her desire to know that the children were healthy, well cared for and loved. It was obvious that both sets of parents were well off, and absolutely adored and spoiled the girls. What Mykola found surprising was that they spoke openly and candidly about the adoptions. It was no secret, nothing to keep hidden under a rug. What shocked them was learning the true circumstances behind the birth of the girls. Brenda Cooper had informed both couples that the biological mother had died from complications during the delivery. The couples were acutely aware of the baby broker's arrest and conviction, having read about it in the newspapers and having been visited by FBI agents. For a while, they were worried sick they might be ordered to surrender the girls, but were later informed this would not happen. They were also more than willing to connect with Halya and send her photographs of the children. Each family added that when the girls were old enough, they would be told about their biological mother and allowed to decide for themselves if they wanted to contact her. The families immediately got in touch which each other by email and Skype. After watching their little girls stare wide-eyed at mirror images of each other on the screen, they couldn't wait to reunite them.

Less than three months after her arrest, Brenda Cooper's high priced legal team brokered a plea bargain. She was sentenced to six months in a federal prison, followed by nine months of house arrest. She was also ordered to pay a $250,000 fine and was disbarred from practicing law.

That same week, the disgraced director of Orphanage 41 pleaded guilty to charges of misuse of power, bribery and fraud. With that muted plea, the details of her reprehensible operation would remain out of the public eye, as would any links to the upper echelons of power in Ukraine. Justice had been bought. Matlinsky alone took the fall, and for that, she was treated with silk gloves. She was immediately sentenced to two years in prison and fined a paltry $5,000. The sham trial was over in less than a half hour.

Matlinsky was ushered out a side door and whisked off in a black SUV to serve her time at what was known in certain circles as the Hotel Hilton – the prison for the privileged outside Odessa. Melekov, who had been sitting in the judge's chambers throughout the proceeding, left unseen through a back door.

"I can't believe it!" Mykola vented into the phone when Petrenko told him the news. "Two years for all that? And a $5,000 fine? Her shoe collection is worth than that! What the hell is wrong with that country? Is justice really so blind? This is a colossal joke!"

Mike Petrenko held the phone away from his ear until Mykola calmed down. He shared Mykola's sentiments. There was no doubt in his mind that Viktor Yurkovich had dispatched his head puppeteer to the chief prosecutor's office and judge's chamber to pull the strings.

"Mykola … Mykola! Listen to me," Petrenko shouted into the phone. "You know Ukraine feeds on corruption. What did you expect? I've seen this happen so many times – in so many countries – even *here* in good old

Canada. Look what those slime bucket thieves got away with in the Senate. They suck at the public trough, commit fraud and get exposed. You think you've nailed the crooks, taken them down, and they end up getting a slap on the wrist. They laugh and you retreat into the sunset one pissed off dude. It happens everywhere. But you can't allow yourself to focus on that. All it ends up doing is bringing you down. You should be proud of what you accomplished. You broke this baby selling scandal wide open and shut down one heck of a sleazy operation."

"It still pisses me off."

"I hate to tell you this, but don't be surprised if after all this, Matlinsky gets out in a few months."

"What do you mean a few months?"

"I'd bet my month's rent that once the attention has died down, Matlinsky will be quietly released in two or three months tops. I'm sure it's all part of the backroom deal. That woman knows too much, and there's no doubt in my mind that she's probably got all kinds of incriminating documents tucked away in a safe place to sink her so-called friends at the top in case things go sideways. A woman like that always has an insurance policy. And all the President's lackeys know it."

Mykola could not believe what he was hearing. "So that's it. She pleads guilty and wins."

"No!" Petrenko was emphatic. "She lost. We won. She's done like burned toast. We exposed her and shut her down."

"But when she gets out she'll still be set for life with all the money she's socked away."

"Yeah, but look at her. She's now a social pariah. No one will want to be seen with her. For a woman like that, that's a fate worse than death. The best thing for you now is to just let it go. It's over. Try to move on."

CHAPTER THIRTY-SIX

But Mykola couldn't move on. He couldn't let it go. Instead, he indulged his anger. Nursed it like a hangover as he desperately tried to fight off the relentless guilt that washed over him like giant, ocean swells battering a capsized boat. With every day, he felt himself sinking lower and lower. A sound sleep was impossible. He managed one or two hours a night, max. When he finally dozed off, his mind was attacked by an eerie canvas of macabre images: Natalka Matlinsky, a devious grin on her malevolent face; Kateryna, her lifeless body shrouded in a black tarpaulin on the street outside her apartment; his father Stepan, a mocking sneer on his lips and cold loathing in his eyes; his mother Iryna lying dead in her white casket. Mykola would wake up drenched in a hot sweat. His brain was in constant overdrive; his conscience screaming that Kateryna was murdered because he couldn't leave well enough alone. His ego had propelled him to believe he was invincible, strong enough to withstand whatever Matlinsky could throw his way. He never once considered Kateryna's safety in this Shakespearean tragedy that had become his life.

How could he have been so stupid, so blind? Kateryna's safety should have been his penultimate priority. Her very existence perched on the edge of a deadly abyss. He should have recognized the danger he was bringing to her door in his vain pursuit of the woman who had stolen him from her. Exposing Matlinsky had become his goal, his obsession, fuelled by an implacable desire to come out on top. She was the bad. He was the good. Good had to triumph over evil. It had seemed as simple as that; so crisply black and white.

Now, through the unforgiving lens of hindsight, under the glaring spotlight of his battered conscience, his black and white palate melded into shades of gray. It wasn't about doing the right thing. The right thing would have led him down a completely different path, one that would never have ended so violently. He had allowed himself to be seduced by the anger that had pulsed through his veins, and he had indulged his darker side, which drove him to strike back . . . to seek revenge. Like anyone wronged by what seemed a supremely unjust fate, he wanted to give Matlinsky – that despicable *shell* of a woman – what she truly deserved. And now, in the tragic aftermath, he realized that in his fight for so-called justice, he had allowed himself to become blinded to the risks that were clearly staring him in the face.

In pursuing his reckless boxing match with Matlinsky, poisoned by visions of a triumphant knockout, he had failed to notice that he had dragged another person so carelessly – so perilously – into the ring. It was only when he saw her body laid out on the gurney that the full impact of his actions hit him. In his relentless quest to be the champ, he had gotten Kateryna killed.

A loud, insistent pounding snapped Mykola from a deep sleep. As he came to, he realized it was coming from somewhere in the house. Rubbing his eyes, he looked at the clock on his bedside table. It was three in the afternoon. He had finally slept, *really* slept, or more to the point, passed out from sheer exhaustion. He had been out cold for fifteen hours. No dreams. No nightmares. No shadows of the past.

Disoriented, he shook his head and realized the pounding was coming from the front of the house. Stumbling towards the door, he yanked it open, throwing up his arm to block the sunlight.

"Mykola! Are you alright? What in the world has happened to you? Why aren't you answering our calls?"

His godmother didn't wait for him to answer. She swept by him and planted herself in the foyer. As he closed the door behind her, he could feel her watchful gaze take him in from head to toe. He was quite a sight. He hadn't showered in six days or had a proper meal. His face looked sallow. But it was his eyes that shocked her. She saw the torment and swiftly pulled him into her arms.

"Mykola," she whispered softly. "Whatever it is, you'll be okay."

He buried his head in her shoulder.

"You have got to stop shutting us out. You can't deal with whatever is troubling you alone. You need help and we're here to support you. You have got to stop torturing yourself."

They stood for a moment, neither daring to move. Then Mykola pulled away, straightened himself up, and walked past her into the kitchen.

"I'm ok," he called out. "It's just been a rough few months."

Sonia followed him and sat down at the kitchen table. He could tell she wasn't buying it. He poured them each a tall glass of iced tea, then plopped down on the chair across from her.

"I'm tired. That's all. Ukraine was an insane whirlwind. And I've been having a little trouble sleeping. But it's nothing to worry about" he said, averting her eyes.

"Mykola," she said in a calm voice. "I know you. *Really* know you. I haven't seen you like this … ever. Look at you. You're a mess."

Mykola shrugged and directed his gaze out the back window, trying to focus on the branches of the maple tree in the yard swaying in the breeze.

"You've skipped school."

"A day or two."

"Lesia tells me three weeks."

"I've lost track."

Sonia said nothing more, waiting for Mykola to look directly at her. After several minutes, he finally drew the courage to face his godmother.

"What about Lesia?" she continued. "She's worried sick over you. You haven't answered her calls, her texts. She's starting to believe you two are through."

"No, Teta. That's not it at all. Tell her I'm okay . . . we're okay. I just need some time."

"No, *you* tell her. She needs to hear from you. And I have to tell you that Orest and I don't like seeing her torn up over you like this."

He looked up, surprised at the firmness in her voice, and realized that she was now speaking as a concerned mother.

"I can't tell you what to do, Mykola. You need to take responsibility for yourself. But I can tell you, as Lesia's mother, that if you don't reach out to her, you'll lose her." Her voice trailed off, and he could see tears starting to well in her eyes. "Is that what you want?"

He shook his head.

"Whatever it is that's eating at you, you have to get it off your chest. You have to talk about it, if not with me or Lesia, then maybe with a therapist."

"I don't need a therapist."

"Spoken like a man in denial."

As she reached out to take his hand, Mykola felt the brick wall he had built up since his return from Ukraine come crumbling down. He fell to the kitchen floor and dissolved into tears. He couldn't hold them back.

Sonia knelt down beside him. "What happened, Mykola? What really happened in Ukraine?"

"It's my fault," he began in a hoarse whisper. "She's dead because of me. I had her killed."

The look on Sonia's face turned to one of panic. "What do you mean you had her killed? What are you talking about?"

"It's not what it sounds like. I didn't kill anyone. But it's because of me that she's dead."

Sonia was confused. "What do you mean?"

"Kateryna! She'd be alive if I had just left well enough alone."

For the next three hours, Mykola recounted in finite detail what had really happened in Ukraine. He poured out his soul until there was nothing more to say.

Sonia looked at him tenderly. "Mykola. I love you. I've always cared for you the way I would a son. So I hope you'll take my words for what they're worth. You never meant your birth mother any harm. Nor are you responsible for her death."

Mykola squeezed his eyes shut. "Yes I am."

"You tried to help her. You know it, and she knew it. There was no predicting how it would all turn out."

"But Matlinsky would never have gone after her if it hadn't been for me."

"Mykola, stop it!" She shook him by the shoulders. "You need to stop this. Now! If you don't, you will dig yourself deeper and deeper into depression, and it will destroy you. You need to be stronger than that. You are stronger than that."

It was true. He had allowed himself to tumble so deep into the muck of misery that he had lost sight of the way out.

"You need to forgive yourself," his godmother added. "And then, you need to find the strength to move on."

"Move on how? I can't help feeling that all the pain and suffering Kateryna went through in her life, the humiliation ... it was all for nothing."

"Then make something of it."

"How?"

"I don't know," Sonia replied, watching him closely. "But I know it has to come from you. You've had quite a journey, one that has marked you for life. It has changed you. Learn from it. Take lessons from it. Find a way to honour Kateryna's life. Find a way to preserve her memory and make all that happened to her mean something."

"How do I do that?" Mykola asked, desperate for some guidance. His mind was blank.

Sonia smiled at him. "You'll find a way. Open your heart. It will speak to you. But first you have to let go of the blame. You will never move forward if your feet are stuck in the misery of the past."

Mykola knew she was right, and for the first time since his return from Ukraine, he felt as though a heavy weight was being lifted from his shoulders.

"I'll try," he promised. But he knew it would be difficult, particularly since the guilt he suffered went hand in glove with his anger. Sonia picked up on it.

"Is there anything else?"

Mykola walked past her into the living room and settled down on the couch. His godmother followed him.

"It's Matlinsky," he said finally. "She got away with it all. She was arrested, pleaded guilty and got what amounts to a slap on the wrist. She'll be out of prison in a few months. Everyone else involved in the selling of orphan babies got off."

"What you did was incredible," Sonia countered. "And you did it with hard work, and at risk to your life. That reporter, Mike Petrenko, wrote about you in an online Web article for CTN. He gave you full credit for exposing that despicable baby trade. Everyone in the community knows what you did, and they're all very proud of you."

"Yeah. They think I'm a regular chip off the old block."

"No, Mykola. You're not like your father. Not like him at all."

Sonia hesitated mulling over whether to say more. "You probably don't realize this," she continued, "but what you've managed to accomplish actually outweighs what your father did."

Mykola laughed. "That's not even remotely possible! Just look at Blind Defiance. Tato's legacy! What I did doesn't even close."

Sonia drew a deep breath, exhaled slowly and glanced up at a photograph of Iryna on the mantel. It was as if she was looking for a sign.

"I'm going to tell you something your mother told me in the strictest confidence but given the circumstances, I think she would want you to know."

Mykola steeled himself, praying he wasn't about to be hit by yet another disquieting family secret.

"You worked hard to get to the bottom of what was going on at that orphanage. You took risks, *real* risks, and it could have cost you your life. But that didn't stop you. You were tenacious, and you kept at it until you got all the answers. Mykola, what you accomplished is truly remarkable. It is something you should be proud of."

Sonia paused momentarily, watching her godson carefully. "Your father … he didn't do any of that."

Mykola looked up. "What do you mean?"

"Exactly that. He *paid* for his discovery. He didn't uncover it or take any risks like you did."

Mykola shifted to the edge of the sofa. "Teta, that doesn't make sense. Paid what? Paid how?"

"Your father bought all those files from a retired NKVD agent in Kyiv. He didn't dig for them. He didn't spend years combing through archives. In fact, he did very little independent research. Your father became famous, that's true, and he was enormously respected. But his fame and fortune came from a check book."

Mykola was stunned. "That can't be."

"It is. The agent who sold him the documents could have sold them to anyone. To the highest bidder, had he wanted or maybe he did. Your father happened to be in the right place at the right time with the right amount of U.S. dollars in his bank account."

"Who else knows about this?" Mykola asked, feeling somewhat light-headed by the revelation.

"Only your mother, me, and now you. Even Orest doesn't know. Your father would have had a coronary had anyone ever found out."

"I bet," Mykola exclaimed, wondering how the famed professor would have reacted *had* anyone ever found out and raised it during one of his lectures. He would have gone ballistic. His reputation was everything to him. This was his dirty little secret and there was no doubt in Mykola's mind that his father shredded all traces of the bank withdrawal records. In fact, it was the only documents the professor had ever destroyed.

Mykola's eyes wandered over to the mantel, fixing on the last photograph taken of him with his mother. It was at his high school graduation. She was beaming, looking proudly at her son in his burgundy cap and gown.

"She loved you more than anything in the world. You were her world," Sonia said softly. "You have to believe she would have never done anything to hurt you. Iryna never knew about Kateryna. Had she known, there is no doubt in my mind that she would have done something to help her. Kateryna's life was a tragedy, and I feel in my heart that she truly loved you. She got to see her son and see the wonderful and caring young man you turned out to be. You have to believe that and now you have to find a way to make both your mothers proud."

She gave his hand a gentle squeeze. "I want you to think about what we've talked about and tomorrow I want you over at the house for dinner. Is that understood?"

"Yes, teta. It's understood."

That night, Mykola tumbled into yet another dream-troubled sleep. And once again his father appeared. He was as intimidating in death as he had been in real life. A menacing scowl on his face, his unspoken message was clear: *Do not dare dishonor my name. Do not dare impugn my reputation. Do not dare reveal what you now know.* Then something very strange occurred. From nowhere, Kateryna and Iryna appeared. They were composed, a look of firm resolve on their faces. The professor tried to drive them away, but the two women fought back and began to swirl around him, spinning faster and faster. Then, in a blinding flash of black, Stepan Yashan vanished. At that moment, Mykola realized that the professor would never return to torment him any longer. Holding hands, the two mothers turned and smiled lovingly at their son. He could feel their love warm his soul, but most of all he could feel Kateryna's forgiveness. They held his gaze for a moment, and nodded gently. Mykola wanted the moment to last forever. In prayer, he asked them to stay. Then slowly, they began to retreat.

Don't go! Not yet! He pleaded. *I need you. Both of you!* His pleas were for naught. He watched helpless as they faded into the grayish blue mist. Suddenly, his mind was engulfed by a vision of the Carpathia – the mountains in western Ukraine, so lush and green ... so tranquil and inviting.

Mykola awoke with a start. For the first time in months, he felt an inner calm. More importantly, he had his answer. He knew what he needed to do.

CHAPTER THIRTY-SEVEN

Mykola paced nervously in his mother's study going over and over in his head what he wanted to say. Lesia sat quietly on the sofa watching him. She was worried and trying not to show it. She knew Mykola was stepping out on a limb. She was praying it wouldn't snap.

Sonia was in the living room greeting the guests as they arrived for the 2 p.m. Sunday meeting. Coffee, tea and an assortment of homemade pastries were set out on the antique oak desk in the professor's office. It was the only piece of furniture in the room. Every single vestige of the late, great Dr. Yashan had been removed and dispatched to the Shevchenko Foundation.

"There's a buzz out there. I bet they're all wondering about the two posters," Lesia said.

Mykola didn't hear a word. He was staring out at the back garden. Large clusters of tall daisies were swaying in the summer breeze. He remembered his mother's smile when they came into bloom. It was her favorite flower.

"What was that?" he asked.

"The posters! I bet all the women are wondering about them."

"Well, they'll get the answer soon enough."

"Are you okay?"

"I don't know. I'm really nervous," he said, wiping his palms on his pants.

"Just keep in mind why you're doing this. Speak from your heart and you'll be fine."

There was a rap on the door and a moment later, Orest poked his head inside. "How are you doing?"

"I'm all knots," Mykola said.

"But they're good knots," Lesia offered with a smile.

"It looks like everyone is here. I figure about 30 people, all women. We're the only guys," Orest said with a wink.

Lesia grabbed Mykola's hand as he made his way to the living room. "I want you to know that what you're doing takes a lot of courage. I'm very proud of you. Your mothers would have been proud of you."

As he entered the room, the chatter immediately ceased. All eyes were riveted on Mykola as he stopped and gazed adoringly at the poster blow up of Iryna perched on a chrome easel. Across the top was one word: Mama. He then looked over at the second poster resting on an easel beside it and said a short prayer. It was a blow up photograph of Kateryna. Across the top was the caption: Mother.

Sonia gave her godson a warm hug and turned to address the gathering.

"Iryna was a good friend to us all. She worked with each and every one of you on so many, many projects in the community. She always gave unselfishly of herself. That was the kind of person she was, and now her son wants to carry on her good works. What he is about to tell you will no doubt shock many of you. But I want you to hear him out. I want you all to keep an open mind and more importantly, an open heart. Mykola!"

His mouth dry with apprehension, Mykola nervously cleared his throat and began. "I've asked you here for two reasons. The first is to celebrate the life of Mama. The other is to celebrate the life of someone you did not know existed, my mother."

Several of the women looked at each other in total bewilderment.

Mykola continued. "I love mama. I always will. I will forever honor her in my soul and in my memory. She is my guiding light. I am her son. She loved me with all her heart and there is not a day that goes by that I don't think of her. I miss her so much."

He gazed over at the mantel, taking in the framed photographs of mother and son. Closing his eyes, he dug deep for the courage to keep going. He was now at the point of no return. From this moment on, his life would take on a new meaning.

Sitting on the edge of the sofa, Lesia held her breath.

"Soon after my parents died in the car accident, I learned that they had adopted me from an orphanage in Ukraine."

There was a collective gasp.

"Not too long ago, I went to Ukraine and found my mother, that is, my biological mother."

The room went dead silent.

"While I am the son of Iryna Yashan, I am also the son of Kateryna Chumak," Mykola said, pointing to her photograph. "Before I get into the reason why I asked you all here today, I want you to know a little bit about her and how I came into this world. At the age of 17, Kateryna was abducted, trafficked into Italy and brutally forced into a life of prostitution. While in Italy, she became pregnant by a young man she had fallen in love with and planned to run away with. Her pimp brutally beat the man, sending him to hospital. Kateryna was told he had been killed. Her pimp then threatened to abort the baby. Kateryna ran into the streets begging for help and was rescued by a nun. She helped my mother to return to Ukraine. By this time Kateryna was seven months pregnant. Two months later and moments after I was born, I was taken from her and given to my parents. My birth mother was told I had died. Mama was told Kateryna had died during the delivery. Both my mothers were totally unaware of my true circumstance."

Mykola went on to describe his first encounter with Kateryna.

"I was shocked to discover that she was working in a bar as a prostitute. I was so disgusted and upset. I wanted to run as far away from Ukraine as possible. I couldn't believe my biological mother was doing this. It was like the worst possible nightmare. All I wanted was to get on a plane and come home but something stopped me. Something made me go back to that bar. I wanted to confront Kateryna. I wanted to know why she had chosen this life. I wanted to know why she had given me up. I wanted to tell her off.

"Instead, I ended up spending several hours at her apartment. She told me about her life, about how her family and friends turned their backs on her when she came home pregnant. How everyone in her community totally abandoned her and left her to fend for herself. After she left the hospital, her own brother took her to a town far from the village and dumped her in the square. The only avenue open to her was to go back to doing what she hated most. It was either that or death. No one held out a helping hand.

"When I left her apartment, I felt so ashamed. Like everyone else in her life, I had rushed to judge her without ever knowing or taking the time to find out about her true situation. I decided then and there that I wanted to help her, to save her, to bring her here to my home and keep her safe. But before I could make it happen she was murdered."

Several women were weeping. Others were wiping tears from their eyes, overcome with sadness for a woman they'd never met and empathy for the young man standing before them bearing his soul.

"Before I returned home, I went to Milan where I met with Sister Eugenia Benedicta, the nun who rescued Kateryna. I was confused and completely devastated by everything that had happened during my trip to Ukraine. Mostly, I still could not get over the fact that Kateryna was a prostitute. The very thought tormented me day and night. All that kept eating away at me was that I was the son of a prostitute. In my brief encounter with Sister Eugenia, she told me how she had come upon Kateryna, and how that chance meeting transformed her life. From that moment on, she said her mission became the rescue of women from prostitution. She never once judged them. She simply opened her heart to them. Where all I could see was the stiletto heels, the cheap clothes, the gaudy makeup, and the hard eyes, she saw young, innocent women trapped in a world that was not of their making. She looked into their eyes and saw the terror and desperation. She saw the suffering. She saw the soul in torment and she reached out to them. Sister Eugenia explained to me that these women are not prostitutes. Her phrase was that they are *prostituted women*. Slowly the jumble in my head started to unravel and I began to understand the incredible tragedy that had been Kateryna's terrifying reality. Sister Eugenia opened my eyes and lifted the shame that clawed at my soul. She was the one who got me to accept the fact that Kateryna is my mother. She was the one who got me to understand that my mother never chose the life of a prostitute. She had been forced into it. She was an innocent victim."

Mykola stared hard at the ceiling fighting not to lose his composure. He closed his eyes for a moment to gather his thoughts.

"I'm sure most of you have heard accounts of young women from Ukraine being trafficked into prostitution around the world. Every year thousands of young women are forced to be sex slaves in foreign lands, and the sad reality for those who manage to escape the clutches of their captors is that once they return home they're looked upon as whores. They come home traumatized by what they've had to endure … the rapes, the torture, the fear, the humiliation and above all, the shame. And the very people they had hoped would understand and help them – their family, friends and community - turn their backs on them."

Mykola reached for a glass of water. "Now I'll get to why I've asked you here today. I want to do something to honor my two mothers. Mama would have been broken hearted to learn the truth about Kateryna. My mother was just 17 when her life and dreams were ripped away from her. Her youth was stolen and destroyed. Mama would have done everything in her power to help Kateryna. I just know it. I don't want the tragedy that was Kateryna's life to be in vain. I want to do something to honor her memory."

Mykola paused and looked at the faces around the room. He thought about the journey that had brought him to this point and how much it has changed him. He was no longer a naive young man. He had braved a baptism by fire and barely survived. Now he was a man with a mission. From the back of the room, Lesia smiled warmly, her heart filled with admiration and love. Mykola smiled back, glad that he had finally opened up to her and amazed at her strength of character and support. She had always been his girlfriend and his one true love but now she was more than that. She was his confidant, his rock and best friend. The two had talked for weeks about Mykola's idea. Lesia helped shape it and guide it along on the drawing board. It was no longer Mykola's project. It was their project, and he was about to reveal the details.

"What I want to do is build a place, a safe haven in Ukraine for women like Kateryna who have been rescued from prostitution. It will be a place where they can recover from their horrific ordeal. It will be a place where they can get much needed medical and psychological help. It will be a place where they can be trained in something that will enable them to get a real job and have a real chance at a normal life. But most importantly, it will be a place where they can begin to heal spiritually. This place will be called Kateryna's House, and I'm asking every one of you here to help me make this a reality. Mama would have wanted it. My mother deserves this tribute."

EPILOGUE

In a rustic farm village deep in the heart of the Carpathian Mountains invited guests and curious villagers gathered in a spacious courtyard for the official opening of Kateryna's House. Yellow and blue ribbons strung on the wrought-iron fence surrounding the white-washed, three-story structure fluttered in the warm summer breeze. Alex, his wife, Tamara, and Petro, Mykola's sister, Olenka along with her parents Markian and Ruslana were on hand for the ceremony. Sonia and Orest led a strong contingent of women and men from Edmonton, Saskatoon and Winnipeg. Shooting the event for an upcoming documentary on CTN was Mike Petrenko, thrilled for once to be working on a positive, inspirational story.

The first of 22 house guests – eight young women who had been rescued from sexual bondage in The Netherlands, Italy, Greece, Germany, Spain and Kosovo – hovered discreetly in the background.

There was the traditional Ukrainian welcoming of bread and salt presented by a group of local girls in colorful Hutzul dress. At Mykola's request, Father Ihor flew in from his Edmonton parish to bless the safe house.

After the brief service, Mykola made his way to the entrance. He stopped and ran his fingers across the brass plague attached to the outside wall. It read: "Kateryna's House". With scissors in hand, he looked up at the clear blue sky, whispered a prayer and then turned to the crowd. He smiled as he spotted Antonio Rinaldo standing proudly by the fence.

"This is for my mother, Kateryna," he began. "It is to honor her and all women like her who have been victims of human trafficking. While it is a small gesture against the backdrop of this overwhelming, global crisis, I'm hoping that Kateryna's House will be an inspiration to other groups to do the same. The victims of human trafficking need a safe place, a refuge where they can rehabilitate after their ordeal. We need to reach out and help them, not judge them or blame them for something that was never of their making. I believe with all my heart that if we each reach out and touch the soul of even one suffering human being on this planet, then we've done something truly special. I want to thank everyone who has helped to make this a reality."

To an enthusiastic applause, Mykola turned to cut the bright red ribbon taped across the entrance but suddenly stopped. He quickly scanned the crowd and spotted her.

"I want my sister, Olenka, to come up here and help me."

Olenka made her way to the door. Taking her brother's hand, together, they officially opened Kateryna's House.

ACKNOWLEDGMENTS

First off, I want thank Sandie Rinaldo. She has been my eyes on so many re-writes, giving me advice, suggestions and constant positive support throughout the entire process. I also want to thank Lesia Stangret who assisted me with her diligent research, insights and critical editorial direction. Lastly, I want to acknowledge Chris Casuccio, my agent at Westwood Creative Artists, for all his help and encouragement on this my first foray into the world of fiction.

After a lot of reflection and research into my publishing options, I decided to go "indie" on my first novel. I chose FriesenPress as my publisher. I want to thank the folks there for their professionalism, and for making the process an easy, supportive and painless one.